Harlequin Books is proud to offer
classic novels from today's superstars
of women's fiction. These authors have
captured the hearts of millions of readers
around the world, and earned their place
on the *New York Times, USA TODAY* and
other bestseller lists with every release.

As a bonus, each volume also includes a
full-length novel from a rising star of series
romance. Bestselling authors in their own right,
these talented writers have captured the qualities
Harlequin is famous for—heart-racing passion,
edge-of-your-seat entertainment
and a satisfying happily-ever-after.

#1 *New York Times* Bestselling Author

LINDA LAEL MILLER

Only Forever

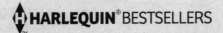

Recycling programs
for this product may
not exist in your area.

ISBN-13: 978-0-373-60606-1

ONLY FOREVER
Copyright © 2011 by Harlequin Books S.A.

The publisher acknowledges the copyright holders
of the individual works as follows:

ONLY FOREVER
Copyright © 1989 by Linda Lael Miller

THUNDERBOLT OVER TEXAS
Copyright © 2006 by Barbara Dunlop

This edition published by arrangement with Harlequin Books S.A.

For questions and comments about the quality of this book,
please contact us at CustomerService@Harlequin.com.

Printed in U.S.A.

CONTENTS

For Debbie Korrell, beloved friend.
Remember that serenity
is never more than twelve steps away.

ONLY FOREVER

#1 *New York Times* Bestselling Author

Linda Lael Miller

LINDA LAEL MILLER

The daughter of a town marshal, Linda Lael Miller is a #1 *New York Times* bestselling author and a *USA TODAY* bestselling author of more than one hundred historical and contemporary novels, most of which reflect her love of the West. Raised in Northport, Washington, the self-confessed barn goddess now lives in Spokane, Washington. Linda recently hit #1 on the *New York Times* list with *A Creed in Stone Creek,* the first title in her series The Creed Cowboys, which was followed by *Creed's Honor* and *The Creed Legacy.*

Linda has come a long way since leaving Washington to experience the world. "But growing up in that time and place has served me well," she allows. "And I'm happy to be back home." More information about Linda and her novels is available at www.lindalaelmiller.com. She also loves to hear from readers by mail at P.O. Box 19461, Spokane, WA 99219.

Chapter 1

This particular strain of flu, Nick DeAngelo decided, had been brought to Earth by hostile aliens determined to wipe out the entire planet—starting, evidently, with an ex-jock who owned one of the best Italian restaurants in Seattle.

Sprawled on the couch in the living room of his apartment, he plucked a handful of tissues from the box on the floor beside him and crammed them against his face just in time to absorb an explosive sneeze. He was covered in mentholated rub from his nose to his belly button, and while his forehead was hot to the touch, the rest of him was racked with chills.

He wondered when Mike Wallace would burst through the door, wanting the story. It was time to alert the masses to impending doom.

Did you actually see these aliens, Mr. DeAngelo?

Call me Nick. Of course I didn't see them. They must have gotten me when I was sleeping.

The imaginary interview was interrupted by the

jangling of the telephone, which, like the box of tissues, was within reach. Hoping for sympathy, he dug the receiver out from between the cushions and rasped out a hoarse hello.

"Still under the weather, huh?" The voice belonged to his younger sister, Gina, and it showed a marked lack of commiseration. "Listen, if I wasn't afraid of catching whatever it is you've got and missing my exams next week, I'd definitely come over and take care of you."

Nick sagged against the back of the sofa, one hand to his fevered forehead. "Your concern is touching, Gina," he coughed out.

"I could call Aunt Carlotta," Gina was quick to suggest. She was a bright kid, a psychology major at the University of Washington, and she knew which buttons to push. "I'm sure she'd love to move into your apartment and spend the next two weeks dragging you back from the threshold of death."

Nick thought of his aunt with affectionate dread. It was in her honor that he'd slathered himself with mentholated goo. "This is not your ordinary, run-of-the-mill flu, you know," he said.

Gina laughed. "I'll alert the science department at school—I'm sure they'll want to send a research team directly to your place."

Privately Nick considered that to be a viable idea, but he refrained from saying so, knowing it would only invite more callous mockery. "You have no heart," he accused.

There was a brief pause, followed by, "Is there anything I can get you, like groceries or books or something? I could leave the stuff in the hallway outside your door—"

"Or you could just drop it from a hovering helicopter," Nick ventured, insulted.

Gina gave a long-suffering sigh. "Why don't you call one of your girlfriends? You could have a whole harem over there, fluffing your pillows and giving you aspirin and heating up canned chicken soup."

"My 'girlfriends,' as you put it, are all either working or letting their answering machines do the talking. And chicken soup is only therapeutic if it's homemade." Nick paused to emit another volcanic sneeze. When he'd recovered, he said magnanimously, "Don't worry about me, Gina, just because I'm putting you through college and paying for your car, your clothes, your apartment and every bite of food that goes into your mouth. I'll be fine without…any help at all."

"Oh, God," wailed Gina. "The guilt!"

Nick laughed. "Gotcha," he said, groping for the remote control that would turn on the TV. Maybe there was an old Stallone movie on—something bloody and macho.

Gina said a few soothing words and then hung up. It occurred to Nick that she was really going to stay away, really going to leave her own brother to face The Great Galactic Plague alone and unassisted.

There was, Nick decided, no human kindness left in the world. He flipped through the various movie channels, seeing nothing that caught his fancy, and was just about to shut the set off and try to focus his eyes on a book when he saw her for the first time.

She was a redhead with golden eyes, and the sight of her practically stopped his heartbeat. She was holding an urn that was suitable enough to be someone's final resting place, and there was a toll-free number superimposed over her chest.

With quick, prodding motions of his thumb, Nick used the control button on the remote to turn up the volume. "My name is Vanessa Lawrence," the vision told her viewing audience in a voice more soothing than all the chicken soup and mentholated rub in the world, "and you're watching the Midas Network." She went on to extol the virtues of the hideous vase she was peddling, but Nick didn't hear a word.

He was too busy dredging up everything he knew about the Midas Network, a nationwide shopping channel based in Seattle. One of his friends—an executive with the company—had urged him to invest when the economy had gone south, claiming that the new home-shopping network would be a hit with newly spendthrift consumers.

Nick shoved one hand through his hair, causing it to stand on end in ridges that reeked of eucalyptus. Undoubtedly, he thought, he was experiencing some kind of dementia related to the virus that had been visited upon him.

Without taking his eyes away from the screen, he groped for the telephone and punched out the office number. His executive assistant, a middle-aged woman named Harriet, answered with a crisp, "DeAngelo's. May I help you?"

"I hope so," wheezed Nick, who had just finished another bout of coughing.

"You don't need me, you need the paramedics," remarked the assistant.

"At last," Nick said. "Someone who understands and sympathizes. Harriet, find Paul Harmon's number for me, will you please? I'm in no condition to hunt through the contacts on my phone."

It was easy to picture Harriet, plump and efficient, searching expertly for the number. "His office number is 555-9876," she said.

Nick found a pencil in the paraphernalia that had collected on the end table beside the couch and wrote the digits on the corner of the tissue box, along with the home number Harriet gave him next.

The woman on the screen was now offering a set of bird figurines.

"Oh, lady," Nick said aloud as he waited for Paul Harmon to come on the line, "I want your body, I want your soul, I want you to have my baby."

The goddess smiled. "All this can be yours for only nineteen-ninety-five," she said.

"Sold," replied Nick.

Vanessa Lawrence inserted her cash card into the automatic teller machine in Quickee Food Mart and tapped one foot while she waited for the money to appear. A glance at her watch told her she was due at her lawyer's office in just ten minutes, and the drive downtown would take fifteen.

Her foot moved faster.

The machine made an alarming grinding noise, but no currency came out of the little slot, and Vanessa's card was still somewhere in the bowels of the gizmo. From the sound of things, it was being systematically digested.

Somewhat wildly, she began pushing buttons. The words *Your transaction is now completed,* were frozen on the small screen. She glanced back over one shoulder, hoping for help from the clerk, but everyone in the neighborhood seemed to be in the convenience store that afternoon, buying bread and milk.

"Damn!" she breathed, slamming her fist against the face of the machine.

A woman wearing pink foam rollers in her hair appeared at Vanessa's side. "You're on TV, aren't you?" she asked. "On that new shopping channel, the something-or-other station."

Vanessa smiled, even though it was the last thing she felt like doing. "The Midas Network," she said, before giving the machine another despairing look. "Just give me back my card," she told the apparatus, "and I won't make any trouble, I promise."

"I watch you every day," the woman announced proudly. "I bought that three-slice toaster you had on yesterday—there's just Bernie and Ray and me, now that Clyde's gone away to the army—and my sister-in-law has four of the ceiling fans."

In her head, Vanessa heard the production manager, Paul Harmon, giving his standard public-relations lecture. *As the viewing audience expands, you'll be recognized. No matter what, I want you all to be polite at all times.*

"Good," she said with a faltering smile.

She took another look at her watch, then lost her cool and rammed the cash machine with the palms of her hands. Miraculously two twenty-dollar bills popped out of the appropriate slot, but Vanessa's cash card was disgorged in three pieces.

She dropped both the card and the money into the pocket of her blazer and dashed for the car, hoping the traffic wouldn't be bad.

It was.

Worse, when Vanessa reached her attorney's modest office, Parker was there with his lawyer and his current girlfriend.

Vanessa prayed she didn't look as frazzled as she felt and resisted an urge to smooth her chin-length auburn hair.

Parker smiled his dazzling smile and tried to kiss her cheek, but Vanessa stepped back, her golden eyes clearly telling him to keep his distance.

Her ex-husband, now the most sought-after pitcher in the American League, looked hurt. "Hello, Van," he said in a low and intimate voice.

Vanessa didn't speak. Although they had been divorced for a full year, Parker's presence still made her soul ache. It wasn't that she wanted him back; no, she grieved for the time and love she'd wasted on him.

Vanessa's attorney, Walter, was no ball of fire, but he was astute enough to know how vulnerable she felt. He drew back a chair for her near his desk, and gratefully she sank into the seat.

Parker's lawyer immediately took up the conversational ball. "I think we can settle this reasonably," he said. Vanessa felt her spine stiffen.

The bottom line was that Parker had been offered a phenomenal amount of money to write a book about his career in professional baseball and, with the help of a ghostwriter, he'd produced a manuscript—one that included every intimate detail of his marriage to Vanessa.

She was prepared to sue if the book went to press.

"Wait," Parker interceded suavely, holding his famous

hands up in the air, "I think it would be better if Van and I worked this thing out ourselves…in private."

His girlfriend shifted uncomfortably on the leather sofa beside him, but said nothing.

"There is nothing to work out," Vanessa said in a shaky voice she hated. Why couldn't she sound detached and professional, like she did when she was selling ceiling fans on the Midas Network? "If you don't take me out of that book, Parker, I'm going to drive a dump truck into your bank account and come out with a load of your money."

Parker went pale beneath his golden tan. He ran a hand through his sun-streaked hair, and his azure blue eyes skittered away from Vanessa's gaze. But after a moment, he regained his legendary poise. "Van, you're being unreasonable."

"Am I? That book makes me sound like some kind of sex-crazed neurotic. I'm not going to let you ruin me, Parker, just so you can have a few more annuities and condominiums!"

Parker flinched as though she'd struck him. He rose from his chair and came to crouch before hers, speaking softly and holding both her hands in his. "You feel threatened," he crooned.

It was all Vanessa could do not to kick him. She jerked her hands free, shot to her feet and stormed out of the office.

Parker caught up to her at the elevator, which, as luck would have it, was just arriving. "Baby, wait," he pleaded.

Vanessa was shamed by the tears that were flowing down her face, but she couldn't stop them. She dodged into the elevator, trying to escape him.

Parker squeezed into the cubicle with her, oblivious, apparently, of the fact that there were two men in suits, a cleaning woman and a maintenance worker looking on. He tried again, "Sweetheart, what do you want? A mink? A Corvette? Tell me what you want and I'll give it to you. But you've got to be reasonable!"

Vanessa drew her hand back and slapped the Living Legend. "How dare you assume you can buy me, you pompous jackass!" she cried. "And stop calling me sweetheart and baby!"

The elevator reached the ground floor, and Vanessa hurried out, hoping Parker wouldn't give chase. As it happened, however, he was right on her heels.

He looked exasperated now as he lengthened his strides to keep pace with her on the busy downtown sidewalk. He straightened the lapels of his tailored suit jacket and rasped out, "Damn it, Vanessa, do you know how much money is at stake here?"

"No, and I don't care," Vanessa answered. She was almost to the parking lot where she'd left her car; in a few minutes she could get behind the steering wheel and drive away.

With sudden harshness, Parker stopped her again, grasping her shoulders with his hands and pressing her backward against a department store display window. "You're not going to ruin this deal for me, Vanessa!" he shouted.

Vanessa stared at him, appalled and breathless. God knew Parker had hurt her often enough, but he'd never been physically rough.

Parker's effort to control his temper was visible. "I'm sorry," he ground out, and because he seldom apologized for anything, Vanessa believed him. "I didn't mean to manhandle you like that. Vanessa, please. Sit down with me somewhere private and listen to what I have to say. That's all I'm asking."

"There's no point, Parker," Vanessa replied. "I know what you want to tell me, and my answer won't be any different. The way you portrayed me in that book is libelous—I wouldn't be able to hold my head up in public."

"And I thought you'd be proud when I sent you a copy of that manuscript." He paused to shake his head, as if still amazed at her negative reaction. "Van, people will know I made most of that stuff up," Parker went on presently with a weak smile. "They're not going to take it seriously."

Vanessa arched one eyebrow. "Oh, really? Well, I'd rather not take the chance, if you don't mind. I have dreams of my own, you know."

Passersby were beginning to make whispers that indicated they recognized Parker. He took Vanessa's arm and squired her into a nearby coffee shop. "Two minutes," he said. "That's all I want."

She smiled acidly. "That's you, Parker—the two-minute man."

He favored her with a scorching look and dropped into the booth's seat across from her. "I'd forgotten what a little witch you can be, Van." He paused to square his shoulders. "Darla hasn't complained."

Darla, of course, was the girlfriend. "People with IQs under twenty rarely do," Vanessa answered sweetly. Then she added, "Your two minutes are ticking away."

A waitress came, and Parker ordered two cups of coffee without even consulting Vanessa. It was so typical that she nearly laughed out loud.

"The advance on this book," Parker began in a low and reluctant voice, "is seven figures. I can't play baseball forever, Van. I need some security."

Vanessa rolled her eyes. Most oil sheiks didn't live as well as Parker; he certainly wasn't facing penury. "I'll drop you off at the food bank if you'd like," she offered.

A muscle bunched in his jaw. Vanessa could have lived for years on the money that Parker's face brought in for commercials alone. "You know," he said, "I really didn't expect you to be so bitter and frustrated."

The coffee arrived, and the waitress walked away again.

"Watch it," Vanessa warned. "You're trying to get on my good side, remember?"

Parker spread his hands in a gesture of baffled annoyance. "Van, I know the divorce was hard on you, but you have a job now and a life of your own. There's no reason to torture me like this."

He sounded so damnably rational that Vanessa wanted to throw her coffee in his face. "Is that what you think I'm doing? I want nothing from you, Parker—no money, no minks, no sports cars—and no lies written up in a book and presented as the truth."

"So I was a little creative. What's wrong with that?"

"Nothing, if you're writing a novel." Vanessa could see that the conversation was progressing exactly as she'd expected. "I don't know why I even came down here," she said, glancing at her watch and sliding out of the booth.

"Hot date?" Parker asked, giving the words an unsavory inflection.

"Very hot," Vanessa lied, looking down at Parker. She was meeting her cousin Rodney for dinner and a movie, but what Parker didn't know wouldn't hurt him. She made a *sssssssss* sound, meant to indicate a sizzle, and walked away.

Much to her relief, Parker didn't follow.

Rodney was waiting in the agreed place when she reached the mall, his hands wedged into his jacket pockets, his white teeth showing in a grin.

"Hi, Van," he said. "Bad day?"

Vanessa kissed his cheek and linked her arm through his. "I just came from a meeting with Parker," she replied. "Does that answer your question?"

Rodney frowned. "Yeah," he said. "I'm afraid it does."

Vanessa smiled up at the handsome young man with the thick, longish chestnut brown hair and warm eyes. Her first cousin—and at twenty-one, five years her junior—Rodney was the only family she had in Seattle, and she loved him. She changed the subject. "Aren't you going to ask me about the apartment?"

Rodney laughed as they walked into the mall together and approached their favorite fast-food restaurant, a place that sold Chinese cuisine to go. The apartment over Vanessa's garage was empty since her last tenant had moved out, and Rodney wanted the rooms in the worst way.

"You know I do, Van," he scolded her good-naturedly. "Living over a funeral home has its drawbacks. For one thing, it gives new meaning to the phrase, 'things that go bump in the night.'"

Van laughed and shook her head. "Okay, okay—you can move in in a few weeks. I want to have the place painted first."

Rodney's face lighted up. He was a good kid working

his way through chiropractic school by means of a very demanding and unconventional job, and Vanessa genuinely enjoyed his company. In fact, they'd always been close. "I'll do the painting," he said.

It was late when Vanessa arrived at the large colonial house on Queen Anne Hill and let herself in the front door. She crossed the sparsely furnished living room, kicking off her high heels and rifling through the day's mail as she moved.

In the kitchen, she flipped on the light and put a cup of water in the microwave to heat for tea. When the brew was steaming on the table, she steeled herself and pressed the button on her answering machine.

The first message was from her boss, Paul Harmon. "Janet and I want you to have dinner with us a week from Friday at DeAngelo's. Don't bring a date."

Vanessa frowned. The Harmons were friends of hers and they were forever trying to fix her up with one of their multitude of unattached male acquaintances. The fact that Paul had specified she shouldn't bring a date was unsettling.

She missed the next two messages, both of which were from Parker, because the name of the restaurant had rung a distant bell. What was it about DeAngelo's that made her uncomfortable?

She stirred sweetener into her tea, frowning. Then it came to her—the proprietor of the place was Nick DeAngelo, a former pro football player with a reputation for womanizing exceeded only by Parker's. Vanessa shuddered. The man was Paul's best friend. What if he turned out to be the mysterious fourth at dinner?

Vanessa shut off the answering machine and dialed the Harmons' home number. Janet answered the phone.

"About dinner at DeAngelo's," Vanessa said, after saying hi. "Am I being set up to meet Mr. Macho, or what?"

Janet laughed. "I take it you're referring to Nick?"

"And you're hedging," Vanessa accused.

"Okay, yes—we want you to meet Nick. He's a darling, Vanessa. You'll love him."

"That's what you said about that guy who wanted to be 'friends with benefits'," Vanessa reminded her friend. "I really don't think this is a good idea."

"He's nothing like Parker," Janet said gently. She could be very perceptive. "It isn't fair to write Nick off as a loser without even meeting him."

The encounter with Parker had inclined her toward saying no to everything, and Vanessa knew it. She sighed. She had to be flexible, willing to meet new people and try new things, or she'd become stagnant. "All right, but if he turns out to be weird, Janet Harmon, you and Paul are off my Christmas-card list for good."

That damned sixth sense of Janet's was still evident. "The appointment with Parker and his attorney went badly, huh?"

Vanessa took a steadying sip of her tea. "He's going to publish that damned book, Janet," she whispered, feeling real despair. "There isn't anything I can do to stop him, and I'm sure he knows it, even though he seems to feel some kind of crazy need to win me over to his way of thinking."

"The bastard," Janet commiserated.

"I can say goodbye to any hopes I had of ever landing a job as a newscaster. I'll never be taken seriously."

"It's late, and you're tired," Janet said firmly. "Take

a warm bath, have a glass of wine and get some sleep. Things will look better in the morning."

Exhausted, Vanessa promised to take her friend's advice and went off to bed, stopping only to wash her face and brush her teeth. She collapsed onto the mattress and immediately fell into a troubled sleep, dreaming that Parker was chewing her cash card and spitting the plastic pieces out on the pitcher's mound.

She awakened the next morning in a terrible mood, and when she reached the studio complex where the Midas Network was housed, her cohost, Mel Potter, looked at her with concern in his eyes.

A middle-aged, ordinary-looking man, Potter was known as Markdown Mel in the business, and he was a pro's pro. He had ex-wives all over the country and a gift for selling that was unequaled in the field. Vanessa had seen him move two thousand mini food-processors in fifteen minutes without even working up a sweat, and her respect for his skill as a salesman was considerable.

He was, in fact, the one man in the world, besides her grandfather, who could address her as honey without making her hackles rise.

"What's the matter, honey?" he demanded as Vanessa flopped into a chair in the makeup room. "You look like hell."

Vanessa smiled. "Thanks a lot, Mel," she answered. "You're a sight for sore eyes yourself."

He laughed as Margie, the makeup girl, slathered Vanessa's face with cleansing cream. "I see by the papers that that ex-husband of yours is in town to accept an award at his old high school. Think you could get him to stop by the studio before he leaves? We could dump a lot of those baseball cake plates if Parker Lawrence endorsed them."

Now it was Vanessa who laughed, albeit a little hysterically. "Forget it, Mel. Parker and I aren't on friendly terms, and I wouldn't ask him for the proverbial time of day."

Mel shrugged, but Vanessa had a feeling she hadn't heard the last of the subject of Parker Lawrence selling baseball cake plates.

Twenty minutes later Vanessa and Mel were on camera, demonstrating a set of golf clubs. Vanessa loved her job. Somehow, when she was working, she became another person—one who had no problems, no insecurities and no bruises on her soul.

The network had a policy of letting viewers chat with the hosts over the air, and the first caller was Parker.

"Hello, babe," he said, after carefully introducing himself to the nation so that there could be no doubt as to who he was. "You look terrific."

Vanessa's smile froze on her face. She tried to speak, but she couldn't.

Mel picked up the ball with admirable aplomb. "Thanks, Parker," he answered. "You look pretty good yourself."

Even the cameraman laughed at that.

"Giving up baseball for golf?" Vanessa was emboldened to say.

"Never," Parker answered confidently. "But I'd take ten of anything you're selling, baby."

Vanessa was seething inside, but she hadn't forgotten that several million people would be watching this. She wasn't about to let Parker throw her in front of a national audience, and she knew the network wouldn't pass on airing a segment with *the* Parker Lawrence in it, even if she beggcd. "Good," she said, beaming. "We'll put you down for ten sets of golf clubs."

Parker laughed, thinking she was joking. Vanessa wished she could see his face when the UPS man delivered his purchases in seven to ten working days.

Chapter 2

The man was impossibly handsome, Vanessa thought ruefully as she watched Nick DeAngelo approach the table where she and the Harmons had been seated. He was tall, with the kind of shoulders one might expect of a former star football player. His hair was dark and attractively rumpled as though he'd just run his fingers through it. But it was the expression in his eyes that took hold of something deep inside Vanessa and refused to let go.

Suddenly Vanessa's emotional scars, courtesy of Parker Lawrence, got the best of her. She could have sworn they were as visible as stitch marks across her face and she was positive that Nick DeAngelo could count them. Her first instinct was to run and hide.

Grinning, Paul stood to greet his friend. "You survived the flu," he remarked. "From the way you sounded, I didn't think you were going to make it."

A half smile curved Nick's lips, probably in acknowledgment of what Paul had said, but his gaze was fixed on Vanessa. He seemed to be unwrapping her soul, layer by layer, and she didn't want that. She needed the insulation to feel safe.

She dropped her eyes, color rising to her cheeks, and clasped her hands together in her lap. In a matter of moments, a decade of living, loving and hurting had dropped away. She was as vulnerable as a shy sixteen-year-old.

"Vanessa," Paul said gently, prodding her with his voice. "This is my friend, Nick DeAngelo."

She looked up again because she had to, and Nick was smiling at her. A strange sensation washed over her, made up of fear and delight, consolation and challenge. "Hello," she said, swallowing.

His smile was steady and as warm as winter fire. Vanessa was in over her head, and she knew it. "Hi," he replied, his voice low and deep.

The sound of it caressed the bruises on Vanessa's soul like a healing balm. She was frightened by his ability to touch her so intimately and wondered if anyone would believe her if she said she'd developed a headache and needed to go home to put her feet up. She started to speak, but Janet Harmon cut her off.

"I hear you're opening another restaurant in Portland next month," she said to Nick, her foot bumping against Vanessa's under the table. "Won't that take you out of town a lot?"

The phenomenal shoulders moved in an easy shrug. Nick DeAngelo was obviously as much at home in a tailored suit as he would be in a football jersey and blue jeans. His brown eyes roamed over Vanessa, revealing an amused approval of the emerald-green silk dress she was wearing. "I'm used to traveling," he said finally in response to Janet's question.

Vanessa devoutly wished that she'd stayed home. She wasn't ready for an emotional involvement, but it seemed to be happening anyway, without her say-so. She was as helpless as a swimmer going down for the third time. In desperation, she clasped on to the similarities between Parker and Nick.

They were both attractive, although Vanessa had to admit that Parker's looks had never affected her in quite the same way that Nick's were doing now. They were both jocks, and, if the press could be believed, Nick, like Parker, was a veritable legend among the bimbos of the world.

Vanessa felt better and, conversely, worse. She lifted her chin and said, "I don't think a jock—I mean, professional athlete—ever gets the road completely out of his blood."

Nick sat back in his chair. His look said he could read her as clearly as a floodlighted billboard. "Maybe it's like selling electric foot massagers on television," he speculated smoothly. "I don't see how a person could ever put a thrill like that behind them."

Vanessa squirmed. How typically male; he knew she was responding to him, and now he meant to make fun of her. "I'm not ashamed of what I do for a living, Mr. DeAngelo," she said.

Nick bent toward her and, in that moment, it was as though the two of them were alone at the table—indeed, alone in the restaurant. "Neither am I, Ms. Lawrence," he replied.

A crackling silence followed, which was finally broken by Paul's diplomatic throat clearing and he said,

"Vanessa hopes to anchor one of the local news shows at some point."

Vanessa winced, sure that Nick would be amused at such a lofty ambition. Instead he merely nodded.

Dinner that night was delicious, although Vanessa was never able to recall exactly what it was, for she spent every minute longing to run for cover. After the meal, the foursome drifted from the dining room to the crowded cocktail lounge, where a quartet was playing soft music. Vanessa found herself held alarmingly close to Nick as they danced.

He lifted her chin with a curved finger and spoke in a velvety rasp. "Your eyes are the size of satellite dishes. Do I scare you that much?"

Vanessa stiffened. The man certainly had an ego. "You don't scare me at all," she lied. "It's only that I'm—I'm tired."

He smiled, and the warmth threatened to melt her like a wax statue. "You were married to Parker Lawrence, weren't you?"

Suddenly it was too hot in the place; Vanessa felt as though she'd suffocate if she couldn't get some fresh air. "Yes," she answered, flustered, searching for an avenue of escape.

True to form, Nick read her thoughts precisely. "This way," he said, and, taking Vanessa by the hand, he led her off the dance floor, down a hallway and into a large, tastefully furnished office. She was about to protest when she realized there was a terrace beyond the French doors on the far side of the room.

The autumn night was chilly, but Vanessa didn't mind. The crisp air cleared her head, and she felt better immediately.

The sky was like a great black tent, pierced through in a million places by tiny specks of silver light, and the view of downtown Seattle and the harbor was spectacular. Vanessa rested her folded arms against the stone railing and drew a deep, delicious breath.

"It's beautiful," she said, smiling.

Nick was beside her, gazing at the city lights and moonlit water spread out below them. "I never get tired of it," he said quietly. "The only drawback is that you can't see the Space Needle from here."

Vanessa shivered as an icy breeze swept off the water, and Nick immediately draped his jacket over her shoulders. She thanked him shyly with a look, and asked, "Have you lived in Seattle all your life?"

He nodded. "I was born here."

Vanessa marveled that she could be so comfortable with Nick on the terrace when she'd felt threatened inside the restaurant. She sighed. "I grew up in Spokane, but I guess I'm starting to feel at home."

"Just starting?" He arched a dark eyebrow.

Vanessa shrugged. "Seattle is Parker's hometown, not mine." Too late she realized she'd made a mistake, reopening a part of her life she preferred to keep private.

Nick leaned against the terrace and gazed at the circus of lights below. "I've been married before, too," he confided quietly. "Her name was Jenna."

Vanessa was practically holding her breath. It was incomprehensible that his answer should mean so much, but it did. "What happened?"

"She left me," Nick replied without looking at Vanessa.

"I'm sorry," Vanessa said, and she was sincere because she knew how much it hurt when a marriage died, whether a person was left or did the leaving. "A lot of women can't handle living with a professional athlete," she added, and although she'd meant the words as a consolation, she immediately wished she could take them back.

"Jenna bailed out before I got into the pros," Nick said in tones as cool as the wind rising off the water. "When I started making big bucks, she wanted to try again."

Before Vanessa could make any kind of response to that, Nick put an arm around her waist and ushered her back inside. She lifted the jacket from her shoulders while he closed the French doors that led out onto the terrace.

"Did you love Jenna?" she asked, and the words were the most involuntary ones she'd ever spoken.

Nick's expression was unreadable. "Did you love Parker?" he countered.

Vanessa bit her lower lip. "I honestly don't know," she answered after a few moments of thought. "I was in college when I met him, and he was already breaking records in baseball. I'd never met anyone like him before. He was—overwhelming."

Nick grinned somewhat sadly and leaned back against the edge of his desk, his arms folded. "I'd like to know you better," he said.

Vanessa was aware that such straightforwardness was rare in a man, and she was impressed. She was also terrified by the powerful things this man was making her feel. She placed his jacket carefully over the back of a chair, searching her mind for a refusal that would not be rude or hurtful.

She was unprepared for Nick's sudden appearance at her side, and for the way he gently lifted her chin in his hand and said, "It's time to let go of the pain and move on, Vanessa."

The low, rumbling words, spoken so close to her mouth, made her lips tingle with a strange sense of anticipation. When Nick kissed her, she swayed slightly, stricken by a sweet malaise that robbed her of all balance.

Nick was holding her upright, though whether by means of the kiss or his gentle grasp on her waist, Vanessa couldn't be sure. She knew only that she was responding to him with her whole being, that she'd let him take her then and there if he pressed her. Being so vulnerable when she'd been so badly hurt before was almost more than she could bear.

When Nick finally released her, having kissed her more thoroughly than Parker ever had in even the most intimate of moments, she was so dazed that she could only stare up at him in abject amazement. She made up her mind that she absolutely would not see him again, no matter what.

He was too dangerous.

"Are you working tomorrow?" he asked in a sleepy voice, toying with a tendril of titian hair that had slipped from her hair clasp.

Vanessa struggled to remember, her throat thick, her mind a razzle-dazzle of popping lights. Finally she shook her head.

Nick grinned. "Good. Will you spend the day with me.

No, no, no, cried Vanessa's wounded spirit. "Yes," she choked out.

Nick smiled at her, tracing the curve of her cheek with one index finger, then reached for his jacket and shrugged into it. "We'd better get back out there before Paul and Janet decide we're doing something in keeping with my image."

They went back to the dance floor, and Nick held her. It was an innocent intimacy but it stirred Vanessa's senses, which had been largely dormant for the better part of a year, to an alarming pitch of need.

Every time she dared to meet Nick's eyes, it was as though he had taken away an item of her clothing, and yet she could not resist looking at him. The dilemma was at once delicious and maddening, and Vanessa was relieved when Nick didn't offer to drive her home at the end of the evening.

Paul lingered on the sidewalk for a few minutes, talking with Nick, while Vanessa and Janet settled themselves in the car.

"Well," Janet demanded the moment she'd snapped her seat belt into place, "what did you think of him?"

Vanessa drew in a deep breath and let it out in an agitated rush. "I think I should have stayed home with my needlepoint," she said.

Janet turned in the car seat to look back at her. "You've got to be kidding. The man is hot!"

Only now, when her nostrils weren't filled with the subtle scent of his cologne and her body wasn't pressed to his could Vanessa be rational and objective where Nick DeAngelo was concerned. "He's also a jock," she said miserably. "Do you have any idea how egotistical those men can be? Not to mention callous and self-serving?"

Janet sighed. "Not every man is like Parker," she insisted.

The conversation was cut off at that point because

Paul came back to the car, whistling cheerfully as he slid behind the wheel. Vanessa shrank into the corner of the seat, wishing, all in the same moment, that the night would end, that she could go back in time and say no to Nick's suggestion that they spend the next day together and that tomorrow would hurry up and arrive so she could see him again.

"Thanks," she said ruefully when Paul saw her to her door a few minutes later.

He smiled as she turned the key in the lock and pushed the door open. "Sounds as if you have mixed feelings about Nick," he commented.

Vanessa kicked off her high heels the moment she'd crossed the threshold. "I have *no* feelings about Nick," she argued, facing Paul but keeping her eyes averted. "Absolutely none."

Her boss chuckled. "Good night, Van," he said, and then he was gone, striding back down the front walk to his car.

Vanessa locked the door, slipped out of her velvet coat and bent to pick up her discarded shoes. Her calico cat, Sari, curled around her ankles, meowing.

Sari had already had her supper, and even though she had a weight problem, Vanessa couldn't turn a deaf ear to her plaintive cries. She set her purse, coat and shoes down on the deacon's bench in the hallway and allowed herself to be herded into the kitchen.

Even before she flipped on the lights, she saw the blinking red indicator on the answering machine. Vanessa was in no mood to deal with relationships of any kind that night; she wanted to feed the cat and go to bed. Her own innate sense of responsibility—some calamity could have befallen Rodney or her aging grandparents—made her cross the room and push the play button.

She was opening a can of cat food and scraping it into Sari's dish when Parker's voice filled the kitchen.

The first message was relatively polite, but, as the messages progressed, Parker grew more and more irate. Finally he flared, "Why did you change your cell number? And don't you ever stay home? Damn it, call me!"

Vanessa had washed her hands and was about to turn off the machine when Nick's voice rolled over her like a warm, rumbling wave. "You're a terrific lady," he said. "I'm looking forward to seeing you again tomorrow."

Vanessa moaned faintly and sank into a chair, propping her chin in both hands. With a few idle words, the man had melted the muscles in her knees.

"Good night," he said, his voice deep and gentle, and then the machine was silent.

After a few moments of sheer bewilderment, Vanessa got up and checked the locks on both the front and back doors. Then, taking her coat and shoes with her, Sari padding along beside her, she went upstairs.

She hung her coat carefully in the closet and put the shoes back into their plastic box. Soon she was in bed, but sleep eluded her.

She kept imagining what it would be like to lie beside Nick DeAngelo, in this bed or any other, and have him touch her, kiss her, make love to her. Just the thought made her ache.

Sometime toward morning, Vanessa slept. The telephone awakened her to a full complement of sunshine, and she grappled for the receiver, losing it several times before she managed to maneuver it into place.

"Hello," she accused, shoving one hand through her rumpled hair and scowling.

After knowing him such a short time, it seemed impossible, but she recognized Nick's laughter. "Don't tell me, let me guess. You're not a morning person."

Vanessa narrowed her eyes to peer at the clock and saw that it was nearly nine o'clock. She was glad Nick had called, she decided, because that gave her a chance to cancel their date. "Listen, I've been thinking—"

He cut her off immediately. "Well, stop. You're obviously in no condition for that kind of exertion. I'll be over in ten minutes to ply you with coffee."

"Nick!" Vanessa cried, afraid of being plied. But it was too late, he'd already hung up and she had no idea what his number was.

Grumbling, she got out of bed, stumbled into the bathroom and took a shower. By the time Nick arrived, she was clad in jeans and a blue knit sweater and was fully conscious.

She greeted him at the front door, holding a cup of therapeutically strong coffee in one hand. "You didn't give me a chance to tell you on the phone, but…"

Nick grinned in that disarming way he had and assessed her trim figure with blatant appreciation. "Good, you're dressed," he said, walking past her into the house.

"You expected me to be naked?" Vanessa wanted to know.

He laughed. "I'm allowed my share of fantasies, aren't I?"

Vanessa shook her head. Nick was impossible to shun.

He was wearing jeans and a hooded sweatshirt, and he had the look of a man who knew where he was going to spend that chilly, sun-washed Saturday. "Come in, come in," she chimed wryly as he preceded her down the hallway to the kitchen. "Don't be shy."

He grinned at her over one shoulder. "I've never been accused of that," he assured her.

Vanessa had no doubt he was telling the truth. She gave up. "Where are we going?"

"Running," he said. "Then I thought we'd take in a movie…."

Vanessa was holding up both hands in a demand for silence. "Wait a minute, handsome—rewind to the part about running."

Nick dragged his languorous brown eyes from the toes of her sneakers to the crown of her head. "Bad idea? You certainly look like someone who cares about fitness."

She sighed and poured her coffee into the sink. "Thank you—I think."

"I guess we could skip running—just for today," he said, stepping closer to her.

Vanessa's senses went on red alert, and she leaped backward as though he'd burned her. "On second thought, running sounds like a great idea," she said, in a squeaky voice, embarrassed. "You seem to have a lot of—of extra energy."

He favored her with slow, sensuous grin. "Oh, believe me," he said with quiet assurance, "I do."

Vanessa swallowed. It was beyond her how accepting a single blind date could get a person into so much trouble. She swore to herself that the next time Janet and Paul wanted to introduce her to someone, she was going to hide in the cellar until the danger passed.

"Relax," Nick said, approaching and taking her shoulders into his big, gentle hands. "You are one tense individual, Value Van."

Vanessa blinked. "What did you call me?"

"I've gotten kind of caught up in this home-shopping thing," he replied, his dark eyes twinkling. "I thought you should have a professional nickname, like your friend Markdown Mel. The possibilities are endless, you know—there's Bargain Barbara, for instance, and Half-price Hannah…"

Vanessa began to laugh. "I never know whether to take you seriously or not."

He bent his head and kissed her, innocently and briefly. "Oh, you should take me seriously, Van. It's the rest of your life that needs mellowing out."

She gave him a shove. "Let's go running," she said.

They drove to the nearest park in Nick's Corvette. He led the way to the jogging path and immediately started doing warm-up exercises.

Vanessa eyed him ruefully, then began, in her own awkward fashion, to follow suit. "One thing about dating a jock," she ventured to say, breathing a little hard as she tried to keep up, "a girl stays skinny, no matter what."

Nick started off down the path after rolling his eyes once, and Vanessa was forced to follow at a wary trot. "Are you saying that I'm not a fun guy?" he asked over one shoulder.

"What could be more fun than this?" Vanessa countered, already gasping for breath. She'd dropped her exercise program during the divorce, and the effects of her negligence were painfully obvious.

When they reached a straight stretch, Nick turned and ran backward, no trace of exertion visible in his manner or voice. "So, how long have you been a member of the loyal order of couch potatoes?" he asked companionably.

"I hate you," huffed Vanessa.

"That really hurts, Value Van," Nick replied. "See if I ever buy another pair of Elvis Presley bookends from you."

There was grass alongside the pathway, and Vanessa flung herself onto it, dragging air into her lungs and groaning. She couldn't believe she was there in the park, torturing herself this way when she could have slept in until noon and sent out for Chinese food.

Nick did not keep running, as she'd expected. Instead he flopped down on the cold grass beside her and said, "I appreciate the offer, but we haven't known each other long enough."

Vanessa gave him a look and clambered to her feet. "Tired so soon?" she choked out, jogging off down the pathway.

At the end of the route, which Vanessa privately thought of as The Gauntlet, the ice-blue Corvette sat shining in the autumn sunlight. She staggered toward it and collapsed into the passenger seat while Nick was still cooling down.

When he slid behind the wheel, she barely looked at him. "What did I do to Janet to make her hate me like this?" she asked.

Nick chuckled and started the car. "I'll answer that when I've had a shower."

Vanessa's eyes flew open wide. Showering was an element she hadn't thought about, even though it seemed perfectly obvious now.

Nick's expression was suddenly serious. "Relax, Van," he said. "It's a private shower, and you're not invited."

To her everlasting chagrin, Vanessa blushed like a Victorian schoolgirl. She was a reserved person, but not shy. She wondered again what it was about this man that circumvented all the normal rules of her personality and made her act like someone she didn't even know.

"It never crossed my mind that you might expect me to share a shower with you," Vanessa lied, her chin at a prim angle, her arms folded.

"Liar," Nick replied with amused affection.

He lived in a condominium on the top floor of one of the most historic buildings in Seattle, and the place had a quiet charm that surprised Vanessa. She had expected a playboy's den with lots of leather, glass accents and stark colors, but the spacious rooms were decorated in earth tones instead. There was an old-fashioned fireplace in the living room and a beautiful Navaho rug graced the wall above the cushy sofa.

"Make yourself at home," Nick said casually, ducking through a doorway and leaving Vanessa to stand there alone, feeling sweaty and rumpled and totally out of place.

She went to the window and looked out on busy Elliot Bay. A passenger ferry was chugging into port, large and riverboatlike, and Vanessa smiled. In the distance, she heard the sound of running water and an off-key rendition of a current popular song.

The view kept her occupied for what seemed like a long time, but when Nick didn't return after ten minutes, Vanessa began to grow uneasy. She approached the big-screen television in one corner of the room and pushed the power button on the nearby remote.

Immediately the Midas Network leaped out at her in living color, life-size. She turned the set off again and began to pace, tempted to sneak out before this nonrelationship with Nick DeAngelo grew into something she couldn't handle.

She was just reaching for the doorknob when his voice stopped her.

"Don't go," he said quietly. "I'm not going to hurt you in any way, Vanessa. I swear it."

She couldn't move, couldn't drop her hand to her side or turn the knob and make her escape.

"Something really important is happening here," he went on. "Can't you feel it?"

Vanessa let her forehead rest against the cool panel of the door. "Yes," she confessed in a strangled voice, "and that's what scares me."

He stepped closer to her and laid his hands very gently on her shoulders. She was filled with the scent of his clean hair, his freshly washed skin. "I won't let anything happen that you're not ready for," he promised, and when he turned her around to face him, Vanessa was powerless to resist.

She looked up at him with eyes full of trust and fear, and he let his hands drop to her waist. He was careful not to hold her too close, and yet she was achingly aware of his total, unreserved masculinity.

"I'm going to kiss you," he said matter-of-factly. "That is, if you're ready."

She slid her arms around his neck and stood on tiptoe, exhilarated and, at the same time, terrified. "I'm ready," she answered, her mouth only a whisper away from his.

Chapter 3

"Want a shower now?"

Vanessa, her energy drained by the kiss, had sagged back against the door when it was overz Her eyes opened wide, however, when Nick's words registered. "I beg your pardon?"

He turned and walked off toward the open kitchen, looking too good for comfort in his jeans and T-shirt. His biceps bulged when he lifted his arm to open a cupboard door, and Vanessa felt vaguely dizzy.

At that moment there was only one thing in the world she wanted more than a shower. She followed him, careful to keep the breakfast bar between them. "I don't have any clean clothes to put on," she ventured to say.

Nick shrugged. "Some of Gina's things are still here. You're about her size, I think."

The name made Vanessa round the breakfast bar. "Gina?" she asked, looking up at him.

He kissed her forehead. "My sister," he assured her.

The relief Vanessa felt was embarrassing in its scope. "I've never had to shower on a date before," she confessed.

Nick chuckled at that. "Never?"

Vanessa looked up into his dancing eyes and felt a painful tug somewhere in the region of her heart. She wanted to appear glamorous and sophisticated, but the truth was far different. She'd never been with any man besides Parker, and, when and if she went to bed with Nick, it was going to be almost like reliving the first time. At last she shook her head and answered, "Never."

He started to put his arms around her and then stopped. "Do you like Chinese food?" he asked.

Vanessa nodded.

"Good. You'll find the clothes and the shower down the hall—first room on the right. I'll go get our lunch while you're changing—okay?"

"Okay," Vanessa answered, not knowing quite what to make of this man. She knew Nick was attracted to her, and yet when he had an advantage, he didn't press it.

The room Nick had directed her to was large, though it obviously wasn't the place where he slept. There was a private bathroom, however, and Vanessa locked herself in before stripping off the clothes she'd worn to run in the park.

When she finished showering, she found the promised clothes in closets and bureaus and finally helped herself to yoga pants and a hoodie. She zipped it to her eyeballs and was just entering the living room when Nick returned with cartons of fragrant sweet-and-sour chicken, chow mein and fried rice.

He smiled and shook his head when he saw the outfit. "Feel better?" he asked.

Vanessa felt a number of things, and she wasn't ready to talk about any of them. She went to the cupboards and opened doors until she found plates for their food. They ate at the breakfast bar, perched on stools, and Nick insisted on using chopsticks.

"Show off," Vanessa said, spearing a succulent morsel of chicken with her fork.

He surprised her by laying down his chopsticks, reaching out and pulling down the zipper on the hoodie to her breastbone. "The weather's getting nasty outside," he commented, "but it's warm enough in here."

Vanessa blushed, embarrassed. She knew Nick thought she was a hidebound prude, but she didn't have the nerve to prove she wasn't. Not yet.

He leaned over and gave her a nibbling kiss on the lips. "Everything is okay, Van," he promised her quietly. "Just relax."

A light rain spattered the windows, and Nick left his stool to light a fire on the hearth. The crackling sound was cozy, and the colorful blaze gave that corner of the room a cheery glow.

Something Vanessa could not name or define made her leave her place at the breakfast bar and approach Nick. She knelt beside him, facing the fireplace, and said, "I'm not like you p-probably think I am. It's just that you scare me so much."

He turned to her, smiling softly, and slid four fingers into her hair, caressing her cheek with his thumb. "I won't tell you any lies, Vanessa," he replied. "I want you—I have since I turned on the Midas Network and saw you standing there with a toll-free number printed across your chest—but I'm willing to wait."

"Wait?" Vanessa asked. Nothing in her relationship with Parker had ever prepared her for this kind of patience from a man. He had to want something. "You're admitting, then, that there is a plan of seduction?"

He laughed. "Absolutely. I intend to make you want me, Vanessa Lawrence."

Vanessa figured he had the battle half won already, but she wasn't about to say that to him. In fact, she didn't say anything, because Nick DeAngelo had rendered her speechless.

He got up, leaving her kneeling there by the fire, and returned after a few minutes with two glasses of wine. After handing one to Vanessa and setting his own down on the brick hearth, he glanced pensively toward the rain-sheeted windows. "Do you want to go out to a movie, or shall we stay here?"

Even though Vanessa was still wishing that she'd stayed home, indeed that she'd never met Nick at all, she had no desire to leave the comfort and warmth of his fire. She was, in fact, having some pretty primitive and elemental feelings where he and his comfortable home were concerned. It was almost as though she'd been wandering, cold and hungry and alone, and he'd rescued her and brought her to a secret, special place that no one else knew about.

Vanessa shook her head. She hadn't even had a sip of her wine yet, and it was already getting to her.

"Van?" Nick prompted, peering into her face, and she realized that she hadn't answered his question.

"Oh. Yes. I mean, I'd like to sit by the fire and watch the storm." Even as she spoke, blue-gold lightning streaked across the angry sky and a fresh spate of rain pelted the glass.

Nick came back and sat down beside her on the rug. "Tell me about your life, Van," he said, his voice low.

She immediately tensed, but before she could frame a reply, Nick reached out and squeezed her hand.

"I'm not asking about Parker—I know a little about him because we traveled in some of the same circles. You're the one I'm curious about."

Vanessa took a sip of her wine and then told Nick the central facts about her childhood; that her father had died when she was seven, that her very young mother had been overwhelmed by responsibilities and grief and had left her daughter with her parents so that she could marry a rodeo cowboy. There had been cards, letters and the occasional Christmas and birthday gifts, but Van had rarely seen her mother after that.

The expression in Nick's eyes was a soft one as he listened, but there was no pity in evidence, and Vanessa appreciated that. Her childhood had been difficult, but there were lots of people who would have gladly traded places with her, and she had made a good life for herself—generally speaking.

"You've always wanted to be on television?" Nick asked, plundering the white paper bag he'd brought home from the Chinese restaurant until he found two fortune cookies at the bottom.

Vanessa sighed and shook her head. "Not really. I wanted to be Annie Oakley until I was six—then I made the shattering discovery that there was very little call for trick riding and fancy shooting except in the circus."

Nick grinned at that. "My childhood dream pales

by comparison. I wanted to run my Uncle Guido's fish market."

Vanessa laughed. "And you had to settle for a career in professional football. My God, DeAngelo, that's sad—I don't know how you bore up under the disappointment!"

He had drawn very close. "I'm remarkable," he answered with a shrug.

"I can imagine," Vanessa confessed, and as he touched the sensitive, quivering flesh of her neck with his warm and tentative lips, she gave a little moan. "Is this the part where you start making me want you?" she dared to ask.

Nick nipped at her earlobe and chuckled when she trembled. "Yes. But that's all, so don't get nervous."

"What about what you want?" Vanessa asked.

"I can wait," he replied, and she knew she should push him away, but she couldn't. The attention he was giving her neck felt entirely too good.

Presently his hands came back to the zipper of the hoodie. Vanessa closed her fingers over his, realizing with a sleepy sort of despair that she wasn't wearing either bra or panties beneath the soft blue cotton, but Nick would not be stopped. He was a gentle conqueror, though, and she had no more thoughts of fear or of escape.

She was lying on her back before the popping fire when he bared her breasts and watched the shimmer of the blaze and the flash of lightning play over them. Vanessa had never felt so feminine, so desirable.

With a low, grumbling groan, Nick lowered himself to chart the circumference of her breast with a whisperlight passing of his lips. Vanessa watched in delicious dread as he moved toward the peak he meant to conquer, in an upward spiraling pattern of kisses. A whimper of long-denied pleasure escaped her as he touched her budding nipple with his tongue, causing it to blossom like some lovely, exotic flower.

Beyond the windows, lightning raged against the sky as though seeking to thrust its golden fingers through the glass and snatch the lovers up in fire and heat. Vanessa shuddered involuntarily as Nick's hand made a slow, comforting circle on her belly, his lips and tongue continuing to master her nipple.

He'd said his goal was to make her want him, and he'd succeeded without question. Vanessa longed to give him the kind of intolerable pleasure he was giving her, to be joined with him in a fevered battle that would have no losers. But he was setting the pace, and Vanessa had no power to turn the tables.

Her breasts were moist and pleasantly swollen by the time he brought his mouth back to hers and consumed her in a kiss as elemental as the lightning tearing at the afternoon sky.

"Do you want me to make love to you, Van?" Nick whispered against her throat when the kiss had at last ended.

Vanessa could barely lie still, her body was so hungry for his. "Yes," she admitted breathlessly, her fingers frantic in his hair. "Oh, yes."

He gave a heavy sigh and circled a pulsing nipple with the tip of his tongue before saying the unbelievable words. "You're not ready for that, darlin'."

Although he'd spoken without a trace of malice, Vanessa still felt as though she'd been slapped. "You can't just—just leave me like this…."

"Don't worry," he said, still toying with her nipple. "I don't intend to."

Moments later, he drew her pants down over her hips and legs and tossed them away. He kissed Vanessa thoroughly before trailing his mouth down over her collarbone, her breasts, her belly.

When he reached his destination, the lightning would wait no longer. It reached into the room, scooping Vanessa up with crackling fingers and bouncing her mercilessly in its palm. Only when she cried out in primitive satisfaction did it set her back on the rug in front of Nick's fireplace and leave her in relative peace.

She was crying, and she couldn't bring herself to look at the man who had unchained the lightning.

He covered her gently with an afghan as though she were a casualty of some sort and kissed her on the forehead. "I'll be back in a few minutes," he said.

By the time Nick returned, Vanessa had rallied enough to get back into her clothing. She was standing at the window, looking out on the gloomy spectacle of a city dressed in twilight gray, hugging herself. Nick stood behind her, putting his arms around her, and she felt the chilly dampness of his bare chest against her back and guessed that he'd taken a cold shower.

"Why?" she asked, not looking at him because she couldn't. "I would have given myself to you. Didn't you want me?"

"Oh, I wanted you all right."

"Then why? Why didn't you take me?"

"Because this is your time, Vanessa. Because I think you're hiding somewhere deep inside yourself and you need to be coaxed into the world again. That's what I want to show you—that it's safe out here."

She turned in his arms, sliding hers around his waist. He wore nothing but a pair of jeans and an impudent half grin. She rested her forehead against his cool, muscular chest.

"It was as though the storm came inside," she confessed. "I've never felt anything like it."

Nick simply held her and listened.

"I'm not some kind of neurotic, you know," she went on. "And I'm not a prude, either."

He chuckled, and his lips moved softly at her temple. "No prude would have responded the way you did."

Vanessa looked up at him. "You were right earlier, Nick DeAngelo—you are a remarkable man."

He favored her with a cocky grin. "You have no idea how remarkable," he teased.

"I think I'd like to go home before I decide to find out," Vanessa replied.

Nick didn't argue, get insulted or try to convince her to stay. He simply put on a shirt and shoes, got her a paper bag for her jeans and sweater and drove her home.

"Will you come to dinner on Friday night?" Vanessa asked him, when they were standing in her kitchen and he'd just given her a goodbye kiss that brought faint flickers of lightning to her mind.

"Do I have to wait that long to see you again?" he countered, albeit good-naturedly.

Vanessa nodded. "I'm afraid so. If you're around, I won't get any rest at all, and when that happens, I don't do well on television."

Nick touched the tip of her nose with an index finger. "Okay." He sighed. "I'll content myself with watching you sell cordless screwdrivers and stainless steel cutlery for a week, but be forewarned, when Friday night comes around, you're in for another lesson on why I'm the only man for you."

Vanessa felt a pleasant little thrill at the prospect and hoped he didn't notice. "Eight o'clock," she said.

He kissed her again. "Seven, and I'll bring the wine."

"Seven-thirty," Vanessa negotiated, "and you can also build the fire."

Nick laughed. "Deal," he said, shaking her hand. And then he was gone, and Vanessa's big, empty house seemed bigger and emptier than ever.

She fed Sari, who had been telling a long and woeful tale in colloquial meows from the moment Vanessa and Nick had entered the house. She had just tossed her jeans, sweater and underwear into the utility room when someone began pounding at the front door.

Thinking Nick had come back, she hurried through the house, worked the lock and pulled the door open wide.

Parker was standing on the step, looking apoplectic. "Do you realize how many messages I've left for you since last night?" he demanded furiously.

Not wanting the neighbors to witness a domestic drama of the sort they'd learned to expect and relish during the last days of the marriage, Vanessa grasped Parker by the arm and pulled him inside the house.

"I've been busy," she hissed, annoyed. She started off toward the kitchen again, leaving Parker to follow. "What did you want, anyway?" she demanded, reaching into a cupboard for two mugs and marching over to the sink.

"I'm going to be on a talk show day after tomorrow," her ex-husband answered in grudging tones, hurling himself into a chair at the table. He named a very famous host. "She wants you to appear, too, since you're in the book."

So that was it. Vanessa's feelings of being cherished was displaced by a sensation of weariness. She wondered who, besides Parker, would have had the gall to suggest such a thing.

"No way, slugger," she breathed, setting the mugs full of water in the microwave and getting out a jar of instant coffee.

"It will mean more sales, Van," Parker whined, "and more sales means more money!"

Vanessa was standing by the counter, her arms folded, waiting for the water to heat. "You live in a fantasy world, don't you, Parker? A place where nobody ever says no to anything you want. Well, listen to this—I'm not going to help you promote that book, I'm going to sue you for writing it!"

The bell on the microwave chimed, and Vanessa took the mugs out and made coffee by rote. She set one in front of Parker with a thump and sat down on the opposite side of the table from him.

He was staring at the hoodie in baffled distaste. "Good grief, Vanessa," he said, "don't you make enough money to dress decently? Whatever that thing is, it's a size too big."

Vanessa sighed. Some things never changed. "I knew you were coming over and I dressed for the occasion," she said sweetly, taking a sip from her mug. Sari made a furry pass around her ankles, as if to lend reassurance.

Parker was a master of the quicksilver technique, and he sat back in his chair and smiled warmly at Vanessa. "I hope I didn't make you feel inadequate," he said.

He'd made a specialty of it in the past, but Vanessa

had no desire to hash over the bad old days. She thought of the hours she'd spent in Nick DeAngelo's company and smiled back. "That's about the last thing I'm feeling right now," she answered.

Parker looked disappointed. "Oh."

Vanessa laughed at his frank bewilderment. "Listen," she said after recovering herself, "our marriage has been over for a long time. We don't have to do battle anymore."

He sat up straight. "The things I'm asking for are very simple, Vanessa," he said, sounding almost prim.

"And they're also impossible. I'm not going on any talk show to promote a book I'd like to see fade into obscurity."

His expression turned smug. "Suing me will only make sales soar," he said.

"I know," Vanessa confessed with a sigh. "Just tell me one thing, Parker—why did you describe me that way? Was that the kind of wife you wish I'd been?"

Parker averted his eyes, then pulled back the sleeve of his expensive Irish woolen sweater to glance at his Rolex. "What would I have to do to get you back?" he asked without even looking at her.

Vanessa was thunderstruck. Not once in her wildest imaginings had it ever occurred to her that Parker had been harassing her in a sort of schoolboy attempt to get her attention. She put her hands to her cheeks, unable for the moment to speak.

At last Parker met her gaze. "I thought things would be so much better without you," he told her gruffly. "Instead my whole life is going to hell."

Vanessa resisted an urge to take out the brandy she'd used to make fruitcake the year before and pour a generous dose into her coffee. "I'm flattered," she said in a moderate voice, "but I don't think getting back together would be good for either of us."

"You're in love with somebody else," Parker accused.

It was too soon to say that what Vanessa felt for Nick was love, but his appearance in her life had made some profound changes. "That's got nothing to do with anything," she answered. "There is no future for you and me—there shouldn't even have been a past." She got out of her chair and went to the back door, opening it to the chilly autumn wind and standing there looking at Parker.

To his credit, he took the hint and slid back his chair. "If you'd just let me stay, I could prove to you that getting divorced was a mistake for us."

Vanessa shook her head, marveling. "Good night," she said, and she closed and locked the door the moment Parker stepped over the threshold.

The telephone rang just as she was taking their cups from the table to the sink.

"Was that The Living Legend I just saw leaving your place?" her cousin Rodney demanded.

Vanessa smiled, looking out the kitchen window at the lighted apartment over the garage. "Yes. All moved in, are you?"

"Absolutely," Rodney replied. "I've been painting all day, and the fact is, I think if I close my eyes tonight I'm going to wake up asphyxiated."

"If you're asphyxiated, you don't usually wake up," Vanessa pointed out.

"I'd forgotten how nitpicky you get when you're tired," Rodney teased. "Are you going to invite me to sleep on your couch tonight or what?"

Vanessa laughed. "I haven't got a couch, remember? Parker took it. But you're welcome to spread out a sleeping bag and breathe free."

"I'll be right down," came the immediate response.

Rodney arrived within seconds, carrying a rolled-up sleeping bag and a paper sack with the name of a favorite delicatessen emblazoned on the side. "Have you had dinner?" he asked.

Vanessa realized that she hadn't had anything to eat since the Chinese lunch at Nick's, and she was hungry. "Actually, no," she answered.

Rodney pulled out the cutting board and slid the biggest hero sandwich Vanessa had seen in recent memory out of the bag. Her cousin reached for a knife and cut the huge combination of bread and lettuce, cheese and turkey into two equal pieces. "Share and share alike," he said.

Grinning, Vanessa took plates from the cupboard and brought them over to the counter. "I'm overwhelmed by your generosity."

"It's the least I can do for the woman who saved me from spending another night above Jergenson's Funeral Parlor," he replied.

Vanessa put half the sandwich onto her plate and went back to the table. "Someday, when you're a successful chiropractor, you'll look back on living there as a growth experience."

Rodney dropped into the chair directly across from hers. "You're trying to evade the real issue here, which is what did Parker want?"

"I don't think he knows," Vanessa confided, dropping her eyes to her sandwich.

"Damn," Rodney marveled, "he's trying to get you

back, isn't he? I wonder how he found out you were seeing Nick DeAngelo. Bet it's eating him up—"

Vanessa gazed directly at her cousin. "How do you know about Nick?" she broke in.

"I saw him," Rodney answered with a shrug. "I go out with his sister Gina sometimes."

Vanessa blushed, remembering that she was wearing Gina's clothes and wondering if Rodney recognized it. "Then you know him?" she speculated.

Rodney shrugged again. "You could say that, I guess. I've been on a few family picnics—when that tribe heads for the island, it's like some kind of Italian exodus."

Vanessa swallowed a weary giggle. "The island?" she asked, trying to sound casual.

The mischievous look in Rodney's eyes said she'd failed roundly. "Nick owns a big Victorian house in the San Juans," he answered. "Don't you ever read the tabloids? He's famous for the parties he gives."

A picture came into Vanessa's mind, the image of herself walking into Parker's condominium on Maui, planning to surprise him by arriving for their vacation a day ahead of time. She'd surprised him, all right—along with the Polynesian beauty sharing his bed.

Her thoughts turned to the storm of that afternoon, and the searing, crackling lightning. Vanessa felt betrayed.

The fiery gentleness of Nick's lovemaking had eased many of her doubts about him, but now she realized that the patience and caring he'd shown had probably been nothing more than pretense. If he liked to party and play the field, a relationship with her wasn't likely to change him any more than it had changed Parker.

Every self-help book on the market was screaming

the message that men are an as-is proposition, once a rogue, always a rogue.

Vanessa put her hands over her face, her appetite gone.

"Van?" Rodney sounded worried. "What's the matter? Are you okay?"

Vanessa got out of her chair, carried her sandwich to the counter, wrapped it carefully and tucked it into the refrigerator. Although she didn't say a word, she was shaking her head the whole time.

Rodney's chair scraped against the floor as he pushed it back. "I said something wrong, didn't I?"

"No," Vanessa said, unable to meet her cousin's eyes, "you brought me to my senses, that's all. I'd forgotten that a jock is a jock is a jock." She paused at the base of the back stairway, her hand resting on the banister. "Good night," she said.

Words, Vanessa discovered, did not make it so. The night was not a good one, and the morning showed every sign of being worse.

Chapter 4

The porcelain statuette of a Grecian goddess toppled precariously when Vanessa bumped into it, and it would have shattered on the studio floor if Mel hadn't been so quick to grab it.

Paul Harmon signaled from off-camera, and Vanessa was grateful for the respite.

"Are you all right?" her friend and employer asked, when she left Mel to sell the goddess unaided.

Vanessa drew a deep breath and let it out slowly. She'd been a klutz all morning, crashing into props and sales items, saying nonsensical things, getting prices and details wrong. She splayed her fingers and shoved them through her hair, thus spoiling the coiffure Margie in Makeup had spent twenty minutes styling. "Let's just say I'll be glad when this day is over." She sighed loudly.

Paul grinned. "Nick?" he asked.

Vanessa squared her shoulders. *What egotists men are,* she thought. *One of them comes along and screws up your life, and all his friends think "what a guy."*

"Nick who?" she countered coolly, turning around and marching back on camera.

An elderly lady from Tucson, calling in to order the statuette for her daughter, was on the air. "I've got all my credit cards up to their limits, but I can't help myself," she enthused. "I just had to get Venus for Allison. She'll love this for her bathroom."

Distracted, Vanessa forgot the cardinal telemarketing rule and said worriedly, "Maybe you shouldn't buy anything for a while. After all, there will be other statues, and you've worked hard to build up your credit…."

Mel looked at Van as though her nose had just grown an inch and elbowed her aside. "Vanessa's kidding, of course," he boomed in his best it's-me-and-you-against-those-guys-who-charge-high-prices voice. "This is a unique piece of art that would grace anybody's bathroom."

Paul was signaling again, but this time he didn't look quite so friendly. When Vanessa reached him, he took her arm and squired her into the makeup room, where fast-talking Oliver Richards was being prepared to go on.

He glanced up at the monitor to let Vanessa know he'd witnessed her gaffe and wriggled his eyebrows. Since the day he'd made a pass at her and she'd set him straight, Oliver had taken pleasure in every setback she suffered, be it major or minor.

"Good work, Van," he said. "Keep this up, and we'll all be in the unemployment line."

Paul gave the former sportscaster a dark look. "Go out and take over for Mel. He's got a dental appointment and has to leave early." Oliver immediately left.

Vanessa lowered her head, braced for a lecture. "My mind hasn't been on my work this morning," she said. "I'm sorry."

Paul sighed. "This kind of thing happens to everybody at one point or another," he reasoned. "One thing is a given—the board isn't going to be pleased about that little speech you just made. Van, what possessed you to do that?"

"I told you, I wasn't thinking." Vanessa looked up at her friend, feeling defensive. "Besides, what I said was true, even if it wasn't a good sales technique. There are a lot of people out there running themselves into serious debt so they can put statues of Venus in their bathrooms.

"And I should pity the wretched masses and shut down the cameras?" Paul shot back, annoyed. "Is everybody supposed to do without the convenience of home shopping because a few people can't control themselves?"

"I didn't say that!" Vanessa cried.

Just then Nick walked in, looking reprehensibly handsome in gray slacks, a navy blue sweater and a charcoal sports jacket.

"What are you doing here?" Vanessa demanded.

"I'm going out to lunch with a friend," he answered calmly, his eyes dancing with amusement.

"We agreed not to see each other again until Friday," she reminded him.

"You're not the friend," Nick replied in reasonable tones. He looked over her head at Paul. "Ready to go, old buddy?"

Vanessa's face was flushed, and she turned away to hide it. "I'm due on camera," she muttered, striding purposefully toward the door.

"Try not to put us out of business before your segment's over," Paul called after her.

Although Vanessa was seething inside, she smiled at the camera and at Oliver Richards when she stepped back onto the set. A rowing machine had been brought on as the next item to be featured, and Oliver beamed as an idea came to mind.

"The lovely Vanessa Lawrence rejoins us, folks," he announced. "Just in time to demonstrate the rowing machine."

Determined not to lose her composure, Van kicked off her high heels and sat down on the machine's seat, trying to be graceful as she tugged the straight skirt of her cashmere dress modestly over her thighs.

Despite the blinding glare of the studio lights, Vanessa was painfully aware of Nick's presence as she rowed and chatted with customers from all over the country. He'd lingered to watch her make a fool of herself in front of Middle-America.

By the time her replacement arrived, she had developed a megaheadache, but Nick was nowhere in sight when she left the studio complex to drive home.

Upon reaching the house, she felt better, and, seeing Rodney's car in the driveway, she decided to drop in to see if he was settled into the apartment over her garage.

Music was blaring through the open door when Vanessa reached the top of the stairs, and she was smiling when she knocked.

"Come in!" cried a feminine voice.

With a slight lift of one eyebrow, Vanessa went inside. A lovely dark-eyed girl, dressed in blue jeans and a T-shirt, with chocolate-colored hair tumbling to her waist, was sitting in the middle of the living-room floor. She was breaking a thread with her teeth, a tangle of fabric and sequins resting in her lap.

Rodney arrived from the kitchen, carrying two cans of diet pop, just as Vanessa was about to introduce herself. He took over the task with admirable grace. "Van," he said proudly, "this is Gina DeAngelo. Gina, my cousin and landlady, Vanessa Lawrence."

"Hi," Gina said, holding out a hand.

Vanessa was charmed. After returning the greeting, she sank into a chair. "What is that?" she asked, referring to the fabric Gina had been working with.

"It's Rodney's costume," the girl answered, holding up the blue stretchy fabric. "He's got a new act. Why don't you show her, Rod?"

Rodney blushed. Despite the fact that he earned his living, as well as his tuition, by working as an exotic dancer, he was shy. "No way," he answered.

Gina let the subject drop, smiling at Vanessa. "You're dating my brother," she said, her brown eyes twinkling.

Vanessa sighed. "I wouldn't exactly say—"

"It bothers her that he used to be a pro athlete, like her first husband," Rodney put in, speaking as though Vanessa weren't there.

Gina shrugged prettily. "To each her own," she said.

Vanessa felt called upon to say something positive about Nick. "Your brother is the most self-assured person I've ever met," she remarked.

Gina shrugged again. "He'd face down the general membership of Hell's Angels without batting an eye," she said, "but let him get sick or hurt himself and he goes to pieces. Last month he cut his finger chopping vegetables for a salad, and you'd have thought there'd been a chainsaw massacre."

Vanessa laughed. It was good to know the idol was human with feet of clay, she thought to herself. But then she remembered his reputation and the parties he was allegedly so famous for and decided he was probably *too* human. Her expression sobered.

"You look so sad," Gina said, exhibiting her brother's propensity for perception. That she could read minds was evident when she went on. "Nick is a really nice man, Vanessa. And he's mellowed out a lot since the old days."

Vanessa was not comforted, nor could she help drawing certain correlations between Nick and Parker. They were both attractive, sought-after men. While finding Parker in bed with another woman had been devastating, she knew that if history repeated itself with Nick, she would be shattered.

Somewhat awkwardly she told Gina that it had been nice to meet her, made an excuse and fled.

As usual, the light on her answering machine was blinking when she let herself into the house. Dreading more of Parker's nonsense, she nonetheless played back the messages.

The first call was from her grandmother, who wanted to know if she and Rodney would be coming to Spokane for Thanksgiving and Christmas that year. The second was from a local television station, where Vanessa had put in an application just before Paul had hired her to be on the Midas Network.

Her heart practically stopped beating, she was so excited. In the middle of Parker's diatribe on how the divorce had been a mistake, she stopped the playback and listened again. She hadn't imagined it; Station

WTBE was interviewing potential hosts for a new talk show and they wanted her to come in to see them.

Vanessa had to take three deep breaths before she was steady enough to return the call. When the producer's assistant answered, her voice elevated itself to a squeak.

The assistant was patient. "What did you say your name was again, please?" she asked.

Van closed her eyes, rehearsing her answer. The way things had been going that day, there was every possibility she'd get it wrong. "Vanessa Lawrence," she managed to reply at some length.

"Would a week from Friday be convenient for you?"

Any day would have been convenient, but Van knew better than to make herself sound desperate by saying so. "That would be just fine," she said coolly.

"Two-thirty?" the woman suggested.

"Two-thirty," Vanessa confirmed, frantically scribbling the date and time on the back of a phone bill even though the information was emblazoned in her mind for all time.

The moment she'd hung up the receiver, she dashed breathlessly up the rear stairs and into her sparsely furnished bedroom. There, she slid open the closet door and flipped on the light, looking for the perfect outfit, the clothes to convince the producers of *Seattle This Morning* that their search for a host was over.

Soon the bed was piled high with dresses, suits, skirts and blouses—none of which quite met Vanessa's specifications. She had just decided to head for the mall when the telephone rang.

Her cheerful hello brought a burst of blustering frustration from Parker.

"Didn't you get my message?"

"Yes…" Vanessa sighed. "Parker, I don't have time to tango right now, okay? Something really important has come up, and I'm going out."

"You've got a date with DeAngelo, I suppose," Parker immediately retorted. "I could tell you a few things about that son of a—"

The pit of Vanessa's stomach twisted. She wasn't ready to hear the things Parker would say about Nick, not yet. "I've got to run," she interrupted, almost singing the words, "'Bye!"

The telephone started to ring again almost immediately after she'd hung up, and it was still jangling away when she dashed out of the house without turning the answering machine on.

Five hours later she returned with a fitted suit in a shade of ice blue. There was a Corvette to match sitting behind Rodney's battered sports car in her driveway.

Memories of the way she'd behaved in Nick's apartment combined with a not-so-instant replay of the words they'd exchanged at the studio to make her cheeks hot. The man didn't know the meaning of the word Friday, she fretted. Well, maybe it was just as well that he was there. Now would be as good a time as any to tell him that they shouldn't see each other anymore.

She unlocked the back door, let herself in and waited. Nick was obviously up in Rodney's apartment, passing the time of day. In a matter of minutes he would realize that she was home and appear on some flimsy pretext.

Twenty minutes passed with no sign of Nick. Vanessa had put away her new outfit, changed into jeans and a flannel shirt and even brewed herself a cup of tea when she finally heard an engine roar to life in the driveway.

He was leaving without even saying hello!

Incredulous, Vanessa raced through the house to peer out one of the front windows. Sure enough, Nick was backing the Corvette out into the road, Gina beside him and, as far as Vanessa could tell, he didn't even glance in her direction.

"I'm becoming obsessive," she told the cat, who had come to steer her back toward the kitchen.

Sari made her usual noncommittal comment, and Vanessa gave the animal supper before setting aside her pride and going outside to climb the stairs to Rodney's apartment.

"Hi," he said, looking surprised to see her.

Vanessa took in the very abbreviated cowboy costume he was wearing, raising an eyebrow.

"I was just practicing a new number," he told her, sounding defensive.

His cousin smiled. "Speaking of numbers, I wonder if you'd mind giving me Nick's?"

Rodney eyed her curiously, then shrugged. "Sure, I've got it here somewhere. Are you going to ask him out or what?"

"That's kind of a personal question, isn't it?" Vanessa countered.

"Touchy lady," drawled Rodney as he searched through the contact list on his phone. "Here it is," he said, scrawling the number onto a piece of scrap paper and holding it out to Vanessa.

She took it, thanked him and left with as much dignity as she could manage.

She gave Nick plenty of time to get home, systematically building up her courage as she waited, and then dialed his number. It was an irony of sorts that she got his answering machine.

The message she left was simple and to the point. "Nick, this is Vanessa. I don't think we should see each other anymore, and that includes dinner on Friday. Goodbye."

It was a long evening for Vanessa, spent with the nervous expectation that Nick would either call or drop by, demanding an explanation for her decision. As it happened, neither the telephone nor the doorbell rang once.

The rest of the week and following weekend was peaceful, too.

On Monday morning, Margie complained about the shadows under Vanessa's eyes as she applied her makeup. "Keep losing sleep like this, kid," the cosmetologist warned, "and you're going to look like a raccoon."

Despite everything, Vanessa laughed. "The beginning of another lovely day," she said.

Just then, Oliver Richards dashed in and switched the channel on the monitor from the Midas Network to a popular national talk show. Vanessa stiffened in her chair as she saw the handsome face of her ex-husband fill the screen. She'd forgotten all about Parker's guest spot.

The program had obviously been in progress for a few minutes, and Parker was smiling boyishly at the applause of the predominantly female audience. "I'm happy to say that Van and I are getting back together," he said. "This time I'm going to be the best husband any woman ever had."

The paper cup in Vanessa's hand dropped to the floor, coffee and all.

"Tell us a little about your ex-wife," the program's

famous host prompted, watching Parker with a certain speculation in her eyes.

"It's all in the book," Parker answered proudly, and, to Vanessa's abject horror, he held up a copy for the whole world to see.

Vanessa hadn't expected the book to be published for weeks, so her first shock was compounded by a second. "Oh, no!" she cried.

Oliver, standing beside her chair, was wiping Van's coffee from his pants legs with a wad of tissue.

Parker looked directly into the camera, a besotted expression on his face. "I will say this—I love you, Vanessa. And I forgive you for all the times you've... hurt me."

Vanessa could bear no more. She lunged for the monitor's off button and then covered her face with both hands and groaned in helpless despair.

"Congratulations on the reconciliation, Van," Oliver boomed. "Does this mean we'll be forced to get along without you here at the old network?"

Vanessa glared at him, pointedly ignoring his remark, and stormed out.

That stint on camera was the most difficult of Vanessa's brief career, and when it was over she had to sit through a long meeting with the buyers. The products that would be featured for the next few days were demonstrated in detail, and price lists were passed out.

When she got home, the cleaning lady was there, and the living room was filled to the rafters with flowers. If Rodney had been around, Vanessa reflected ruefully, he'd have thought he was back at the funeral parlor.

As she'd expected, the carnations, roses and daisies

were all from Parker, who thought surely he'd won her heart by forgiving her on national television. A headache pulsed under Vanessa's left temple, and she snapped at the cleaning lady when the doorbell rang.

"Shut that vacuum cleaner off!"

Looking wounded, Marita kicked the switch and stomped off into the kitchen. Vanessa opened the door, expecting another shipment of flowers, and found Nick standing there instead of a delivery man.

His jawline looked like granite. "When did you make the decision not to see me anymore, Vanessa?" he demanded, pushing past her when she didn't invite him inside. "Before or after you came to my apartment and let me make love to you? Before or after you decided to go back to Lawrence?"

Vanessa shoved her hands into her hair. "You didn't make love to me," she said lamely. It was a moot point, but she was desperate. "And I don't have any intention of reconciling with Parker. He made the whole thing up to sell books."

Nick was visibly relieved, but only for a moment. "Just how firm is this decision that we shouldn't see each other again?" he asked quietly, facing her now, standing so close that she could feel the heat and power of his body.

She remembered what Gina had said about the way Nick acted when he was sick or hurt, and a wave of tenderness swept over her. She couldn't help smiling a little. "Why do you ask?" she countered, because she didn't know what to say.

He laid his hands on her shoulders. "Because I'm crazy about you, Value Van."

Vanessa stepped back, lifting one eyebrow. "So

crazy that you didn't even return my call when I left that message on your machine. Or was it just that you didn't go home that night?"

Nick sighed. "I went to Portland, Van—I'm opening a new restaurant there."

Marita peered tentatively around the door jamb. "Can I come back now?" she queried, poised to run.

"Yes," Vanessa said, closing her eyes.

Nick took her elbow gently into his hand. "What do you say we go somewhere and talk?"

Vanessa could only nod, and they'd reached the sensible solace of Nick's apartment before she spoke. "Do you have any aspirin?"

After favoring her with a grin and a kiss on the forehead, Nick disappeared down the hallway, returning momentarily with two white tablets and a glass of water. Vanessa swallowed the aspirin gratefully and then staggered across the room and threw herself down on his cushy sofa.

"The day was really that bad, huh?" Nick said, sitting down on the sofa and placing her feet in his lap. He slipped her shoes off and tossed them away, then began massaging her aching arches and insteps.

"It was terrible!" Vanessa wailed, her arms folded across her face.

Nick went right on rubbing her feet, saying nothing, and she felt compelled to hurl something into the conversational void.

"Why did you leave football?"

Nick chuckled. "I'd made all the money I needed and I wanted to get out before I ruined my back or one of my knees."

The massage felt sinfully good—in fact, it was

beginning to arouse Vanessa, though she would never have admitted that. "Sensible," she said with a sigh. "That's you, Nick DeAngelo."

"Um-hmm," he answered, gently working the taut muscles of Vanessa's left calf.

She gave an involuntary whimper. "Stop," she said with such a lack of sincerity that Nick didn't even hesitate.

"Let's go out to the island tonight," he suggested in a reasonable tone.

Vanessa raised her head to look at him. "I have to work tomorrow," she said.

"So do I. There's ferry service—we can be back in plenty of time."

"But we would spend the night?"

Nick didn't look at her. "Yes."

She pulled her leg free and sat up. "I thought we had an understanding about that," she said tautly.

Nick reached out and hauled her easily onto his lap. "I didn't say we'd sleep together," he said in a deep, sleepy voice.

"Then what's the point of going?"

He laughed. "Get your mind out of the gutter, Lawrence. We could walk on the beach, listen to music by the fire and talk. We could play cribbage, drink wine and bake brownies...."

Vanessa rolled her eyes. "You are weird."

"Saturday I was remarkable. What happened?"

Van was feeling harried, and the idea of spending a peaceful night in an island hideaway was not without appeal. But there were those correlations. "I got to thinking that you're probably a whole lot like Parker," she confessed, looking away.

He took her chin in his hand and made her look at him. "I hate it when you do that," he said in a low, angry voice. "Don't compare me to him, Vanessa."

She shrugged. "He's a jock, you're a jock. He's a party animal, you're a party animal—"

"Tell me one thing, Vanessa," Nick interrupted, his dark eyes hot with quiet anger. "Did he let you decide when the two of you would make love for the first time?"

Vanessa looked away. "I don't see what that has to do with anything."

"Did he?" Nick insisted.

"No," she was forced to admit after a long time. Tears welled in her lashes. "No! I had too much wine on our second date and the next morning I woke up in his bed! Are you happy now?"

Nick closed his eyes. "I'm sorry," he said hoarsely.

Vanessa sniffled and started to get off his lap, but his arms tightened around her and the thought of rebelling didn't even cross her mind.

"Are you still in love with him?" he asked.

"No," Vanessa answered without hesitation.

"Then come to the island with me."

"I have a cat to think about, you know," Vanessa pointed out, as Nick began kissing her neck in much the way he had on Saturday.

"Rodney will feed it," he said.

Vanessa trembled. She wasn't ready for a physical relationship, and yet she wondered how she would endure spending a whole night on an island with Nick without offering herself to him. "Our deal still holds? That I get to choose the time, I mean?"

Nick opened the top button of her blouse. "Yes, but

it's only fair to tell you that I'm going to make it hard to wait."

"Oh," Vanessa answered inanely as another button gave way. He slid his hand inside her blouse to caress her breast, and she thought she was going to go insane with wanting him.

As it happened, though, the doorbell rang. Vanessa scrambled to her feet and began righting her blouse while Nick strode, grumbling, across the living room to open the door.

The wonders of the jet age, Vanessa reflected, staring at the visitor in amazement.

Parker glared at Nick as he stepped back to admit him. "It's good to see that you haven't changed, DeAngelo," Parker said furiously.

Nick sighed and ran a hand through his hair. "Is that what you came here to say?" he asked.

Parker had already turned his attention to Vanessa, and he looked for all the world like a betrayed husband, stricken at the discovery of his wife's faithlessness. "How could you, Van?" he rasped. "After the flowers and—"

Vanessa was incensed. "And your generous offer over national television to 'forgive' me?"

"I love you!" Parker bellowed.

"You don't know what love is," Vanessa cried, her chin high and her shoulders square. She took comfort from Nick's presence, but it was even better realizing that she could handle the situation on her own. "Once and for all, Parker, it's over. Now go away and leave me alone."

Parker glowered at Nick, obviously seeing him as the

villain of the piece, and then left in a rage, slamming the door behind him.

Vanessa glanced at her watch. "If we're going to the island," she said, "we'd better get started. I need to pick up some of my clothes and feed the cat before we leave."

Nick grinned. "Whatever you say, lady," he teased. "I wouldn't dare cross you."

Chapter 5

Nick's island house was gray with white trim and latticework, and it was enormous. Standing hardly more than a stone's throw from the beach, the place had a friendly look about it, and Vanessa's first impression was favorable.

Still, what she knew of Nick's reputation haunted her subconscious, but she refused to entertain the thought. She was tired, even frazzled, and she needed the peace Nick and his grand old house were offering.

The inside was furnished in the same comfortable way as his condominium in Seattle; the sofas and chairs were soft and welcoming, the carpets deep. The paintings were watercolors in muted shades.

Nick led the way through the living room and up the stairway to the second floor. He passed several closed doors, then opened one on the right. "You can sleep in here," he said.

Vanessa bit her lip and slipped past him into a room decorated for a woman. The curtains and the comforter on the bed were a pastel floral print, and there were two white wicker chairs in front of the window, their seats upholstered to match.

"It's Gina's," Nick said, laying an index finger to Vanessa's lips just as she was about to open her mouth to ask.

He set her overnight case and garment bag on the bed and gestured toward the hall. "Come on, I'll show you where my room is—just in case."

Vanessa laughed. "Just in case what?"

Nick gave her a look. "Did I forget to tell you? The place is haunted. If you hear anything spooky, all you'll have to do is climb in bed with me and you'll be safe."

"I've heard some lines in my time, buddy," Vanessa replied, preceding him out into the hall, "but that one beats them all."

His room was really more of a suite with a fireplace and six floor-to-ceiling windows that overlooked the sea. Vanessa glanced at the bed and quickly shifted her eyes away.

Nick shook his head and pushed up the sleeves of his sky-blue sweater. A look at the half-open door of the closet explained why he hadn't brought spare clothes.

"What we need is some exercise," he said resolutely. "Let's go out for a run before it gets dark."

The way he'd phrased the suggestion made Vanessa feel like an Irish setter, and she did not share Nick's passion for running, but she wanted to be a good sport. She'd brought along an old set of sweats and some sneakers, and she went to put them on.

When she descended, Nick was already downstairs, warming up.

They followed the beach until Vanessa was near

collapse, then started back. She knew Nick was adjusting his pace to hers, and she tried not to slow him down too much.

Returning to the house was a vast relief. Vanessa threw herself onto the porch steps, gasping for breath, only to be hauled back to her feet again by Nick. She did seemingly endless cooling-down exercises before he was satisfied that he'd tortured her enough.

"I'm not sure I have the stamina for a relationship with you," she said when they were in the kitchen a few minutes later.

"Why do you think I'm trying to build up your endurance?" Nick got a bag of cookies down from a cupboard and took a carton of milk out of the refrigerator. Sniffing the milk, he made a face and poured it down the sink.

Vanessa grinned, shaking her head. "Your self-confidence overwhelms me."

Nick took two cookies from the bag and stuffed them into his mouth, one right after the other. "I was hoping it would be my charm and good looks," he said. He was standing right in front of Vanessa before she realized that he'd been approaching her.

She brushed a few chocolate crumbs from his lips. "That, too," she conceded.

Her back was to the counter—that was another fact that had sneaked up on her—and Nick had only to lean against her gently to imprison her. He did that without any apparent attack of conscience, and Vanessa ached in response to the hard grace of his body. He bent his head and kissed her, and his mouth tasted deliciously of chocolate cookies and controlled passion.

Vanessa was dazed when he finally broke away,

propelled her toward the back stairway and swatted her playfully on the bottom.

"To the showers, team," he said in a hoarse voice, and when Vanessa looked back over her shoulder, she saw him shove a hand through his hair in frustration.

Since Gina's room didn't come with its own bath like its counterpart in the condominium, Vanessa took her shower in the main bathroom. She put on gray pants and a kelly-green shirt, along with a light touch of makeup.

Nick was dropping an armload of wood onto the hearth in his bedroom when Vanessa finally gathered the nerve to creep to the doorway and look inside. He was wearing jeans and a plaid shirt that he hadn't bothered to button over his T-shirt.

Vanessa cleared her throat to let him know she was there, and he gave her a sidelong grin that said he'd been aware of her presence from the first.

"There's a storm coming in from the north," he said, laying a fire in the grate.

Vanessa's eyes widened, the lightning that had changed her forever still fresh in her mind. Her gaze skittered nervously to the big bed and back again.

Nick saw her trepidation and smiled. "Come in and sit down, Van. You ought to know by now that I'm not going to hurl you down and have my way with you."

There were comfortably upholstered chairs in front of the fireplace, and Vanessa went to sit in one of them, watching the motions of Nick's back as he finished building the fire, and thinking.

Ever since she'd met Nick, she'd been pondering the powerful effect he had on her senses and emotions, and she understood at least one thing, Nick DeAngelo was the kind of man most women dreamed of meeting—

strong, handsome, successful and far too good to be true.

There had to be a glaring fault that would come leaping out at her when she let down her guard and trusted him—and that was the moment Vanessa feared most. She drew her bare feet up onto the chair and wrapped her arms around her legs.

"Tell me about Jenna," she said, tilting her head to one side.

Nick sighed and reluctantly turned from the fire. "Okay. What do you want to know?"

"Why she left you, for one thing."

"She had a big problem with trust," Nick recalled, looking not at Vanessa but beyond her, it seemed, into the distant past. "I couldn't go anywhere without having her call or drive by to see if I was really where I said I'd be. We started to fight, the marriage fell apart and we went our separate ways."

Vanessa swallowed, remembering her own experience with Parker. "Did you give Jenna reason not to trust you?"

Nick looked insulted that she would even ask the question. "No," he replied with biting directness.

A few moments passed before Vanessa had the courage to speak again. "There was more to it than that, I think," she mused aloud.

"We disagreed about a lot of fundamental things," Nick admitted. "Kids, for instance."

Vanessa sat up straighter. This was a subject that mattered to her. She wanted children of her own more than anything else in the world, including the job on *Seattle This Morning* or a place on a television news team. "She wanted them and you didn't," she blurted out, braced for the worst, expecting Nick to feel as Parker had.

She got another angry, heated look for her trouble. "Wrong," he replied, turning away to throw an unnecessary chunk of wood onto an already thriving fire. "Jenna wanted to be the only child in my life. She was afraid a baby would steal the show."

Vanessa bit her lower lip and looked down at her lap, wishing she'd allowed Nick to tell her what he felt without holding him up against Parker first and then taking her clues from the comparison.

The silence stretched, and Nick finally got to his feet and pushed the screen up close to the fireplace. "What about you?" he asked, keeping his back to her. "Do you want children, Vanessa?"

She swallowed. Here was her chance to distance herself from Nick DeAngelo once and for all, to eliminate him and all the danger he represented from her life. Here was her opportunity to go back to being safe and ordinary.

She couldn't lie to him.

"A houseful," she answered, dropping her eyes when she saw him start to turn toward her.

"What about your career?" he asked. "What about selling foot massagers and wicker birdcages and porch lights?"

He was crouching in front of Vanessa's chair, grasping both its arms in his hands, and there was no way she could escape. "I don't intend to spend the rest of my life selling birdcages and porch lights," she said. "I—I have an interview for another job on Friday, as a matter of fact."

"You're hedging," Nick accused, and the timbre of

his voice and the scent of his freshly showered skin combined to make Vanessa slightly dizzy.

"I want to work, Nick," she said quietly, purposefully. "And I want babies, too. When—and if—I remarry, my husband will have to do more than help make children. He'll have to help raise them, too."

"Fair enough," he replied, his voice a husky rumble low in his chest. He drew Vanessa out of her chair, and she ended up kneeling astride his lap.

"Don't we need to go to the store and buy milk or something?" Vanessa queried, her voice an octave higher than usual.

The sound of Nick's laughter seemed to brush against the hollow beneath Vanessa's right ear. "Milk?" he echoed.

"T-to go with the cookies." Vanessa knew she sounded desperate.

He chuckled and began kissing the delicate flesh of her neck. "Cravings already?" he teased.

Vanessa wondered how in the name of heaven she was going to resist this man until she'd reached that mysterious point of readiness that so eluded her. "Nick," she pleaded.

"Hmm?" He pulled out her tucked-in shirt and then proceeded to unbutton it. The tingling pattern his lips painted on her neck continued without interruption.

"This isn't fair," she whispered breathlessly. Her head fell backward as he pushed the front of her blouse aside.

He unfastened the front catch on her lace-trimmed, silky pink bra, freeing her. "Life is never fair," he reminded her.

Against her better judgment, Vanessa leaned back

even farther when his hands rose to cup her breasts. "Ooooooh," she said.

Nick was kissing his way down over her collarbone. "My sentiments exactly," he replied just before he closed his mouth over one straining nipple.

Vanessa clasped both hands behind her head, increasing both her vulnerability and her pleasure. Her lips were parted, and her eyes closed as she reveled in nurturing Nick; she could feel and hear his desire, and it heightened her own.

He was moaning as he enjoyed her like a man wild with fever, and when she would have lowered her hands, he held them in place. The fingers of his left hand rubbed Vanessa's bare back, at once positioning her for his own unrestricted access and stroking her reassuringly.

The moment he released her wrists, Vanessa was peeling off his shirt and tossing it away, tearing at the T-shirt beneath. She would have undressed him completely if his position hadn't made that impossible.

His chest was muscular and, as Vanessa had, he leaned back slightly, in effect surrendering at least a part of his body to her explorations. He gave a powerful shudder and moaned low in his throat as she kissed, caressed and nibbled at him.

After a long time he rose gracefully to his feet, drawing Vanessa with him, clasping her close even as he stripped her of her shirt and dangling bra and began unfastening her pants.

"If you want to stop this, Vanessa," he warned, "turn around and walk out of the room right now. Whatever self-control I might have had is gone, and all bets are off."

Looking up into his smoldering brown eyes, Vanessa

remained where she was and opened the top button of his jeans. "All bets are off," she repeated, to let him know that she understood what was about to happen, that she welcomed it.

He kissed her then with all the passion he'd been holding back, and Vanessa could only guess at the strength it had taken to restrain such a torrent. She was hardly aware of being carried to the bed or undressed, and even though the sky outside was clear and quiet, the room crackled with lightning.

Nick was poised above her, his mouth covering hers in another mind-splintering kiss, the mattress giving slightly beneath her. Vanessa ran gentle hands up and down his broad, sinewy back, telling him without words that she wanted him.

He took her in a long, slow thrust that set her to twisting her head from side to side on the pillow, delirious in her need.

"Easy," he rasped out, and she could feel the struggle between Nick's mind and his body as he lay perfectly still inside her. "Take it easy, sweetheart. We have all the time in the world...."

Vanessa tried to force him to provide the friction, the motion, that she needed so desperately, but he was too big and too powerful and she could not move him. "Oh God, Nick. Why do you do this to me—why do you love making me wait?"

He chuckled and gave her a single, searing stroke metered to drive her insane, but his expression was serious when he spoke. "I want you to remember this always—it has to be special."

Vanessa arched her neck, felt his lips descend to the fevered skin there. "It is—I swear it. I'll remember..."

His laugh vibrated through his vocal cords and captured her heart like a warm summer wind. "So this is the secret to making you agree to my terms, is it?" he teased.

But he began to move upon her after that, quickening his pace heartbeat by heartbeat, stroke by stroke until Vanessa was covered from head to foot in a fine sheen of perspiration, until she was moaning and flinging her head from side to side.

"Let go," Nick whispered raggedly near her ear. "Stop fighting it and let go." His words broke down the last flimsy wall enclosing Vanessa's soul.

With a series of straining cries, she surrendered all that she was to Nick, all that she'd ever been or ever would be. The relief was exquisite; for a time, her soul escaped its bonds and flew free.

There was no restraint in Nick's release. He trembled, lunged deep inside her and cried out in satisfaction as pleasure induced its unique seizure.

For a long time afterward there were no sounds in the room except for their breathing and the popping of the fire. Then inexplicably, uncontrollably, Vanessa began to weep.

Nick groaned and rolled over to look down into her face. "Don't do this to me, Van," he pleaded, wiping away a tear with one thumb. "Please, don't be sorry for what we did."

She shook her head. "I'm not," she managed to say. "It's just that—"

He kissed her briefly on the mouth. "It's just that we don't know each other well enough, right?"

She nodded. "Right."

He leered at her and wriggled his eyebrows. "Okay, I'm a modern guy, I can relate. What's your sign, baby?"

Vanessa gave a shout of laughter through her tears. "Stop," she pleaded. "This is a sensitive moment."

Nick squinted at the clock on the bedside stand. "It's also dinnertime, and I'm hungry as hell. Let's make spaghetti."

Vanessa was too relaxed to contemplate getting up and doing any kind of work. "Make spaghetti? I *am* spaghetti."

"I have a hot tub," Nick wheedled, sliding downward and beginning to kiss her neck again.

Vanessa knew where that would lead. She twisted free and sat up. "You have a hot tub," she mused, looking at Nick with shining eyes. "What the devil does that have to do with cooking spaghetti?"

Nick declined to answer that and said instead, "On second thought, let's go out to dinner. I don't want you to get the idea that I'm a cheap date."

They took a shower, this time sharing the same stall, and dressed in the clothes that had been strewn from one side of the bedroom to the other. Vanessa reapplied her makeup and styled her hair.

"I hope this place is casual," she said, giving Nick's jeans and shirt a look.

The restaurant was a few miles away on the edge of the only town the small island boasted, and the spaghetti there was good.

"The owner must be Italian," Vanessa guessed, stabbing a meatball with her fork and lifting it to her mouth.

"Paddy O'Shaughnessy?" Nick teased. "Definitely. He probably grew up in Naples, or maybe Verona."

It was a night full of nonsense, restorative and precious, and Vanessa didn't want it to end. She knew, of course, that it would, and that the morning would bring painful regrets. She concentrated on enjoying Nick, the spaghetti and, later, the hot tub.

There were plants in the glass-walled room where the hot tub bubbled and churned, and Vanessa wrapped herself in the night sky with its glittering mantle of stars. "This must be what it's like when you're on safari," she said after swallowing a sip of wine. "I can just imagine that we're camped alongside a steaming river with crocodiles slipping by, unseen, unheard…"

"Now that's a romantic thought," Nick observed.

Vanessa hiccuped and looked accusingly at her wine. "I've had too much *vino,*" she told Nick seriously. "I'd better sleep in Gina's bed tonight."

If Nick was disappointed, he didn't show it. "Whatever you say, princess," he said quietly, taking the glass from her hand and setting it on the tiled edge of the large square tub. "I don't want you to have any regrets when you look back on today."

"I won't," Vanessa said, even though she knew she would. The wounds Parker had left were only partially healed, and she wouldn't be able to disregard the similarities between him and Nick forever.

When she yawned, Nick lifted her out of the tub. "Time for bed," he said. "We have to get up early."

Vanessa scrambled for a towel, not because she was naked, but because she was chilled, and she watched unabashedly while Nick got out of the tub and switched off the jets. He was so incredibly secure in his masculinity that he didn't reveal the slightest qualm about being nude.

When he pulled on a blue terrycloth robe, it was an unhurried action, meant for comfort and not modesty. In fact, when Vanessa came to him he opened the garment long enough to enfold her inside, against his ribs.

They walked upstairs that way, talking idly of spaghetti and hot tubs, and parted after a brief kiss in the doorway of Gina's room.

The sheets were cold. The moon and stars must have all gathered on the other side of the house, for there was no light for Vanessa to dream by. She missed Nick, even though they had parted only a few minutes before and he was just one room away.

Snuggling down determinedly, she closed her eyes and commanded herself to sleep. Despite her utter weariness, oblivion eluded her. She tossed, turned and tossed again.

Finally she got out of bed, put a robe on over her striped silk pajamas and padded across the hall.

"Nick?" she questioned softly from the doorway of his room.

He sounded sleepy. "What?"

"I think I heard something."

A motion in the moon-shadowed bed and a throaty groan of contentment told her he was stretching like some cocky panther. "Like what?" he asked innocently.

Vanessa shrugged. "You said there were ghosts…."

"Yup," Nick agreed, "I did." He threw back the covers to make a place for her beside him. "There's only one thing to do, lady. Circle up the wagons and share a bunk."

Vanessa was across the room and between Nick's sheets in a wink. She snuggled up against him, reveling in his warmth and his strength. "I'm going to hate myself when I wake up in the morning," she confessed with a contented sigh.

Nick kissed her forehead. "I know," he answered sadly. "And me, too, probably."

Vanessa rested her head on his shoulder. "Probably," she said, and then she dropped off to sleep.

When she awakened at dawn, Nick was gone. She knew he was probably out running, and she was grateful for the time to sort out where she was and what she'd done the night before.

She'd had her shower and dressed for work by the time Nick returned. Clad in running shorts, a tank top and a jacket, despite the fact that November was fast approaching, he looked at Van warily as he crossed the kitchen. He opened the refrigerator and took out the milk he and Vanessa had stopped for on the way home from O'Shaughnessy's the night before.

"Let's hear it," he started. "You hate me, you had too much wine last night and waking up the morning in my bed was an instant replay of the first time with Parker. Right?"

Vanessa was eating a slice of whole wheat toast slathered with honey. "Do I look traumatized?" she asked, chewing.

He cocked his head to one side, frowning. "No," he said, sounding surprised. "Are you saying you don't regret letting me make love to you?"

"Excuse me," Vanessa said, pouring herself a cup of the coffee that had been waiting when she came downstairs, "but you didn't do everything, you know. I was half of that little encounter." She paused and drew a deep breath, then let it out. "To answer your question, yes and no."

Nick gave her a wry look. "Yes and no. I like a decisive woman."

"It was too soon," she said. "I probably wasn't ready."

He set the milk back in the refrigerator and put his hands on his hips. "You seemed ready to me," he replied.

Vanessa blushed at the good-natured jibe and sipped her coffee to avoid having to say something.

"That takes care of the yes. What about the no? What don't you regret, Vanessa?"

Vanessa dropped her eyes. "The passion," she answered after a long time. "You brought me back into the world, Nick, and I'm grateful."

"Gratitude isn't exactly what I had in mind, but it'll do for now," he answered, and then he disappeared up the stairs. When he came back, he was wearing tan cords, gleaming leather shoes and a green sweater.

Vanessa assessed him appreciatively. "How much time have we got before the ferry leaves?"

Nick took in her blue dress and sighed heavily. "Not enough," he lamented. He took her in his arms and kissed her with knee-weakening thoroughness before whispering hoarsely, "I wish we could stay here forever."

Vanessa laid her head against his chest. "Me, too," she said, but she knew the magic was already slipping away.

It seemed sadly fitting that, when they drove aboard the ferry to return to Seattle, dark clouds were gathering in the northern sky.

The storm Nick had predicted was almost upon them.

Chapter 6

When Vanessa finished her segment that morning, Parker was waiting at the door of the women's dressing room. His arms were folded across his chest, and his features were set in a sour scowl.

"Where were you last night?" he demanded in a furious whisper.

Vanessa sighed. "We're divorced, Parker, and that's all I'm going to say about last night or anything else." She started to walk around him, but he reached out and took her arm in a painful grasp.

His nose was an inch from Vanessa's as he rasped, "You slept with him, didn't you?"

Vanessa wrenched free of his hold, her face hot with color. A receptionist was approaching with a folded piece of paper in her hand, looking scared.

"Sh-should I call security, Ms. Lawrence?"

Vanessa saw nothing to fear and everything to pity in Parker's eyes at that moment, and she shook her head as he made a visible effort to control himself. "Everything is fine, Karen," she lied.

Karen darted an uneasy glance at Parker and held out the paper to Vanessa. "Mr. DeAngelo called while you were on the air," she explained.

Vanessa scanned the note and suppressed a sigh. There was some kind of problem at the new restaurant in Portland, and Nick would be away until Friday. She bit her lower lip and crumpled the message into a ball. "Thank you," she said to the receptionist, who promptly hurried away.

"Have lunch with me," Parker said.

Vanessa stared at him. "You must be insane."

He treated her to his most endearing smile. "Look at it this way—if you don't, I'll just follow you home and you'll have to feed me anyway."

"I'd be more likely to call the police," Vanessa said.

Parker shrugged. "Whereas a restaurant would be a safe, neutral place—very public."

Vanessa sighed. She was in a glum mood and Parker was the last person she wanted to spend time with, especially when she knew he was going to tell her something she didn't want to know, but she finally nodded. She couldn't hide forever.

While her ex-husband waited, she toned down her makeup, gathered up the list of times she would be selling the next day and braced herself for the worst.

A soft rain was falling as Parker and Vanessa hurried across the employee parking lot to her car. Parker had arrived in a cab, which said a lot about his confidence in his powers of persuasion.

Unable to stand it any longer, Vanessa looked at him out of the corner of her eye as she snapped her seat belt into place. "You're going to tell me something about Nick, aren't you? Something awful."

Parker's expression was one of regretful gallantry. "This thing between you and him is getting serious, and I can't let it go any further."

"What?" Vanessa cried, frustrated beyond all bearing. "What's so terrible about Nick?"

Parker sighed. "All I'm going to say for right now is that he's not husband material. DeAngelo is ten times the bastard I ever was."

Vanessa offered no comment on that, and as she drove out of the studio compound, she gnawed nervously at her lower lip. Normally she wouldn't have given Parker's words any credence—he was, after all, a lying, manipulative cheat. But she had a spooky, gut-level feeling that this time he had something valid to say.

"Where do you want to go for lunch?" she asked even though every trace of her appetite was gone.

He named a nearby bar and grill, and Vanessa drove toward it.

They were settled in a booth with cushioned leather seats and roast beef sandwiches and glasses of beer in front of them, when Parker grinned at her and said, "Just like old times, huh, Van?"

Vanessa rolled her eyes. "Stop it, Parker. Too much has happened for us to be sitting here pretending to have fond memories."

Parker looked hurt. "You don't have any happy memories of us? Not even one?"

Vanessa thought of the early part of their marriage when she'd adored Parker, when everything he said had made her either laugh or cry. She'd lived on an emotional seesaw in those days, believing herself to be happy. In retrospect, she knew she had suffered. "Don't push, okay?" she said, averting her eyes. She hadn't been able to touch her sandwich, but she reached for the glass of beer with a trembling hand.

"You're really nervous, aren't you?" Parker's features darkened, indicating an approaching storm. "Are you that crazy about DeAngelo?"

Vanessa saw no point in lying. "Yes," she said straight out. "I am."

"Why?" Parker demanded, and some of the shaved beef slid out of his sandwich because he was squeezing it so hard.

Vanessa shrugged, trying to look nonchalant even though her stomach was roiling and her throat was closed tight. It wasn't fair of her to try to convict the man she loved on whatever it was Parker was going to say, especially when Nick wasn't there to defend himself.

"This is a mistake," she blurted, sliding across the bench to stand and shrug into her coat. "I shouldn't have come here—"

"Vanessa, sit down," Parker said, and something in his tone made her meet his gaze.

Her courage failed at what she saw there, and she dropped back into the seat, covering her face with both hands for a moment and sighing. "Tell me, Parker. Stop playing games and say it."

"He's using you to repay me for something that happened a couple of years ago."

The statement sounded so preposterous that Vanessa almost laughed out loud. Almost. "Like what?"

Parker sighed heavily and, for just a second or so, he looked honestly reluctant. "Did he mention Jenna—his ex-wife?"

Vanessa nodded. "Yes."

The expression in Parker's blue eyes was distant and vaguely arrogant. "What did he tell you about the divorce?"

Powerful forces battled within Vanessa, one faction wanting to stay and hear Parker out, the other clamoring for escape. "He said she had a problem with trusting him, and that she didn't want to have children."

Parker shook his head, as though marveling at some tacky wonder. Then, without further ado, he dropped the bomb. "She and I had an affair, Vanessa. Nick caught us together and he's been out to get me ever since."

For a moment the words just loomed between Vanessa and Parker, quivering with portent. Then they exploded in Vanessa's spirit, and tears of pain filled her eyes. She put a hand to her throat and rose shakily to her feet.

"Tell me it's a lie, Parker."

He shrugged and, incredibly, reached for his sandwich. "I'd like to, babe, but I can't. The truth will out, and all that."

Vanessa turned and stumbled toward the door. The storm had come and rain was pounding on the sidewalk as she stood in the cold wind, heedless and broken. She walked slowly to the car, her hands trembling so that it took several attempts to get the key into the lock and open the door.

When she was inside, she let her forehead rest against the steering wheel and drew deep breaths until the desire to scream had abated a little. She was just fitting the key into the ignition when the door on the passenger side opened, and Parker flopped into the seat, sopping wet.

"You shouldn't be alone right now," he said somehow managing to look as though he really gave a damn.

"Get out," Vanessa said. She was soaked to the skin, her hair was dripping rainwater and she knew her mascara was running down her face in dark streaks. She didn't care about any of those things. She wanted to be alone; she needed it.

Parker actually had the gall to reach out and grip her hand. "It's okay, Van—I'm going to take care of you. You'll forget about DeAngelo in no time."

Vanessa was cold and her teeth were beginning to chatter. "Get out," she said again, and after a second's hesitation Parker left the car, slamming the door behind him.

She drove home by rote, tears streaming down her face, and she hadn't had time to pull herself together before Rodney appeared. He let himself in through the kitchen door, took Vanessa by the shoulders and pressed her into a chair.

"Good God," he breathed, "you look awful! What happened? Did somebody die?"

Vanessa nodded. "Me," she answered. "I died, Rodney—fifteen minutes ago in Toddy's Bar and Grill."

Rodney put a hand to her forehead and then went to the cupboard for a mug. He promptly filled it with water and shoved it into the microwave. While it was heating, he plundered the cabinets until he found Vanessa's fruitcake brandy.

When he'd made a cup of instant coffee liberally laced with brandy, he set it on the table in front of Vanessa and sat down in the chair beside hers. "Talk to me," he said quietly.

Vanessa reached for the mug, holding it in both hands, letting it warm her fingers. "I can't," she said. "Not yet."

The door opened, and Gina slipped in. "Is everything okay?" she asked.

Vanessa averted her eyes, humiliated. She didn't want Gina to go to her brother and report that he'd broken her. His plan of revenge had succeeded beyond his wildest expectations.

"It's got to be about Nick," Rodney mused.

A strangled sob escaped Vanessa.

Gina spoke softly to Rodney. "I'd better go. I'll call you later."

"Sure," Rodney replied with affection, and he kissed Gina's forehead before she left the house.

Vanessa took a steadying sip of the brandied coffee.

"So," Rodney said, dropping back into his chair at the table, "tell me about the murder of Vanessa Lawrence back there at Toddy's Bar and Grill."

Vanessa shook her head. "Not now."

"Okay," her cousin said, "if you won't talk, at least go upstairs and get out of those wet clothes before you catch pneumonia."

Thinking of the important interview scheduled for Friday, Vanessa nodded woodenly. "Okay." She got up and walked up the stairs, stiff and slow of movement, carrying her coffee with her. She took a brief hot shower, then put on flannel pajamas and collapsed on her bed.

"You love Nick that much, huh?" Rodney asked from the doorway. He'd brought another cup of coffee, probably doctored, and he proceeded toward Vanessa's bedside.

She took the cup. "That's ridiculous. I've only known him a few days." And in that short length of time he had recreated her world.

Rodney sat down on the foot of the bed since Parker

hadn't left any of the chairs when he moved out. "Why do I get the feeling that your ex-husband had something to do with this?"

Vanessa set her coffee on the bedside table and wriggled under the covers. "Nick's been using me," she said, ignoring her cousin's question. "God, Rodney, what an actor he is—you should have seen him!"

"What did Parker tell you?" Rodney persisted.

"That he had an affair with Jenna DeAngelo and Nick caught them together," she said, and a new wave of pain washed over her as she said the words out loud.

"And you bought that?" Rodney bit off each word, clearly annoyed. "Van, you know Parker would rather climb the tallest tree and lie than stand flat-footed on the ground and tell the truth!"

Their grandfather had said those very words right after Van had introduced Parker to him. She wished she could be in Spokane now and be held in the old man's strong, gentle arms. "What Parker said was true," she said sadly. "I can't explain how I know, but I do."

Rodney rolled his eyes. "Great. You're not even going to give Nick a chance to tell his side of the story, are you?"

The mention of his name went through her like a lance. As soon as Rodney left, she would roll herself into a fetal ball and die. "He used me to get back at Parker," she said miserably. "Now go away and leave me alone. I'm terminal."

Rodney gave the telephone beside her bed a pointed glance. "I'll be in my apartment if you need me," he told her, and then he was gone.

Vanessa drank the rest of her coffee with brandy and

slipped under the covers to wait for the hurting to stop. It followed her relentlessly, even into her sleep.

She awakened hours later, when the room was glowing with moonlight, to find Nick sitting on the side of the bed, looking down at her. She started to pull the covers over her head, but he caught her wrists in an inescapable grasp and held them on either side of the pillow.

"What are you doing in my house?" she spat, struggling, to no real avail, against the hands that imprisoned her with such gentle effectiveness. "Get out, and don't ever come back!"

Even in the half darkness she saw the pain in Nick's eyes. God, how calm and collected he was. He should have been the one to work in the broadcasting business, not her.

He spoke in a steady, though hoarse, voice. "I'm here because Gina called me and told me you were in pieces. Rodney filled me in on the rest."

"It's true, isn't it?" Vanessa ventured to ask, looking at him with wide eyes.

Nick sighed and released her hands. He shoved splayed fingers through his rain-dampened hair. "Part of it. I did come home one night and found Jenna and Parker together."

Vanessa felt herself breaking apart inside. "And you swore revenge?"

"Hardly. I beat the hell out of him and left. He didn't tell you that part of the story, though, did he?"

"You lied to me," Vanessa accused. "You used me to get back at him!"

"I didn't care enough about Jenna to do that, Vanessa," Nick replied, still avoiding her eyes. "In one sense, I was actually relieved that it was finally over between us."

"You're glossing over the fact that you wanted revenge."

"I told you," Nick said with cold patience, "I had all the vengeance I wanted that night. Can you say you don't remember a night when your devoted husband came home with a few cuts and bruises?"

Vanessa shuddered. She remembered all right. Parker had claimed he'd been mugged, but refused to report the incident to the police. He and Vanessa had been married a little over six months at the time. "My God," she whispered.

Nick reached out to touch her face, and she slapped his hand away.

With a sigh, he got up and walked over to one of the windows that overlooked the street. "I think we'd better stop seeing each other for a while," he said after a long time.

Vanessa was stunned and infuriated. If anybody was going to break off this relationship, it was going to be her. She was the one who had been wronged!

She threw back the covers and struggled out of bed. "Wait just a minute, Nick DeAngelo!" she shouted, waving her finger at him.

Instantly he was facing her, and his face was taut with fury. "Listen to me," he ground out. "I won't play these games, Vanessa. I'll be damned if I'll involve myself with another woman who refuses to trust me!"

Vanessa's mouth dropped open.

"Goodbye," Nick said bluntly, and then he walked out, leaving her standing there, in the middle of her bedroom, feeling even worse than she had before.

Throughout the rest of the week, Vanessa functioned like an automaton. She got up in the mornings, fed the cat, got dressed and went to work. When that was done, she went home, fed the cat again and crawled into bed, usually without supper.

By Friday, the day of her interview, she looked less than her best. Wearing some compound Margie had given her to cover the shadows under her eyes, she presented herself at WTBE-TV in her new suit.

The front she put on must have been effective because the interview went very well. Although the program wouldn't actually go into production until after the first of the year, she was informed, the final decision would be made before Thanksgiving. Would she be able to leave the Midas Network by the middle of December?

Vanessa answered yes, thanked the woman who had interviewed her and left. Some fundamental instinct told her she was going to get the job. She still wanted it very much, but the excitement was gone.

Since Nick had walked out of her bedroom three days before, so many things had stopped mattering.

She glanced at her watch and saw that it was three-fifteen. She'd promised to meet Janet Harmon for a drink, so she set out for the Olympic Four Seasons at a very reluctant pace.

Janet would probably grill her about the breakup with Nick, and Vanessa didn't want to burst into tears in the bar of a swanky hotel.

Sure enough, her friend looked grimly determined when Vanessa met her in the elegant lobby.

"Paul and I stayed here on our wedding night," she said to make conversation, but it was plain that Janet's mind wasn't on her own relationship. "How did the job interview go?"

"I think they're going to hire me," Vanessa answered dispiritedly as they entered the cocktail lounge and seated themselves.

"Paul will be beside himself," Janet answered, "and not with joy, either."

Vanessa sighed and averted her eyes for a moment. "Stop pretending you didn't ask me here to find out what happened between Nick and me," she said.

Janet, a pretty woman with shoulder-length dark hair and blue eyes, folded her arms on the table top and leaned forward slightly. "I don't have to ask, Vanessa—I already know. Paul is Nick's best friend, remember?"

A waitress came, took their orders and left again.

"I'd be very interested to hear Nick's side of the story," Vanessa said stiffly.

"Then why don't you go over to DeAngelo's after you leave here and ask him to tell it to you?" Janet replied in clipped tones.

"Oh, great," Vanessa complained. "You're mad at me, too!"

"I'm furious. Nick DeAngelo is the best thing that's ever happened to you, and you're not even going to fight for him."

The waitress returned, setting a glass of white chablis in front of Vanessa. Janet was having a martini, and she made a small ceremony of eating the olive.

At any other time Vanessa would have been amused. As it was, she just wanted to go home, feed the cat and slink back into bed. To get it over with, she said, "I admit it. I was going to break off with Nick, and he beat me to the punch."

"He's a wreck," Janet informed her. "Paul says he's never seen Nick so low."

Vanessa took a certain satisfaction in knowing she wasn't the only one suffering. She lifted her wineglass to her mouth and sipped the chablis before answering, "He'll get over it, and so will I."

"I don't understand this," Janet pressed. "You fell in love with Nick the first night you met him—I know because I was there and I saw it happen. And now you're just going to walk away without looking back?"

"I'm not going to crawl to him," Vanessa said firmly. "I still think he used me to get back at Parker and I despise him for it."

"You don't know Nick very well." Janet sighed, sounding resigned at last. "He'd never do a thing like that. He's too open, and he hates games and little intrigues."

"He also hates me," Vanessa said, remembering the look in his eyes when he'd told her goodbye. "Let's drop the subject, please, because if we don't, I'm going to fall apart right here."

Janet must have believed her because she didn't mention Nick's name again. The two women finished their drinks and parted, vowing to meet for lunch before the holidays got into full swing and there was no time.

It was four-thirty when Vanessa got home—too early to go to bed and hide from her depression. She changed into jeans and a Seahawks T-shirt, fed Sari and proceeded to the living room, which was still choked with Parker's flowers.

She dropped one fading bouquet after another into a large plastic garbage bag and carried it out to the curb, where Rodney had already set the trash for morning pickup. She was stuffing the bag into one of the plastic cans when an ice-blue Corvette slipped sleekly into her driveway and Nick got out.

He looked as bad as she felt.

"Hi," he said, rounding the car to stand beside Vanessa and effectively block any retreat to the house.

Even though she'd rehearsed this moment through a thousand varying versions, she wasn't prepared to face Nick. She averted her eyes and said nothing at all.

Nick sighed, and out of the corner of her eye she saw him wedge his hands into the hip pockets of his jeans. "Damn it, Van, will you at least listen to me? I'm willing to admit I was wrong—I should have told you about Parker and Jenna."

"Why didn't you?" Vanessa asked, raising wary, pain-filled eyes to his face.

His formidable shoulders moved in a shrug. "It was water under the bridge to me. I didn't think it mattered."

Vanessa bit her lower lip. "You don't want to be involved with a woman who doesn't trust you— remember?"

Nick swore under his breath. "And you still don't, right?"

Vanessa sighed. "When you've been married to a man like Parker, it doesn't come easy."

"Speak of the devil," Nick marveled as a cab swept up to the curb and Parker got out.

He probably wouldn't have been so brave if he hadn't had another man with him. "That's the idea, Van," her ex-husband said, smiling as he approached, "Toss DeAngelo out with the trash and get on with your life."

Parker's friend, a yuppie-type wearing a three-piece suit, looked at him as though he'd gone mad.

Nick favored Parker with a slow, leisurely grin. "Keep talking," he said. "Right now I'd like nothing better than stuffing you into one of these cans and stomping you down like a milk carton."

Parker paled a little beneath his health-club tan, but he recovered his aplomb quickly enough. "Vanessa," he said, evidently choosing to pretend that Nick wasn't there, "this is Harold Barker. You're getting a second chance, baby."

Vanessa folded her arms, unconsciously protecting herself. "At what?" she asked in suspicious tones.

Parker looked enormously pleased with himself as he explained that Harold was the executive producer of yet another nationally syndicated talk show. "They want you to go on with me next week and help pitch the book."

The idea was born in a rebellious area of Vanessa's mind. She cast a sidelong look at Nick before saying expansively to Parker and Harold, "Come in, come in. This sounds like an interesting proposition."

Nick muttered another swearword, joining them even though Vanessa had made a point of not inviting him.

"Did you want something, Mr. DeAngelo?" she asked coolly when the four of them were standing in her half-furnished living room.

Nick gave her a look that would have made a vampire cower, planted himself in front of the fireplace and folded his arms across his chest. He was clearly staying for the duration, and that pleased Vanessa, even though she felt a conflicting desire to march over there and kick him in the shins.

Over a drink, solicitously served by a doting hostess, Harold explained his concept of a show including both

Parker and Vanessa. He was sure the viewing audience would enjoy hearing her reactions to the things her ex-husband had written about her.

"Of course," he finished, casting a nervous glance toward Nick, "we'll want to discuss your—er—reconciliation with Mr. Lawrence, too."

Vanessa beamed, perching behind Parker on the back of one of the two easy chairs he'd left her and ruffling his hair. "It's a romantic story," she said, well aware that Nick was seething even though she didn't dare look at him.

Parker was obviously baffled, but his tremendous ego served him well in his hour of need. He swelled up like a peacock and then shrugged in that aw-shucks-folks way that had made him such a hit with the fans. "I guess we were just swept away by passion," he said.

At last Vanessa risked a glance in Nick's direction. It was obvious from his grin that he was on to her game, even if Parker and Harold weren't.

Vanessa was still looking at Nick when she responded to Parker's remark. "It was incredible," she said.

Chapter 7

"It's Friday night," Nick said stubbornly, standing in Vanessa's kitchen with his arms folded. "We had a date, remember?"

Vanessa sighed. It was dark outside, even though it was still early, and there was a wintry chill in the air. She took her old sweater from the peg inside the pantry door and put it on. "We can't just go on as though nothing happened, Nick," she reasoned, wishing they could do exactly that.

"Because you still don't trust me," he ventured to guess.

She gently bit her lower lip for a moment. "I want to, but you're so much like Parker...."

His eyes darkened. "I didn't come over here to be insulted," he informed her. "Furthermore, damn it, I'm nothing like that bastard!"

Vanessa took a can of vegetable-beef soup from the cupboard. Since the argument with Nick, she'd been virtually living on the stuff. "You are," she insisted.

When he started to speak, she held up a hand, palm outward, to silence him. "Besides the pro-athletics aspect, there's your reputation. Do you deny that you're known far and wide as a rounder and a ladies' man?"

Nick jerked the soup can out of her hand, stuck it up against the can opener and pushed down on the handle so that an angry whir filled the kitchen. "Who the hell told you that?" he demanded. "Parker?"

Vanessa shook her head, reclaiming the soup, dumping it into a saucepan and adding water. "I'm not sure where I heard it. I just know, that's all." She studied him pensively as she put the mixture on the stove to heat. "You know, I think it's very interesting that Jenna didn't trust you when she was the one who was fooling around. Was yours an open marriage, Nick?"

He rolled his eyes, looking more annoyed by the moment. "Not on my end, it wasn't. As for Jenna, her own guilty conscience made her suspect me."

"Want some soup?" Vanessa asked, getting two bowls down from the shelf even as she spoke because she knew he wasn't about to leave.

Nick sighed. "No, but I'll eat it," he answered. While Vanessa was stirring the broth, he called DeAngelo's and instructed someone to send over two orders of clam linguine and a bottle of white wine.

She was grinning when she brought the steaming bowls of soup to the table. "A man of sweeping power and influence," she commented, as much to keep the conversation moving as anything.

Nick was frowning as he sat down. "How did your job interview go?" he asked.

"They're going to hire me, I think," she answered, reaching for a basket of saltine crackers she'd set out earlier and squashing a handful into her soup. "Of course, if they see me on national television with Parker, they may change their minds."

For a few moments, Nick said nothing. He was busy adding crackers to his soup. When he finally spoke, his tone was serious. "You're really going to do that? I thought you were just stringing Parker along to get rid of him."

Vanessa swallowed. "Yes, I'm really going to do that," she confirmed. "And I'm pretty sure he'll stop being a problem from then on."

"What about us, Vanessa?" Nick wanted to know, and there was a vulnerability in his voice that made her love him all the more hopelessly. "Where do we go from here?"

Inside Vanessa ached. She knew there could be no relationship without trust, and as much as she longed for things to be different, she hadn't reached the point where she could let herself rely on any man's integrity. She looked away, unable to answer.

He reached out and took her hand in his. "Okay, lady. So be it. I'll back off for a while."

The prospect made Vanessa's world seem as dark as deep space. "Don't you dare leave me here to eat two orders of linguine all by myself," she warned, on the verge of tears.

He smiled sadly and stayed, but Vanessa was conscious of the vast distance between them—one that might never be bridged.

Presently he found another subject, seemingly a safe one, and asked, "How did you get into home shopping?"

It was a relief to think about something besides her own mixed-up emotions, doubts and fears. "I majored in broadcast journalism in college," she said. "Parker insisted that I drop out when we got married. He was traveling all the time, and I didn't have much to do once the house was clean and everything, so I started looking for work." She paused and lowered her head for just a moment, then went on. "Janet Harmon has been my friend for a long time. When the Midas Network came to Seattle and Paul was hired as production manager, he gave me a job."

"Selling gold chains and kitchen gadgets to the masses," Nick remarked, setting his empty soup bowl aside and regarding Vanessa with puzzled eyes, "is a far cry from broadcast journalism."

She was instantly defensive. "Some of us don't just fall into our dream jobs and become instantly successful," she pointed out tartly. "I had to take what I could get."

The doorbell chimed in the distance like the ringing of the gong between rounds of a boxing match. Nick must have deemed it a good time to retreat to his own corner, for he slid back his chair and disappeared toward the front of the house.

Vanessa hastily rinsed out their soup bowls and put them into the dishwasher, wondering what would happen between her and Nick and how it would be if he did indeed back off for a while.

She had a feeling that life would become as dull a chore as cleaning out an oven or stripping years of wax from a linoleum floor.

When Nick returned he was carrying a sizable white bag and a bottle of wine. Plundering the cupboards and drawers, he brought forth plates, silverware and a pair of dusty wineglasses.

Vanessa immediately took the glasses from him and carried them to the sink, where she washed them in hot soapy water while Nick set out the meal he'd had sent over from his restaurant.

"This house reminds me of your life," he observed when she finally rejoined him at the table and took up her fork to eat linguine. "Lots of empty spaces."

She glared at him as she chewed the most exquisite pasta she'd ever tasted.

He opened the wine bottle and poured chablis into her glass. "Well?" he prompted, arching one dark eyebrow. "Aren't you even going to fight back?"

"No," Vanessa responded after a few moments of tight-jawed deliberation. "If you want to be a jackass, that's your prerogative. I don't have to jump on the proverbial bandwagon and become one, too."

Nick grinned at her, more in amazement than good humor, and shook his head. "At least you're not denying that there are some gaps that need filling. I guess that's progress."

Although Vanessa was furious, she managed to keep her temper under control. "Thank you for your analysis. And to think some people actually pay psychiatrists when all they'd need to do is ask the great Nick DeAngelo to tell them how to run their lives!"

He sighed, and the sound conveyed an infinite sadness. "It isn't going to work, is it?" he asked, setting down his fork and leaning back in his chair.

A massive, hurtful lump formed in Vanessa's throat. She closed her eyes for a moment, then shook her head. "I don't think so," she said.

Nick stood, taking his leather jacket from a peg on the wall and shrugging into it. "I know it sounds crazy," he said hoarsely, keeping his back to her, "but I love you, Vanessa. When and if that ever means anything to you, call me."

With that, he opened the back door and went out.

Vanessa sat still in her chair for a long time, stunned and utterly confused. Then she got up and scraped the remains of their dinner down the garbage disposal, taking grim satisfaction in grinding it up. She just wished that she could throw in her memories of Nick as well to be pulverized and washed down the drain.

Trying to sleep proved to be a useless effort that night. At the first glimmer of dawn, she called Nick.

He answered on the second ring, sounding wide awake and quietly desolate.

"How could you tell me you love me and then just walk out like that?" Vanessa asked.

"Who is this?" he countered, and she could practically see his wonderful, dark eyes dancing with mischief.

Vanessa laughed miserably. "Damn it, Nick, don't make this any more difficult than it already is."

He sighed. "The whole thing is pretty confusing to me, too, if that makes you feel any better."

"It doesn't."

"You made the call, Vanessa," Nick pointed out. "The ball's in your court."

She shoved a hand through sleep-tangled auburn hair, then bit down on her thumb nail. "I'm in love with you," she finally admitted.

"That's progress," he conceded, but he still sounded the way Vanessa felt—sad.

She closed her eyes against an ocean of scalding

tears. "What I'm trying to say, I guess, is that I need some time."

"Fine," he retorted. "How does a hundred years strike you?"

"That was mean!"

Nick was silent for a few moments, and when he went on his voice was low and ragged. "I've told you before," he explained with a slow patience that was patently insulting, "I don't play games. If I can't be totally committed to this relationship, I don't want any part of it."

Vanessa felt as though he'd slapped her. "I see," she said.

"Should you ever feel ready to take the risk, get in touch with me. If I'm not involved with someone else, we'll see what happens."

Outrage replaced shock. "Of all the arrogant—"

"I'm through shadowboxing with you, Vanessa. I want a wife and a family and I'm not going to wait forever."

"How dare you threaten me that way!"

"It isn't a threat," Nick answered, his words grating together like rusty nails in the bottom of a bucket. "It's a fact."

"Goodbye," Vanessa said after a brief interval.

He hung up without returning her farewell.

Vanessa was determined not to fall apart again. She was a modern woman, she told herself, independent with a career. She didn't need Nick DeAngelo to be whole.

Oh, but she wanted him. She wanted him.

When a few hours had passed and she'd recovered her composure to some degree, she dialed the Harmons' number. Paul answered.

Vanessa explained that she had some personal business to take care of and asked for a few days off.

"Are your grandparents all right?" her employer asked, his voice full of concern.

At the mere mention of them, Vanessa ached with homesickness. She would have given a lot to be back in Spokane, pouring out her heart to the people who had raised her, but there wasn't going to be time for that. "They're fine," she answered belatedly, feeling strangely tongue-tied. "It's—it's something else."

Paul sighed. "All right," he said in his kind and quiet way. "Take as much time as you need."

"Thanks," Vanessa replied. She asked Paul to give her best to Janet and then hung up.

She had finished packing and was just carrying her suitcase downstairs when Rodney arrived to check up on her.

"I saw Nick's car here last night," he said, standing in the doorway to the kitchen and eying the suitcase. "I guess the two of you are going away together for a few days, huh?"

Again, Vanessa felt a hollowness inside. "Wishful thinking, Rod," she answered in resigned tones. "I'm flying to New York with Parker."

Seeing Rodney's mouth fall open was the only fun Vanessa had had in days. "What?" he croaked.

Vanessa smiled. "He's been pestering me to tell the world what I think of his book, and that's what I plan to do," she said.

Rodney's eyes rounded, and a grin broke over his face as her meaning struck him. "Wow," he breathed. "He'll kill you."

"He'll want to," Vanessa agreed, and just then the doorbell rang.

"I'll get it," Rodney volunteered, loping toward the front door. Even though he was in his second year of chiropractic school, there were times when he was still the gawky boy Vanessa remembered.

She stood up a little straighter when she heard him talking to Parker. Since there was no love lost between the two men, the exchange was terse.

Seeing Vanessa, Parker smiled fondly as though there had been no ugly divorce and then kissed her cheek. "You are as lovely as ever," he said.

Gag me, Vanessa thought. "Thank you, Parker," she said aloud. "So are you."

He gave her a bewildered look and then glanced at his Rolex.

You'd think a man who could afford a watch like that would at least let his ex-wife keep all the furniture, Vanessa reflected.

"Let's go," Parker boomed in sunny, all-hail-the-conquering-hero tones. "We've got a plane to catch. Thought we'd have dinner at the Plaza."

Why not? Vanessa thought. *He's paying.* "Sure," she enthused. A cloud passed overhead as she considered potential problems. "You did book separate rooms, didn't you, Parker?"

He cleared his throat and looked away for a moment. "Thanks to my agent, we have a penthouse suite. Nothing but the best for you, darlin'."

She arched one eyebrow as they started toward the door, but didn't pursue the point. They could agree on sleeping arrangements later. "You'll feed Sari until I get home and bring in the mail?" she asked of Rodney, who lingered in the entryway, watching her and Parker with a worried expression in his eyes.

He nodded. "Sure."

Some impulse made her hurry back and plant a kiss on Rodney's cheek. *Don't worry,* she mouthed before turning back to Parker.

There was a taxi waiting at the curb, and Parker made a great show of squiring Vanessa to it and sweeping open the door. She almost—not quite, but almost—felt guilty for what she was going to do to him.

They were at the airport, about to board their plane, when Nick suddenly appeared, moving gracefully through the crowds of travelers as he approached. Vanessa felt a lump of dread rise in her throat and averted her eyes momentarily.

Parker was cocky, shoving his hands into the pockets of his tailored trousers and rocking back on the heels of his Italian leather shoes. "I thought you had more pride than this, DeAngelo," he dared to say.

Vanessa gave her ex-husband a wild look and elbowed him, but when she turned her amber eyes to Nick, she was smiling.

"What is it?" she asked sweetly.

Nick took her arm in his hand and pulled her around a pillar, his nose an inch from hers. "You're not actually going through with this, are you?" he demanded in a sandpapery whisper.

She widened her eyes, well aware that Parker, while feigning arrogant disinterest, was actually listening. "I have to," she answered. "Thank you for coming to see me off and goodbye!"

"Goodbye, hell," Nick rasped. "I have half a mind to buy a ticket on this plane and go to New York with you. Wouldn't that be romantic—just you, me and your ex-husband."

Vanessa drew in a deep breath, then let it out in a hiss. It was a technique she'd learned once in a relaxation seminar. "Go away." She smiled. "Please?"

Nick bent around the pillar to glare at Parker. "Are you going to sleep with that rat?" he demanded.

"Talk about a lack of trust," Vanessa pointed out, lifting her chin.

Nick closed his eyes for a moment. "You're right," he admitted at length. "I shouldn't have asked you that."

They were calling for the first-class passengers to board the plane, and Vanessa had to leave.

She told him the name of the hotel where she would be staying, adding, "I'll call you as soon as I'm settled."

But Nick shook his head. "I'll be in Portland. We'll talk when you get home."

Vanessa stood on tiptoe to kiss him lightly on the mouth, and Parker took her arm and dragged her away toward the boarding gate.

She was feeling a confused sort of hope when she and her ex-husband were settled in their seats, the coach passengers trailing past them into the body of the airplane.

Some of them recognized Parker and clogged the aisles, asking for autographs, but Vanessa paid little attention to them. She was staring out at the terminal, wondering what Nick was thinking.

For the first time, she allowed herself to hope that things might eventually be all right between them, once she'd dealt with Parker and his book. That would close one chapter of her life, and she'd be able to begin another.

Parker spent most of the trip flirting with a particularly attractive flight attendant; it was only when they had landed at JFK that he turned his efforts back to Vanessa.

A long silver limousine had been sent to fetch them, and Vanessa smiled as she settled into the leather-covered seat. She meant to enjoy every possible luxury while she could since she would undoubtedly leave town on a rail, covered in tar and pigeon feathers.

Twilight was falling as they drove toward the hotel, and Vanessa gazed out through the tinted windows, drinking in the spectacle of light and the cacophony that is New York.

Twice she had to pull her hand out of Parker's fingers. She began to regret the act she'd put on a couple of days before.

"This trip is strictly business," she whispered, hoping the driver wouldn't hear. "So keep your hands to yourself, Parker Lawrence!"

Parker looked wounded. "How are we going to reconcile if I can't touch you?" he inquired.

Vanessa was tired and hungry and she was beginning to have serious doubts about the wisdom of this venture. "We're not going to get back together ever, and you damned well know it," she said irritably.

She glanced in Parker's direction and saw that he was watching her with a disturbing sort of shrewdness in his blue eyes. "Then why did you come with me?" he asked.

Vanessa sighed. Maybe she should just forget her plan and go home—by way of Portland. The deception seemed too big to carry off now. "I wanted to come to New York," she hedged.

Parker didn't speak to her again until they'd reached their hotel, which overlooked Central Park, and checked in.

The suite was spacious with a breathtaking view of the city and it came equipped with its own bar—and even a glistening black grand piano. There were flowers everywhere, compliments of Parker's agent, and a bottle of Dom Perignon was cooling in a bed of ice.

Vanessa made sure there were two bedrooms and that hers had a lock on the door before taking off her coat and unpacking the few clothes she'd brought with her.

She changed into a figure-hugging silk dress for dinner and saw a familiar light in Parker's eyes when she returned to the suite's living room. He was standing by the piano and, grinning, he ran one hand over the keyboard, filling the place with a discordant exclamation.

There was a pop as a waiter opened the champagne. After accepting a tip from Parker, the whip-thin young man—an aspiring dancer, no doubt—slipped out of the suite.

Once again, Vanessa had misgivings. In fact, she wished she'd run after Nick at the airport and made him take her to Portland with him. Her yearning for his voice, his smile, his touch, was an ache deep within her.

"You look troubled," Parker observed, his eyes discerning. "What is it, Vanessa?"

She wrung her hands together and drew upon all her courage. The idea that had seemed so just and so wise had turned foolish somewhere along the line. Even infantile. "I was going to humiliate you, Parker," she confessed. "I meant to denounce your book on that talk show tomorrow and tell the whole world what a lie it is."

To her surprise, Parker threw back his handsome head and laughed. "Your innocence never ceases to amaze me, Vanessa," he crowed when he'd recovered a little. "Do you think I didn't know that from the first?"

Vanessa's mouth dropped open.

Suavely Parker poured champagne into a crystal glass and extended it to his ex-wife. "Friends?" he said, his voice a throaty rumble.

Vanessa accepted the glass, took an unseemly gulp of its contents and retreated a step, her eyes still wide. She was confused about almost everything in that moment, but one thing was clear as the icicles that lined the eaves of her grandparents' house every winter: Parker had no interest in being her friend.

"Why are you staring at me that way?" he pressed, tilting his head to one side and looking ingeniously baffled.

She finished off her champagne and ignored the question. "Let's go to dinner. I'm starved."

Parker consulted his watch. "Our reservations are for an hour from now, but I guess we could have a few drinks while we wait." Even though the restaurant was within walking distance, he went to the telephone and summoned the limousine.

Vanessa didn't question the gesture, reasoning that people didn't go into Central Park on foot at night if they could avoid it, but her mind and heart were far away as one of the hotel's elevators whisked them to the ground floor.

The Plaza's restaurant was an oasis of light in the darkness, and Vanessa felt more at ease when she and

Parker were settled inside with cocktails and a table between them.

"You're still seeing DeAngelo," Parker speculated flatly, and Vanessa was amazed to realize that he'd restrained himself from asking that question for most of the day. Patience wasn't his long suit.

"Yes and no," Vanessa said, her throat hurting. She wondered what Nick would say if she caught a plane to the west coast, took a cab to the restaurant in Portland and surprised him.

"What do you mean 'yes and no'?" Parker demanded. "Damn it, I hate it when you do that!"

Vanessa could be charitable, thinking of how Nick would welcome her. They'd probably go somewhere private, right away, and make love for hours. "We're trying to negotiate some kind of workable agreement," she said.

"You make it sound like a summit meeting," Parker grumbled, looking like a disgruntled little boy. "Doesn't it matter that he was using you?"

Vanessa took a sip of her drink, a fruity mixture that barely tasted of liquor. She was so hungry that she was beginning to feel a bit dizzy. "I'm not sure he was," she said. She looked at her ex-husband pensively, champagne and the cocktail mingling ominously in her system. "He swears he's nothing like you, and sometimes I believe him."

Parker looked roundly insulted. "Am I that terrible?" he demanded.

"You're not a man I'd want to have a lasting relationship with," Vanessa answered with a hiccup.

"Good Lord," Parker grumbled, squinting at her. "You're drunk!"

"I am not," Vanessa protested.

Just then a flash went off, blinding her. For one awful moment, she thought a bomb had gone off. Then she realized that some reporter had recognized baseball's very own bad boy.

For once, Parker didn't look pleased at being noticed. "Get out of here," he said to the hapless person-of-the-press, glaring.

The reporter took another picture before two waiters came and discreetly evicted him from the premises.

"We're very sorry for the annoyance, Mr. Lawrence," a man in a tuxedo came to say. "Your table is ready."

Vanessa was wildly grateful at the prospect of eating. Light-headed, she staggered slightly when she rose too quickly from her chair, and Parker had to steady her by putting an arm around her waist.

Dinner must have been delicious, although Vanessa was never able to recall exactly what it was. She knew only that she consumed it with dispatch and then ordered dessert.

When they reached the hotel, there was a party going on in the suite. Vanessa skirted the room full of laughing, smoking, drinking strangers to let herself into her private chamber and lock the door.

She noticed the message icon was blinking on her cell phone, and she smiled as she read the text. Nick had sent it about an hour before and left his cell number. He was in Portland but he wanted to talk to her.

She punched out the digits on the hotel phone with an eager finger, and when Nick said hello, Vanessa replied with a hiccup and a drunken giggle.

Chapter 8

"Put Parker on the line," Nick said, sounding irritated.

Vanessa raised three fingertips to her mouth to stifle another hiccup. "You sent me a text because you wanted to talk to Parker?" she asked, bitterly disappointed.

An exasperated silence followed, and then Nick swore. Completely ignoring her question, he posed one of his own. "How much have you had to drink, Vanessa?"

A hiccup escaped. "Too much," Vanessa admitted. The noise outside her room seemed to be getting louder with every passing moment, and she was developing a headache. "There's some kind of party going on in the living room," she observed out loud.

"Get Parker," Nick reiterated in an ominously quiet voice.

With a sigh, Vanessa laid the receiver on her bedside table and ventured into the next room, weaving her way through the happy revelers until she finally came to Parker.

"Nick wants to talk to you on the telephone," she said.

Parker grinned and touched her cheek, as though she'd brought him good news. "Fine," he replied, and started off toward the nearest extension.

Nick was speaking when Vanessa got back to her room and picked up the receiver again.

"If you take advantage of her, Lawrence," he warned, "what happened two years ago will be nothing compared to what I'll do to you this time."

"The lady made her choice," Parker replied smoothly, no doubt drawing courage from the fact that Nick was on the opposite coast. "She came to New York with me, and she's staying in my suite. If you can't pick up on the meaning of that, maybe you'd better go back to hawking cod at the fish market."

Vanessa sucked in a breath, horrified and furious. They were discussing her as though she were a half-wit, unable to look after herself or make her own decisions. "Wait a minute, both of you!" she cried, her headache intensifying as the music and laughter got louder in the living room. "It just so happens that I have a thing or two to say about all this!"

"Whatever, darlin'," Parker said in a bored tone, and then he hung up. His confidence in his own powers of seduction was an affront Vanessa would not soon forgive.

"Nick," she said, "don't you dare hang up."

"I'm here," he answered, a sort of broken resignation in his tone.

"None of this is at all the way it sounds. I have my own room, even if it is in Parker's suite, and there's no way he and I are going to get back together. Understood?"

Nick gave a ragged sigh. She knew intuitively that

he was remembering what she'd told him about her first time with Parker—that she'd had too much wine and woke up in his bed.

"I don't have any claim on you, Vanessa," he said at last. "You can do what you want."

While Nick's words were perfectly true, they were not the ones Vanessa had hoped to hear. She wished devoutly that she'd listened to him and stayed in Seattle, where she belonged.

Vanessa sat up a little straighter on the edge of the bed, thinking of all the women who probably chased after Nick whenever the opportunity presented itself. "Are you telling me that you think we should both see other people?"

Nick made a grumbling sound of frustration and weariness. "Is that what you want?" he retorted.

Vanessa closed her eyes. "No," she admitted.

"Good," Nick replied. "When are you coming home?"

"Monday," Vanessa vowed. The door of her room opened, and a woman wearing a leather jumpsuit and stilettos peered in. "I'm sorry, this room is private," she told the intruder.

The woman mouthed an oops and slipped out, closing the door behind her.

"What the hell was that all about?" Nick demanded.

"You'd never believe it," Vanessa replied, yawning. "Shall I just go to Seattle, or make it Portland?"

Nick was quiet for a moment. "Portland. But you have the show to do tomorrow, don't you?"

Vanessa held her breath briefly in an effort to put down another attack of the hiccups. "I'm not staying for that," she said. "I realize now that all my protests will do is make more people rush out and buy the book."

He chuckled, and the sound was warm and low and so masculine that Vanessa ached to be close to Nick. "Speaking of the book, there are a few things I'd like to know about the incident in Chapter Three," he said.

Vanessa sighed. "A circus acrobat couldn't do that," she replied.

Nick laughed outright. "I love you," he said.

She hiccuped again.

"Strange that he didn't write about your drinking problem," Nick teased.

"Good night, Mr. DeAngelo," Vanessa said with feigned primness. "I'll see you in Portland sometime tomorrow."

"Text me the flight number, and I'll pick you up."

Vanessa nodded, her mind fuzzy, and then remembered that Nick couldn't see her. "Okay. And Nick?"

"What?"

"I love you, too."

"Good night, sweetheart," he said, and his voice was a caress.

After hanging up, Vanessa went immediately to her bedroom door and locked it. Then, after laying out the trim royal blue suit she planned to wear on the flight home the next day, she slipped into her private bathroom and took a long, soothing bath.

When she returned to her room, sleepy and comfortable in her favorite pair of flannel pajamas, Parker was sitting on the end of her bed and the party was still going on full blast in the living room.

"What are you doing here?" she demanded in a

furious whisper, pulling on her robe and tying the belt tightly. "How did you get in?"

Parker held up a key. "Relax, Vanessa—for all my sins, I've never forced myself on you, have I?"

Vanessa had to admit that he hadn't, though sometimes his methods had been almost that low-down. She shook her head, still keeping her distance.

"You're not going to do the show tomorrow, are you?" Parker asked, sounding resigned.

"No," she answered. "Are you angry?"

Parker sighed. "It might be to your advantage to go on and show the world that you're not a drunk," he announced.

"A what?" Vanessa demanded, her eyes rounding. With Nick the reference had been a joke, but Parker was coming from a different place altogether.

"You remember that reporter at the restaurant tonight, I'm sure—the one with the blinding flash attachment on his camera? He's from the *National Snoop,* and your delightful face will be propped up beside every checkout counter in America within a week to ten days." He drew in a deep breath and let it out again, his eyes narrowed in speculation. "I can see the headlines now: TOSS-AWAY BRIDE DROWNS HER SORROWS, it will say—or something to that effect."

Vanessa felt the color drain from her cheeks. She had a career of her own to think about, and she couldn't afford publicity of that kind. No one would ever take her seriously if she were seen in such an unflattering light.

"Go on the show tomorrow, Van," Parker said quietly, coming to her and taking her hand in his to pat it. "Show the world who you really are."

Vanessa wrenched free of his grasp. "You don't give

a damn what the public thinks of me," she hissed, "so spare me the performance. All you care about is selling that rotten book of yours!"

Parker shrugged. "The choice is yours, Vanessa. Go or stay."

She thought of Nick waiting for her in Portland and imagined how it would be to be held in his arms again, to lie beside him in the darkness as he quietly set her senses on fire. She closed her eyes for a moment, torn.

"I'll stay," she said, averting her eyes.

"Um-hmm," Parker agreed smugly, and then he tossed Vanessa the key to her room, went out and closed the door.

She promptly locked it, then hurried back to the telephone, planning to call Nick and explain that she'd changed her mind about doing the talk show with Parker.

As it happened, though, Vanessa set the receiver back in its cradle without pushing the sequence of buttons that would connect her with Nick. She couldn't explain the situation to him when she didn't completely understand it herself.

There was no time to call the next morning because a limousine arrived to collect Parker and Vanessa at an ungodly hour. She rode to the studio in a daze, sipping bitter coffee from a Styrofoam cup.

She promised herself that she would call Nick as soon as she had a chance, but it seemed that the talk show people had every moment planned. The instant they arrived, Vanessa was whisked away to have her makeup redone and her hair styled.

As the cosmeticians worked their wonders, a production assistant briefed her on the structure of the show and the line the host's questioning would probably follow.

None of it was anything like Vanessa expected. In fact, when she and Parker were seated before an eager audience and the lights flared on, all her broadcasting experience seemed to slip away into a parallel universe. It was as though she had never appeared before a camera in her life.

To make matters worse, she had slept very badly the night before, and she probably looked like a zombie.

The audience, mostly female, was clearly interested in Parker. It was amazing, Vanessa reflected, how the man could flirt with so many women at once.

Numbly Vanessa groped her way through the hour. She answered the questions presented by the host and the audience as best she could and was grateful when the program ended.

Vanessa fled the studio immediately afterward, caught a cab outside and sped back to the hotel. There, she picked up her suitcase and went straight to the airport.

She had to wait three hours for a flight to Portland, and that was routed through Denver and San Francisco with a long layover at each stop. She called Nick from Colorado and told him that she would be in at six that evening.

He didn't sound particularly enthusiastic, and Vanessa could only assume that he'd watched the show, seen her sitting there as stiff as a board, letting Parker display her like a sideshow freak.

A glum, drizzling rain was falling when Vanessa reached Portland, but the moment she saw Nick, her spirits lifted. Although he gave her a rueful look and shook his head at some private marvel, he took her in his arms and held her close, and that made up for a great many things.

"I've had a terrible day," she said, letting her cheek rest against the front of his cool, rain-beaded leather jacket.

He kissed her forehead. "I know," he replied gruffly, and then he put an arm around her waist and ushered her toward the baggage claim area.

After reclaiming Vanessa's suitcase, they went outside and Nick hailed a cab. All the way to his restaurant, they made small talk, avoiding the issues of Parker and her appearance on television. There were long, stiff gaps between their sentences.

"You're angry with me," Vanessa said when the cab had stopped in front of a towering Victorian building with a view of the water and an elegantly scripted sign that read, *DeAngelo's.*

Nick paid the driver and waited until the cab had pulled away before answering, "Does it matter, Vanessa?"

She sank her teeth into her lower lip. "Yes," she said, after they'd mounted the steps and entered the interior of the restaurant. "Of course it matters."

Wonderful aromas greeted Vanessa, reawakening her appetite.

Nick gave her a look. "Whatever you say," he replied, putting his hand to her back and propelling her toward a set of sweeping, carpeted stairs.

Vanessa decided to save the serious issues they needed to talk about for later when she'd had some aspirin and something to eat. "Do you stay right here at the restaurant when you're in Portland?" she asked, trying for a smile.

He nodded, opening a pair of double doors to admit her to an office that was the size of some hotel suites. "Sit down and relax," he ordered, setting down her suitcase and striding toward the telephone on his desk. "I'll have some dinner sent up. What do you want?"

"Spaghetti," Vanessa answered without hesitation, thinking of the night in the San Juan Islands.

Nick nodded again and placed the order in clipped, brusque tones. It was obvious that he was distracted.

"I thought you weren't going to be on the talk show," he said, when the silence had lengthened to its limits.

So he'd seen the debacle. Vanessa lowered her eyes, embarrassed that she'd been so tongue-tied on the program. Everyone who'd watched—and the producers of *Seattle This Morning* might well have been among them—was probably thinking that she had all the personality of a secondhand dishrag.

"I changed my mind," she replied almost in a whisper.

Nick sighed. "That was your prerogative," he replied. "You're here, and that's all that matters."

Vanessa looked at him with wide, weary eyes full of relief. "You were right," she conceded in a small voice. "I shouldn't have gone. I only made things worse."

Nick crossed the room to sit beside her, and the moment he took her into his arms she burst into tears.

He kissed her eyelids and her wet, salty cheeks before taking her mouth and taming it with his own. Vanessa's exhausted body was captured in an instant and largely involuntary response, and she gave a strangled moan when he lifted one hand to caress her breast.

"The spaghetti will be here in a few minutes," Nick muttered against the warm flesh of her neck.

Vanessa laughed even as she tilted her head back in pagan enjoyment of his attentions. "You're so romantic, DeAngelo."

He drew away from her very reluctantly and shoved one hand through his hair. "You'd better reserve judgment on that, lady," he warned.

A sweet tingle went through Vanessa, but she was cool and composed as she arched an eyebrow and queried, "Until when?"

"Until I take you to bed, which will be about sixty seconds after you finish your spaghetti."

Vanessa looked around. "You have a bed here? This is an office!"

Nick pointed toward a closed door on the other side of the room, but said nothing.

She felt her temper flare. "How convenient," she said, folding her arms.

Nick sighed, shook his head and grinned at her. "We party animals like to be prepared," he said.

Vanessa honestly tried, but she couldn't sustain her anger. She was too tired and she wanted him too badly. "Don't tease me," she pleaded.

He touched her nipple and, even through her blouse, it came instantly to attention. "No promises," he said just as a knock sounded at the door.

The spaghetti had arrived, but there was no wine. Diet cola was served instead and Vanessa, who was seated at the small table in front of the windows, gave Nick a knowing glance while the waiter poured it for her.

"Are you afraid I'll lose control of myself?" she asked the moment they were alone again.

"Afraid? Hardly," Nick said, folding his arms and watching as Vanessa ate. "I'm looking forward to it, if you must know."

Vanessa blushed. She did tend to shed her inhibitions when Nick made love to her. "I'm serious, Nick," she said.

"So am I," he replied.

Vanessa tried not to gobble down her spaghetti, but there was no hiding the fact that she was eager to be taken to Nick's bed and driven beyond her own restraints. He was grinning at her when she dabbed hastily at her mouth with the napkin and shoved her empty plate away.

"Go ahead and—er—get settled. I'll be in in a few minutes."

Vanessa was possessed of such virginly shyness all of a sudden that she couldn't even look at Nick. She picked up her suitcase.

Those few steps toward the door he'd pointed out earlier seemed to take half an hour to execute, and when she was finally out of his view, she sagged with relief.

The room was not as large as his suite on the island, but it was full of Nick's personality and his scent, and Vanessa felt at home there. With a sigh, she sat down on the edge of a large bed covered with an old-fashioned patchwork quilt and kicked off her high-heeled shoes. It had been a long day.

In the adjoining bathroom, Vanessa took a hot, hasty shower, then put on her pyjama bottoms and a camisole, wishing she'd brought something sexier. She brushed her teeth and misted herself with cologne, and when she returned to the bedroom Nick was there, waiting for her.

"I missed you so much," she confessed, her chin at a proud angle.

"And I missed you," he answered gruffly, making no move to approach her.

Vanessa knew she would have to go to him this time, but now that they were alone and she was ready for him, it didn't matter. She crossed the shadowy room, which was lit only by the stray glimmers of street lamps outside, and slid her arms around his lean waist.

"Love me, Nick," she whispered, looking up at him, knowing her whole soul showed in her eyes and not caring. "I've been fantasizing about you so much that I'm going to go crazy if you don't touch me."

He cupped his strong hands on either side of her head, stroking her satiny cheeks with the edges of his thumbs. After searching her face with his dark, smoldering eyes for several seconds—as though to commit every feature to memory—he bent his head and kissed her.

His seductive kiss was a gentle kind of mastery, and Vanessa swayed as Nick gave her a foretaste of the fiery conquering she knew he would make her earn.

When he finally broke away, it was only to slide her camisole over her head and toss it into a chair. Her breasts seemed to swell as he admired them.

Vanessa's knees went weak when he reached out to cup her breast in one hand, the pad of his thumb teasing the nipple. She wanted to lie down and abandon herself to Nick, but he wouldn't allow that. He put his free arm around her waist to support her, and she bent backward by instinct, silently offering herself.

With a groan, Nick bent to taste the nipple he'd already taught to obey him. His hand moved away, sliding down over Vanessa's ribcage to the place where her waist dipped inward to tug at the waistband of her pants.

She trembled as she felt the last barrier give way, cried out softly when he caressed her. The excitement was building steadily, and Vanessa didn't want it to be over so soon.

"Stop," she pleaded, her head bent back. But he didn't stop. With his hand he taught her new levels of pleasure. First he beckoned, then he soothed, now he taunted. "Oh, Nick, please—please—I'm going to…" There was a fierce explosion inside Vanessa, and her hips convulsed as Nick extracted every trace of response from her.

She was still gasping for breath, still so bedazzled that she could barely see when he laid her gently on the bed and began taking off his own clothes. When he was naked, Nick joined her.

Although most of the tension had left her body, Vanessa gave herself up gladly to the slow, skillful massage Nick treated her to. She caught the scent of some fragrant oil, felt it seeping into her skin as he applied it with circling motions of his fingertips.

She asked Nick to take her, but he only turned her onto her stomach and repeated the process with the oil.

Vanessa was in an odd state of mingled excitement and sweet satiety, and the thrumming need inside her increased until she couldn't wait any longer. She twisted onto her back again and gasped a fevered plea.

Her hands moved over Nick's chest, his back, his buttocks in a wild, soft urging, and finally, blessedly, his resistance snapped. He took her in a hot, sweeping stroke that made her cry out in welcome and arch her back to receive him as completely as possible.

Her name was a ragged rasp torn from his throat, and though his mouth dipped to hers in an attempt at a kiss, he was too frantic to linger. With a desolate groan, he began quickening his pace by degrees until Vanessa's hips were rising to meet his.

His magnificent head was tilted back in triumph and surrender as he strained, visibly, to prolong the sweet anguish that consumed them both. Finally with a growl of lust he joined Vanessa in the core of a flaming nova. Even when their bodies parted much later, their souls remained fused together.

Vanessa was the first to recover, and she gave Nick a teasing kiss on the belly before sitting up and moving to slide off the bed.

"Don't go," he said, taking her wrist in a painless grasp and holding on.

She allowed him to pull her back down beside him, to kiss and caress her until the treacherous heat was building inside her again. In this second joining, there was no control on either of their parts, no withholding from the other and no teasing. It was fast and it was primitive, and when it was over Vanessa didn't even try to leave the bed because she couldn't move.

She awakened in the depths of the night to find herself alone, and an incomprehensible, unfounded dread forced her heart into her throat. "Nick?" she called, getting up and groping for her robe.

She found him in the adjoining office, half dressed and sound asleep in his desk chair.

Full of love and relief, Vanessa went to him and laid her hands on his shoulders. "Nick?" she said again.

He woke with a start and pulled her deftly onto his lap. "Hi," he greeted her with a rummy yawn.

Vanessa kissed his forehead. "Come back to bed," she said.

He gave another yawn. "This reminds me of page 72," he said.

"Page 72?" Vanessa echoed, completely puzzled.

Nick pulled a copy of Parker's book from underneath a stack of papers and held it two inches from her nose.

Vanessa snatched the volume from his hand and flipped through it until she'd found the page in question. Hot color pooled in her cheeks as she read, and her eyes grew wider with every passing word. She'd forgotten this passage.

"I never did any such thing!" she cried, slamming the book closed and flinging it away.

Nick smiled wickedly. "Are you against trying it?" he teased.

Vanessa laughed, her anger fading. "Wretch," she said, giving him a quick kiss on the mouth and a push to the chest, both at the same time.

He rose out of the chair, forcing Vanessa to stand, too, and gave her a little shove toward the bedroom.

There, Vanessa undressed Nick after shedding her robe, but there was no more lovemaking that night. They slept, legs and arms entangled, heads touching.

The moment she opened her eyes in the morning, however, all Vanessa's doubts and fears were back, lined up at the foot of the bed like an invisible army. This time she sent them packing, determined to enjoy her time with Nick. Things were still far from settled between them, and she didn't want to waste a moment.

He was singing in the shower and she joined him under the spray, although she was nowhere near as brave in the daylight as she had been in darkness.

Nick greeted her with a resounding kiss, then proceeded to lather every inch of her body. The water ran cold long before they came out.

Chapter 9

Until that day, Vanessa's impression had been that Nick dabbled at running his restaurants since he obviously didn't need to earn a living. By noon she knew he worked the same way he made love—with a quiet, thorough steadiness neither hell nor high water could deflect him from.

Watching him fascinated Vanessa, but it also made her restless. She had her own fish to fry, and her thoughts began turning in the direction of Seattle, the Midas Network and the decision being made at WTBE-TV. Leaving Nick in the middle of a loud argument with the chef, she went upstairs where there was privacy and silence and accessed her voicemail to listen to the messages she'd accumulated.

Her eyes widened as she listened. Representatives of six different stations, in that many different cities, had called with requests to "discuss" her career plans. Parker had left word that he'd realized he loved Darla after all and was off to Mexico to be married, and the cleaning lady had imparted that she was going to quit if Vanessa didn't buy a new vacuum cleaner.

When Nick entered the room a few minutes after the messages had ended, Vanessa was still sitting on the corner of his desk with the receiver in one hand, staring off into space.

He frowned as he hung up the telephone and peered into her eyes. "Is everything all right?" he asked.

Dazed, Vanessa nodded. "Parker is getting married and my housekeeper is going to quit," she said.

Nick put a hand under her chin. "You can always get another housekeeper," he said, looking worried.

Vanessa realized that he thought she was shattered by the news of her ex-husband's remarriage, and she laughed. She wanted to reassure him. "I'm glad Parker is tying the knot, Nick," she said truthfully. "Now maybe he'll leave me alone."

"Your eyes are glazed," Nick insisted. "If it isn't unrequited love, what's making you look like that?"

She told him about the messages from the six television stations. "I have to go home, Nick," she finished, resting her hands lightly on his shoulders.

He sighed, and while he didn't seem threatened by her news, he wasn't pleased, either. "You can call them from here, can't you?"

She shook her head.

Nick looked toward the window for a few moments, but Vanessa knew he wasn't seeing the glum weather or the modern skyline. "None of those stations are in Seattle?"

Again, Vanessa shook her head.

He kissed her lightly on the lips. "I've got to stay here until I can replace this chef," he said reluctantly.

Vanessa felt bereft inside, as though some great chasm had opened between them, and maybe it had. She called the airport and made a reservation on a flight leaving in an hour, then hastily packed her clothes.

Nick offered to see her off, but she declined, needing time and space to think about the future and the unexpected changes it might bring.

Sari greeted her with an annoyed *reoooww* when she arrived home, but was appeased by an early supper. Vanessa returned the calls on her answering machine in a methodical and professional fashion.

Her appearance on national television, far from ruining her in the broadcasting business as she had feared, had sparked considerable interest among the powers-that-be. By the time she'd placed the last call, she had agreed to six interviews, five of which would take place in Seattle for her convenience.

The sixth, in San Francisco, was scheduled for her day off.

Still in something of a daze, Vanessa took a TV dinner from the freezer and shoved it into the microwave. She was eating it when the telephone rang.

"Job offers?" Nick asked, without extending a greeting or even identifying himself.

Vanessa sighed. "Interviews," she corrected. "Did you find a new chef?"

"No," he snapped, and his tone stung like a hard flick from a rubber band. "Did you find a new cleaning lady? Damn it, Vanessa, for once let's not evade the issue here. I'm in love with you, and you're about to be offered a job that takes you to another part of the country. It's half-time, and I'd like to know whether my team is winning or losing."

Vanessa's front teeth scraped her lower lip. "One of us could commute," she said, knowing the idea wasn't going to please him.

She could see Nick shove his hand through his hair so clearly that she might as well have been standing in the same room with him. "No way," he ground out.

Vanessa stood up very straight, bracing herself. Nick had been so gentle with her, so understanding, but now he was showing his true colors. Now he was going to be the demanding male, trying to dictate her lifestyle and the course her career would take.

He really was as arrogant and egotistical as Parker, he was just more subtle about it.

"I guess we don't have anything more to talk about," Vanessa said, and it took all her strength not to fall apart right then and there.

"We have everything to talk about," Nick argued. He sounded calmer, but there was a note of despair in his voice that told Vanessa they weren't going to be able to work out a compromise this time.

"Goodbye," she said brokenly, and then she hung up and covered her face with both hands.

For two weeks, Vanessa didn't see or talk to Nick. She met with the people sent to recruit her for their local newscasts and talk shows and spent the rest of her time selling merchandise over the Midas Network and telling herself that some people just weren't meant to have it all.

Of the offers she received, the one in San Francisco was the most promising. Her salary would be twice what she was earning at the Midas Network, and she had always had a special affection for the city by the bay.

Vanessa had chosen not to make any hard and fast decisions until she'd gotten her emotions on a more even keel, and she felt like a tightrope walker with no balance pole.

The day before Thanksgiving, Vanessa's grandmother called. "Are you absolutely positive you can't come over for dinner?" she asked plaintively. "It's been so long since your grampa and I have seen you, and you've been looking a little peaky lately. Either that or you shouldn't wear peach."

Vanessa smiled, despite the feeling of quiet despondency that had possessed her since the day she left Portland. "You've been watching the shopping channel again," she said, evading the question her grandmother had asked her about Thanksgiving.

Alice Bradshaw chuckled, but the sound was a little hollow. "I watch every day, sweetie. Last week, I even ordered a cordless screwdriver for your grandfather. Now, are you going to change your mind and come home or not?"

"I have to work," Vanessa apologized, pushing her hair back from her forehead and letting out a long breath. Actually that statement was slightly wide of the truth because she had had the day off but offered to fill in so that another host could spend the holiday with family. Even so, she wasn't in the mood to celebrate anything since Nick was out of her life.

Her grandmother was clearly disappointed. "Can we look for you to visit at Christmas, then?" she pressed.

Vanessa swallowed. Christmas seemed far away, though she knew it wasn't. Maybe by then she'd have a grip on herself. "Okay," she agreed, looking distractedly at the wall calendar on the pantry door. "It's a date."

Alice was clearly pleased and excited. "You could bring that young man of yours along—the one Rodney's been telling us about."

Vanessa closed her eyes, feeling as though she'd just been struck a blow to the midsection. *When I get through with you, Rodney Bradshaw,* she thought venomously, *it will take every chiropractic instructor in that school to put you back together.* "Nick and I aren't seeing each other anymore," she said with cheery bleakness. "How's Grampa?"

"What do you mean you aren't seeing Nick anymore?" Alice demanded, not to be put off by questions about the hearty health of her husband. "Rodney said this was *it!*"

"Rodney doesn't know what he's talking about," Vanessa said tightly.

Alice sighed. "I knew something was wrong by the way you looked. That man went and did you dirty, didn't he?"

Saying yes would have satisfied Alice, but Vanessa couldn't bring herself to lie. Nick had been stubborn and unbending, but he hadn't made a deliberate effort to break her heart. "Nothing so dramatic," she confessed. "There were a few fundamental things we couldn't agree on, that's all."

The conversation ended a few minutes after that and, just as Vanessa was hanging up, Rodney rapped at the back door and let himself in.

He was obviously ready to make the long drive to Spokane. "Sure you don't want to go along?" he asked slyly.

Vanessa glared at him, her hands on her hips. "I wouldn't go anywhere with you, you big mouth," she said. "What did you mean by telling Gramma and Grampa about Nick?"

Rodney sighed. "Every time I called them they asked how you were getting along and whether or not you had a man in your life. I suppose I should have lied?"

"Of course not," Vanessa said, sagging a little.

"Call Nick," Rodney told her. "You're never going to be happy until you do."

Vanessa shook her head. Being a man, Rodney probably wouldn't understand if she explained, so she didn't make the effort.

One of Rodney's shoulders moved in a shrug. "It's your choice, of course. I'll see you on Monday, Van."

She accepted his brotherly kiss on the forehead. "Be careful," she couldn't stop herself from saying. "It's snowing on Snoqualmie Pass."

Rodney grinned. "I'll be okay," he promised, and then, after giving Vanessa a quick hug, he left.

It was time to leave for the studio, so she wrapped herself up in her warmest coat, pulled a fuzzy green stocking cap onto her head and left the house.

When she arrived at work, a message awaited her. Paul wanted to see her in his office immediately.

Vanessa pulled off her stocking cap and coat as she walked down the hallway and knocked at her boss's door. While she hadn't actually given notice, it was common knowledge at the network that she wouldn't be renewing her contract.

Paul was standing when she stepped through his doorway. "Before we get down to business," he said when Vanessa was seated in a chair facing his desk, "I'm under strict orders to invite you to our house for dinner tomorrow night. We're having turkey and pumpkin pie—the whole bit. Say you'll be there and Janet will be off my back."

Vanessa smiled sadly and shook her head. "I'm in no mood to 'accidentally' run into your best friend," she said.

Paul sighed and spread his hands. "I tried. Janet had some idea that if your eyes met Nick's over the stuffing and candied yams, lightning would strike."

"Nick is going to be there, then?" Vanessa asked, unable to stop herself.

Paul shrugged. "I was going to ask him after you went to do your segment. Which brings me to the real reason I called you in here. The network is prepared to offer you a sizeable raise to stay on."

Vanessa lowered her eyes and shook her head, but after a few moments she met Paul's gaze steadily. "I hope you don't think I'm ungrateful," she said. "You gave me my first real job, and I'll never forget that."

There was a short silence, then Paul asked, "Have you made any decisions about where you'll go next?"

She sighed, thinking of her ordeal on that talk show with Parker and of the lurid stories that had come out in the tabloids a week afterward. BASEBALL GREAT RESCUES DRUNKEN EX, one of the headlines had read. It still amazed her that the publicity had helped her career instead of ending it once and for all. "No," she answered at last, "but I am leaning toward the job in San Francisco." It was the first time she'd admitted that, even to herself. She wanted to be a long way from the memories of Nick.

"You never heard from *Seattle This Morning?*"

Vanessa tried to smile as she shook her head. "Ironic,

isn't it? They were probably the only ones who were put off by the article in the *National Snoop*."

"Nobody takes that rag seriously," Paul said, dismissing the subject. "We'll all be very sorry to see you go, Vanessa," he finished.

Vanessa couldn't answer since she had a lump in her throat the size of a football helmet. She paused in the doorway, though, and when she was able to speak again, she asked, "What was Nick's number? When he was still playing ball, I mean?"

Paul thought for a moment. "Fifty-eight, I think. Why?"

Vanessa shrugged. "I don't know," she answered, and when she looked back at Paul over one shoulder, there were tears glistening in her eyes.

Her boss got out of his chair, crossed the room and simultaneously closed the door and drew her into his arms. "Van, no job is worth this," he said.

"You wouldn't say that if I were a man," Vanessa wailed, completely miserable.

Paul chuckled. "I wouldn't be holding you if you were a man, either," he pointed out.

Vanessa began to sob as the enormity of losing Nick washed over her once again. It was like parting with a lung.

Paul led her back to the chair she'd just left, seated her and buzzed his assistant to ask her to bring in a glass of cold water.

"Nick is a reasonable man," he insisted once the woman had gone. "I'm sure you could come to some kind of agreement if you'd just talk things over!"

She dabbed her eyes with a tissue plucked from the box on Paul's desk and then wadded it into a ball. She was a wreck; she had to pull herself together and stop moping around all the time. "When I was married to Parker," she said in the thick lisp of the terminally weepy, "I had to hand over all my dreams like a dowry. He didn't want me to go to college, so I quit. He didn't want children, so I gave up on the idea of having babies. Do you really wonder why I don't want to wake up one morning and find myself in the same trap with Nick?"

Paul sighed. "Take the rest of the day off, Vanessa— you're in no shape to sell ceiling fans. Mel is on a roll today—I'm sure he won't mind filling in for you."

Vanessa refused. She wouldn't have it said that she couldn't pull her own weight.

Fifteen minutes later she went on camera and started pitching musical jewelry boxes. Despite Margie's skill with makeup, a glance at the monitor assured Vanessa that she looked bad enough to scare Hannibal Lecter.

She was demonstrating the ugliest floor lamp in captivity when Oliver smilingly announced that it was time to take a call from a viewer.

"What's your name?" Vanessa's cohost asked, reaching out to touch the lamp fondly.

"Nick DeAngelo," responded the caller. "What's yours?"

Vanessa stepped on the base of the lamp at that moment, causing it to wave madly from side to side. She flung both arms around the thing just as it would have toppled to the floor.

"We've got to talk," Nick said. "Will you have dinner with me tonight, Vanessa?"

"No," Vanessa answered, and it was a struggle to get the word out.

"You're being stubborn," Nick insisted.

"Do you want a floor lamp or not?" Vanessa yelled, wondering when the director was going to cut them off. It was obvious that this was no ordinary viewer.

Nick laughed. "I've missed you, too, lady," he said, and his voice was a brandy-and-cream rumble that brought pink color pulsing to Vanessa's cheeks.

Instead of being angry, the floor director seemed delighted. He stood beside one of the cameramen, signaling Vanessa to continue. Her chest swelled as she drew a deep, deliberate breath in an effort to keep her composure. She tried to smile, but the effort was hopeless.

"This is really not the time or place for this," she said, speaking as pleasantly as she could. "Some of our other viewers are probably anxious to talk to us about these lamps."

Again the item in question teetered dangerously; again Vanessa caught it just in time.

"Far be it from me to stand in the way of free enterprise," Nick replied. "I'll pick you up at seven-thirty."

Vanessa squared her shoulders and looked directly into the camera. "I've moved," she lied, hoping he would take the hint.

"I'll find you," Nick replied.

It was all she could do not to stomp her feet and scream in frustration. "All right, all right. If I agree to see you, will you hang up?"

"Absolutely," was the generous response.

"Then I'll see you at seven-thirty," Vanessa said moderately, seething inside.

The cameramen cheered and, at the end of her shift the director told Vanessa he was sure the orders would fly in when they aired the segment. Everybody loved a lover, apparently.

Vanessa stepped through her front door at five-fifteen, screamed in a belated release of her temper and hurled her purse across the living room. Her cat gave a terrified meow and fled up the stairs, and Vanessa was instantly contrite.

"I'm sorry," she called out, but it was no use. Sari would not forgive such a transgression unless Vanessa groveled and made an offering of creamed tuna.

Nick arrived promptly at seven-thirty, wearing the tailored suit he'd had on the first time Vanessa met him. He was as handsome as ever, although there was a hollow expression in his eyes.

He took in Vanessa's glimmery blue dress with appreciation as she stepped back to admit him. "I half expected that you would have moved out of state before I got here," he said.

Vanessa averted her eyes. She'd fantasized about seeing Nick again for days but, despite all those mental rehearsals, the reality was nearly overwhelming. She couldn't help hoping that he was ready to give some ground where their relationship was concerned so that they could forge some kind of future together.

"You look very dapper," she commented, ignoring his remark. The suit emphasized the broadness of his shoulders, and it was difficult not to touch him.

"Thank you," he replied with a slight inclination of his head.

Vanessa, who earned her living by thinking on her feet, talking for as long as three hours virtually nonstop, was tongue-tied. All the things she longed to say to Nick were caught in her throat, practically choking her.

He seemed to be looking into her soul and reading her most private emotions. "It's all right," he said, touching her face briefly with one hand. "We'll find our way through all this somehow. I promise."

Vanessa wished she could be so sure. As he laid her evening coat over her shoulders, she fought to hold back tears of confusion and fear.

A lot of people would have said she was crazy, she thought, as she and Nick whisked through the rainy night in his Corvette. Jock or no jock, this was a rare and gentle man, the kind most women would have tackled and hog-tied. And Paul had been right when he'd said that no job was worth the kind of pain the loss of Nick DeAngelo had caused her. As if that weren't enough, Vanessa knew she loved the man to distraction.

She'd been holding him at arm's length since the night they met, comparing him to Parker. Down deep, she'd known all along that Nick was as different from her ex-husband as salt was from sugar.

There could be only one reason for her failure to make a commitment, and that was fear—fear of loving and then losing, trusting and being betrayed.

The end of her relationship with Parker had been bitterly painful, even though she'd wanted the divorce and known that she had no other choice. If that happened with Nick, she knew she wouldn't be able to endure it.

She closed her eyes and let her head rest against the back of the seat.

"Don't be afraid, Vanessa," Nick said softly. "Please."

Vanessa looked at him, drew in the scent of his cologne. "That's like asking a burn victim not to be be scared of fire," she replied in a sad voice.

Nick sighed. "I'm not the guy who burned you," he reminded her. "Doesn't that mean anything?"

"You have more power over me than Parker ever dreamed of having," Vanessa admitted, unable to keep the words back. "If you wanted to, you could crush me so badly that I'd never find all the pieces."

He turned his head and glowered at her. "You're stronger than you think you are," he said, clearly annoyed. "Give yourself—and me—a little credit."

An uncomfortable silence settled over the car after that, and neither Nick nor Vanessa spoke until they'd reached DeAngelo's and been seated inside a private dining room.

Vanessa had never seen a more elegant room. There was a single table in front of a view of Elliot Bay. The streets were lighted up like a tangle of Christmas tree lights, the colors smudged by the rain that sheeted the windows. Candles provided the only light, and a violinist serenaded Nick and Vanessa as they sat looking at each other, comfortable with the music.

When the music stopped the first waiter appeared, bringing champagne. He popped the cork and poured the frothy liquid into their glasses, being very careful not to look at either Vanessa or Nick.

Vanessa arched an eyebrow the moment they were alone. "No diet cola?" she joked.

Nick grinned. "I'm trying to get past your defenses here, in case you haven't noticed."

"I've noticed," Vanessa said with a sigh, clinking her glass against Nick's as he lifted it in a toast.

"To page 72," he said.

Vanessa laughed and sipped her wine. For the first time in days she felt whole and human. It would be so easy to give herself to Nick body and soul, and that was exactly why she had to keep herself under control.

"I saw a shadow in your eyes just now," Nick said, reaching across the table to take her hand in his. "What were you thinking about?"

"Guess."

His jawline tightened then relaxed again. "The perils of loving Nick DeAngelo?" he ventured.

Vanessa nodded and looked away toward the harbor. "Did Paul and Janet invite you over for Thanksgiving dinner?" she asked in an attempt to change the subject. God knew, the one at hand was a blind alley.

His hand gripped hers for a moment, then moved away. "Yes," he said. "Vanessa, look at me."

She hated the fact that her first impulse was always to do exactly what Nick told her. Before she could do anything about it, her gaze had shifted to his face. "Don't make this any more difficult than it already is," she pleaded. "Please."

"Will you come home with me tonight?"

Vanessa wanted to be flippant. "You move fast," she said, and immediately felt like a bumbling teenager.

"Vanessa."

"No," she said quickly. "No, I won't sleep with you, Nick."

"Why not?"

The nerve. "Because pilgrims don't sleep around, that's why."

Nick tilted his head to one side and studied her. "What?" he asked, looking honestly puzzled.

She smiled, albeit very sadly. "We're doing a special, live show and tomorrow morning I have to get up, put on a pilgrim costume and sell my little heart out. Does that answer your question?"

"Not by a long shot," Nick grumbled as a second waiter appeared with enormous salads.

Vanessa ate with good appetite, having learned her lesson about too much wine on an empty stomach, and by the time the broiled lobster had been served, she felt almost human.

Dessert made her positively daring. When Nick took her home, she invited him in for a drink.

The living room was dark, but Vanessa didn't bother to turn on a light since there was virtually no furniture to bump into. She was leading the way toward the kitchen when a crash and groan behind her made her leap for the switch.

Nick was sprawled on the floor on his back, looking for all the world like someone who had fallen off a ten-story building.

Vanessa dropped to her knees beside him. "Are you all right?" she cried.

"My back is out," he answered, moaning.

There was no time to be wasted. Vanessa went right to the heart of the matter and panicked. She scrambled for the afghan her grandmother had knitted and covered him with it as if he were a war casualty. His eyes were closed, and he was pale.

"Nick, say something!" she cried.

"I may sue," he replied.

Chapter 10

Vanessa tapped one foot nervously while she waited for Gina to answer the telephone. Finally she heard a breathless "hello" at the other end of the line.

Huddled in her kitchen, speaking in a whisper, Vanessa explained that Nick was lying in the middle of her living room floor, apparently immobilized. "What should I do?" she asked. "Call the paramedics?"

Gina laughed. "It would serve him right if you did. Nick's faking, Vanessa—he probably wants to spend the night."

Vanessa sighed. Of course Nick was pretending, indulging his hypochondria. After all, this was the man who carried on like a victim of Lizzie Borden's when he cut himself. "Thank you," she said.

"See you tomorrow," Gina responded lightly. "Have fun getting Nick off the floor."

"*Tomorrow?*"

"At Uncle Guido's dinner, of course," came the answer.

Vanessa's hackles rose. Evidently Nick had committed her to a family gathering without so much as consulting her. She said a polite goodbye to Gina and, after gathering her dignity, walked back into the living room.

There, standing beside Nick's prone body, she folded her arms across her chest and nudged him with one foot. "What's happening at your Uncle Guido's place tomorrow, Nick?"

With great and obvious anguish, Nick raised himself to a sitting position. "I could have been killed," he fretted, avoiding her question.

"That could still happen," Vanessa allowed.

Laboriously the man who had once struck fear into the heart of every linebacker in the National Football League hauled himself to his feet. He gave the vacuum cleaner he'd tripped over a look that should have melted the plastic handle, and then sighed. "I suppose you're mad because I told my family you'd come to dinner tomorrow afternoon," he said.

Vanessa was tapping one foot again. "That kind of high-handed presumption is exactly what keeps me from marrying you, Nick DeAngelo!"

He leaned close to her, and she was filled with the singular scent of him. His dark eyes were snapping with annoyance. "Who asked you to get married, Lawrence?" he countered.

Crimson heat filled Vanessa's face. No one, not even Parker, could make her as furious, so fast, as Nick co~~~
"You wanted to shack up?" she seethed.

Nick sighed again heavily. "Time o~~
making the signal with his hands~~
You're the one who brought up ~~~

Vanessa looked away, her eyes filling with sudden embarrassing tears. She had no idea what to say.

Nick took her arms into his hands and made her look at him. "It's time we stopped playing games," he said hoarsely. "I love you, Vanessa, and I'd like nothing better than to marry you. Tonight, tomorrow, whenever you say."

Vanessa bit into her lower lip. She wanted to say yes so badly that she could barely hold the word back, but fear stopped her. Mortal fear that gripped her mind and spirit like an iron fist, cold and inescapable. She tried to get past it, like a mountain climber working her way around an obstacle by inching along a narrow ledge.

"Maybe I wasn't so far off a minute ago," she ventured to say, "when I asked if you wanted to live together."

Nick stared at her in wounded amazement. "You said 'shack up,' if I remember correctly," he replied.

Vanessa winced at the dry fury in his tone and rushed headlong into her subject. "It seems to me that it would be a good idea for us to live together for a while, just until we could make sure we really love each other."

Nick's eyes glowed with dark heat. "Sure," he mocked, shrugging. "That way you wouldn't have to make a commitment. If you got a job offer in another city, or decided you wanted a different roommate, you could just bail out!"

"That isn't what I meant at all!" Vanessa cried, horrified at the picture he was painting.

"Isn't it?" he demanded. "Tell me, Vanessa—where were we going to set up this romantic little love nest?"

She swallowed. "I thought San Francisco would be ⁿ ᵢ itted in a very small voice.

"I'll bet you did," Nick retorted, and, unbelievably, he turned and strode toward the door.

Vanessa hurried after him, not wanting to let him go again so soon. "Nick, wait…"

He stopped and turned to face her, but there was a cold distance in his eyes that made her heart ache. "I want a wife and a family, Vanessa—I've told you that. If you can't make a commitment, then for God's sake let me go."

"You're being a prude," Vanessa accused, as he opened the door to an icy November wind.

"Imagine," Nick marveled, spreading his hands. "Me—the party animal. Go figure it."

"Don't be so stubborn and unreasonable!" Vanessa cried, knowing how lonely her world was without him. "Lots of people are living together these days, and they're making their relationships work!"

"Good for them," Nick replied. "As for me, I'm ready for a wife, not a perennial girlfriend. Sleep tight, Vanessa." With that, he went out, closing the door crisply behind him.

Feeling bereft, Vanessa shot the bolt into place and wandered witlessly back to the kitchen, meaning to console herself with a cup of tea. She noticed the light on her answering machine blinking and, after putting a mug of water into the microwave, she pressed the play button on the machine.

There was only one, but it might have made all the difference in the world if she'd only heard it a few minutes earlier. The producers of *Seattle This Morning* wanted her to host the show, not with a partner, but on her own.

Vanessa would have jumped for joy at any other time,

but she couldn't forget that Nick had just walked out the front door. She dreaded facing the rest of her life without him.

Thursday was long and it was lonely. Vanessa did her stint on the shopping channel—dressed as a pilgrim—and turned down numerous invitations to friends' houses opting instead to go home alone and cook a frozen turkey dinner in her microwave.

There were messages on her machine and her cell from everyone in the world except Nick DeAngelo. She returned a happy-holiday call to her grandparents and left the others unanswered. All night she lay staring up at the ceiling, trying to imagine herself living with Nick as his wife, bearing his children, sharing his joys and his problems.

The pleasant pictures were all too fleeting. It was easier to imagine him packing to leave her on some rainy afternoon.

All night Vanessa tossed and turned. Long before morning she knew what she had to do. If she stayed in Seattle, she would keep having destructive encounters with Nick, which would break her heart over and over again.

She had to start over somewhere else.

She called the television station in San Francisco first and told them she was accepting their offer, and then she got in touch with a friend in real estate and arranged to put her house on the market. She hoped the new owners would let Rodney go on living in the garage apartment since he liked it so much.

Nick didn't try to contact her again, and Vanessa's feelings about that were mixed. She marveled at her own capacity for conflicting emotions where that man was concerned.

When the fifteenth of December finally arrived, Vanessa's brief career with the Midas Network was over. That evening Mel and the Harmons shanghaied her, dragging her off to a farewell party at, of all places, DeAngelo's.

"How could you?" Vanessa demanded of Janet Harmon in a whisper when the crowd of people from the network had finished congratulating her and gone back to enjoying wine and hors d'oeuvres. It would have been easier if Nick had been away looking after the other restaurant or something, but he was very much in evidence.

"How could I?" Janet echoed. "Vanessa, how could *you?* Leaving the Midas Network is one thing, but leaving Nick is another. Are you out of your mind? The man adores you!"

Vanessa's gaze went involuntarily to Nick. He was talking to a couple on the far side of the restaurant, laughing at something the woman said as he drew back her chair. Knowing all the while that her reaction was silly, Vanessa ached with jealousy. "Bringing me here was a rotten trick," she said miserably, forcing her eyes back to her own circle. "Thanks a lot."

"We were trying to bring you to your senses, that's all," argued Mel, leaning forward in his chair. He was accompanied by a woman half his age with bleached hair and whisk-broom eyelashes.

Vanessa sighed. "Even if I wanted to stay, it's too late. I've already given up my job and sold my house."

Paul, now her former boss, sat back in his chair. "The spot on *Seattle This Morning* is still open," he said.

Vanessa felt a little leap of hope in a corner of her heart, but it died quickly. She was as afraid of commitment as she'd ever been, and Nick probably didn't want her anymore, anyway.

She wasn't about to find out. Going to him with heart in her hands and being rejected would be more than she could bear. She looked down at the glass of chablis a waiter had poured for her moments before and left Paul's remark hanging unanswered in the air.

Vanessa was in a sort of daze from then on, eating her dinner, sipping her wine, making the proper responses—she hoped—to the things the other people around the large table said to her. She told herself that she had only to get through dessert and a round of goodbyes and then she could escape.

She was coming back from the rest room when she encountered Nick in the hallway. He blocked her way like Italy's answer to Goliath.

"Hello, Nick," she managed to choke out, her cheeks coloring. "How are you?"

He gave her a look that said her question was too stupid to rate an answer and sighed. "It would be easier to forget you if you weren't so damned beautiful," he said raggedly.

Vanessa didn't know what to say in response to that. Inwardly she cursed Janet for having her going-away party here where she couldn't have escaped seeing Nick. She tried to step around him but he wouldn't let her pass.

"It's damn easy for you to walk away, isn't it?" he asked in a low, wondering voice. "Didn't any of what happened between us get past that wall of ice you hide behind and touch you?"

Anguish filled Vanessa, but she refused to let her

feelings show. She met Nick's gaze, a feat that nearly brought her to her knees. "It was all a game," she licd coldly.

Nick grasped her shoulders in his powerful hands. "If it was," he bit off the words, "we both lost."

Vanessa was on the verge of tears, but she kept her composure and stepped out of his hold. "Goodbye, Nick," she said in a soft voice. This time, when she went to walk away, he allowed her to pass.

She didn't stop at the table and speak to her friends; that was beyond her. She simply kept walking, crossing the dining room, concentrating on holding herself together.

She paused to collect her coat, but she was practically running when she reached the sidewalk.

Snow was drifting down from the sky in great lacy puffs—an unusual event in Seattle—and the magic eased Vanessa's tormented spirit just a little. She slowed her pace, allowing the weather to remind her of Spokane, of childhood and innocence.

Pike Place Market, with its noise and bustle, reminded her that she was in Seattle. She went inside, making her way through hordes of happy Christmas shoppers, pausing in front of a fish market, watching and listening as salmon and cod and red snapper were weighed and tossed on the counter to be wrapped. Vanessa stepped closer.

"Help you, lady?" asked a young boy with dark hair and eyes. He was wearing a white apron over jeans and a sweatshirt, and Vanessa wondered if he was a part of Nick's vast family.

Vanessa stepped closer, feeling self-conscious in her glittering blue dress, strappy shoes and evening coat.

She opened her evening bag to make sure that she had money. "I-I'll take a pound of—of red snapper, please."

"Red snapper, a pound!" the boy yelled toward the back of the market, and the weighing and tossing process started all over again.

"What's your name?" Vanessa asked.

The young man gave her an odd look. "Mark," he said. "Mark DeAngelo."

She smiled. Nick had told her about working in his uncle's fish market when he was about Mark's age. For Vanessa, it was like looking into the past, seeing Nick as he must have been. "You're Gina's cousin?"

Mark nodded, taking Vanessa's money and making change, still looking puzzled.

Vanessa felt foolish. She put her change back into her purse and reached out for the red snapper, now snug in its white package.

"You a friend of Gina's?" Mark asked just as Vanessa would have turned and walked away.

"Nick's," she confessed.

His wonderful dark eyes narrowed. "So you're the one," he said, and any friendliness he might have shown earlier had faded away.

Vanessa swallowed, wondering what had brought her to this market in the dark of night, what had made her mention Nick in the first place.

"Uncle Guido," the boy said to a heavyset man who had materialized beside him. "This is her—Nick's lady."

Guido DeAngelo gave his nephew a quelling look, then smiled at Vanessa and extended one hand over the counter where crab legs and salmon steaks lay on a bed of ice. "You forgive Mark," he pleaded, beaming. "He got no manners. No good manners at all."

Vanessa shifted her bag and her package of fish so that she could shake Guido's hand. "How do you do?" she murmured, completely at a loss for anything more imaginative to say.

Guido's bright dark eyes took in her evening clothes and her special hairstyle. "You have new fight with Nicky?" he demanded. Despite his stern manner, Vanessa doubted that he had a trace of malice in him.

The tears came back. "I'm afraid it's an old fight," she answered.

Guido rounded the counter and hugged her. "That Nicky. He's a stubborn one. You tell him his Uncle Guido said to quit it out right now!"

"Quit it out?" Vanessa echoed.

"Cut it out," Mark translated from his position at the cash register.

Vanessa smiled and nodded. "I'll tell him," she promised. *If I ever see him again.*

Outside the market, Vanessa hailed a cab. She half hoped to find Nick's Corvette waiting in her driveway, but the only car in evidence was her own. She paid the driver and hurried around to the back door.

The telephone was ringing when she stepped inside the house, and she heard the answering machine kick in.

"Damn it," Janet Harmon said through the machine, "I know you're there, Vanessa Lawrence. Pick up the phone right now or I swear I'll come over and bring the whole party with me!"

Vanessa literally dove for the receiver. "Don't," she cried, "please! I'm here!"

"Well," Janet retorted, "if it isn't the disappearing

guest of honor. You might have told us you were leaving, you know."

Vanessa lowered her head, feeling guilty. Her friends had gone to a great deal of work and expense to say farewell, and she had left them high and dry. "I'm sorry," she said. "It's just that—"

"Don't tell me," Janet interrupted, "I can guess. You ran into Nick, went a few rounds with him for old times' sake and then crawled off to lick your wounds."

Vanessa was incensed. "It wasn't like that at all," she said, even as one part of her insisted that Janet was exactly right. Mostly in self-defense, she began to get angry. "In some ways, Janet, it serves you right. If you'd picked any other restaurant besides DeAngelo's, this wouldn't have happened!"

Janet was quiet for a moment while Vanessa regretted having spoken so sharply.

"I'm sorry," they both said in unison. After that they laughed in chorus, and then cried.

"What are your plans for the holidays?" Janet wanted to know when they'd each gotten a hold on themselves.

"I'm going home to visit my grandparents," Vanessa said.

"After that?"

"I'm due in San Francisco on January second."

"Do you have an apartment?"

Vanessa glanced at the clock, stretching the telephone cord so that she could walk to the refrigerator and toss the package of red snapper inside. "No," she answered. "The station is putting me up in a hotel until I can find something. Where are you calling from?"

"Nick's office," Janet replied. "The party's still in full swing—why don't you come back?"

Vanessa relived the encounter she'd had with Nick in the hallway and nearly doubled over from the pain the memory caused her. "I couldn't," she said.

"What did you say to each other?" Janet wanted to know. "You sound like someone in Intensive Care, and I think Nick is out on a ledge even as we speak."

"What do we always say to each other?" Vanessa countered. She knew the question would confuse Janet, and that was exactly what she wanted. "Listen, my friend—Nick DeAngelo is old news, all right? I don't want to talk about him anymore. Not tonight, at least."

Janet sighed heavily. "Okay," she conceded. "But let me go on record as one who thinks some of your wires are stripped."

Vanessa smiled sadly, though there was no one there to see her. "Thank you for giving the party—I really appreciate it, even though I didn't behave as if I did."

"I understand," Janet said. And that was why she was such a good friend—Vanessa knew without a doubt that she really did. "Will we see you again before Christmas?"

Vanessa promised not to leave Seattle without saying goodbye and hung up. She didn't sleep well that night, but that was nothing new.

In the morning she was up early. Dressed in jeans, sneakers and a hoodie, she was busy packing in the living room when Rodney startled her out of her skin by bursting into the room from the kitchen.

He was dragging an enormous Christmas tree behind him.

"You didn't," Vanessa said painfully, looking at the evidence. The lush scent filled the near-empty room.

Rodney beamed. "Yes, Lady Scrooge, I did. You're going to have a tree whether you like it or not!"

"I'm not even going to be here!" Vanessa wailed.

"Where's your Christmas spirit?" Rodney demanded, looking hurt.

Vanessa had never been able to take a hard line with Rodney. Loving him was a lifetime habit. She shoved a hand through her hair. "Do you promise to take it down before we go home? The Wilsons want to move in the first week in January."

Rodney was mollified. "You have my word, Van. I'll not only take it down, but I'll vacuum up the pine needles and the stray tinsel."

Vanessa laughed. "Wild promises, those," she said just as the doorbell rang.

A delivery man was standing on the porch holding a massive pink poinsettia in a pot wrapped in gold foil and tied with a wide white ribbon. Vanessa accepted the plant, scrounged up a tip and tore open the card the moment she'd closed the door.

"Let's part friends," it read. "Call me. Nick."

A hard, aching lump formed in Vanessa's throat, and tears smarted in her eyes. Against her better judgment and without a word to Rodney, she stepped into the kitchen and dialed the familiar number of his cell.

"Thanks for the poinsettia," she said when he answered.

"I'm sorry about last night," Nick replied.

Vanessa hugged herself with one arm. Just the sound of his voice tied her in knots; she wondered what she was going to do without him. "Me, too," she said.

"You've sold your house," he said, evidently determined to keep the ball rolling.

"I should have done it a long time ago." Vanessa wondered what kind of talk show host she was going to make when she could hardly carry on an intelligent conversation with the man she loved more than life.

"I guess you'll want a small place when you get to San Francisco," he ventured.

So he knew she'd accepted the job there. Vanessa closed her eyes for a moment. "Probably," she responded.

"I'd like to see you before you leave."

Nick's words shouldn't have surprised Vanessa, but they did. It was a long time before she could speak.

"I wonder if that's such a good idea." Her voice was faint and shaky. "We don't seem to do very well on a one-to-one basis."

Nick gave a hollow chuckle. "There's an obvious response to that remark, but I'll let it pass out of chivalry."

Vanessa had to smile. "Is that what you call it?" she countered.

"I hear you met my uncle last night."

She let out her breath. "Yes."

"He gave me a long, loud lecture about mistreating lovely ladies," Nick went on.

Vanessa laughed softly. "I suppose I looked pretty forlorn," she confessed.

"I'm sorry," he responded, his voice a velvety caress.

"Did Uncle Guido tell you to say that?" Vanessa teased.

"Yes," Nick answered. "As a matter of fact, that was part of my penance. Vanessa, will you spend the afternoon with me?"

"I've got to pack and do some Christmas shopping—"

"Please?" he persisted. And when Nick persisted, he was nearly irresistible.

"There's no point—"

"I'm not going to pressure you, Van," Nick broke in gently. "All I'm asking for is this afternoon, not the rest of your life."

It took Vanessa a long time to answer. She wished she had the courage to offer the rest of her life, but she didn't. "Okay," she said.

Nick came to get her at noon, dressed casually in jeans, a sweater and a leather jacket. There was a sad glow in his coffee-colored eyes as he took in Vanessa's gray pants and sweater.

"Hi," he said.

Vanessa resisted an urge to hurl herself into his arms and beg him never to hurt her, never to betray or reject her. "Hi," she answered.

They went to Pike Place Market and walked through it, hand in hand, visiting the different shops and talking about everything but Vanessa's new job and her impending move to California. They had lunch in a fish bar on the waterfront and then drove to a Christmas-tree lot well outside the heart of the city.

Nick inspected tree after tree, consulting Vanessa about each one. She played a dangerous game in her heart, pretending that they would always be together at Christmas, selecting trees, stuffing stockings, putting dolls and tricycles out for little ones to find.

"How are you going to get that home?" Vanessa wanted to know when Nick had at last settled on a seven-foot noble pine with a luscious scent.

Nick looked puzzled by her question. With the help of the attendant, he bound the enormous tree to the top of his Corvette, and Vanessa held her breath the whole time.

She couldn't help comparing Nick's apparent carefree attitude with Parker's paranoia about his car's paint job.

The tree rode with them in the elevator, scratching their faces and shedding its perfume.

"I didn't get any shopping done," Vanessa complained, once they'd dragged the tree inside Nick's condominium and set it up in a waiting stand.

He was dusting his hands together. "I need to get something for Gina," he said. "Let's hit the mall."

Vanessa did a lot more pretending that afternoon, but, like all fantasies, her time with Nick had to end. When he saw her to her door, he didn't even try to kiss her.

"You really didn't pressure me," she marveled as he turned to walk away.

Nick looked back at her over one shoulder, his soul in his eyes. "When I make a promise," he said, "it's good forever."

Vanessa swallowed, thinking of promises that involved loving, honoring and cherishing. "W-will I see you again?" she asked.

He shrugged. "That's up to you," he said. "The next move is yours."

With that Nick walked away without looking back.

Chapter 11

Their grandparents' Christmas tree was a muddle of color in the front window, and Rodney and Vanessa exchanged a look of delight as they pulled into the familiar driveway.

John and Alice Bradshaw had heard the distinctive purr of the sports car's motor and were huddled together on the front porch, waiting. Rodney and Vanessa raced up the walk to greet them with exuberant hugs.

"It's about time you got here," John complained good-naturedly, and then he and Rodney went off to carry in the presents and suitcases that were jammed in the little car.

Vanessa, in the meantime, was led into the kitchen by her spritely redheaded grandmother and divested of her coat and purse. The room was filled with the scents of Christmas—cinnamon, peppermint, a hint of evergreen from the boughs surrounding the striped candle at the center of the table.

"I'm so glad to be home," Vanessa said, and then, remarkably, she burst into tears.

Alice made a clucking sound with her tongue and squired her granddaughter to a seat at the table. "Tell me all about it, sweetheart," she said, patting Vanessa's hand.

Rodney and John had arrived with their arms full by then, and Alice had to go and open the door for them. Vanessa waited with her head down until her cousin and grandfather had passed diplomatically into the living room.

"It's Nick, isn't it?" Alice persisted once they were alone again. She'd brewed a pot of tea, and she poured cupfuls for herself and Vanessa before sitting down.

Vanessa had regained some control of herself. "He's so unbelievably wonderful," she sniffled, plucking a tissue from the little packet that was stuffed into a pocket of her sweater. She was getting to be a regular old maid, carrying on all the time and having to stave off bouts of weeping.

Alice arched one finely shaped eyebrow. At sixty-seven she was still a lovely woman. Her green eyes were as bright and full of humor and love as ever, and her skin was flawless. She wore her rich auburn hair in a braided chignon and dressed elegantly. Vanessa adored her.

"That's what you said about Parker," the older woman remarked.

Vanessa sighed. "I know," she said. "That's part of the problem—what happened with Parker, I mean." She paused to pull in a deep, shaky breath and let it out again. "Nick used to be a professional football player."

Alice was apparently reserving judgment on that,

for she took a sip of her tea and shrugged in a way that meant for Vanessa to continue.

"He was a party animal, too," Vanessa elaborated, thinking, for the first time, how thin her argument sounded. "Surrounded by women," she added uncertainly.

Alice didn't look convinced. "Lots of men carry on like that when they're younger," she observed. "Parker probably won't ever stop."

Vanessa sighed as memories flipped through her mind like rapidly turning pages in a scrapbook—Nick running backward in the park so that she could keep up, eating spaghetti at that café on the island, bringing the lightning inside while he loved her, tying a Christmas tree to the roof of his Corvette.

"I'm so scared, Gramma," Vanessa confessed, and her teacup rattled in its saucer as she set it down.

"But you love him?"

"More than my life," Vanessa answered.

"How about your fear? Is your love greater than that?"

Vanessa bit her lip. "No one in the world has more power to hurt me than Nick DeAngelo does," she said.

"There are two sides to that coin," Alice reminded her with a certain loving sternness in her voice. "No one else could make you happier, either—did you ever think of that? There are times in this life when we come to a crossroad, Vanessa, and we have to make a choice."

Vanessa looked down at her hands. "I've already made the choice," she said, even though she'd told her grandparents about her decision to move to San Francisco soon after it was made.

"Choices can be unmade. Vanessa, if Nick is a good

man—and Rodney certainly seems to think he is—and you love him, then take the risk, for pity's sake!"

"What if he dies?" Vanessa whispered. "What if he decides he doesn't love me anymore and runs off with another woman?"

Alice looked exasperated. "What if you both live to be a hundred-and-four and die loving each other as much as you do today? You're being silly, Vanessa—silly and cowardly.

"Remember how it was when we'd go to the lake in the summertime when you were a little girl? You'd stand on the bank, dipping your toes in the water for an eternity while all your cousins were already swimming. By the time you finally took the plunge, the rest of us were ready to go home and you cried because you'd missed all the fun."

Vanessa smiled ruefully, recalling those incidents and others like them. She'd always been too cautious, except when she'd married Parker and that resounding failure had only made her more careful than ever before. "I am a bit of a coward, aren't I?"

"I don't want you thinking badly of yourself," Alice said firmly. "You're not the most daring person I've ever known, but there's something to be said for thinking things through and taking the slow and steady course, too."

"But I could be more of a risk taker," Vanessa ventured.

"Where this new man is concerned, I think you could," Alice allowed, pouring herself a second cup of tea.

That night, sleeping in her childhood bed in a room where cheerleading pom-poms and pictures of movie stars still graced the walls, Vanessa thought of the last time she'd seen Nick. *The next move is yours,* he'd said.

In the morning, Vanessa awakened and went downstairs in her old bathrobe to find her grandfather in the living room, building the fire in the Franklin stove. John's blue eyes twinkled beneath bristly Santa Claus brows as he looked at her.

"Good morning, sunshine," he said. "You're up early."

A thick Spokane snowfall was wafting past the windows that overlooked the street. Vanessa went to her grandfather and kissed his cheek. "So are you," she pointed out. "But that's nothing new, is it?"

He closed the door of the stove, put the poker away and smiled at her. "We're going to miss tuning in the shopping channel and seeing you there every day," he said.

Vanessa glanced at the clock and wondered if Nick was still in bed or out running through wet, dark streets. Then she slipped her arm through her grandfather's and teased, "You were probably spending too much money trying to make me look good."

John laughed. "You don't need any help to look good, button—you never did." He paused, watching her with wise, gentle eyes. "And the way you keep looking at the clock makes me think maybe there's somebody you want to call."

Vanessa swallowed. She'd been thinking all night, and she'd decided her grandmother was right. It was time she gritted her teeth and took a chance. "There is," she confessed. "But I don't think I'm ready to do it yet."

The old man shrugged. "No one can decide when the time is right but you," he said, and he and Vanessa went into the kitchen where he poured fresh coffee for them both.

"Did you ever wish you hadn't married Gramma?" Vanessa asked, watching the snow through the window above the sink. It gave her a peaceful, secure feeling.

"A thousand and one times," John answered. "And I'm sure she wished she'd never laid eyes on me now and again, too."

Vanessa was staring at her grandfather in surprise, the lovely and mystical snow forgotten. "But you love each other!"

"That's no guarantee that two people are going to get along all the time, Vanessa," her grandfather pointed out reasonably, leaning against the counter as he sipped his coffee. "Show me a marriage where neither party ever gets mad and yells, and I'll show you a marriage where one or both partners just don't give a damn."

Vanessa made swift calculations. Christmas was just three days away. Perhaps, if she were very lucky, she could get a plane back to Seattle, do what she she needed to do and be home in time for the festivities.

She searched online for a flight, but there wasn't an available seat on any of the planes leaving Spokane until after Christmas.

Discouraged, Vanessa called the train station. The prospects were much more encouraging there, but when she hung up she saw her grandmother standing nearby, looking sad.

"I'll be back before Christmas, I promise," Vanessa said.

Alice was a woman who had made bravery a habit. She squared her shoulders. "Bring the football player back with you," she ordered, tightening the belt on her bathrobe and then smoothing her hair with one hand.

"I'll try," Vanessa promised. She took only her purse and coat, leaving her suitcase and gifts as a pledge that she would return.

The train trip was slow—it took eight hours—but the journey gave Vanessa plenty of time to assemble her thoughts. It was six o'clock in the evening when she reached downtown Seattle, and catching a cab turned to be such a competitive pursuit that it might have become an Olympic event.

Finally, however, she reached DeAngelo's and hurried upstairs to Nick's office, where he'd kissed her the night they met.

Nick's middle-aged assistant looked her over warily. "Ms. Lawrence?" she echoed after Vanessa introduced herself. "You're Nicky's friend?"

Nicky. Vanessa bit back a smile and nodded. "Yes."

The woman made a harrumph sound, as if to say "some friend," and then announced, "He's not here. Mr. DeAngelo is sick today."

Vanessa was alarmed. "Sick? What's the matter with him?"

A shrug was the only answer forthcoming, so Vanessa hastily excused herself and ran outside again. Cabs were still at a premium with so many last-minute shoppers in the downtown area, and it wasn't far to Nick's building. She hurried there on foot and was breathless when she fell against his doorbell.

"Who is it?" yelled a thick voice from inside.

Vanessa smiled. "It's Mrs. Santa Claus. Let me in!"

The door was wrenched open, and Nick stood in the chasm, wrapped in a blue terry-cloth robe. He smelled of mentholated rub, and his hair stood up in ridges as though he'd run greasy fingers through it.

Vanessa wrinkled her nose and stepped past him. "Your assistant tells me you're sick," she said.

Nick sneezed loudly. "I've seen colds like this develop into pneumonia," he said.

Vanessa rolled her eyes, but let the remark pass. After slipping out of her coat and laying it across a chair, she started toward the kitchen. "What you need is some hot lemon juice and honey," she said.

Nick stopped her by grasping her arm in one hand and whirling her around to face him. "What are you doing here?" he asked.

Inside she was trembling. She felt like a person standing on the edge of a cliff, about to pilot a hang glider for the first time. "You said the next move was mine. This is it, handsome."

His mouth dropped open. "You mean—"

"I mean that I love you, Nick."

"Wait a second. You've said that before. What's changed?"

"My mind. I'm not going to San Francisco, Nick, and if you still want to marry me…"

He gave a shout of joy, crushed her against him and whirled her around as though she weighed nothing at all. The scent of mentholated rub was nearly overpowering. "If? Lady, you just say when!"

Vanessa made a face as he set her back on her feet. "You smell awful," she said.

"God, this is romantic," Nick enthused, beaming. He sprinted off down the hall, and Vanessa set about finding lemon juice and honey.

When Nick returned minutes later, he'd showered

and pulled on jeans and a T-shirt with the number 58 imprinted on the front. His hair was still damp and tousled, and Vanessa combed it with her fingers, smiling at his miraculous recovery.

He kissed her, and Vanessa knew she would catch his virus—if he had one—but she didn't care. When he lifted her into his arms, she made no protest.

"Just how long do you want me to stick around, woman?" he asked, his lips close to hers.

Vanessa touched his mouth with her own. "Only forever," she replied.

He kissed her again. "You've got it," he promised.

His bed was unmade and rumpled, but Vanessa barely noticed. She gave herself up to sweet anticipation as Nick removed her clothing article by article, making a game of kissing and caressing each part of her as he unveiled it.

Vanessa settled deep into the mattress, giving a sigh of contentment, trusting Nick so fully that she clasped the headboard in her hands and abandoned herself completely to his loving.

He was tender, sensing that she was giving him her whole self this time and not just her body. She whimpered with pleasure as he circled one nipple with the tip of his tongue and held on tight to the headboard lest she drift away.

Nick teased her nipple, rolling it between his tongue and his teeth, then took it hungrily. When he'd had his fill of her breasts, he moved down over her quivering belly, taking tantalizing nips at her satin-smooth skin and deepening her whimper to a soft, steady croon.

And then he lifted her up in both hands, as he might take water from a cool, clean stream, and drank of her. The glory of it stunned her, but soon she was in a delirium of pleasure, tossing her head from side to side and letting go of the headboard to tangle her fingers in his hair. Shameless pleas fell from her lips, which felt dry even though she continuously ran her tongue over them, and her body was in mutiny against her mind, wildly seeking its own solace.

She sobbed his name as he brought her over the brink and introduced her to a new world—a world of unchained lightning and velvet fire. Her face was wet with tears when he finally poised himself above her, asking for her permission with his eyes.

Vanessa nodded, unable to speak, and ran her hands up and down the taut, corded muscles of Nick's back as he eased himself inside her. The pleasure was quiet at first—she'd already been wholly satisfied—but watching Nick's climb toward glory excited her all over again. When he reached the pinnacle, shuddering upon her and giving a fierce lunge of his hips, Vanessa met him there, arching her back to accommodate him, crying out in triumph and submission.

He buried his face in the curve of her neck when it was over, still trembling and breathing raggedly. Vanessa caressed him gently, wanting to soothe him.

Her body was utterly relaxed, but her mind was active. "I did promise my grandparents that I would come home for Christmas," she said. "They want me to bring you."

Nick sighed, his breath warm against her flesh. "Okay, but don't make any plans for next year without consulting me."

"Yes, sir!" Vanessa laughed.

He raised his head and gave her a sound, smacking

kiss on the mouth. "Don't give me the old 'yes, sir' routine," he said, trying not to grin. "You're going to be nothing but trouble, woman, and you know it."

Vanessa was nibbling at his neck, giving him back some of his own. "Um-hmm," she agreed "trouble."

Nick groaned as she slid downward beneath him, tasting first one of his nipples and then the other. "Give me a break," he pleaded. "I'm Italian, not superhuman."

Vanessa giggled beneath Nick and the covers. "Same thing, to hear you tell it," she said. She didn't stop, and Nick was finally forced to submit to her attentions.

He was a very good loser.

The train pulled into Spokane at 11:50 p.m. on December 23, and Nick and Vanessa caught a cab to her grandparents' house.

Golden light spilled onto the snow outside their windows. "They're waiting up," Vanessa said, touched. "That's so sweet."

Nick paid the cabdriver and collected his suitcases, obviously nervous. "What if they don't like me?" he asked.

Vanessa smiled, pulling him toward the front door. "After the buildup Rodney's been giving you, they won't be able to help it," she said.

Her grandmother hurled open the door just as they reached it and hauled them inside. The Christmas tree glittered in front of the window, piled high with gifts, and a cheerful fire danced in the Franklin stove.

"So this is Nick?" Alice demanded looking him over.

"Number fifty-eight," John said reverently, extending a hand to his future grandson-in-law.

Vanessa rolled her eyes. "What will that make me—Mrs. Fifty-eight?"

Only Rodney laughed at her joke. He'd always been a sport.

Nick and Vanessa were properly welcomed with eggnog and cookies, then sent off to their respective beds. For the first night in weeks, Vanessa slept soundly, and visions of sugarplums danced in her head.

When she awakened, her grandmother informed her with glowing eyes that Nick had gone out shopping with Rodney. "He's a fine man," she added, pouring coffee for Vanessa and herself. "You don't need to worry with that one."

Vanessa nodded, her eyes shining as she sat down at the table with Alice. "I love him so much," she said.

Alice's mind had turned to more practical matters. "What about that job in San Francisco?"

"I called and told them I'd changed my mind," she said.

"You're going to stop working then?" Alice asked, trying to be subtle.

Vanessa shook her head, smiling. "I love working. I got in touch with the people at *Seattle This Morning* while I was in town, and we're going into production right after the first of the year."

Alice sighed. "Does that mean there aren't going to be any babies?"

Vanessa patted her grandmother's hand. "There will definitely be babies," she promised. A quick mental calculation indicated that there might be one sooner than anybody expected. She put all the inherent joys and problems of that prospect out of her mind, determined to enjoy Christmas. "Let's go shopping, Gramma. I need to get something for Nick."

The stores were crowded, but Vanessa still enjoyed the displays and the music and the feeling of bustling good cheer. In one shop there were enormous colored balls hanging from proportionate boughs of greenery, and Vanessa felt like a doll standing under a Christmas tree.

She was full of joy when she and Alice arrived home with their packages to find the house crowded with relatives. All of them were gathered around Nick eating take-out chicken and reliving a certain Rose Bowl game.

There was no private time with Nick at all that day, but when Vanessa crept into the living room to put the gifts she'd bought under the tree he was there.

"If you were hoping to catch Santa," he said, turning from the window where he'd been looking out at the steady snowfall, "you're too late. He's already been here."

Vanessa went to Nick and stood on tiptoe to kiss him. "Mistletoe alert," she said, just before her lips touched his.

He laughed and held her very close. "I love you," he said.

Vanessa pretended to pout. "Oh, yeah? Where's my present?" she demanded.

Nick took a small red velvet Christmas stocking trimmed in white fur from a branch of the tree. "Right here," he said.

Vanessa's hand trembled as she pulled a small box from the stocking and looked inside. Nick's gift to her twinkled even in the relative darkness of the living room, and she drew in her breath.

"It's official now," he told her hoarsely. "I'm asking you to marry me, Vanessa. Will you?"

She looked at the ring and then up at Nick and she nodded, her throat too constricted for speech.

He took the ring from its box and slid it on to the proper finger. Christmas magic seemed to shimmer all around them, and it made a sound, too—like wind chimes in a soft breeze. Vanessa hurled her arms around Nick's neck and held on.

Nick stirred a cup of coffee and leaned on the breakfast bar in the kitchen of the house he and Vanessa had bought soon after they were married. His eyes were trained on the television screen that hung under one of the cabinets along with the coffee maker and the can opener.

As many times as he'd watched Vanessa do *Seattle This Morning,* he was never bored. If anything, he found her more appealing now that she was obviously pregnant and so, apparently, did her viewers. The ratings were sky-high.

The theme music filled the kitchen and there was Vanessa looking like a shoplifter trying to make off with a basketball. Nick smiled and took a sip of his coffee.

"Good morning, Seattle," she said. "This is Vanessa DeAngelo, and today we're going to talk about…"

Nick heard the buzzer on the drier go off and wandered into the utility room to take his shirts out before they could wrinkle. He put each one on to a hanger and then meandered back into the kitchen. Once

Vanessa's show was over, he'd go down to the restaurant, but for now he was a house husband.

He grinned, watching out of the corner of one eye as Vanessa chatted with a group of haggard-looking men. Nick wondered what disaster they'd survived, but he didn't stay to find out. He took the shirts upstairs and hung them in his side of the closet. Then, after peering into the master bath, he shook his head.

As usual, Vanessa had left the place looking like a demilitarized zone. He picked up her towels, hung up her toothbrush and scraped her hairbrush, makeup and other equipment into a drawer.

By the time he got back downstairs, a commercial was on. He was just pouring himself a second cup of coffee when the telephone rang.

"Hello," he said into the receiver, waiting to see what Vanessa's subject for the morning was. She'd told him, but he'd been half asleep and the information had slipped his mind.

"Nick?" The voice belonged to Gina. "I'm calling to remind you about the baby shower. You're supposed to get Vanessa to the restaurant by seven. Can you handle that?"

Nick chuckled, thinking the whole thing sounded like a scene in an espionage novel. "I think so," he said as Vanessa came back on the screen, smiling and telling everybody to stay tuned.

Nick had every intention of doing just that. "Don't worry, Gina," he reassured his sister. "All systems are go."

"Great," Gina said. "What are you doing?"

Terrific. The kid felt sociable. "I'm trying to watch Vanessa's show," he answered pleasantly.

"Oh. Well, goodbye, then."

"See you tonight," Nick responded.

After laying the receiver back in its cradle, he went back to the TV and turned up the volume slightly.

"Don't you think this is a case of plain and simple hypochondria?" Vanessa was asking of one of her guests.

The man looked, as one of Nick's many aunts liked to say, as if he'd been dragged backward through a knothole. "Absolutely not. If my wife gets a cold, I get a cold. If she stubs her toe, mine hurts."

Nick grinned. The world was full of nut cases.

"When my wife was pregnant," offered the next guest, "I was the one who suffered morning sickness."

Just then, Vanessa was shown in full profile. She was probably going to have twins, Nick thought, and just that morning she'd been a little on the queasy side.

He slapped one hand over his mouth and ran for the bathroom.

* * * * *

For Angie

THUNDERBOLT
OVER TEXAS

USA TODAY Bestselling Author
Barbara Dunlop

BARBARA DUNLOP

writes romantic stories while curled up in a log cabin in Canada's far north, where bears outnumber people and it snows six months of the year. Fortunately she has a brawny husband and two teenage children to haul firewood and clear the driveway while she sips cocoa and muses about her upcoming chapters.

Barbara loves to hear from readers. You can contact her through her website at www.barbaradunlop.com.

Chapter 1

Most people loved a good wedding.

Cole Erickson hated them.

It wasn't that he had anything against joy and bliss, or anything in particular against happily-ever-after. It was the fact that white dresses, seven-tiered cakes and elegant bouquets of roses reminded him that he'd failed countless generations of Ericksons and had broken more than a few hearts along the way.

So, as the recessional sounded in the Blue Earth Valley Church, and as his brother, Kyle, and Kyle's new bride, Katie, glided back down the aisle, Cole's smile was strained. He tucked the empty ring box into the breast pocket of his tux, took the arm of the maid of honor and followed the happy couple through the anteroom and onto the porch.

Outside, they were greeted by an entire town of wellwishers raining confetti and taking up the newly coined tradition of blowing bubbles at the bride and groom.

Somebody shoved a neon-orange bottle of bubble mix into Cole's hand. Emily, the freckle-faced maid of honor, laughed and released his arm, unscrewing the cap on her bottle and joining in the bubble cascade.

Grandma Erickson shifted to stand next to Cole. She waved away his offer of the bubble solution, but threw a handful of confetti across the wooden steps.

"Extra two hundred for the cleanup," she said.

"Only happens once in a lifetime," Cole returned, even though the soap and shredded paper looked more messy than festive.

"I've been meaning to talk to you about that."

Cole could feel his grandmother's lecture coming a mile away. "Grandma," he cautioned.

"Melanie was a nice girl."

"Melanie was a terrific girl," he agreed.

"You blew that one."

"I did." Grandma would get no argument from Cole. He'd loved Melanie. Everyone had loved Melanie. There wasn't a mean or selfish bone in her body, and any man on the planet would be lucky to have her as a wife.

Problem was, Cole had plenty of mean and selfish bones in his body. He couldn't be the husband Melanie or anyone else needed. He couldn't do the doting bridegroom, couldn't kowtow to a woman's whims, change his habits, his hair or his underwear style to suit another person.

In short, there was no way in the world he was getting married now or anytime in the foreseeable future. Which left him with one mother of a problem. A nine-hundred-year-old problem.

"You're not getting any younger," said Grandma.

"I've been thinking," said Cole as Kyle and Katie

climbed into a chauffeur-driven limousine for the ten-mile ride back to the ranch and the garden reception.

"About time." Grandma harrumphed.

"I was thinking the Thunderbolt of the North would make a perfect wedding gift for Kyle and Katie."

Even amid the cacophony of goodbye calls and well wishes, Cole recognized the stunned silence beside him. Heresy to suggest the family's antique brooch go to the second son, he knew. But Kyle was the logical choice.

Cole had already moved out of the main house. He'd set up in the old cabin by the creek so Kyle and Katie would have some privacy. Soon their children would take over the second floor, making Kyle the patriarch of the next Erickson dynasty. And the Thunderbolt of the North was definitely a dynastic kind of possession.

As the wedding guests moved en masse toward their vehicles, Grandma finally spoke. "You're suggesting I throw away nine hundred years of tradition."

"I'm suggesting you respect nine hundred years of tradition. Kyle and Katie will have kids."

"So will you."

"Not if I don't get married."

"Of course you'll get married."

"Grandma. I'm thirty-three. Melanie was probably my best shot. Give the brooch to Katie."

"*You* are the eldest."

"Olav the Third came up with that rule in 1075. A few things have changed since then."

"The important things haven't."

"Wake up and smell the bridal bouquets. We're well into the twenty-first century. The British royal family is even talking about pushing girls up in the line of succession."

"We're not the British royal family."

"Well, thank God for that. I'd hate to have the crown jewels on my conscience."

Grandma rolled her eyes at his irreverence. She started down the stairs, and Cole automatically offered his arm and matched his pace to hers.

She gripped his elbow with a blue-veined hand. "Just because you're too lazy to find a bride—"

"Lazy?"

She tipped her chin to stare up at him. "Yes, Cole Nathaniel Walker Erickson. Lazy."

Cole tried not to smile at the ridiculous accusation. "All the more reason not to trust me with the family treasure."

"All the more reason to use a cattle prod."

He pulled back. "Ouch. Grandma, I'm shocked."

"Shocked? Oh, that you will be. Several thousand volts if you don't get your hindquarters out there and find another bride." Then her expression softened and she reached up to pat his cheek. "You're my grandson, and I love you dearly, but somebody has to make you face up to your weaknesses."

"I'm a hopeless case, Grandma," he told her honestly.

"People can change."

Cole stopped next to his pickup and swung the passenger door open. He stared into her ageless, blue eyes. "Not me."

"Why not?"

He hesitated. But if he wanted her support, he knew he had to be honest. "I make them cry, Grandma."

"That's because you leave them."

"They leave me."

She shook her head, giving him a wry half smile.

"You leave them emotionally. Then they leave you physically."

"I can't change that."

"Yes you can."

Cole took a deep breath. "Give Kyle the brooch. It's the right decision."

"Find another bride. That's the right decision. You'll thank me in the end."

"Marital bliss?"

"Marital bliss."

Cole couldn't help but grin at that one. "This from a woman who once threw her husband's clothes out a second-story window."

Grandma turned away quickly, but not before he caught a glimpse of her smile.

"You know perfectly well that story is a shameless exaggeration," she said.

His grin grew. "But you admit there were men's suits scattered all over the lawn."

"I admit no such thing, Cole Nathaniel." She sniffed. "Impudent."

"Always."

"You get that from your mother. May she rest in peace."

Cole helped Grandma into the cab of the truck. "The Thunderbolt would make a perfect wedding gift."

"It will," Grandma agreed, and he felt a glimmer of hope.

Then she adjusted the hem of her dress over her knees. "You just have to find yourself a bride."

So much for hope. "Not going to happen," he said.

"You need some help?"

Cole's brain froze for a split-second, then it sputtered back to life. "Grandma…"

She folded her hands in her lap and her smile turned complacent. "We're late for the reception."

"Don't you dare."

She turned to him and blinked. "Dare what?"

"Don't you try to match me up."

"With whom?"

"Grandma."

"Close the door, dear. We're running late."

Cole opened his mouth to speak, but then snapped it shut again.

His grandmother had inherited the stubbornness and tenacity of her ancestors. He knew all about that, because he'd inherited it, too.

He banged the door shut, cursing under his breath as he rounded the front grill. There was no point in arguing anymore today. But if she started a parade of Wichita Falls' fairest and finest through the ranch house, he was going bull riding in Canada.

Cultural Properties Curator Sydney Wainsbrook felt her stomach clench and her adrenaline level rise as Bradley Slander sauntered across the foyer of New York's Laurent Museum. A champagne flute dangled carelessly from his fingers and that scheming smile made his beady brown eyes look even smaller and more ratlike than usual.

"Better luck next time, Wainsbrook," he drawled, tipping his head back to take an inelegant swig of the '96 Cristal champagne. His Adam's apple bobbed and he smacked his lips with exaggerated self-satisfaction.

Yeah, he would feel self-satisfied. He had just outbid

her on an antique, gold Korean windbell, earning a hefty commission and making it the possession of a private collector instead of a public museum.

It was the third time this year he'd squatted in the wings like a vulture while she did the legwork. The third time he scrabbled in at the last second to ruin her deal.

Sydney had nothing against competition. And she understood an owner's right to sell their property to the highest bidder. What galled her was the way Bradley slithered around her contacts, fed them inflated estimates to convince them to consider auction. Then he bid much lower than his estimate, disappointing the owner and keeping important heritage finds from the community forever.

"How *do* you sleep at night?" she asked.

Bradley leaned his shoulder against a marble pillar and crossed one ankle over the other. "Let's see. I spend an hour or so in my hot tub, sip a glass of Napoleon brandy, listen to a bit of classical jazz, then crawl into my California king and close my eyes. How about you?"

She pointedly shifted her gaze to the stone wall beside them. "I fantasize about you and that broad ax."

He smirked. "Happy to be in your fantasy, babe."

"Yeah? The broad ax wins. You lose."

"Might be worth it."

"Gag me."

His lips curved up into a wider smile. "Whatever turns your crank."

A shudder ran through Sydney at the unbidden visual. She took a quick drink of her own champagne, wishing it was a good, stiff single malt. It might have been a long dry spell, but she wouldn't entertain sexual thoughts about Bradley if he was the last man on earth.

Bradley chuckled. "So, tell me. What's next?"

She raised an eyebrow.

"On your list. What are we going after? I gotta tell you, Wainsbrook, you are my ticket to the big time."

"Should I just email you my research notes? Save you some trouble?"

"Whatever's most convenient."

"What's most convenient is for you to stick your head in a very dark place for a very long time."

"Sydney, Sydney, Sydney." He clucked. "And here I tell all my friends you're a lady."

"It'll be a cold day in hell before I voluntarily give you any information."

He shrugged. "Suit yourself." Then he leaned in. "I have to admit. The chase kind of turns me on."

Fighting the urge to fulfill her broad-ax fantasy, Sydney clenched her jaw. What *was* she going to do now?

She was on probation at the Laurent Museum due to her lack of productivity this year. If Bradley scooped one more of her finds, she'd be out of a job altogether. Her boss had made that much clear enough after the auction this afternoon.

What she needed was some room to maneuver. She needed to get away from Bradley, maybe leave the country. Go to Mexico, or Peru, or…France. Oh! She quickly reversed the smile that started to form.

"See?" purred Bradley. "You like the game, too. You know you do."

Sydney struggled not to gag on that one.

He held up his empty glass in a mock salute. "Until next time."

"Next time," Sydney muttered, having no intention whatsoever of giving him a next time. She figured the odds of Bradley following her overseas were remote, which meant the Thunderbolt of the North was wide open.

She had three years' worth of research notes on the legendary antique brooch, including credible evidence it was once blessed by Pope Urban the Fifth.

Forged by the Viking King, Olav the Third, in 1075, the jewel-encrusted treasure had journeyed into battles and crossed seas. Some claimed it was used as collateral to found the Sisters of Beneficence convent at La Roche.

Most thought it was a legend, but Sydney knew it existed. In somebody's attic. In somebody's jewel case. In somebody's safe-deposit box. If even half the stories were true, the Thunderbolt had an uncanny knack for survival.

And if it had survived, she'd pick up its trail. If she picked up its trail, she'd find it. And when she found it, she'd make *sure* it stayed with the Laurent Museum— even if she had to hog-tie Bradley Slander to keep him out of the bidding.

Life was looking up for Cole. He'd spent the past three days at a livestock auction in Butte, Montana, with his eye on one beauty of a quarter horse. In the end, he'd outbid outfits from California and Nevada to bring Night-Dreams home to the Valley.

He might not be in a position to produce the next round of Erickson heirs, but he was sure in a position to produce top-quality cutting horses. That had to count for something.

Cole tossed his duffel bag on the cabin floor and kicked the door shut behind him. Of course it counted for something. It counted for a lot. And he had to get his grandmother's voice out of his head.

It had been months since the wedding. He wasn't a stud, and she could only make him feel guilty if he let her.

He pulled a battered percolator from a kitchen shelf and scooped some coffee into the basket. As soon as Katie was pregnant, he'd make his case for the Thunderbolt again. If Olav the Third could start a tradition, Cole the First could change it.

He filled the coffeepot with water and cranked the knob on his propane stove. The striker clicked in the silent kitchen. Then the blue flame burst to life.

A four-cylinder engine whined its way down his dirt driveway, and Cole abandoned the coffeepot to peer out the window. His family drove eight-cylinder pickups. In fact everybody in the valley drove pickups.

He leaned over the plaid couch and watched the little sports car bump to a halt beneath his oak tree.

He didn't recognize the car. But then a trim ankle and a shapely calf stretched out the driver's door and he no longer cared.

He moved onto the porch as a telltale hiss of steam shot out from under the hood and a spurt of water dribbled down the grill. The engine gurgled a couple of times, then sighed to silence.

Another shapely leg followed the first. And a sexy pair of cream heels planted themselves in the dust.

The slim woman rose to about five-foot-five. She wore a narrow, ivory-colored skirt and a matching jacket. Thick, auburn hair cascaded over her shoulders in shimmering waves. Her cheeks were flushed and her skin was flawless. She hadn't even been in the valley long enough to get dusty.

She smiled as she turned, flashing straight white teeth and propping her sunglasses in her hair. Cole sucked in an involuntary breath.

"Hello." She waved, stumbled on the uneven ground, then quickly righted herself as she started toward him.

He trotted down the three steps to offer his arm.

"Thank you," she breathed as her slim fingers tightened against his bare forearm.

A jolt of lightning flashed all the way to his shoulder and he quickly cleared his throat. "Car trouble?" he asked.

She turned to look at the vehicle, frowning. "I don't think so."

He raised a brow. "You don't?"

She blinked up at him with jewel-green eyes. "Why would I? It seemed fine on the way in."

He stared into those eyes, trying to decide if she was wearing colored contacts. No. He didn't think so. The eyes were all hers. As was that luscious hair and those full, dark lips.

"I think you've overheated," he said, breathing heavily. He knew he sure had.

She gazed up at him in silence and her manicured nails pressed against him for a split second. "You, uh, know about cars?"

He pulled himself up a fraction of an inch. "Some."

"That's good," she said, her gaze never leaving his, the tip of her tongue flicking over her bottom lip for the barest of moments. "I mostly use taxis."

"I take it you're not from around here?" Stupid question. If she lived anywhere near Blue Earth Valley, Cole would have spotted her before now.

"New York," she said.

"The city?"

She laughed lightly and Cole's heart rate notched up. "Yes. The city."

They reached the porch and a loud spattering hiss came through the open door. The coffee. "Damn."

"What?"

"Hang on." He took the stairs in two bounds, strode across the kitchen and grabbed the handle of the coffeepot, moving it back on the stove as he shut it down.

"You burned the coffee?" she asked from behind him.

"Afraid so." He wiped up the spilled coffee then rinsed and dried his hands. Then he held one out to her. "Cole Erickson."

Her smile grew to dazzling. "Sydney Wainsbrook."

She shook his hand and the jolt of electricity doubled.

"You want me to take a look at your car?" he asked, reluctantly letting her go.

"I'd rather you offered me a cup of that coffee."

"It's ruined," he warned.

She shrugged her slim shoulders. "I'm tough."

He took in her elegant frame and choked out a short laugh. "Right."

"Hey, I'm from New York."

"This is Texas."

"Try me."

Cole bit down on his lip. Nope. Not going there.

Her eyes sparkled with mischief and she shook her head. "Walked right into that one, didn't I?"

He quickly neutralized his expression. "Walked right into what?"

She brushed past him and retrieved two stoneware mugs from the open shelf. "Don't you worry about my delicate sensibilities." She held them both out. "Pour me some coffee."

"Yes, ma'am."

Sydney ran her fingertip around the rim of the ivory coffee cup. Even by New York standards, the brew was terrible. But she was drinking every last drop. Black.

She needed Cole to know she meant business, because he looked like the kind of guy who'd walk right over her if she so much as blinked.

She contemplated him from across the table. He was a big man, all muscle and sinew beneath a worn, plaid shirt. His sleeves were rolled up, revealing tight, corded forearms. He had thick hair, a square chin, a slightly bumped nose and expressive cobalt eyes that turned sensual and made her catch her breath.

He was going to be a challenge. But then, anything to do with the Thunderbolt of the North had to be a challenge. She'd have been disappointed if it had gone any other way.

"So what brings you to Blue Earth Valley, Sydney Wainsbrook?" he drawled into the silence.

She smiled, liking her audacious plan better by the second. She'd worried he might be obnoxious or objectionable, but he was a midnight fantasy come to life. Why some other woman hadn't snapped him up before now was a mystery to her.

"You do," she said.

"Me?"

She took a sip of her coffee. "Yes, you."

"Have we met?"

"Not until now."

He sat back, blue eyes narrowing. Then a flash of comprehension crossed his face and he held up his palms. "Whoa. Wait a minute."

"What?" Surely he couldn't have figured out her plan that quickly.

"Did my grandmother put you up to this?"

Sydney shook her head, relieved. "No, she didn't."

"You sure? Because—"

"I'm sure." The only person who had put Sydney up to this was Sydney. Well, Sydney and a thousand hours of research in museum basements across Europe.

She moved her cup to one side and leaned forward, her interest piqued. "But tell me why your grandmother might have sent me."

He tightened his jaw and sat back in purposeful silence.

Sydney wriggled a little in her seat. "Hoo-ha. I can tell this is going to be good."

He didn't answer, just stared her down.

"Dish," she insisted, refusing to be intimidated. She had a feeling people normally gave him a wide berth. And she had no intention of behaving like normal people. Surprise was one of her best weapons.

He rolled his eyes. "Fine. It's because she's an incorrigible matchmaker."

Sydney bit down on a laugh. "Your grandmother is setting you up?"

He grimaced. "That sounded pathetic, didn't it?"

"A little."

"She's a meddler. And…well…" He seemed to catch

himself, and he quickly shook his head. "Nah. Not going there. You tell me what you're doing in Blue Earth Valley."

Sydney wrapped her hands around her coffee cup. Right. Stalling wasn't going to change a thing. She'd plunge right in and hope to catch him off guard. "I'm a curator from the Laurent Museum."

He didn't react. Didn't show any signs of panic. That was good.

"I've just finished three months' research in Europe."

He waited. Still no reaction.

"It supplemented three years of previous research. My thesis, actually."

"You wrote a thesis?"

"Yes, I did. On the Thunderbolt of the North."

Okay. That got a reaction from him. His eyes chilled to sea ice and his jaw clamped tight.

"I understand you're the current owner."

His palms came down hard on the table. "You understand wrong."

"Let me rephrase—"

"Good idea."

She leaned in again. "I know how it works."

"You know how *what* works?"

"The inheritance. I know it goes to your wife. And I'm here to offer to marry you."

Chapter 2

Everything inside Cole stilled.

He opened his mouth, then he snapped it shut again.

He stared at the perfectly gorgeous creature in front of him and tried to make sense out the situation. Was this a joke?

"Did Kyle put you up to this?" he asked.

"Who's Kyle?"

"My brother."

She shook her head and all that auburn hair fanned out around her perfectly made-up face. "It wasn't your brother, and it wasn't your grandmother."

"Then who?"

"Me."

He paused again. "You seriously expect me to believe you came all the way from New York—"

"Yes, I do." She reached into her clutch purse and pulled out a business card.

He read it. Sure enough, Laurent Museum. Okay, now

he was just getting annoyed. The Thunderbolt wasn't a commodity to be bartered. It was a trust, a duty. "So was that breakdown nothing but a setup?"

"What breakdown?"

"Your car."

"My car is fine."

"Your car is fried."

"You know, I just proposed to you."

He stood up. "And you thought I'd say yes?"

"I'd hoped—"

"In what universe?" His voice rose, bouncing off the cabin walls. He was offended, offended on behalf of his grandmother, his ancestors and his heirs. "In what *universe* would I agree to marry a complete stranger and give away a family heirloom?"

She stood, too. "Oh, no. I didn't mean—"

"I have horses to shoe." He was done listening. She could fix her own car for all he cared, or call a taxi or hoof it up to the main road.

"Right now?" she asked.

"Right now." He scooped a battered Stetson from a hook on the wall and stuffed it on his head.

Sydney watched Cole march out of the small log cabin. Okay, that hadn't gone quite as well as she'd hoped. But then again, he hadn't really given her a chance to explain. She wasn't trying to *steal* the Thunderbolt. She merely wanted to display it for a few months.

She was pulling together a Viking show exceptional enough for front gallery space at the Laurent. With the Thunderbolt as the centerpiece, she would thwart Bradley Slander and save her career. All she needed was the cooperation of one cowboy.

She moved to the cabin door and watched him head up a rise while she contemplated her next move.

The man had the broadest shoulders she'd ever seen. Solid as an oak tree, he had a confident stride and a butt that could stop traffic. She watched for a few more steps, then she forced her gaze away. His butt was irrelevant. The marriage would be in name only.

Her focus had to be on the brooch, not on the man. It wasn't as if she could put Cole on display in the front gallery. Although…

She squelched a grin and glanced at the rental car.

A breakdown, huh? Car trouble could be her ticket to more time with him. Swallowing the dregs of her coffee, she made up her mind. If that baby wasn't broken down now, it soon would be.

She waited until Cole disappeared over the hill. Then she popped the hood, yanked out some random wires and closed it up again, hoping she'd done some serious damage.

Dusting off her hands, she tucked her clutch purse under her arm and headed up the hill.

Three-inch heels were definitely not the best choice for the Erickson Ranch. Neither was a straight skirt and loose hair. By the time she closed in on Cole, she was disheveled and out of breath. She'd scratched her hand ducking through a barbed-wire fence, got a cactus stuck to the toe of her shoe and attracted a pair of horseflies that were now moving in for the kill.

Cole looked completely unfazed by the climb. He stood a hundred yards away, on the crest of the hill, with a coiled rope in one hand. He raised his thumb and index finger to his mouth and let out a shrill whistle that she was willing to bet would get the attention of every cab driver on Fifth Avenue.

The ground rumbled beneath her feet and she took an involuntary step backward. Then she forced herself to hold still and sucked in a bracing breath. If it was a stampede, it was a stampede.

The Thunderbolt had the power to launch her career to the stratosphere. And she'd studied too long and too hard to quit now. Better to be trampled to death trying to get her hands on it than give up and become a tour guide.

A herd of some twenty horses appeared on the ridge, their manes and tails flowing in a wave of black, brown and silver. In the face of their onslaught, Cole stood his ground. He lifted his battered cowboy hat and waved it in the air. The herd slowed, parted around him, then shuffled to a stop.

Okay. Now *that* was sexy.

And she wasn't dead.

The day was looking up.

Cole captured a big gray horse and led it through a gate. Sydney quickly followed. She was intimidated by the big animal, but she was more frightened of the two dozen of his friends they were leaving behind.

Cole tied up the horse then ran his hands soothingly along its neck. "Was there something about my *no* that was ambiguous?" he asked Sydney.

She found a log to perch on and gingerly plucked at the little round cactus on her shoe. Her skirt would probably be ruined, but that couldn't be helped. She played dumb. "You said no?"

He turned to stare at her for a moment. "Just in case you missed it the first time, no."

"You haven't heard me out."

"You're trying to steal my family heirloom. What's to hear out?" With a firm pat on the horse's neck, he headed for a nearby shack.

She scrambled to her feet and followed. "I wasn't going to keep the brooch."

He opened the door. "Ah. Well, in that case..."

Her spirits rose. "Yes?"

"No." His answer was flat as he retrieved a wooden box and a battered metal stand.

Once again, he hadn't let her give enough information for a logical decision. "Are you always this unreasonable?"

"Yes."

"You are not."

He pulled the door shut. "Are you always this stubborn?"

"Will you at least listen to my offer?"

"No."

"Why not?"

"Have *you* ever listened to the wedding vows?"

"Of course."

He started back to the horse. "There's a little thing in there about loving and honoring and till death do us part. And there's generally a preacher standing in front of you, along with your family and friends when you make those promises."

Sydney hesitated. She hadn't actually thought through the details of the ceremony. She'd pictured something in a courthouse, a minimum number of words, mail-order wedding bands and a chaste kiss at the end.

"I could honor you," she offered.

He stopped and turned, leaning slightly forward to pin her with a midnight-blue stare. "Could you love me?"

Sydney stilled. What kind of a question was that?

His gaze bore into hers, searching deep, as if sifting through her hopes and fears.

She knew how to love. She'd loved her foster parents. She loved her mother. But those loves turned bittersweet when her parents died in the house fire and her aging foster parents passed away five years ago.

"Hey there, Cole," came a laughing feminine voice.

Sydney quickly pulled back, shaking off the unsettling memories.

Cole focused his attention over her shoulder.

"Hey, Katie." He nodded.

"You been holding out on us?" asked the voice.

Sydney turned to see a woman on horseback come to a stop in front of the little shed. She had shoulder-length brown hair tied back in a ponytail. A cowboy hat dangled between her shoulder blades, and her burgundy shirt and crisp blue jeans made her look as if she had ridden out of a Western movie.

Her saddle leather creaked as she dismounted.

"What?" asked Cole. "You wanted to shoe the horses?"

The woman smirked as she led her chestnut horse forward. Then her smile turned friendly and she stretched her hand out to Sydney. "Katie Erickson. Cole's sister-in-law."

Sydney reached out to shake the woman's surprisingly strong hand. "Sydney Wainsbrook."

"Nice to meet you," said Katie. She glanced specu-

latively at Cole for a split second before returning her
attention to Sydney. "And what brings you to Blue Earth
Valley?"

Sydney took in Cole's determined expression and
decided she had little to lose. "I'm here to marry Cole."

He sputtered an inarticulate sound.

But Katie shrieked in delight and her horse startled.
"So you *were* holding out on us."

"She's only after the Thunderbolt," said Cole, plant-
ing the metal stand with disgust.

But Katie's attention was all on Sydney. "How long
have you known him? Where did you meet?" Her gaze
strayed to Sydney's bare fingers. "Did he propose yet?"

"I proposed to him."

"She's after the Thunderbolt," Cole repeated. "She's
a con artist."

"I'm a museum curator. I want to display the Thunderbolt. But I really am willing to marry him."

"She's—" Cole threw up his hands, turning to pace
back to the horse. "Forget it."

Katie called after him. "Don't be so hasty, Cole. It
sounds like a good offer. And you're not getting any
younger, you know."

He muttered something unintelligible.

Katie laughed, turning back to Sydney. "From a museum, you say?"

"The Laurent."

"In New York?"

"Yes."

Katie's reaction to the proposition wasn't nearly as
negative as Cole's. Maybe she would listen to reason.
Maybe she would even have some influence over her
brother-in-law.

"I was planning to display the Thunderbolt temporarily," said Sydney, keeping her voice loud enough to be sure Cole would hear. "It would only be a loan."

"How did you know it went to his wife?" asked Katie.

"Research."

"And how did you know he wasn't already married?"

"More research." Sydney raised her voice again. "I was thinking of something simple and temporary. At the courthouse."

"A marriage of convenience," Katie nodded.

"Right."

"And how would that be convenient for me?" Cole's hammer came down on a metal horseshoe and the rhythmic clanks echoed through the pasture.

"You could think of it as a public service," said Sydney.

"I'm not altruistic."

"You'd bring an important antiquity to the attention of the world."

"It's a private possession."

"It would only be a loan."

"Why don't you give up?"

While Sydney formulated a response, Katie spoke up. "Why don't you come for dinner instead?"

"Katie," Cole stressed, wiping the sweat from his brow.

"We can talk about it, Cole," said Katie. "No harm in talking about it."

Sydney felt a surge of hope. She definitely had an ally in Katie.

"You two can do whatever you want," said Cole, going back to hammering. "But I'm not coming to dinner."

"Of course you are," said Katie.

"Nope."

"I'll send Kyle after you."

"Good luck with that."

Katie put her hands on her hips and arched one eyebrow.

"You really need to do something about your wife," said Cole as he leaned on the rail next to the barbecue where his brother was grilling steaks.

Kyle closed the cast-iron lid and joined Cole. "It's not my fault you can't say no to her."

"Can *you* say no to her?"

"Why would I want to say no to her?"

"Not ever?"

"Not ever."

Cole folded his arms over his chest. "Don't you ever need to just put your foot down and lay out the logic?"

Kyle laughed. "You're joking, right?"

"How can a man live with somebody orchestrating his every move?"

"Are we talking about Katie or Sydney?"

"Katie's helping Sydney. And we're talking about women in general."

"And your fear of them."

"Don't be absurd."

"Then why are you freaking out over Sydney's idea?"

Cole peered at his brother, squinting in the dying light of the sunset. "Are you seriously suggesting I marry a stranger and give her the Thunderbolt?"

"She's from a museum, not some crime family. I'm only suggesting you hear her out."

Katie appeared in the doorway, a big wooden salad bowl clasped in her hands. "Hear who out?"

"Sydney," said Kyle.

"Oh, good," said Katie. "We're just in time."

Sydney appeared behind her with a basket of rolls, and Cole did an involuntary double take. She'd removed her jacket and her silk, butter-yellow blouse highlighted the halo of her rich, auburn hair. Her rounded breasts pressed against the thin fabric, and a small flash of her stomach peeked out between the hem of her blouse and the waistband of her skirt.

"Can you open the wine?" Katie asked Cole.

"Uh, sure," said Cole, with a mental shake, telling himself to quit acting like a teenager. He reached for the corkscrew.

"I was the high bid on Night-Dreams," he said to his brother, not so subtly changing the direction of the conversation.

Kyle shot him a knowing grin but played along. "Planning to use Sylvester as a sire?"

Cole popped the cork on the bottle of merlot. "Come next spring, it's the start of a whole new bloodline."

After Sydney set the rolls down on the table, Cole automatically pulled out her chair. She accepted with a smile of thanks, and the scent of her perfume wafted under his nose.

"That reminds me," said Kyle from the other side of the table. "I need your signature on a contract with Everwood." He transferred the sizzling steaks from the grill to a wooden platter. "Gave me my price. He'll take all the beef we can supply."

Cole masked a spurt of frustration by focusing on the wine-pouring. He hated that Kyle had to run to him for every little signature. His brother was an incredibly talented cattleman, and the tradition that put the ranch solely in the name of the eldest son was archaic and unfair.

"Way to go," he said to Kyle, setting out the glasses. "You always were the brains of the outfit."

Kyle scoffed. "Yeah, right."

Cole pulled out his own chair and held up his glass in a toast to his brother's advantageous deal. "I'm dead serious about that."

"Are we going to talk shop all night?" asked Katie, sitting down.

Simultaneously, Cole said yes while Kyle said no. They both sat down.

Sydney leaned forward. "Maybe we could talk about my shop."

"I'm deeding you half the ranch," Cole said to Kyle, without so much as glancing in Sydney's direction.

Those words had the effect he was looking for. The air went flat-dead silent. The barbecue hissed once, and a sparrow chirped from the poplar trees.

"I talked to a tax lawyer in Dallas last week," Cole continued, reaching for a roll. "About our options."

"Cole," Kyle cautioned.

"I figure we can subdivide along Spruce Ridge, then follow the creek bed to the road."

Kyle planted the butt of his steak knife on the wooden table. "Stop."

"I'm going to do it," said Cole.

"Oh, no, you're not."

"You can't stop me."

"Boys," Katie interrupted.

"Oh, yes, I can," said Kyle. "I won't accept."

"It's not up to you." Cole took a breath. The guilt on this one had been burning inside him for a long time.

He wasn't about to back off. "Sometimes a man has to put his foot down and make decisions that are in the best interest of his family."

"Was that a slam?" asked Kyle.

"No."

"It sounded like a slam."

Cole dropped the roll to his plate, regretting his choice of words. "I didn't mean that. I meant, a man needs his own land."

"Kyle?" Katie tried again. "Cole?"

"You saying all these years I haven't had my own land."

That threw Cole. "Of course not."

"There you go."

"What about your kids?"

Kyle clenched his jaw but remained silent.

Cole hoped that meant his brother was running low on arguments. "You need to build a legacy for your kids." He rushed on. "You need to leave them something. If you won't think of yourself, think about your children."

Sydney's hand touched Cole's thigh. His muscle immediately convulsed and he shot her a stunned look.

"Let's move on," said Kyle, a steely thread to his voice.

Cole looked back at his brother. "Let's agree to go to Dallas and talk to the lawyers."

Sydney's fingernails tightened, jolting Cole's nervous system.

What the hell was she doing?

"It's not just you anymore," Cole said to Kyle. "You have a family—"

Sydney pinched him. It actually hurt.

He swung his gaze back to her, but caught Katie's expression on the way,

He stopped.

He stared at his sister-in-law's white lips. "Katie?"

Kyle pulled back his chair as Katie started to tremble.

Katie stood and Kyle rose with her.

"What?" Cole jumped up. "What's wrong?"

Katie gave a little shake of her head and waved away their concern. "I'm fine."

"You're not fine," said Cole.

She placed her hand on Kyle's arm. "I'm really okay. I'm just going to get a glass of water."

Kyle put an arm around her shoulders and gave her a little squeeze. "You sure?" he whispered.

She nodded. "Really. The less fuss, the better. I'll be right back."

Kyle watched her disappear into the kitchen.

Cole raked a hand through his hair, trying to sift through the turn of events. "I'm sorry," he said. "What the heck…"

"Can I help?" Sydney asked Kyle.

Kyle closed his eyed and dropped back into his chair. He shook his head. "It's the talk of kids."

Cole slowly sat, opening his mouth to ask for an explanation, but Sydney's fingers closed on his thigh again.

He felt like a bull in a china shop. What was he missing here?

"She hoped to be pregnant by now," said Kyle.

Cole went cold.

Sydney tossed her napkin onto the table. "I am going to make sure she's okay."

Both men rose with her.

After Sydney disappeared, Kyle moved restlessly to the rail, taking a long, steady swig of his wine.

Cole followed, not sure of what to say. He and Kyle didn't exactly have heart-to-heart talks about their sex lives, never mind their sperm counts. Was this a medical problem? Did they need to see a doctor?

"Are you…" he began. "Uh, do you…"

"The doctor thinks it's stress," said Kyle. "But we don't know anything for sure, and Katie's worried she'll never have kids."

Cole could have kicked himself. "And I was a big help."

Kyle snorted out a dry chuckle as he gazed out over the Blue Hills. "Next time, watch my expression and grab a clue."

"Next time I'll pay attention when Sydney mangles my thigh." Cole regretted his bull-headed stupidity. "Is there anything I can do to help?"

"Get married and have some babies so Katie doesn't have this whole dynasty thing on her shoulders."

"That would be a trick."

"Hey, you've got a bona fide offer in my kitchen."

"We could have a bona fide con artist in your kitchen. Besides, Sydney doesn't want babies, she wants the Thunderbolt. I'm pretty sure this is a platonic offer."

Kyle turned to face Cole. He braced his elbow on the rail and a speculative gleam rose in his eyes.

"What?" asked Cole, dragging the word out slowly, trepidation rising.

"You wouldn't *really* have to have babies with Sydney," said Kyle. "You'd just have to let Katie *think* you'll have babies with Sydney."

"That's insane." And even if it wasn't, Katie knew

why Sydney was here. There's no way they'd ever convince her they were having babies together.

"No." Kyle shook his head. "It's brilliant. You pretend
to fall in love with her, pretend to marry her for real.
She gets the brooch and Katie relaxes enough to get
pregnant."

"And I get a wife I don't know, who doesn't love me,
won't sleep with me but takes my jewelry?"

Kyle took another swig of his wine. "I'm sure you're
not the first guy that's happened to."

Cole snorted.

Kyle clapped him on the shoulder. "You get the satisfaction of knowing you put your foot down and made
a decision that was best for your family."

"Somehow I don't think this is me putting my foot
down."

"So you'll do it?"

"I never said that." How could Cole justify getting married on the off chance it would help Katie get
pregnant? Then again, how could he justify not getting
married if there was a chance it could help Katie get
pregnant?

"We'd be lying to your wife," he pointed out to Kyle,
looking for some loophole that didn't make him the bad
guy.

"No, we wouldn't. We wouldn't have to say a thing.
Katie's a hopeless romantic. Trust me, she's going to
throw you and Sydney together no matter what you and
I decide. All you'd have to do is hang around and look
besotted."

"I don't do besotted."

"Just look at Sydney the way you were looking at her
before dinner."

"I haven't—"

"That was more aroused than besotted, I'll admit. But it should work."

"You're out of your mind."

"She's hot, Cole. It's not like it would be this huge hardship."

Alarm crept into Cole's system as Kyle's words started to make some kind of bizarre sense. He couldn't consider this. Then again, he couldn't *not* consider this.

"This is the dumbest plan I've ever heard," he said. "Take Katie on a vacation. She can relax on the beach. I'll pay."

"She'll worry about you."

"She doesn't have to worry about me."

"I know that, and you know that, but Katie…"

It was Cole's turn to gaze at the dark hillsides across the lake. "You know, this morning things were looking pretty good for me. I'd just bought a new mare. I was minding my own business, thinking about shoeing, thinking about building a new hay shed, maybe buying a combine…"

Kyle started to laugh.

"Then along comes Sydney Wainsbrook and suddenly she's taking over my life."

"Kyle?" Katie called from the kitchen.

"Yes, sweetheart?" he called back.

"Do you think it's too late for Sydney to drive to Wichita Falls all by herself?"

"Of course it's too late." Kyle waggled a victorious eyebrow at Cole. "It's way too late."

"She's going to stay over," Katie called.

"Sounds good."

"I haven't agreed to anything," Cole muttered to his brother.

"You have the easy part," said Kyle. "Just hang around and look besotted."

"I'm going home."

"Come back for breakfast."

"Nope."

"I'll send Katie after you."

"Good luck with that."

Chapter 3

Cole was steadfastly chowing down on hotcakes and coffee when a knock came on his cabin door.

"Come in," he called gruffly, ready to take on Kyle or Katie or both.

But it was Sydney who poked her head around the door. "Hey, Cole."

Cole cringed, cussing inside his head. *Low blow, Kyle.* "Good morning, Sydney."

She gestured inside. "May I?"

No, never. "Of course."

Her lips curved into that brilliant, sexy smile. "Thanks," she breathed, messing with both his equilibrium and his libido.

Katie had obviously lent her some clothes. Instead of her impractical suit, Sydney wore a tight pair of faded blue jeans, a short T-shirt, and her hair was pulled back in a perky ponytail. Her makeup was more subtle than yesterday but, if anything, it made her sexier.

"Coffee?" he asked, finding his voice and rising from his chair.

"Love some."

"It's a little better than yesterday." One cup of coffee. That was it. And no matter what, he wasn't letting her talk him into going back to the house for breakfast.

Kyle's plan might be crazy, but Cole knew he'd cave—even if there was only a slight chance it would help Katie get pregnant. Because Katie without babies was positively unthinkable. She'd be the greatest mother in the world.

"Yesterday's coffee was fine," said Sydney.

"You lie," said Cole.

She shrugged. "I've had worse."

"Don't know where." He put a fresh, steaming mug on the table in front of her.

"Sherman's on West Fifty-second. Ever been to New York?"

"Never have. You hungry?"

"Katie made eggs."

He nodded and sat back down. "How's she doing?"

Sydney wrapped her hands around the mug. "Sad, I think."

Cole nodded, trying not to feel like a heel.

"You know your brother's come up with a plan to fix this, right?" she asked.

Every muscle in Cole's body contracted. His brother had brought Sydney into the loop? Why, that low-down, sneaky…

He bought a few seconds by taking a swallow of his coffee. "What kind of a plan?"

"He said he'd explained it all to you last night."

Of course he did. "What did he tell you?"

"That my timing couldn't have been better. That you and I should get married and let Katie think we're expanding the Erickson dynasty."

It was a conspiracy. It was a bloody conspiracy. "You actually think Katie will fall for it?"

Sydney gazed knowingly at him from under her thick lashes. "You don't think she'll believe you're interested in me?"

"Fishing?"

Her smile turned self-conscious and she gave a shrug. "Maybe."

"Or cornering me, perhaps?"

Her smiled widened then. "Maybe that, too."

Cole sighed. "I meant no disrespect to you." He simply didn't want to marry a stranger. Was that such a horrible thing?

Sydney was assessing him with those gorgeous green eyes. "Okay, I'll go first. You're a good-looking, sexy guy. It's not a big stretch for Katie to think I might go for you."

Cole's chest tightened on the word *sexy*.

It was Sydney who wrote the book on sexy. The way she moved with such fluid grace. The way her husky voice caught on that trembling laugh.

He could still feel her touch on his arm, on his thigh. Okay, so the thigh one wasn't the most pleasant memory in the world. But it was still sexy. Which was pretty pathetic.

"Cole?"

"Hmm?"

"I think it's a good plan."

"Of course you do."

"If we're lucky, it'll help Katie. It'll definitely help the

Laurent—a respected public institution, I might point out. So where's the harm?"

"Don't you have places to go? Things to dig up?"

"That's archeologists. There's nothing higher on my priority list than the Thunderbolt."

Cole pushed aside his pancakes.

She wanted to take this seriously? Okay. They'd take it seriously for a minute. "What about your family? You'd lie to them about getting married?"

She waved a hand. "Not an issue."

"You're not close to them?" That surprised Cole. She was such a smart, perky, good-natured woman. What kind of a family wouldn't want to stay close to her?

A shadow crossed her face. "My foster parents died five years ago."

Cole's stomach clenched in sympathy. He knew what it was like to lose parents. "I'm sorry to hear that."

She shook her head. "It's okay."

"What about brothers and sisters?"

"None."

His sympathy rush escalated. Now he had a sexy, vulnerable little orphan Annie challenging him to do right by his sister-in-law.

He stood up and took his dishes to the sink.

She followed. "Cole?"

"Yeah." And there was that elusive scent again. He didn't dare turn around.

"Why are you hesitating? We can draft whatever legal documents you want to protect the Thunderbolt."

"It's not that." Well, actually, it was that. At least, that was part of it. He didn't know Sydney, and he'd be a fool to trust her.

But there was more to it than the legal risks. It was a

marriage, a marriage to a woman he didn't love, didn't even know. Maybe he was an old-fashioned guy, but he just couldn't bring himself to do it.

"The Laurent is a very reputable institution," she said.

"I believe you."

"Is it lying to Katie, then?"

Cole turned. And there was Sydney, mere inches away. A slight movement of his hand and he'd be touching her. A tip of his head and he'd be kissing her.

"It's lying to Katie," he said. "Lying to Grandma. Lying to God."

"We could have a civil service."

"Not a possibility."

She tipped her head, looking perplexed.

He moved in, just a little, pressing his point, hoping he could make her understand and give up on this ridiculous idea. "We're talking about my family here, and they know me very well. They know that if I loved someone—if I *truly* loved someone—I sure wouldn't say so in a civic office in front of a clerk and two impartial witnesses."

Sydney bit down on her bottom lip. Her cat-green eyes narrowed in concentration, but she didn't respond.

"You ready to walk down the aisle in a white dress, promise to love me and honor me, then kiss me and throw a bouquet?"

As he outlined the scenario, an unexpected vision bloomed in Cole's mind. Sydney in a white dress. Sydney in a veil. Sydney with a spray of delicate roses trembling in her hands. He could feel her skin, smell her perfume, taste the sweetness of her lush lips.

"We'd both know it was fake," she said.

Cole startled out of the vision and gave a short nod. "Yeah. Right. We'd both know it was fake."

"And that's what would matter. That's what would count." She squared her shoulders. "Knowing the benefits, I could do it."

Cole clenched his jaw. He'd hand the Thunderbolt over to her tomorrow if he could. But Olav the Third was specific, and Cole's grandfather's will was ironclad.

He examined the idea from every angle. From his, from Kyle's, from Katie's, from Sydney's.

She could do it? Of course she could. It wasn't as if it would be physically painful. And nobody would die. And nobody would ever be the wiser. Marriages failed all the time. After a decent interval, he and Sydney could simply divorce.

"Then so can I," said Cole, just as he'd known he would from the second his brother conceived the plan. His family needed him, and that was an unconditional trump card.

A brilliant smile lit Sydney's face. "Where do we start?"

"First thing we have to do," said Cole two hours later while Sydney watched him saddle a horse outside his cabin, "is convince Katie I'm falling for you."

Sydney eyed up the big animal from the safety of his porch, having second and third and fourth thoughts. Oh, not about marrying Cole; she was completely convinced that was the right thing to do. She was having second thoughts about getting on the back of an animal that could crush her with one stomp of its foot.

"Tell me again why that has to involve horses?" she said.

"Don't you watch the movies?" Cole pressed his knee into the horse's ribs and pulled snug on a leather strap. His strong, calloused hands worked with practiced ease, and she had a sudden vision of them against her pale skin.

He released a stirrup and secured a buckle. "People who are falling in love gallop their horses along the beach all the time."

Maybe so. But there was no way in this world Sydney was galloping any horse anywhere anytime soon. "Couldn't we just go to a movie?"

He rocked the saddle back and forth on the horse's back. "Where?"

"I don't know."

"It's a long way to Wichita Falls."

"What about a picnic? You, me, some ants, maybe a bottle of wine?"

"We want Katie to see us."

Good point. Cole and Sydney alone in a meadow didn't do anybody any good. Well, except maybe for the cowboy Viking fantasy she was working on. The one where Cole dragged her into his strong arms and kissed her until she swooned.

"Maybe you could double me on your horse?" That ought to give Katie something to think about.

"I wouldn't do that to my horse."

"Hey!"

He rolled his eyes. "Don't be so sensitive. I'm the heavy one, not you."

She scrambled for an alternative, any alternative. "I know. We could mess up our clothes and our hair and let Katie think we had sex."

He walked the smaller of the two horses over to the porch. "On our first date?"

"What? Are you a prude?"

"No, I'm not a prude. Come over here and get on."

She shook her head, moving backward until she came up against the cabin wall. "Then why not on a first date?"

"Because I'm supposed to be falling in love with you. Come on. Clarabelle won't hurt you."

He couldn't have sex if he was falling in love? "Don't tell me this is a good girl, bad girl thing."

His eyes darkened to cobalt and a shiver ran up her spine. "This is a horseback-riding thing."

"Because, if you've got some hang-up—"

"What? You'll refuse to marry me." His look turned challenging.

But then, Sydney was up for a challenge. There was nothing wrong with sex on a first date. Not that she'd ever done it. But she could have if she'd wanted to.

"I won't refuse to marry you," she answered, striking a pose. "But you'll have to tell me which kind of girl you want me to be."

His nostrils flared.

There. Now he was the one off balance. She took a few bold steps forward and her breasts came level with his eyes.

She made a show of reaching past his shoulder to pat the horse. It twitched at the contact—a warm muscle jumping against her fingers. She let her voice go husky. "Which kind do you want me to be, Cole?"

"Sydney."

"Hmm?"

"Don't do this."

"Don't do what?"

"Don't flirt with me."

She blinked in mock innocence. "I'm simply asking a question."

"No, you're not." He swung up on the porch, positioning himself behind her, speaking very close to her right ear, making her skin vibrate with his gravelly, sensual voice. "What you're asking for is trouble."

He was right. Tall, strong, sexy and right. And if that was trouble, bring it on.

But his voice went back to normal. "Hold on to the saddle horn," he instructed, placing his hand on the back of hers and moving it into place. "You're going to put your left foot in the stirrup and swing your leg over the saddle."

Sydney tensed. Flirting, she knew. Horses were something else entirely. "Listen, I've never, ever—"

"It's easy."

She fought his grip. "Cole."

"She's calm and gentle, and she'll follow right along behind me."

"I'm scared," Sydney admitted. What if the horse bucked? What if she fell? What if she was trampled?

"Tighten your grip." He pressed her hand against the hard leather of the horn. His palm was warm and sure, and for a moment she relaxed.

"I'm right behind you." He nudged her forward, urging her closer to the horse. "Foot in the stirrup now."

She took a deep breath and did it.

"Up and over." He placed a broad palm under her butt and all but lifted her into position.

It was a quick thrill, but a thrill all the same. And now she was straddling a shifting horse, staring down at a rough-and-ready cowboy with a knowing glint in his blue eyes.

She could feel the heat coming off her cheeks and tiny quivers jumping in her thigh muscles.

"For the record," he said, back to husky and sexy.

"Yeah?"

"You should feel free to be good *and* bad."

It was a long mile from Cole's cabin near the creek up to Katie and Kyle's house on the hill. They took it at a slow walk, and Clarabelle followed the black horse along a faint trail through a wildflower meadow. Sydney's thigh muscles grew tight, but otherwise the ride went without incident.

"Katie said you used to live up here," she called to Cole as the two-story house rose up in front of them.

He twisted in the saddle to look back. "I moved out when Kyle got married."

"Was it just the two of you?"

He nodded, then did something to drop his horse back so they were side by side. "My parents died when I was twenty. Kyle was eighteen."

"I'm sorry."

"It was tough. But at least we had Grandma."

"The matchmaking grandmother."

Cole smiled. Then his eyes dimmed. "She's going to be really excited about you."

Sydney felt a twinge of guilt. Grandmas didn't seem like the kind of people you should lie to.

"Will it be okay?" she asked.

He seemed to ponder the question. "Well, she'll definitely book the church. Probably start baking the cake."

He brought the horses to a halt but didn't dismount.

"You know, if we want to pull this off, we'd better make sure we have our stories straight."

Trying to lighten the mood, she tossed her hair over her shoulders. "How about you fell head over heels and I'm marrying you out of pity?"

"That'll work."

"Cole, I was only—"

"It *will* work."

Katie appeared at the back door, giving an exuberant wave. "Sydney. You're still here?"

Sydney smiled at Katie. "Cole offered to teach me how to ride," she called back, deciding it was better to stick to the truth as far as they could.

Katie skipped toward them. "That's fantastic."

Sydney shifted in her saddle. "It's pretty hard on the butt. I don't know how you guys do it."

"Callouses," said Cole as he dismounted. Then he grinned at her. "You'll be developing some soon."

Was he flirting?

He looked as though he was flirting.

And she'd sure felt a shiver at the reference to her butt.

He walked a few paces and tied his horse. Then he came back for her. "You want some help down?"

"Sure," she said. It wasn't as if she had a hope of getting off by herself. Plus, her skin was already tingling in anticipation of his hands.

"Kick out both feet," he instructed. "We don't want you getting hung up."

She kicked free of the stirrups.

Katie grabbed the bridle and held the horse steady.

"Lean forward and bring the other leg over his back," said Cole.

She did.

Cole wrapped his hands around her waist and slowly lowered her to the ground.

It wasn't nearly as exciting as mounting the horse, but she got to inhale his scent, and for a second there his body was pressed full length against her back. She shivered deep down inside.

He didn't immediately step away.

"She's catching on pretty well," he said to Katie. Then he leaned around and brushed a lock of hair from Sydney's cheek. "She'll be running barrels in no time." He gave her shoulders a little squeeze before shifting away.

Sydney blinked at him in amazement. She'd never met anyone so caring and attentive. It was almost as if… She stopped herself. He was playacting. Wow. He was very good at it.

Katie let go of the horse's bridle and reached for Sydney's hand. "So you *are* staying for a while?"

"Okay with you?" Cole asked.

"Of course it is." Katie gave Sydney's hand a quick squeeze. "You're welcome to stay with us as long as you like."

Cole led Clarabelle to the post and tied her alongside his black horse while Katie insisted they come in.

The visit didn't last long before pillars of black clouds moved down the valley. Soon, fat raindrops plunked onto the warm earth and battered against the windows.

Kyle arrived, taking refuge from the storm, shaking his hat and wiping raindrops off his face.

Katie greeted him with a hug and a kiss, and Cole moved up close to Sydney's ear. "Okay," he whispered, glancing surreptitiously at his brother and sister-in-law. "This is perfect."

"What? You mean me?" Was she hitting just the right note here?

"No. I mean the rain."

Oh. Sydney glanced out the window. *Perfect* wasn't exactly the word she'd use to describe the growing torrent. "Is there a forest fire or something?"

"No. But the horses are all wet now. And so is the tack. It's going to be a miserable ride back to my place." Cole sounded unnaturally excited by the prospect.

Sydney grimaced. "Well, it doesn't get much more perfect than that, does it?" Her inner thighs chafed at the thought of getting back on a dry saddle, never mind a wet one.

He patted one of her shoulders. "You need to think strategically."

"Okay." She nodded slowly, trying to figure out how the rain fit into their plans. Would it flood the road? Maroon them together?

"When Kyle and Katie break it up back there," said Cole, "I'll suggest we ride home. Kyle will offer to ride Clarabelle, but you insist on doing it yourself."

Sydney watched the raindrops battering the window pane. "And why would I do that?" Other than a latent masochistic streak.

"You want to be with me, of course. You're dying to spend time with me, because I'm so sexy and irresistible."

Sydney cocked her head to one side. "How could I possibly forget?"

"I don't know. Thing is, if you're willing to ride a wet horse through a rainstorm, Katie will know you're in deep."

It made sense, in a wet, squishy, ugly kind of way.

Sydney steeled herself. So be it. She was prepared to take one for the Thunderbolt.

"So Kyle knows about the plan?" she asked.

Cole shook his head. "I just came up with it."

"What if he doesn't offer?"

"Don't be ridiculous."

She gave him a questioning look.

"If he didn't offer, we'd have to kick him out of Texas. Now, no matter what he says, you ride that horse."

"This is secretly revenge, isn't it?"

Cole tapped the tip of her nose with his index finger. "Nah. When it's revenge, you'll know it."

Cole's plan worked like a charm.

Soon Sydney stood dripping wet and saddle sore in the middle of his cabin. And, though he was just as soaked as her, he had gallantly lit a fire then gone back outside to take care of the horses.

She'd briefly considered offering to help. But she was exhausted. Instead, she shook the droplets from her hands, finger-combed her hair and glanced around the little room.

She had to admit, the cabin was charming and homey in the rain. It was built of peeled logs that had mellowed to a golden yellow. The floor was hardwood, scattered with rugs, and the walls were decorated with antique pictures and hurricane lamps. The pieces weren't valuable, but she suspected Cole's ancestors had purchased them and handed them down over many generations.

She ran her finger along the stone fireplace mantel as she moved closer to the heat. It was only September, but there was a definite chill in the air. A plaid armchair with a folded knit blanket looked inviting. Too bad she'd soak the upholstery.

Cole returned, banging the door shut behind him.

"You should go get dry," he said as he pulled off his dripping Stetson and hung it on a peg. "There are a couple of robes on the back of the bathroom door. I'll make us a hot drink."

"I should do something to help." Not that she didn't appreciate this gallant he-man stuff. But she was beginning to feel like a dead weight.

He shook off the sleeves of his denim shirt. "Don't worry about it."

But she did worry about it. He'd agreed to marry her, and she didn't want him to change his mind because he thought she was high maintenance. "Am I keeping you from work?"

He jerked his thumb toward the kitchen window. "In *that?* Are you going to be a nagging wife?"

Sydney couldn't help but smile. "Sorry."

"Get dried off. I can't marry you if you've got pneumonia."

She gave up. She left Cole to the teakettle and closeted herself in the tiny bathroom, stripping off her wet clothes. There was barely room to turn around in there. She banged her butt against the pedestal sink and nearly fell into the claw-foot tub. But she managed to strip down, find some towels and rub her skin dry.

She chose a three-quarter-length, plaid flannel robe with buttons all the way up the front. The shoulders drooped halfway to her elbows, and she had to roll up the sleeves, but it was warm and comfortable. She hung her wet clothes over the shower curtain.

They reminded her that she needed to get back to

Wichita Falls and check out of her hotel room. She couldn't keep wearing Katie's clothes, and she should really return the rental car.

She cringed, remembering the wires she'd yanked out of the motor. Should she confess the sabotage to Cole, or just wait until it was discovered and pay the damages? Hard to say. Ultimately, she'd rather give up money than mess up her chances with Cole.

She rubbed her hair dry and found a comb. Makeup, she'd have to do without.

When she wandered back into the living room, Cole's gaze slid down her body, lingering on her bare feet. He cleared his throat. "You want some socks?"

She glanced down at the billowing flannel. The tails hung past her knees. "You might have hit on the one way to make this outfit less attractive."

"You look fine."

"I look like a refugee from *Little House on the Prairie*."

Cole chuckled low. "Who cares? I'm a sure thing, remember?"

"That's an excellent point. I've never had a man see me at my worst and not had to care about it." She sat down in the big armchair and eased her saddle-sore legs under her. This was restful, in a bizarre sort of way.

All those years she'd spent fussing and primping and worrying. Cole could see her in a gunny sack and it wouldn't make a bit of difference. Come to think of it, this was pretty close to a gunny sack.

"This is your worst?" asked Cole.

She smoothed back her wet hair and nodded. "Pretty close."

"At least there'll be no surprises in our marriage." He headed into his bedroom.

Sydney leaned back into the soft cushions. He was forcing her to think past the wedding. What would they do? She had to take the Thunderbolt to New York. But what if Katie didn't get pregnant right away?

Would they keep up the charade? And if they did, would Sydney stay *here?*

She scanned the cabin again. It was a quaint little place. Maybe too quaint.

The kettle let out a shrill whistle. She waited a couple seconds, but Cole didn't appear. Finally she flipped off the blanket, groaned and straightened, then hustled toward the kitchen, nearly colliding with him as he appeared out of the bedroom.

He was shirtless. His feet were bare. And the button at the top of his clean jeans was undone, revealing a flash of skin below his washboard abs.

"Sorry." She put up her hand to forestall the collision and it came flat against his chest.

His fingers closed over her elbow to steady her and his thighs brushed up against hers.

"You okay?" he asked

She nodded, her heart skipping double-time. This was one good-looking cowboy. He looked great in his clothes, but out of them… Hoo, boy.

He reached over and shut off the burner.

Then his hand came up to cover hers, pressing it into his chest. His skin was warm and smooth. She could feel his heart thudding against his rib cage.

Her fingers made out the ridge of a horizontal scar. It was an uneven gash, three inches long, and she wondered what had happened.

From the little she'd seen of his life, she knew it was rough and physical. But what had caused this? And what other secrets were there on the body she'd admired for two days?

Before she could voice a question, their gazes met. His eyes turned a deep, ocean blue, and she inhaled his scent, marveling at how familiar it had become.

He slowly reached out to stroke her hair. Sensations washed over her like warm rain, and she longed to lean into him and absorb the full warmth of his strength. She held his gaze instead, finding flecks of gray among the storm-tossed blue. His look was turbulent, challenging.

He dipped his head ever so slightly. Then he stopped and his eyelids came down in a long blink.

"Is it just me?" he asked, refocusing. "Or is this a really stupid idea?"

She couldn't stop the slow, sultry smile that grew on her face. "It is a really stupid idea…"

His lips parted. "But…"

"Have we ever let that stop us before?"

Chapter 4

Cole was going to kiss this woman.

Stupid decisions were his stock-in-trade around her, and he saw no reason to give that up now.

"You're gorgeous," he said in all honesty, brushing the pad of his thumb across her cheek.

"So are you," she responded.

He grinned at that, sliding spread fingers through the thickness of her hair.

To his surprise, she rocked forward and placed a hot, moist kiss on his chest.

He sucked in a tight breath, and she kissed him again, her soft lips searing into his skin. It took a second to realize she was tracing the scar on his breastbone. She was kissing away his pain, soothing what was once a gaping wound, calming a memory he'd sworn he'd have to fight forever.

His hands convulsed and he tilted her head, searching

her eyes for the reason behind her caring touch. What he saw was smoky jade and simmering passion.

Lightning exploded in the sky above them. Rain crashed down on the shake roof and clattered against the windowpanes. The oak trees creaked and the willows rustled as the wind whipped the world into a frenzy.

That same storm swirled to life inside him. He couldn't wait another second to taste her lips. He dipped to capture them, touching, tasting, savoring. They were as lush as he'd imagined, but sweeter, more giving, the perfect shape and size and pressure.

He kissed her again, this time pulling her soft body against his, opening wide, praying she'd follow suit. His skin was on fire and his chest tightened with a deep longing.

She parted her lips and a small moan escaped. The sound tugged at him, surrounded him, buried itself deep inside him as she wrapped her arms around his neck and hung on tight.

He inhaled her scent, wishing the moment could go on and on. He wanted to close his eyes, block out the world, lose himself in her, pretend nothing existed outside their cocoon.

But that was impossible.

The world did exist. The world of Kyle and Katie and the Thunderbolt. He slowly pulled back.

Her face was flushed and her eyes were glazed.

He suspected he looked exactly the same way.

She rubbed his chest and eased off with a deep breath. "Guess it's good to get that out of the way," she said.

"Our first kiss?"

She nodded, her gaze fixed somewhere below his

neck. "Yeah. Could have been awkward in front of Katie."

"I'll say." He stepped back, raking a hand through his damp hair. "Now at least I'll know what to expect."

"Me, too."

"So it wasn't such a stupid idea after all."

"I think it was quite brilliant."

"Yes." He nodded. "Brilliant." He took a tight breath. "I'm, uh…" He gestured vaguely toward his bedroom door then escaped quickly and grabbed a clean shirt, stuffing his arms into the sleeves.

Brilliant was just the word. *Brilliant.* Now he wouldn't be able to look at her without getting aroused.

When he returned to the living room she was curled up in the armchair again with a pen and paper in her hands.

"We should talk logistics," she said.

Cole's steps faltered.

Maybe her mood could shift one-eighty in the blink of an eye, but he needed a few minutes to recover. He made a show of securing his buttons and tucking the shirt into his waistband, before he dropped down onto the couch and met her eyes.

"What have you got so far?" he asked, struggling to get back on an even keel, trying to ignore that fact that she was wearing his clothing.

She tucked her auburn hair behind one ear. It was beautiful even when it was wet.

"How fast do you think we can pull this off?" she asked.

"Why? You in a hurry?"

She glanced up in surprise. "Yes. I've got a whole display to coordinate. Dozens of pieces."

"I don't think Katie's going to buy love at first sight."

"I didn't mean this afternoon. It'll take a couple weeks to prepare the gallery."

"A whole two weeks?"

"Probably a little more."

Cole tamped down his annoyance at her business-like approach. They'd shared one kiss. Nothing had changed. There was still nothing more to their relationship than a commercial transaction.

"What's wrong?" she asked.

"Nothing." He neutralized his expression.

"You sure?"

"What could be wrong?"

She nodded. "Okay. Where's the Thunderbolt now?"

"In a lawyer's safe in Wichita Falls."

"Can we get it?"

"Not until after the wedding."

Sydney nodded again. "I'm going to need to make a few calls."

"Kyle has a land line at the house. So does Grandma." You couldn't pick up a cell signal in the Valley.

"You don't have a phone?"

Cole shrugged. "I only moved in after Kyle and Katie got married. Haven't updated much."

"No problem." Sydney flipped the page. "Okay. So what's our next move with Katie?"

"You might not want to takes notes on that."

"Why?"

He raised a brow.

"Oh. Right. We don't want to leave an evidence trail."

"Rain's stopping," Cole noted. "How about I drive you back to her place and you can wax poetic about me for a while?"

A slow smile grew on Sydney's face and Cole relaxed for the first time since the kiss.

"Let me see…" She began counting off on her fingers. "You are a good-looking guy. Smart, funny and oh—" She snapped her fingers and laughed. "I can tell her you're sexy."

Cole wasn't sure how to take that. Was Sydney saying she thought he was sexy, or that she was willing to lie about it? He couldn't ask. It would sound stupid. And there was no logical reason for him to care.

Still, he couldn't help but wonder if she meant it.

When Katie found out Sydney was still checked into the hotel in Wichita Falls, she offered to drive her in to pick up her suitcase. The rental car was down for the count, and it was looking as though they'd need a tow truck to retrieve it. Exorbitantly expensive, but the drive alone with Katie seemed like a perfect opportunity to go all moony-eyed over Cole.

Not that it was such a huge stretch. That man could kiss like there was no tomorrow. She still got a little flushed thinking about it. In fact, she was hoping for an excuse to do it again. Soon.

The next morning, Katie's pickup truck bumped over the ruts of the ranch's access road.

"That's Grandma's house at the top of the hill," she said. "Kyle and Cole's dad grew up there. Kyle and Cole, too, for a while. But after the boys were born, their dad built the house where we live now."

"Cole mentioned his parents had died."

Katie nodded, gearing down to negotiate a series of potholes. "Light plane crash."

"Oh, no." A pain flashed through Sydney's chest, her

mind going back to the horrible day when she'd learned her own parents had been killed in a house fire.

"Cole was in the plane," Katie continued. "He was the only one who lived."

"Was he all right?"

"Cuts, bruises, broken ribs. He was really lucky."

"But he lost his parents." And he had at least one scar to remind him. She was glad now she hadn't asked him about it.

Katie nodded again, keeping her gaze fixed on the road. "He's a good man, Sydney."

"I know he is."

"He's been through a lot."

"Yes, he has." Sydney understood better than most the horrible pain of losing your parents.

Katie cleared her throat. "I can understand…"

Sydney turned to try to gauge the odd tone of Katie's voice.

"I can understand that you might be tempted to, uh, romance the brooch from under—"

"Katie!"

"I'm not judging you. I have a sense of how important it is."

"I would *never*—"

"Like I said, I'm not judging. Women make choices all the time." Katie glanced at Sydney, a mixture of pain and awkwardness in her eyes. "I just don't want to see him hurt again."

Sydney frantically shook her head. "I've been completely honest and up-front with Cole."

"I saw how he looked at you."

"And I like him, too, Katie." Sydney's stomach clenched with guilt.

"He's falling for you."

"Maybe. I don't know." Sydney had to remind herself that she was being honest with Cole. She wasn't conning him, and she wouldn't hurt him.

"I don't know where this is going," she told Katie honestly. "But I won't lie to him about my feelings. I promise you."

"He's a good man," Katie said in a quiet voice.

"He's a very good man," Sydney agreed. "And he's lucky to have you."

Katie cracked a small smile.

Sydney reached out and touched her shoulder. "I'm serious, Katie. You are a terrific sister-in-law. Cole knows full well that I want the Thunderbolt. If anything happens between us, we'll both go into it with our eyes wide open."

Katie wiped her cheek with the back of her hand, giving Sydney a watery smile. "So, you think there might be a chance for the two of you?"

Sydney took a deep breath, turning back to the windshield as she chose her words. "I think Cole and I are going to have a very interesting relationship."

Sydney's answers must have satisfied Katie, because at the end of the day, Katie suggested stopping at her grandmother's for dinner. She said Saturday night was traditionally for family, and a perfect opportunity for Sydney to meet Grandma.

Cole had warned Sydney that his grandma was an incorrigible matchmaker, and that she'd go for broke the minute she laid eyes on Sydney. So Sydney was prepared for anything.

What she got was a sharp, funny, sweet-natured, little

woman in a floppy hat and bright gardening gloves with a dream of a period house. Circa 1940, it had an octagonal entry hall, with an archway that led to a living room, while another doorway led to what looked like the master bedroom.

The wallpaper was yellowed and russet tiles were faded with age. But the wood trim shone with a dark patina and the leaded windows were definitely original.

"Your home is beautiful," Sydney said to Grandma, peering into the living room. The couch and armchair were burgundy, looped brocade, dotted with doilies that Sydney would bet Cole's grandmother had crocheted herself.

Grandma glanced around. "Never thought of it as beautiful before."

"It's *gorgeous*," said Sydney, smiling at the incongruous wide-screen television and the personal computer perched on an antique, rolltop desk. Oh, how she'd love to check her email.

"Sydney's here to visit for a few days," said Katie. "She's interested in the Thunderbolt of the North."

Sydney stole a quick glance at Katie, trying to decide if she was giving Grandma a subtle warning about her possible motives.

"Have to marry Cole to get the Thunderbolt," said Grandma as she led the way through the living room.

"So I understand," said Sydney.

They passed into a second octagonal hallway in the middle of the house, and then through a doorway to the kitchen at the back.

"Good news is that he's available," said Grandma.

"You know, he told me that himself."

Grandma looked back and cocked her head. "Did he, now?"

Sydney nodded.

The older woman smiled. She took a blue enamel kettle out of a painted cupboard and filled it with water from the deep, old-fashioned sink. "From New York, you say?"

"Yes."

"Like it here in Texas?"

"So far I'm having a wonderful time."

"That's good." Grandma nodded her head. "Cole's mother passed away, you know."

"Katie told me about that."

"His dad, too. My Neil."

"I'm very sorry."

"Well, I'm still here. And I've always figured that meant I've still got a job to do with one wayward grandson."

Sydney grinned, assuming she was in for the full court press. "You mean Cole or Kyle?"

"Cole, of course." Grandma paused. "You want to help me?" Then a split second later she gestured to a bowl of freshly picked blueberries so that the question could be interpreted either way.

"I'd love to help." Sydney was ready to give her all on both fronts.

"Good!" Grandma winked. "You can wash the berries. Katie, you get down a mixing bowl."

Katie opened a high cupboard and retrieved a large stoneware bowl. "Grandma's scones are renowned in this part of Texas."

"Recipe is a family secret," said Grandma. "Handed down from generation to generation."

"Can't wait to try them," said Sydney, pushing up the sleeves of her shirt.

"Grandma?" Katie ventured. "Why don't you explain to Sydney why the Thunderbolt goes to the wives?"

"I'll do that," said Grandma with a nod.

Katie turned to waggle an eyebrow at Sydney. "I love this story."

"Near as I can figure," said Grandma, scooping into a tin flour canister, "it started around the middle of the fourteenth century."

Sydney was instantly riveted. There was nothing she liked better than family lore. As far as she was concerned, stories were as important as antiquities.

"The family went through a streak of good-for-nothing eldest sons," Grandma continued. "Worry was, if the young scoundrels got control of the Thunderbolt, they'd sell it for wenches and ale."

Sydney ran some water over the blueberries.

"Old Hendrik wanted to make sure they earned their money the Viking way," said Grandma, her practiced hands cutting a block of butter into the flour mixture. "By raiding and pillaging."

Sydney longed for a pen. She'd have to ask permission, of course, but she'd love to write this down for the museum.

"So, that's why Cole can't get the Thunderbolt until his wedding?" Sydney worked the stubby green stems off the berries.

"Can't have Cole going after ale and wenches," said Grandma with a wink and a sparkling smile.

"Do you have a lot of stories?" asked Sydney.

"Some," said Grandma.

"I'd love to hear them."

"And I love to talk. We'll get along just fine."

Grandma opened a drawer beneath the counter and pulled out a wooden rolling pin. "Berries ready?"

Sydney quickly turned her attention to the bowl, picking out the last of the stems, draining the water. Then she rolled the blueberries onto a clean towel.

"So, what do you say?" asked Grandma. "You willing to give my grandson a go?"

The front door slammed. "Grandma?" called Cole.

Grandma winked at Sydney again as she rolled out a round of dough. "That man needs a strong, intelligent woman," she stage-whispered.

Cole sauntered into the kitchen. "There you are." He gave his grandma a hug. He nodded to Katie. Then he clasped Sydney around the shoulders and gave her an affectionate squeeze. Good compromise.

"How was the trip?" he asked.

"Bought a Stetson and some blue jeans," said Sydney, finding it ridiculously easy to act excited about Cole's presence.

"Can't wait to see them." He dropped his arm from her shoulders and turned back to his grandma. "Need anything from the garden?"

"Potatoes and carrots," she answered.

"Want to help?" he asked Sydney.

"Sure."

Cole strode for the kitchen door, opening it and motioning for her to go first.

As she crossed the back deck to the stairs, she took in the spectacular panorama. She could see the roof of Cole's cabin, the winding creek, the blue-green lake and Katie and Kyle's house on a distant hill. Evergreens on the mountain ridges spiked up to a crackling turquoise sky.

"Be careful. They're steep," Cole warned from behind.

Sydney put her hand on the painted rail as she started down the long staircase that led to a lawn and a huge vegetable garden.

"How did it go?" Cole kept his voice low.

"Your grandma's definitely on board," said Sydney. "But Katie thought I was trying to romance the brooch out from under you."

Cole moved up beside her as they hit the bottom. "How do you know that?"

"She didn't pull any punches. She flat-out accused me of pretending to fall for you in order to get the Thunderbolt."

Cole shook his head, placing a hand on the small of Sydney's back and guiding her to the far side of the garden. "That Katie's more than just a pretty face."

"I'll say." His warm hand felt good against her back. It felt sure and strong. This chivalrous streak might be annoying in another man, but somehow it suited Cole. It wasn't put on and it wasn't a put-down. He was genuine. Genuine was nice.

"What did you tell her?"

"I swore up and down that I was being completely honest with you."

Cole grinned. "Good one. You're more than just a pretty face, too."

She stopped at the edge of the garden, telling herself he was just being polite. "Thank you. I may have a brain, but I'm not a gardener. What do we do?"

"I'm thinking something silly and romantic."

"What?"

"I can guarantee you they're watching us from the window." He picked a plump tomato from a vine and tossed it meaningfully in the air, catching it with one hand and advancing toward her with an evil grin.

She took a step back. "That doesn't look very romantic, Cole."

"I'm teasing you. Guys in love do that all the time."

"You stay back."

He kept advancing. "It's plump and ripe and very juicy."

She took another step backward and stumbled on a clump of grass. "Cole."

He lunged, and she shrieked, covering her eyes, expecting a face full of tomato juice. But he snaked an arm around her waist, pulling her up tight against his back, holding the tomato a safe distance away.

Guys in love. Cole did guys in love very, very well.

He kissed her neck. The heat of his lips and the puff of his breath made her knees go weak. She grabbed at his arm to support herself.

"Nice move," he whispered, kissing her again.

Oh, no. Her hormones surged to life. Her head dipped back to give him better access. The mountains blurred and the sound of cicadas magnified in the long grass.

"Sydney," he breathed, and she turned to meet his lips.

The world instantly shrank to the two of them. She'd been thinking about this all day, missing this all day, every second she was in Wichita Falls, every second she'd been away from Cole.

She couldn't understand it, but nor could she deny it that his kisses seemed the center of the universe. The world pulsated out from the moisture of his lips, the touch of his hands. He lowered them slowly to the soft, fragrant grass, released the tomato and wrapped his arms fully around her.

She closed her eyes. The afternoon sun heated her skin, soaked into her hair. Cole was a delicious weight on top of her, and his lips were working magic. She needed to stay here, just another second, just another minute.

Somebody cleared their throat.

Sydney's eyes flew open and a pair of worn boots came into focus. She squinted up to where Kyle's Stetson blocked the sun.

"Much as I admire your dedication to the cause," he drawled, "I think you two might be overacting."

Cole eased his weight off her.

"Sorry," said Sydney, adjusting her shirt. Where exactly had Cole's hands roamed? What had Kyle seen?

Cole rolled to his feet and held out a hand for Sydney. "Just trying to do our part," he said to Kyle.

Kyle fought a grin. "Next time get a room."

"What would be the point in that?" asked Cole.

Kyle glanced at Sydney and snorted before turning away.

Cole pulled her into a standing position and patted her on the back. "Way to go, partner."

She smoothed her hair. "No problem." No problem at all. If that was Cole faking it, some lucky woman was going to live in paradise someday.

Cole scooped his hat from the ground. "Potatoes and carrots."

"You think that was overkill?" she asked.

"Nah. It was romantic."

"So you figure we're getting it right."

He walked into the garden and crouched down. "Aside

from you making Katie suspicious, I think it's going according to plan."

Sydney turned to watch Kyle stride up the staircase. "You know, you three blow me away."

"What do you mean?" Cole dug into the black dirt.

"Katie's protecting you from me. Kyle's protecting his wife from stress. And you're compromising your principles to help them both."

"Something wrong in that?"

"Something nice in that. I'm just trying to save my job." She liked what that said about Cole. She wasn't completely sure she liked what that said about her.

Cole rose to his feet, dusting one hand off on the thigh of his jeans as he made his way out of the garden. "Your job is in jeopardy?"

She nodded. "Yeah," she admitted. "I'm on probation. There's this guy…"

Then she stopped herself and shook her head. She wasn't letting thoughts of Bradley mar the day. "Truth is, I haven't been delivering the way the museum needs. If the Thunderbolt hadn't worked out, I'd have been out of a job."

"Hold these." He filled her hands with long, crisp carrots. "So, do I get extra points for helping you *and* with Katie?"

"Absolutely." She tried to think of something nice she could do for Cole. "You want to come to New York and see the display?"

He shrugged, heading into another section of the garden. "Maybe. If we're still faking it."

Sydney watched Cole unearth a handful of potatoes and tried to imagine him in her Sixth Avenue apartment. He was too big for New York, too raw, too wild. He belonged on horseback in the rain, or half naked in his cabin kitchen.

She shivered at that particular memory. This urge to kiss him was turning into an obsession. And the obsession was moving way past kissing.

Cole was untamable and exciting and exotic. He was sexy as all get-out, and challenged her on every level. Aside from the Thunderbolt, aside from the charade, she wanted him in every way a woman could possibly want a man.

"You'll never get anyone to marry you without a decent house," said Grandma, plunking a well-thumbed catalog down on the low table in front of him.

Cole snapped to attention, pulling his arm from the back of the porch swing where he'd been toying with Sydney's hair. "Huh?"

"I've been after you for months to pick out plans. And with Sydney here, well, it seems like the perfect opportunity to get a female opinion."

"As opposed to yours and Katie's?" Cole wasn't picking out house plans. He had other things to spend his money on, and he had a perfectly good cabin down by the creek.

"Great idea," said Katie, pulling her patio chair closer. Her eyes shone with anticipation as she flipped open the book.

"Cape Cod or Colonial?" asked Kyle, placing his hands on his wife's shoulders.

Cole glared at his brother. "I do not need a new house."

"You're joking, right?" said Katie.

She shifted her attention to Sydney. "Tell him no self-respecting woman would live in that cabin."

Sydney tensed, and Cole automatically reached out to squeeze her hand. "You're putting Sydney on the spot, Katie."

Grandma sidled up next to Sydney. "I'm sure she doesn't mind. We just want to take advantage of your cosmopolitan taste, dear."

Sydney kept her mouth shut tight, and Cole shot Kyle a meaningful glare. Unfortunately his brother's only response was a mocking grin.

"I need a new hay barn," said Cole. "An addition on the tack shed, and an upgrade to the combines. We all agreed in the spring."

"No. *You* agreed in the spring," said Katie primly. "The rest of us thought you needed a new house."

Cole reached out and shut the book. He'd agreed to a marriage of convenience. He'd agreed to pretend it was real. But he wasn't building any damn house just to keep Katie from being stressed.

"The cabin's fine," he said, moderating his voice. "Even if I was to get married—" he turned to Sydney "—that cabin would be okay in the short term. Right?"

She swallowed. "Uh—"

Katie jerked the catalog out from under Cole's hand. "Now you're the one putting Sydney on the spot. If the cabin's so fine, we'll move into it. You take the house."

"Don't be ridiculous."

"Why is it ridiculous when I say it?"

"There are two of you. And you're a woman."

"Now you're sounding sexist."

Cole turned to his brother. "You'd actually let your wife live in the cabin."

"Nope," said Kyle. "But it sounds like you're willing to let yours."

Cole opened his mouth, but he couldn't immediately come up with the right argument. Damn Kyle. This was *not* his opportunity to push the new house agenda.

"And what about the children?" asked Katie. "There's absolutely no room in the cabin for children."

All eyes swung to Sydney. "Maybe an addition?" she offered.

Katie laughed. "Yeah, right. Cape Cod or Colonial?"

Grandma patted her hand. "Don't be shy, Sydney. We value your input."

Sydney hesitated, but she was being stared down by the entire family. "I've, uh, always liked a nice Cape Cod."

"Page thirty-nine," said Grandma.

"Well, you were a big help," Cole said to Sydney as they walked down the ranch road in the moonlight. After her initial protest, she'd plunged into the planning session with gusto.

"I tried to keep quiet."

"And that didn't seem to work out for you?"

"I'm supposed to be falling for you, so I tried to make myself sound like actual wife material. I answered all your Grandma's questions. We swapped recipes—"

"You know recipes?"

Sydney shot him a look. "I made them up. Point is, if I'd balked at planning my future house, it would have looked suspicious."

"Now they're going to want me to build the damn thing."

"So what? The cabin is falling apart."

"What am I going to do with a two-story, octagonal great room?"

"I didn't vote for the octagonal great room. That was Katie."

"Well you voted for the dormer windows."

"They're pretty."

"And a turret?"

"Adds detail."

"And what am I going to do with a hot tub?"

Sydney was silent for a moment. "Uh, bathe?"

"Very funny. I don't need jets and bubblers rumbling under my butt to get clean."

"Ever tried one?"

"No."

She grinned and bumped her shoulder against his arm. "Don't know what you're missing, cowboy."

"Why? Have you?"

"It just so happens I *own* a hot tub."

A visual bloomed in Cole's brain—of Sydney, glistening skin and swirling water.

"Cole?"

He cleared his throat. "Yeah?"

"You ever stop to think there might be some deep-seated, psychological reason you shortchange yourself?"

"No." He didn't shortchange himself, and he didn't have deep-seated reasons for anything. He herded cows. He raised horses. He kept the ranch running. What you saw was what you got.

"You're living in a cabin where you wouldn't let any other member of your family live."

That wasn't true. He turned from the ranch road down his short driveway and the roar of the creek grew louder. "I'd let Kyle live there."

"And you've never been married."

"Lucky for you." If he was married she wouldn't be getting this opportunity with the Thunderbolt.

"See, I have a hard time believing women aren't interested in you. If you'd wanted—"

"Plenty of women are interested in me." He felt ego-bound to point that out. Well, maybe not plenty. But some. Enough. He wasn't exactly a monk out here.

"Then why haven't you settled down?"

"It's not by choice."

"Bet it is."

"Not my choice."

"The women said no?"

He refused to answer, wondering how he and Sydney always ended up having such personal conversations. He was a private man. He liked it that way.

"Come on, Cole," Sydney prompted.

"Why aren't *you* married?" He tried to turn the tables.

Her answer surprised him. "Nobody ever proposed."

"Did you even want them to?" he asked.

"You mean, have I ever been in love?"

"Yeah."

"I don't think so."

"You don't know?" That surprised Cole.

She shook her head. "What about you?"

"I guess not."

She grinned and bumped him again. "But *you're* not sure?"

He cocked his head, considering her. "You know, it's hard, isn't it? To know for sure."

"Is that why you never asked anyone."

"Nah. Never got that far. Truth is, they all left me once they got to know me."

She tipped her head back and gave him a hint of that sexy laugh. "No way. You left them."

He had to squelch an urge to wrap his arm around her. She was just the right height, just the right size, just the right shape for his arms.

Instead he shook his head. "I'm a bit of a selfish jerk deep down inside."

"No. You're the opposite. Just like I said. You're the one sacrificing to take care of everyone around you."

They came to the porch and he preceded her up the three steps. "Do you happen to have a degree in psychology?"

"I have a degree in art history."

"Good." He pushed open the door and stood to one side. "You can decorate the turret and leave my brain alone."

She grinned as she walked past him. "Your brain is beginning to fascinate me."

"I don't want a new house, because I don't need a new house. This is a working ranch, not a Dallas subdivision. Next thing they'll be putting in a pool."

"I've hit on something here, haven't I?"

"You haven't hit on anything." His voice came out unexpectedly sharp as he flipped the kitchen lamp.

Her eyes went wide. "I'm sorry."

Cole swore under his breath. He shook his head and moved toward her. "No. I'm the one who's sorry." He was falling back on defense mechanisms now.

"It's none of my business," she said.

"Of course it's not. But we're playing this silly game." He took a breath. "Ah, Sydney. We should have known it would get complicated."

She gave him a nod and a hesitant smile, and he

found himself easing closer. He inhaled deeply, filling his senses.

Her lips were burgundy in the lamplight. Her emerald eyes were fringed by thick lashes. Her skin was ivory-smooth, flushed from the walk. And the memory of it was indelibly pressed into the nerves of his fingertips.

Unable to stop himself, he smoothed a lock of hair from her forehead.

"Complicated," he whispered one more time.

Her lips parted, softly, invitingly. He should have known the second he got her alone, he'd give in to the cravings. He cupped her cheeks, pulling her closer. His lips closed over hers and relief roared through his body.

He'd been watching her all day, wanting her all day. She was under his skin and into his brain in a way that he couldn't control.

He kissed her harder, stepping toward her, pressing her back against the door. A bronc had blasted off inside him, and there was nothing he could do but hang on for the ride.

He tipped his head to find a better angle, and she came alive under his hands, all movement and sound and scent.

This was good. This was right. This was more than he'd ever found in any other woman. He stopped thinking about the Thunderbolt. He stopped thinking about Katie. He stopped thinking about plots and plans and deceptions.

There was only Sydney, her taste and her touch.

"Cole," she breathed, her fingertips tightening on his shoulders.

"I know." He kissed her eyelids.

"This *is* complicated."

"This is inevitable."

She paused for a second. "Maybe."

"Absolutely." He slipped his hand under her shirt, skimming across the small of her back. Her skin was sinfully warm, sinfully soft. She was a treasure he hadn't earned and didn't deserve.

"We can stop," he whispered reassuringly, kissing his way along the crook of her neck. "You say when."

"Not yet," she whispered back.

"Thank God," he sighed.

Her hand inched its way slowly up between them and, one by one, she popped the buttons on his shirt. When the last one gave way, she burrowed inside the fabric.

He kissed the top of her head and rocked her in his arms. He wanted to carry her to his bed, press himself against her—kiss her, talk to her, make love with her, simply breathe the same air. Whatever she wanted, whenever she wanted it.

She kissed his chest, her hot tongue flicking out to sear his skin.

He struggled for air as passion commandeered his senses. "We're pushing it," he warned.

She kissed him again. "Let's push it further."

He pulled back and gazed down at her. Her lips were swollen, her eyes were slumberous and her hair was tousled out like a halo.

"You want to make love?" he asked.

"Yeah."

"You sure?"

She smoothed her palms up the front of his chest. "You're right. It's inevitable."

Chapter 5

Sydney held her breath, wondering if Cole might actually refuse.

"I want you *so* bad," he said instead.

Her breath whooshed out. "You had me worried there for a second, cowboy."

He shook his head, smoothing back her hair. "Don't you worry. Don't you ever worry."

Something settled deep inside her and her worries vanished.

Cole had to be the most honest and honorable man she'd ever met. Yeah, he was getting in her way over the Thunderbolt. But he was doing it out of respect for his family.

Unlike the men she'd dated in New York, unlike some of her colleagues and contacts at the museum, everything she'd seen, everything he'd done, told her Cole was a man to be trusted.

She'd missed trust.

She'd missed honor.

She wanted him and he wanted her. It didn't get much more honest than that.

She focused on the feel of his rough palm against her scalp. His eyes burned smoky-blue, and she felt like the most desirable woman in the world. Her lashes grew heavy and she tilted her head into the sensation of Cole.

His palm cupped her face and he kissed her eyes. Her body felt as if it were drifting on air, soaring up to the ceiling. The dying fire gave off a faint, distinct tang. The creek roared over boulders outside the window, and Cole left trails of shooting sparks wherever he touched.

She tasted his salty skin, then she squeezed his hard body tighter and tighter until she was safe and surrounded by his warmth. He lifted her into his arms as if she weighed nothing. Nobody had ever carried her before. He started to walk, and she was sorry the bedroom was so close.

"Hold me for a minute," she said when they got there.

His arms flexed. "No problem."

She sighed against his chest. "You think you could stop time? Right here? Right now?"

"I wish I could."

"Try really, really hard."

His chuckle rumbled through her. "I can go slow."

"Easy for you, maybe."

"Nope. Not easy at all."

"But you'd do it for me?"

"I'll do anything for you. Just say the word."

Let me into your world, she wanted to say. *Not just your bed, but your heart and your soul.*

But that was impossible. They had here and now, and that was all. She forced a light note into her voice.

"Get naked."

"Okay. But that might speed things up a little."

"Or I could get naked."

"That would be worse." His voice sounded strangled.

She struggled to push his shirt from his shoulders. "Let's play with fire."

He slowly lowered her feet to the floor. "Sydney, I've been playing with fire since the first second I laid eyes on you."

She took a shaky step back and reached for the hem of her T-shirt. He stared down at her with such longing and reverence that a shudder ran straight through her body. She peeled the shirt over her head, gauging his reaction, loving his reaction.

His nostrils flared and his gaze latched onto her lacy bra. Without a word, he shucked his own shirt.

She stared unabashedly at the play of muscles across his chest. "You think we want this so bad, because we know we shouldn't?"

"Yeah." He nodded. "It probably has nothing to do with the way you look, taste, smell or feel."

"That's it."

"That's what?"

"The way you smell."

"It's bad?"

She shook her head, gliding toward him, burying her face in his chest again. "It's good. So good."

He reached between their bodies and flicked the button on her jeans. "You, too."

She smiled and went on her toes, kissing his mouth as he lowered her zipper. "Let's not tell anyone," she said.

"That we made love?"

She shook her head. "The smell secret."

"You got it."

He rolled off her pants then got rid of his own. Then he gently pressed her back on the bed, covering her with kisses, whispering words of reverence and encouragement, sending her heart rate soaring and her hormones into overdrive.

His fingertips skimmed her stomach, circling her navel with a featherlight touch that made her breath come in a gasp and her muscles contract. Before she could adjust to the sensation, he bent over her breast, taking one nipple into his mouth, swirling and circling the crest with his tongue.

She moaned, and her hands went to his hair. Sensations rocketed through her body as his teeth raked her tender flesh and his hand began a downward spiral.

This wasn't going to be slow. It was going to be lightning fast if she didn't do something.

"Cole," she gasped.

"You're delicious," he answered, fingers dipping lower, increasing the onslaught of sensation.

"Slow…down…" she begged.

She felt his smile. "No way." He crossed the downy curls and pressed into her in one swift motion.

Her hips came up off the bed, and her hands convulsed against his head. "Cole," she wailed.

"Go with it," he said.

"But…"

He moved to look into her eyes, his fingers pulsing in a way that made her world shift to the exquisite touch on her tender, moist flesh. She flexed her hips. He kissed her mouth.

"There's more to come," he rumbled against her. "I promise."

She closed her eyes. She was past the point of resisting. Past the point of coherent thought. She was going where he led her, and there was no way to stop it.

Her world roared, then went silent.

They were skin to skin, soul to soul as he eased inside her. True to his word, he took it slow, watching her closely, gauging her desires. Their breathing synchronized as the corner clock ticked away minutes.

A warm rush of sensation crested up from her toes. He smiled and deepened his kiss, increasing his rhythm until her world imploded, the clock's ticks slowed to a crawl and paradise stretched on and on.

She wrapped her arms around his neck, guilt nipping at her conscience. Nobody had ever done that before. No one had ever set aside their own needs to take her to paradise.

As the power of speech returned, she searched his deep eyes, worried that he'd made some stupid, gentlemanly decision against making love. "We're not…uh… stopping, are we?"

He shook his head and brushed a lock of hair from her cheek, shifting so that his big body covered hers. "Oh, sweetheart. We're just getting started."

He kissed her mouth. His thumb returned to her breast and, against all odds, her desire instantly rallied.

She ran her hands down his back, sliding them onto his taut buttocks and pressing his erection against her stomach, shivering with anticipation. She kissed him harder, swirling her tongue against his.

He opened wide, and she could feel the tension rising in his muscles.

She moaned and wriggled beneath him, shifting her thighs in a clear invitation.

He gasped. "Hey. This is supposed to be the slow part."

"Fast is fun," she assured him, shifting again, even more meaningfully this time.

He grabbed her hip with a broad hand and held her still, pulling back to look into her eyes. "If I go now, I'm going to break a land-speed record."

"Now," she said. "I don't care. Now." Slow had been a stupid idea anyway. Nothing between her and Cole was ever going to be slow.

He flexed his hips and was instantly inside her.

She groaned, nearly melting around his heat.

He buried his hands in her hair, thumbs stroking her temples. His breath came in gasps next to her ear.

She could feel the tension cresting in his steel, hard muscles. Her body tightened and strained and pulsated.

She reached for the comfortor, fisting her hands into the fabric as their rhythm increased.

He repeated her name, over and over again. Then his hands found hers, covered hers, their fingers entwining as the world exploded into black and time ceased to exist.

Cole kissed her damp brow. "You okay?"

She sighed, sinking into his incredibly soft bed. "I don't think okay is exactly the right word."

"You hurt?"

"No. It's fantastic. Fantastic is the right word."

He chuckled low in her ear, easing most of his weight off her. "You give me heart failure all the time, you know that?"

* * *

"You're pushing things too fast," said Kyle as he tapped the remainder of the glass from a broken window in the toolshed.

Cole set a new pane on the ground, leaning it against the wall of the shed before he retrieved a hammer from the toolbox.

Kyle didn't know the half of how fast they'd pushed things. Cole had never done that before—made love after only two days.

"I think we're doing fine," he said, strapping on a leather belt and dumping a handful of nails into the pouch.

Kyle whacked at a stubborn corner of glass and it tinkled into jagged pieces. "First you're necking on the lawn, then you bring her home after midnight."

A grin split Cole's face. "Will you listen to yourself? You sound like her father."

"I'm just saying, Katie's not going to buy it if you don't slow it down."

Cole moved up to the shed wall and dug his claw hammer into the window frame. One by one, the finishing nails popped out. "It's a compromise. Sydney's on a deadline with the Thunderbolt."

"You're worried about her deadline? This from a guy who was willing to throw her off the property two days ago?"

"I'm getting to know her now. And I didn't realize her job was on the line."

Kyle stopped, fixing his attention on Cole. "She told you her job was on the line?"

"Yeah."

Kyle glared at him impatiently.

"What?"

"Cole. What are you doing?"

Had Kyle guessed what had happened last night? Was it that obvious?

"I'm pretending to fall for Sydney," he said with exaggerated patience, trying to gauge his brother's expression.

"You sure about that?"

"I'm positive about that. What are you suggesting?"

Kyle whacked the glass again. "I'm suggesting you watch yourself."

Cole nearly choked on that one. "Hang on. This was *your* idea, little brother."

"Yeah." Kyle tugged his leather work gloves from his back pocket. "And I may have been wrong about that."

"Wrong? Hello? What did I miss?"

"She could be playing you," said Kyle, settling his fingers in the grooves.

"Playing me how? She's been up front and honest about everything." Unlike him and Kyle who were pulling one over on Katie.

"Has she?"

"Yes!"

Kyle brushed shards of glass from the sill. "Think about it, Cole. She's getting exactly what she came for."

"Uh, yeah. That was the deal."

"The deal was Katie would think Sydney fell for you. But now *you* think Sydney's falling for you."

"No, I don't," Cole snapped.

"Yes, you do. And what the hell are the odds of that?"

Cole hadn't honestly thought about the odds last night. But then, he didn't think Sydney was falling for him, either. Not really. It was more a chemical thing. A very powerful chemical thing.

Not that he could tell Kyle he'd slept with Sydney. How suspicious would that look?

"It's under control," he said to Kyle.

"You telling me you're not falling for her?"

"We're faking it for Katie."

"You and I shared a room for fifteen years, Cole. Quite frankly, you're not that good an actor."

"So, what are you suggesting? I call it off? Kick her out?"

"I'm just suggesting you watch your back. Don't trust her too far too soon."

"Fine."

"I'm serious."

"I said fine."

"Just think about the possibilities."

Cole dug in on the upper frame. "What part of *fine* didn't you understand?"

He would think about the possibilities. He was thinking about the possibilities. Because he didn't know Sydney.

Yeah, he felt as though he knew her. But she had an agenda, and that agenda included getting him to the altar.

What he'd interpreted as sweet, sexy vulnerability, could have been cold, calculated manipulation. Maybe she was hot for him, or maybe she was playing to his ego.

As bad as it sucked, Kyle had a point. What *were* the odds of a woman like Sydney wanting to sleep with a man like Cole after only two days?

* * *

Katie had offered Sydney the use of Kyle's office phone to contact the museum. Sydney's heart thumped in her chest as she dialed Gwen Parks's number. Saying it out loud was going to make it real.

"Gwen, here," came her friend's voice over the phone line.

"Hey, Gwen. It's Sydney."

"Hey, Sydney." There was a smile in Gwen's voice. "How's the hunt going?"

Sydney took a deep breath. "Well. I found it."

There was silence on the other end of the line. "Define 'it'."

"The Thunderbolt of the North."

Gwen squealed and Sydney jerked the phone away from her ear.

"You actually found it? Where are you? Where is it? What happened?"

"I'm in Texas."

Another silence.

"Who'd have thought," said Sydney.

"Did you bring it over from Europe?"

"It's been here the whole time."

"Oh, wow. When are you coming back?"

Sydney lowered her voice. "Not right away. It's complicated. Can I get you started on the show?"

"Without you?"

"Yeah."

"Of course. But you *do* have the Thunderbolt, right?"

"It's in a lawyer's office in Wichita Falls. But don't tell a soul. Bradley Slander is still gunning for me, and I don't want him getting wind of this until it's a done deal."

"If it's not a done deal, why am I setting up the show?"

Sydney twisted the phone cord around her hand. "It is. Sort of. Well… I have to marry the owner."

Another silence.

"It's a complicated inheritance thing."

"You're going to *marry* into the Thunderbolt family?"

"It's a marriage of convenience."

"Don't you think that's above and beyond?"

"It's the only way. I'm pretending to fall…" Sydney hesitated over the details. "Anyway, we'll divorce as soon as the show's over."

"I don't know, Sydney."

"Trust me on this. I've got it under control. My notes on the other antiquities are in my computer, along with the contact names. I'm going to reserve the front gallery."

"You're making me nervous."

"I can do this."

"You sure?"

"Yes."

She had to do this. She had no choice but to do this. It didn't matter how complicated her feelings got for Cole. Nor did it matter how much she was starting to love this crazy Texas ranch.

She was here to do a job. Once she got back to New York it would all fall into perspective. She'd be hailed a hero, and her professional reputation would be saved.

"Okay."

"Great. Talk to you in a few days." Sydney let out a sigh of relief and hung up the phone.

It was going to happen. It was truly going to happen.

Then she glanced up, and there was Katie, white-faced in the doorway.

Damn. She opened her mouth, but Katie turned on her heel.

"Katie!" Sydney scrambled around the desk, sprinting to the door. "Katie, it's not what—"

"Don't!" Katie gritted her teeth, her hands balling into fists as she stomped down the hallway. "You lied to me. You lied, straight-faced, and I let you into my family."

"Cole knows."

"Yeah, right."

"He *knows*."

Katie shook her head, her voice quavering. "No, he doesn't. But he's going to. Right now."

She stormed out the door and Sydney took off after her.

The plan was ruined. Sydney had screwed up everything. She should have talked quieter. She should have closed the door.

Cole was going to kill her, and so was Kyle, and now Katie would be more stressed than ever.

"Katie, listen," she gasped, rushing through the open doorway and struggling to catch up. She tried running, but her pace in heels was no match for Katie in her boots. Katie easily outdistanced her to the toolshed.

"She's a con artist and a liar and thief," yelled Katie as Sydney rapidly approached the three.

Kyle dropped a tool onto the ground and wrapped his arms around his wife. "What the hell?"

"She overheard me," Sydney called as she made her way through cacti and range grass.

"She's pretending to fall in love with Cole." Katie's

voice broke. "I heard her. She's only after the Thunder-bolt."

Cole stuffed a hammer into his tool belt and moved toward Katie, laying a hand on her shoulder. "It's okay, Katie. I know that already."

"How could you know that?" she sniffed. "She's lying to you. She's lying to all of us." She shot Sydney a look of venom.

"I am so sorry," said Sydney, her voice shaking, a sick feeling swirling in the pit of her stomach.

"I'll just bet you are," Katie snapped.

"Sweetheart." Kyle spoke against her hair in a soft voice. "This is all my fault."

Katie tipped her chin to look up at him. "How is it your fault?"

Sydney wished the ground would open up and swallow her whole. Katie was such a wonderful human being. She didn't deserve this heartache. She deserved Kyle's love every minute of every day, plus a whole troop of little Ericksons running around her house.

"*I* did something really stupid," said Cole.

"It was *me*," said Sydney. She didn't want to break up this happy family. They loved each other. They meant the world to each other.

"Will you two stop?" asked Kyle.

"Katie," said Cole. "After the baby thing—"

Katie turned a shade paler.

"—I thought your stress level would drop if I got married and had babies."

"We weren't really going to have babies," Sydney put in. "We were just going to let you think we'd have babies. It seemed like the perfect plan. I'd get the Thunderbolt. You'd probably get pregnant. By the time we got divorced, you'd be okay again."

Katie turned to Kyle. "You went along with this?"

"I—"

"We talked him into it," said Cole. "*I* talked him into it. Thing is, Katie. I'm going to make it come true."

The breath rushed from Sydney's lungs and she blinked at Cole's rugged profile. Because of last night? Because of what they'd shared?

Was it possible? Did Cole think there was something growing between them?

Her chest expanded with a warm glow. She had no idea how they'd work it out, but the thought of Cole wanting to try settled around her like a soft blanket.

"As soon as I divorce Sydney," Cole continued, and Sydney's heart went flat, "I'm going to find another wife. A real wife. I'm going to take on some of the responsibility of this damn dynasty."

Cole's words died away to silence and Sydney took an involuntary step back.

Of course he'd find a real wife. What on earth was she thinking? Cole couldn't do New York, and Sydney wasn't staying in Texas. Her career and her life were about to take a quantum leap. The sky would be the limit after the Thunderbolt show.

Katie stared at her, and Sydney forced out a shaky laugh. "See? It'll all work out."

"Cole," said Kyle. "You don't have—"

"My mind's made up." Cole rubbed Katie's shoulder. "I just hope I can find a wife who'll hold a candle to you."

Katie wiped her cheeks with the back of her hand. "I'm sorry," she whispered to Sydney.

Sydney moved closer. "You have absolutely nothing to be sorry about." Katie had come to a perfectly logical conclusion.

She nodded her agreement. "Okay. But we probably shouldn't tell Grandma it's a sham."

Cole looked at Kyle, and Kyle looked at Cole.

"You're right," said Cole. "We still have a wedding to plan."

Sydney parked herself on an old workbench to watch Cole finish the window repair. It had seemed like a good idea to give Katie and Kyle some time alone. She wanted to ask Cole about his marriage promise, but she didn't want him to think she cared.

If she didn't care, would she ask or stay quiet? Hard to know. Probably ask. After all, it was all academic to her.

She made up her mind. "Cole?"

"Yeah?"

"Were you serious? Or were you just trying to make Katie happy?"

"Serious about what?"

"Finding a real wife." She hated the pain that flashed through her chest when she said those words. It was almost as though she was jealous. Which made no sense. She was never going to see Cole again after the museum show. That had always been the plan.

Just because she'd slept with him, she didn't need to get all moony-eyed about it. She'd slept with men before. Men she'd liked and trusted. But she'd never gone around the bend over it. She'd never started imagining forever. Never even been jealous of the women they *might* date in the future.

Cole nodded as he hammered tiny nails around the wood that held the new glass. "I am putting too much pressure on Kyle and Katie. It's time I held up my end of the family."

"Do you think planning to marry some unknown wife is such a good idea?"

He stopped hammering and gave her a long look. "Yes, I do."

"It doesn't strike you as just a little bit self-sacrificing?"

He went back to hammering. "Not really. We Texans take loyalty and honor very seriously."

Sydney shifted on the bench. "Ouch."

Cole shrugged. "Not a criticism."

"Yeah, right." Obviously her values were a question mark in his mind. She might be fine for a night in bed, but she sure didn't meet his standards for a wife.

Good girl, bad girl again. At least this time she knew which one she was.

"We can probably move the marriage plans up," he said.

Sydney nodded. "That's good." The sooner she got away from him, the better.

"If Grandma suspects anything," he continued, "it'll be that you're pregnant and we need a quickie wedding."

"But you've only known me a few days."

He pounded in a final nail and dropped the hammer into his belt. "I travel a lot. She'll assume we've met before."

"Of course." Sydney nodded. Because a bad girl is always good for a one-night stand when a guy's on the road. She gritted her teeth and forced herself to focus on business. "I've asked a colleague to start preparing for the show."

Cole gave a nod.

"Is there any way I could take a look at the Thunderbolt before the wedding?"

"I guess so. What for?"

"It'll help me conceptualize a display for it. It would really help if I could take a couple of pictures to send to the museum." Business, business. All business. She could do this.

Cole stood back to scrutinize the job. "I'll drive you in as soon as I can get away."

Chapter 6

One thing about having Katie in on the marriage plan, it meant Sydney didn't have to see nearly as much of Cole. While she waited for the trip to Wichita Falls, she made museum arrangements by long distance and spent some time visiting Grandma.

Sydney was growing to like the eccentric old woman. Grandma was smart, opinionated and had one zinger of a sense of humor. She also told stories about the Thunderbolt and about her early years in Texas that fascinated Sydney.

Like the time the pack string stepped in a wasps' nest. The first horse through was stung once and did a little crow hop off the trail. His burden of flour and utensils stayed put. The second horse through was a bomb-proof mare. She barely flinched when three wasps stung her rump.

Unfortunately, the third horse through took the brunt of the attack. He was a reliable four-year-old entrusted with the month's supply of whiskey. The horse leapt off the ground, all four feet in the air. His frantic bucking loosened the pack saddle, sending the whiskey swinging under his belly.

The unnatural load spooked him even more, and he ran hell bent for leather into the creek. Though the cowboys raced to his rescue, the precious cargo was washed over the falls.

The cook was so frightened at the prospect of showing up at the cattle drive without a fresh whiskey supply that he rode two days and two nights to restock.

When Cole finally announced he had time to take Sydney to the city, she eagerly hopped into his pickup. She couldn't wait to see the Thunderbolt, even if it meant a two-hour drive alone with him.

"Haven't seen much of you," he commented as they pulled onto the main road.

"Haven't seen much of you, either," she returned, gauging his tone, wondering how to read him and annoyed that she felt the need to try.

He shrugged. "Had work to do."

"Me, too." She did have a life. It wasn't as if she'd been pining away, wondering if he regretted their lovemaking, or if he'd found any likely Susie Homemakers to take her place.

"Have I done something to annoy you?" he asked.

Did he mean other than announce to his family that he was finding a "real" wife just as soon as he dumped her?

"I'm not annoyed," she said.

"So this is the level you've picked for our relationship?"

The level *she'd* picked? "You wanted something more?"

He shrugged, flipping on his right signal and leaving the gravel road behind in favor of the four-lane interstate. "You must admit, it all turned on a dime there after Katie got in the loop."

"Ah." Sydney nodded, wishing she could control the jealousy cresting in her veins. "So you did want more sex."

He twisted his head to look at her. "Excuse me?"

"Sorry about that. I guess I did turn off the tap all of a sudden."

His eyes narrowed, and he glanced to the highway and back to her again. "Was there a particular reason you backed off?"

She shrugged. No reason that was remotely logical, just a horrible, kicked-in-the-gut feeling when he'd rejected her. "We didn't need to pretend anymore," she said.

"You mean, the Thunderbolt was in the bag."

"Yeah. Right. Something like that." She turned her head to look out the window.

"I see."

"Okay."

"Fine." He pressed on the accelerator and turned up the radio.

Neither of them spoke until they hit Wichita Falls.

At a traffic light in the heart of downtown, Cole turned on the left turn signal and waited for a space in traffic. "This is it."

Despite his brooding presence, Sydney's stomach leaped in anticipation. "Which one?"

He pointed to a tall, gray office tower as he angled into a parking spot in front.

Sydney scanned the building. This was it. The treasure of a lifetime was waiting inside for her. Despite her anger with Cole, she felt like a kid on Christmas morning.

They entered the building and took an elevator to the tenth floor. The brass sign on the oversize office doors read Neely And Smythe, Attorneys-At-Law.

"Auspicious," said Sydney.

"It's been the family firm for four generations."

"And the Thunderbolt's been here the whole time?"

"Most of it."

"I'm getting goose bumps."

As he opened the door, Cole gave her his first smile in three days.

It felt good. Way too good. Pathetically good.

She preceded him into the reception area, and a smiling brunette woman greeted them warmly. She sat behind a marble counter in a room decorated with leather furniture and fine art.

"Mr. Neely can see you right away," she said to Cole.

Cole moved to open another doorway that took them to a private hall.

A balding man met them at the far end of the hallway. He shook hands with Cole then turned to Sydney. "Joseph Neely." He offered his hand to her. "I understand you're here to see the Thunderbolt."

"I am," she agreed. "Sydney Wainsbrook."

"I enjoy an excuse to look at it myself," he said, turning his key in the lock and pushing the door inward.

"It's pretty exciting," she admitted.

"I'll leave you two alone then." Joseph Neely gestured to the interior of the office.

Sydney went in first, blinking to adjust her vision to the dimmer light.

Cole came in behind her and pointed to a round, mahogany meeting table.

She followed his signal and everything inside her turned still. Laid majestically out on a purple, velvet cloth, was the Thunderbolt of the North. The brooch of kings. The stuff of legends.

Sydney sucked in a breath. It was large, boldly crafted, magnificent in every way. The polished-gold lightning bolt was scattered almost randomly with rubies, emeralds and diamonds. It was big. It was audacious. It was everything she'd ever hoped for.

She circled it, running her fingers across the soft cloth, letting them get close, but not touching the treasure. "You are one lucky man," she said in a reverent, husky voice.

His voice was equally hushed. "Sometimes I think so."

"This is the thrill of a lifetime."

"You can touch it, you know."

She rubbed her fingertips together, sensitizing them. Then she leaned in ever so slowly, resting her hips against the edge of the table.

After a long minute she dared to touch the bottom point of the brooch.

She immediately snatched her hand back, a chill creeping into her veins. She felt it again, and her world came to a screeching halt.

"Cole?" she ventured slowly, stomach clenching.

"Yeah?" He'd moved closer, but his voice seemed to come from a long way off.

She tested the bottom diamond one more time and her heart went flat, dead cold.

"This is a fake."

"Don't be absurd," said Cole, studying Sydney's shocked expression.

"It's a fake," she repeated more passionately.

"Right," Cole drawled, glancing down at the brooch. Somebody had bypassed the alarm and broken into the lawyer's safe to reproduce the Thunderbolt without anyone noticing. That was likely.

"When was it last appraised?"

Cole tried to figure out where she was going with this.

"When?" she demanded.

"It's been closely guarded for hundreds of years." The odds of it being a fake were ridiculously slim.

Had Kyle been right about her? Was this some kind of an elaborate con?

"What are you up to?" he demanded.

"I'm *up to* giving you my professional opinion."

"Uh, huh." He struggled to figure out her angle. How she could turn this little ruse to her advantage?

She pointed to the brooch. "See those diamonds? The little ones on the points?"

He glanced down. "Sure."

"They're cut."

"So what?"

"So, nobody faceted diamonds until the fourteenth century. They didn't have the tools. The process hadn't been invented. I don't know who made this brooch, but it sure wasn't the ancient Vikings."

Cole's gaze shot back to the Thunderbolt. He'd seen it dozens of times. It looked the same. It always looked the same.

But she was sounding alarmingly credible, and he couldn't for the life of him figure out how lying about its authenticity would help her get her hands on it. His stomach sank. He had to allow for the possibility that she was telling the truth.

Her voice went up an octave. "Cole, you're not reacting."

He lifted it, holding the glittering gold to the light, speaking to himself. "Who would fake it?"

"We need more information," said Sydney, squinting at the jewel. "I have a friend who's a conservator. She could pinpoint the date more closely, give us somewhere to start."

Ah. Okay. There it was. He could see the scam now.

"You have a friend," he mocked, palming the brooch.

"Gwen Parks. She's worked at the Laurent for—"

"And your *friend* is going to come out and value my brooch?"

Sydney's eyes narrowed. "She's not going to value it—"

Cole let out a chopped laugh. "Let me guess." He took a pace forward. "It'll be worthless. You'll offer to take it off my hands. And the next thing I know it'll be on display in New York."

Sydney's expression lengthened in apparent horror. "Cole, I'd never—"

"Never *what?*" He stepped closer to her again. "Never try anything and everything to get your hands on the Thunderbolt? Never lie? Never cheat? Never marry me or sleep with me?"

She clenched her hands into small fists. "I really don't give a damn what you think of me right now. But the brooch is a fake. Get my expert. Get your own expert. Take it to the Louvre. But if you don't find out *when* it was faked, you're never going to find out *why* it was faked, you are never, *ever* going to have a hope in hell of getting the real one back."

Cole stared at her in silence. Was she serious? She looked serious.

He opened his palm and inspected the brooch.

"Think about it, Cole," she stressed. "Run it through your suspicious, little mind. How could I possibly get away with it? How, in the world, could I think for one minute that I could get away *pretending* the Thunderbolt was a fake?"

Cole closed his hand again, letting the points of the brooch dig into his palm.

She was right. But who would fake it? Who *could* fake it? And who could do it so well that nobody had ever noticed?

There were no pictures of it in circulation. It would have to be somebody who had access to it for more than—

A light bulb exploded in his brain. He stomped his way to the office door, flinging it open.

"Joseph!" he bellowed.

The lawyer appeared almost immediately, bustling his way down the corridor. "Mr. Erickson?" His voice betrayed his obvious concern.

Cole stepped back into the office and closed the door for privacy. "We need an appraiser. Now."

"A conservator," said Sydney.

Both men turned to look at her.

"A museum conservator," she repeated. "One who specializes in gems and jewelry."

"Is something wrong?" asked Joseph Neely.

"The brooch has been faked," said Cole, watching the man closely. Somebody at the firm could easily be the culprit.

Neely was silent for a long moment. He didn't look guilty, but his lawyer brain was obviously clicking through the implications. When he finally spoke, his voice was a rasp. "I don't see how it could have—"

"We need to find out when and how and why," said Cole, accepting that Sydney was telling the truth.

This was a catastrophe.

His chest tightened at the thought of his grandmother's distress. He had to help her. He had to protect her.

No matter what happened, she could never find out.

In Neely's office eight hours later, the words on the newly penned conservator's report blurred in front of Cole's tired eyes. Joseph had offered the use of the facilities as long as they needed them. It was probably half generosity, half concern for the firm's liability. Cole didn't particularly care which one. He just wanted some answers.

After gauging the level of expertise at the local museum, he'd given in and flown Sydney's colleague Gwen Parks down from New York. The two women had talked technical for a couple of hours, quickly losing Cole. But it didn't matter. The only thing important to him was the final verdict.

Gwen had just confirmed that the brooch was indeed a reproduction, and that it was made sometime between nineteen fifty and nineteen seventy-five. It didn't tell them who, and it didn't tell them why, but it did tell them that they had at least a small hope of finding the real one.

"I can put out some feelers," Gwen was saying to Sydney while Joseph put the brooch back in its box to be returned to the safe.

Cole dimly wondered why he bothered. Sure the jewels themselves were valuable, but they were also replaceable. A fifty-year-old ruby, emerald and diamond reproduction was hardly something to lock up in titanium.

He clenched his fist, crumpling it around the report.

"If anybody's ever sold it, or offered it for sale…" Gwen continued, leaning against Joseph's wide mahogany desk "…somebody out there will know something."

Gwen might be dressed in blue jeans and a Mets T-shirt, but the woman had convinced Cole she knew her stuff.

"You got a way into the black market?" asked Sydney.

Gwen nodded her pixie blond head.

Both women were silent for a moment. Sydney didn't ask any questions, and Gwen didn't offer an explanation.

Sydney turned her attention to Cole. "I think we should go talk to Grandma now."

Cole jerked his head up. "What?"

"Gwen's going to try her contacts, but we need to get information from Grandma. The sooner, the better."

"We're not telling Grandma." That point was non-negotiable.

Sydney brought her hands to her hips. "Of course we are."

Cole dropped the report on the desk. "Do you have any idea how much this will upset her?"

Sydney took a couple of paces toward him, gesturing with an open palm. "Of course it'll upset her. But never finding the Thunderbolt will upset her a whole lot more."

Cole clenched his jaw. "We'll find it without her."

"She had it during the years it was copied. She's our best lead."

"No."

"Cole. Be reasonable. She can tell us where it was, during what time periods."

"The lawyer's records will tell us that."

"All they can tell us is when it was or was not in their safe. Grandma can tell us if it was ever missing, if anybody borrowed it—"

"My answer is no."

Sydney moved directly in front of him and crossed her arms over her chest. "What makes this your decision?"

A pulse leaped to life in Cole's temple. He straightened to his full height, matching her posture. "You will *not* go behind my back and talk to my grandmother."

"The police might. A crime has been committed here, Cole."

"We'll take care of it privately." There was no way in the world Cole was losing control of the investigation, having it dumped into the lap of some overworked police precinct.

"Cole," came Gwen's voice.

Sydney and Cole both turned. Gwen straightened away from the desk, tucking her blond hair behind her ears and moving her small frame into the thick of the conversation.

"Sydney's right. No matter who you talk to, who you ask for help, public, private or otherwise, the first thing they're going to want to do is talk to your grandma. And if they don't, you should fire them for incompetence."

Sydney spoke up again. "She's our only lead."

It didn't matter. "She's seventy years old."

"She's tough as nails."

"The stress could kill her."

Sydney stared at him levelly with those penetrating green eyes. "It's not going to kill her."

They were intelligent eyes, Cole acknowledged. Clear-thinking, logical eyes. He'd never doubted she was smart. Never doubted she was capable. And this was definitely her field of expertise.

Damn.

If he wanted to keep the police out of it, he needed to keep Sydney and Gwen in, which meant he needed to take their advice.

He hated it, but there it was.

"Okay," he said. "Fine. We'll talk to Grandma."

"Tonight?" asked Sydney.

"Tomorrow," said Cole. He wasn't waking Grandma out of a sound sleep to give her bad news.

Gwen plucked her purse from the desktop. "In that case, I'd better get back to New York."

Cole quickly crossed the room and held out his hand. "Thank you very, very much for coming on such short notice." He was a lot more grateful to Gwen than he'd probably let on.

"Thanks for chartering the plane," said Gwen with a shake.

"Whatever you need," said Cole. "You just call me. Anything. Anytime."

Gwen nodded. "For now, I'll just be making phone calls. But I'll keep you guys posted." She glanced at her watch. "It'll be morning in London by the time I get home."

"You think the brooch is overseas?" asked Cole, his stomach hollowing out all over again. They were looking for a needle in a haystack.

"I'm going to check every possibility," said Gwen.

Sydney moved between them to give Gwen a hug. "Thank you," she whispered.

"Happy to help," said Gwen, glancing sideways at Cole and giving him a final once-over. "Talk to you tomorrow."

As Gwen left the office, Sydney sucked in a deep breath, blinking her exhaustion-filled eyes. But instead of complaining, she touched Cole's shoulder. His muscle instantly contracted beneath his jacket.

"We'll break it to her gently," she said.

Cole felt the weight of forty generations pressing down on him. "I don't see how we'll manage that."

Grandma greeted Sydney with a hug in the octagonal entryway. "Well? Did he do it? Did he pop the question?"

"Grandma," Cole warned.

"I hope he had a ring."

"He didn't have a ring," said Sydney.

Grandma glanced from one to the other. "But Katie said it was love at first sight. I'd hoped that was the point of this special trip."

"We are getting married," said Cole, although Sydney couldn't imagine why he bothered keeping up the charade. Katie knew their secret, and the Thunderbolt might never be found. A quickie wedding sure didn't matter anymore.

She hadn't let the full impact of that sink in yet. The odds of finding the Thunderbolt in time for the show one month away were almost nonexistent. She'd have to call it off. She'd lose her job, and her reputation would be ruined. She'd be lucky to get a position as a tour guide.

"I knew it," said Grandma, clasping her hands together. "I could tell by the way you looked at her."

"Grandma."

"Come in, come in." She backed into the living room. "I'll make tea. Tell me everything. What's the date? Where's the ceremony? Sydney, dear, you'll have to give me a guest list."

"We don't need tea. And there is no date."

"Of course we need tea. There are arrangements to make, plans to finalize. Thank goodness we already picked out the house." She took a deep breath and her grin widened.

Sydney felt sick. This should have been a happy occasion. It should have been a celebration.

"Can we please sit down?" asked Cole in a grave tone.

"Of course." Grandma gestured toward the burgundy couch. "You sit down. I'll be right back."

"Grandma." Cole's tone was sharp.

Sydney squeezed his arm, but he shook her off.

"What?" asked Grandma, blinking.

Sydney shifted between them and took Grandma's hand, trying to diffuse the building tension.

"Grandma," she said, looking into her blue eyes. She tried to let her tone give away the mood of the upcoming conversation. "We need to talk to you about something."

Grandma glanced at Cole then back to Sydney. A sly grin grew on her face. "Will it be a…quick…wedding?"

"You're not helping." Cole ground the words out from behind Sydney.

"We have some…unsettling news," said Sydney.

Grandma glanced from one to the other again. The expectant glimmer in her eyes dimmed slightly. "Oh?"

Sydney eased Grandma onto the couch. Cole crouched down in front of them and took a breath. "There's no easy way to say this," he began.

"Is someone sick?" asked Grandma, looking worried.

"No. Everybody's fine. Grandma. It's the Thunderbolt."

She stilled. After a silent heartbeat, her eyes went wide and her lips paled a shade.

"We stopped at Joseph's office," Cole continued. "The real Thunderbolt is missing. The one that's in the safe is a fake."

Grandma's hand went to her chest and her cheeks turned white as paper.

Cole jumped up. "Grandma?"

Sydney stood, too, mentally cursing herself for not taking Cole's advice. The shock really was too much for Grandma.

"Grandma?" Cole repeated.

But she still didn't answer.

"Let's lay her down," said Sydney, tossing a pillow to the far end of the couch. "Grandma? We should elevate your feet."

Cole stood back while Sydney gently repositioned her.

"I'm calling Dr. Diers," he said.

"Good idea," Sydney agreed, mentally berating herself.

Why had she thought Grandma could take this? The

woman's heritage had been stolen. They should have looked for it themselves, exhausted all other possibilities. But, no, Sydney had gone for speed, and she might have harmed a wonderful woman in the process.

Grandma gripped Sydney's hand, trembling slightly. "I don't need a doctor."

"Don't try to talk," Sydney whispered.

The old woman's eyes fluttered closed. Her wrinkled skin looked frail and transparent. Her gray hair was thin, and there were age spots dotted over her forehead.

Cole hung up the phone. "Dr. Diers is on his way. How is she?"

Grandma's breathing was shallow but steady.

"I don't need a doctor," she rasped.

Cole moved forward. "Well, you're getting one anyway."

"Waste of time," said Grandma.

He crouched down and Sydney shifted out of the way. "Grandma," he said in a gentle voice, taking her hand. "We're going to find it."

Her eyes opened and she stared at him in silence for a long moment. "I know you will." And then tears formed in the corners of her eyes.

"She's resting comfortably," said Dr. Diers, quietly closing the door to Grandma's bedroom. "She's obviously had a shock."

"We gave her some bad news," said Cole, turning from the big picture window. "Probably should have kept our mouths shut."

His shoulders were tense and Sydney knew he blamed himself. But it was her fault. Trying to salvage her career on the back of an old woman was unforgivable.

"I've given her a light sedative," said Dr. Diers. "She's going to be fine. She'd like to see you."

Cole nodded and made a move toward the bedroom.

"Sydney," said the doctor.

"Yes?" asked Sydney.

"Your grandma asked to see Sydney."

Sydney straightened in surprise and Cole blinked.

"Why does she want to see Sydney?"

The doctor gave a slight shrug. "Maybe she'd rather talk to a woman?"

"I can go get Katie," he said.

"She did ask for Sydney."

"I'll go in," Sydney agreed.

Cole took a jerking step toward her.

"I promise," said Sydney, holding up her palm. "I'll just listen to what she has to say."

"I can't let you upset her," said Cole. "We've made enough mistakes already."

"I'm not going to upset her."

Cole's mouth was taut and his knuckles were white; guilt was obviously eating him up.

"We had no choice," said Sydney, trying to reassure him.

"Oh, yes, we did."

True enough. She wasn't about to take on that debate. "I'll go find out what she wants, then we can talk, okay?"

Before he could tell her no, she cut through the entrance foyer to the bedroom door, turning the cut-glass knob as quietly as possible, just in case Grandma had fallen asleep.

Grandma's eyes were open, but the sparkle was gone from their blue depths. The harsh, noonday sun streamed in through the paned window, making her look small and frail beneath the patchwork quilt.

"Sydney," she whispered, reaching for a hankie.

Sydney clicked the door shut and came to her side. "Can I get you anything? A drink of water? An aspirin?"

"I've done something terrible, Sydney," said Grandma, dabbing the hankie beneath her nose.

"Grandma?" Sydney crouched down by the bed. "What's wrong?"

"Everything's wrong."

"Tell me."

Grandma grasped Sydney's hand, searching her eyes. She drew a breath. "I have no right to ask."

"Go ahead and ask."

"What I did. What I'm going to say. Please don't tell my family."

"Of course I won't."

Grandma drew a breath, and there was a catch in her voice as her glance slid away from Sydney's. "It was me."

"What was you?"

"I faked the Thunderbolt."

A jolt of shock ricocheted through Sydney's body. "What? When? How?" Then she quickly shut her mouth, biting back more staccato questions.

She forced herself to moderate her voice. "Do you know where the real one is?"

Grandma shook her head miserably. "No."

"I don't understand," said Sydney, straining not to sound judgmental. Why on earth would Grandma fake her own heirloom? Did she need money?

"It was a long time ago."

Sydney nodded, waiting for this to start making sense.

"I was young, only twenty." Grandma's voice faded and a faraway look came into her eyes.

Sydney carefully lowered herself to the carpet, trying not to interrupt the flow of the story. She rested her back against the small bedside table, placing her hand on Grandma's.

"It was Harold's and my second anniversary, and I was pregnant with Neil. And there was this woman…"

Sydney's heart sank.

"She had a baby. A son." Grandma's voice broke. "He was six months old…"

"I'm sorry."

Grandma shook her head. "She said things. She knew things." She looked into Sydney's eyes. "I could tell it was all true."

Sydney groaned in heartfelt sympathy. What a hurtful secret. What a terrible thing for Grandma to experience. "I am *so* sorry."

"Things weren't like they are now," Grandma continued, "the neighbors would have gossiped, Neil would have been ostracized, sales from the ranch might have dropped."

"Did you talk to him?" asked Sydney. It was Harold's responsibility to make it right.

Grandma shook her head.

"Why not?"

"We'd been through so much. We'd come so far."

Sydney didn't understand.

"I was lonely that first year, and I blamed Harold, and we weren't…" The silence stretched.

"It wasn't your fault," said Sydney. Infidelity was not justifiable, no matter what was going on in a relationship.

Grandma gave a watery smile. "The Thunderbolt was all my doing." She stabbed a finger against her chest. "Me. I was young and inexperienced. Then I was afraid of what people might say. Bottom line, I wanted my husband and our life *more* than I wanted a piece of jewelry."

A cold chill snaked up Sydney's spine. "What are you saying?"

Grandma impatiently swiped at a tear with the back of her hand. "I gave it away."

Oh, no.

"She demanded the Thunderbolt and I gave it to her." Sydney's entire body cringed.

"She said Rupert was the first-born Erickson, and so he was entitled. She promised she'd leave us alone forever."

"She blackmailed you?"

Grandma nodded, her voice quavering. "And I was a willing victim. To save my marriage, I betrayed my family."

Sydney closed her eyes. "Did it work?"

Grandma gave a short laugh. "It worked. It worked for thirty years. Except…"

Sydney dropped her head forward onto her chest. There was nothing she could say, nothing anybody could say. The Thunderbolt was gone.

In her mind she saw a flash of her mother's blond hair, the twinkle of her silver locket—the heirloom that had been snatched away from Sydney. She didn't know for sure, but she thought it was the day before the fire. She was five years old, and it was the last day her mother had held her. The last day she'd seen the silver locket, or anything else her family had ever owned.

"Can you get it back?" Grandma asked in a small voice. "Because if you could get it back…"

Sydney opened her eyes and nodded. "Yes," she promised, although she had no idea how she was going to keep it. Then a vow came from the deepest recesses of her being. "No matter who has it. No matter where it is."

Hope rose in Grandma's eyes, and a little color came back to her cheeks. "I made a mistake."

"No, you made a decision."

"How can I explain—" Grandma's voice broke. "The boys…"

"Cole and Kyle don't have to know." Sydney shook her head. "Your secret is safe with me."

Chapter 7

"Katie?" Cole held the phone to his ear as he watched the dust billow out behind the doctor's deep-treaded SUV tires.

"Hey, Cole," his sister-in-law answered cheerfully around the whistling of a teakettle. "What's going on? Where was Sydney last night?"

"Can you come down to Grandma's right away?"

"Why?" The whistling subsided.

Cole shifted away from the closed bedroom door, dropping his voice to make sure he wasn't overheard. "Because we need you."

A beat went by before Katie spoke. "What's wrong?"

"Is Kyle there?"

"Cole, what's wrong?"

"It's not…" he began. Not what? Not bad? Not major? Not terrible?

The reality was, it was all of those things and more. He straightened the black-and-white picture of his grandfather that hung above the mantel. "Listen, I'd really rather tell you guys in person—"

The tension rose in Katie's voice. "To hell with that."

Cole gripped the carved wood fireplace mantel. "You sure Kyle's not there?"

"He's in the barn. Give!"

"Fine. Okay." Where to start? He couldn't just blurt out that the brooch was missing. "Sydney and I stayed over in Wichita Falls."

The concern in Katie's voice vanished, replaced by interest. "You did? But I thought…"

"Not for that."

"No? Because, you know, she's really a—"

"Can you just come down to Grandma's?"

"Is Sydney still with you?"

"Yes."

Katie paused and he could almost hear her smiling. "Sure. We'll be right there."

"Good." Cole squeezed his eyes shut, trying to alleviate the pounding between his temples.

The door to Grandma's bedroom squeaked open and he punched the off button on the phone.

He turned to face Sydney. "She okay?"

Sydney nodded, blinking glassy, reddened eyes, rubbing her upper arms as if the air-conditioning was too cold for her. "She's fine."

"You okay?" he asked, peering more closely. Was she upset about her career? That would be understandable.

"I'm perfect." She waved away his concern, as if it was a gnat buzzing around her head.

Okay. No sympathy. Fine. "What did Grandma say?"

"She said the brooch was at the ranch for several months in 1978."

"Does she know who faked it?"

"My best suggestion is you talk to the local people who were around back then. Maybe—"

"So, she doesn't know."

Sydney took a sharp breath, as if he was annoying her again. "Maybe you could find out who saw it, if anyone seemed to have a particular interest in it…"

Cole told himself to ignore her mood. She had to be disappointed in the turn of events. Her career was on the line, and he couldn't blame her for thinking about herself.

He nodded. Interviewing the neighbors seemed like as good a place as any to start.

Sydney turned to gaze out the front window, tugging the elastic out of her hair and finger-combing it to redo the ponytail. "While you talk to the local people, I'm going to California—"

"California?" Where the hell had that come from?

She nodded, still gazing at the snowcapped mountain peaks on the far side of the valley. "Gwen is, uh, sending a list of likely antique dealers. There's a concentration of them in California, and I can check—"

"Uh-uh. No way." Cole shook his head. He acknowledged that she was a valuable asset to the search, but he wasn't letting her take over completely. It was his family, his property. She simply had a passing commercial interest.

Sydney turned to face him. "What do you mean no way?"

"I'm going to California."

"You don't know a thing about antiques."

"If you go, I go."

"But somebody has to stay here."

"Kyle can interview the neighbors."

Sydney jerked back. "Kyle?"

"He and Katie are on their way here."

"Now?"

"Yes. Now."

Her eyes narrowed. "You told them?"

"No. But I'm about to."

"But…"

"But what?"

Sydney bit down on her lower lip, the wheels of her brain obviously churning a million miles an hour. "I just think the fewer people who know…"

"Kyle's my brother."

She got a funny look in her eyes.

Was she worried?

Afraid?

Scheming?

Would he ever be able to trust this woman again? She couldn't have predicted the brooch had been faked. But Kyle had pegged her as an opportunist. Was she trying to make this latest turn of events work for her?

"I think this'll work better if you stay here," she said, her gaze darting away from his.

"Not going to happen, Sydney."

"But—"

"Kyle can do the home front. I go with you."

"I, uh, work better alone."

He took two steps toward her. "Tough. Get used to me. Because I'm your new partner."

Cole just had to come to California.

He had to be underfoot. He couldn't have stayed home and interviewed the neighbors like a good little cowboy.

Sydney wriggled beneath the desk in her hotel room at the Sands in Oceanside, searching for the power outlet for her netbook. Why did they always have the electrical plug stashed behind furniture? Did they cater to contortionists?

It took all her strength to inch the desk away from the wall. Then she yanked out the lamp cord, plugged in her computer and shimmied her way back up to the chair.

She pushed her hair off her face and shot an uneasy glance at the connecting door as she flashed up the power. The front desk had given them adjoining rooms, but she hadn't opened the door, and Cole hadn't knocked.

Right now, all she wanted was to get Gwen's emails downloaded. Neither Cole nor Gwen knew Grandma's secret, and handing Gwen's leads to Cole in careful sequence was the only way Sydney could get the job done.

They *were* here canvassing at antiques stores, just as she'd told him. But Oceanside was also the city where Harold's illicit lover, Irene Cowan, had once lived.

As soon as Sydney ditched Cole, she was heading two blocks down to city hall to take a look at the historical property records. Tax rolls could be found online, but Irene Cowan wasn't a current property owner. So if a trail existed in property records, it was going to start on microfiche.

While the files downloaded, a knock sounded on the adjoining door. Sydney stood up, silently urging the email download to hurry.

Cole knocked again.

The word "complete" came up, and Sydney snapped the lid on her laptop before crossing the room.

Cole stood in the doorway in a crisp, white shirt, a burgundy tie and a beautifully cut charcoal suit with polished, black shoes. He was freshly shaved and his hair was neatly combed. If the clerks in the antique stores were female, Sydney was pretty sure they had a shot at getting information from them.

"I thought we'd get more cooperation if we looked like big buyers," he said.

Big buyers nothing, the staff would be too busy flirting with Cole to care whether or not they'd make a sale.

Sydney glanced down at her black jeans and the lacy top that was streaked with dust from her foray under the desk. She was definitely outclassed.

She opened the closet and took an ivory suit in one hand and a little black dress in the other. "Professional or flirtatious?" she asked.

His gaze moved back and forth. "What usually works best for you?"

"Professional," she said. Then she paused. "No. I'm lying." She hung the suit back up and closed the closet. "Flirtatious wins hands down." She rounded the privacy wall to the powder room.

Cole laughed behind her. "I know it would work on me."

"Yeah? Well, you're easy."

"So is most of the male population of this country."

"There's a list of antique stores on the desk," she called, bailing on this conversation before it went bad.

She wiggled out of her jeans and peeled off her blouse, turfing the white bra that would show at her shoulders. "I thought we'd start on Zircon Drive," she called.

"Does Gwen think one of these dealers has seen the Thunderbolt?" he asked in return.

"Nothing specific so far." Sydney ran a brush through her hair and dug into her makeup bag.

"So, what exactly are we doing here?"

"We take the picture of the fake around to the employees and see if they recognize it."

"And if they don't?"

His voice was closer, and Sydney quickly glanced around for the dress. Not that she was afraid he'd come in. He was way too much of a gentleman for that. It was more that his voice and her naked body were a potent combination.

She slipped the dress over her head, the silky fabric teasing her breasts on the way down.

"Sydney?"

"Then we move on to the next store," she said in a voice that was more than a little husky.

Cole was silent for a moment. "You really think this is going to work?"

"I don't know," she answered honestly.

"You almost ready?"

"Just putting on my shoes." She brushed her hair one more time and popped a pair of diamond studs into her ears before heading out to meet him.

His gaze strayed up and down her clingy outfit. His expression gave away nothing, but her skin prickled as if he actually touched her.

"We should go," she said, forcing her thoughts to the search instead of her hormones.

Cole stared at her a minute longer. Then he cleared

his throat. "Right. Zircon Drive." He abruptly turned and headed for the door.

"This is ridiculous," said Cole as they exited from the fourth Oceanside antique store. Despite Sydney's cleavage and Cole's sexy baritone, none of the staff admitted having seen or heard of the Thunderbolt.

"We've barely started," Sydney countered, knowing that no matter what they wore or what they promised, their odds of finding information were almost nil. She was feeling guiltier by the hour for keeping him in the dark about the real search.

"We could blow off a year like this," he said.

"You and I are only one part of the investigation," she argued. "Gwen is checking Europe, and Kyle is interviewing your neighbors."

"While you and I are wasting time."

Sydney skirted around a group of teenage boys who strutted three-wide on the sidewalk in the opposite direction. She hop-stepped in her high heels to catch up to Cole. "Give it a chance."

"We need more manpower," he said as the oncoming crowd parted around him. "I'm hiring a P.I. firm. Somebody national, with lots of investigators."

She ducked in behind him, following in his wake as she fought a spurt of panic. A dozen private eyes? Sticking their noses into the investigation? They'd make it impossible to keep Grandma's secret.

"Let's wait and see instead," she suggested.

"Wait and see what?"

The crowds thinned and she moved back to his side. "Wait and see what Gwen comes up with."

He peered down his nose at her, obviously unconvinced.

"Before we do anything rash," she elaborated. "Okay?"

"Hiring a P.I. firm is *rash?*"

"I think we need to focus our effort."

He turned his palms up, fingers spread wide in a gesture of incredulity. His voice rose as they angled toward the curb. "There's nothing to focus *on.*"

"You're so impatient."

Cole glared his frustration while he unlocked the passenger door. "Impatient? Excuse me, but the Thunderbolt is worth half a million dollars."

Sydney folded herself into the passenger seat, adjusting her dress on the hot leather as Cole clicked the door shut.

She hadn't quantified it from the money angle yet. But the real Thunderbolt represented one of the first documented uses of diamonds as ornamentation in Europe, and the jewels themselves were dozens of carats. It was impossible to put a price on that.

Cole dropped into the driver's side and slammed the door. He cranked the engine and turned the air-conditioning up to full. "For half a million dollars, I think I can be forgiven for a little impatience."

"Fine. You're forgiven."

"And we hire a firm."

"No. Not now. Not yet."

Sydney's cell phone rang.

She could feel Cole working up a counter argument as she hunted through her purse. She hoped it was Gwen with something, *anything.* They needed a bogus lead or a false rumor to distract Cole.

She pushed the talk button. "Yes?"

"Well, well, well," Bradley Slander drawled. "You've been holding out on me, babe."

Sydney stilled, cursing under her breath, eliciting a look of surprise from Cole.

"I'm not your babe, Slander." Her voice grated into the mouthpiece as she turned toward the passenger door in a vain attempt to keep the conversation private.

"The Thunderbolt of the North?" Bradley continued. "That's big even for us."

She flicked her hair back from her sweaty forehead. "There *is* no us." How had he found out so fast? Who did he bribe?

"Oh, there's an us, Sydney," said Bradley. "We're inextricably connected, both cosmically and financially."

"Get over yourself."

"Where are you?"

She glanced back at Cole. He was watching her intently, his hand poised on the stick shift.

"None of your business," she said.

"Gwen's bush league, Sydney," said Bradley.

"Gwen is brilliant."

"What's she found for you so far?"

Sydney clamped her jaw. She wasn't giving Bradley a thing. Not a damn thing.

"Thought so," said Bradley with a self-satisfied chuckle. "Team up with me. I know everybody who's anybody from here to Istanbul."

"Do the words 'cold day in hell' mean anything to you?"

His voice dropped to that reptilian level. "Together, babe, you and I can—"

She straightened, no longer caring if Cole or anyone

else was listening. "Get this through your thick skull, Bradley. I will *not* work with you."

"Sure you will," he purred.

"No."

"You know it's just a matter of time."

"Not now. Not ever—"

Cole snagged the phone from between her fingers.

"I think you heard the lady," he said to Bradley.

Her jaw went slack in amazement.

"Really?" asked Cole mildly, his gaze drifting to Sydney. "Well, I doubt very much you know who you're messing with, either."

Then he took the phone from his ear and hung up on Slander.

He plopped it back into her palm. "Who *was* that?"

"Bradley Slander," she answered, staring at the compact phone, trying to decide whether he was being gentlemanly or controlling. In the end, she decided he was just being Cole. Which was…nice.

She had to admit, she'd experienced a momentary thrill when she pictured Bradley's expression. But now she was thinking about the possible ramifications. Bradley was unpredictable, and they'd just waved a red flag in his face.

"Old boyfriend?" asked Cole, still watching her closely.

She shuddered at the very thought. "Antiquity snake. Now *there's* a guy with contacts in the black market."

"But you're not willing to work with him?"

"I'd rather be dragged naked through an anthill."

Cole quirked a half smile. "Thanks for the visual."

She fought a grin, the tension finally dissipating. She was letting herself get paranoid here. Nothing terrible was going to happen. Bradley was far way, and he didn't have a clue about Grandma's secret.

"So what did he want?" asked Cole.

"He's after the Thunderbolt."

Cole's hand tightened on the shift. "Why? It's mine."

"Possession is nine-tenths of the law."

"That would make him a thief."

"I know." Sydney closed her eyes for a brief second. If Irene Cowan had sold it or given it away, especially if it was overseas, the ownership issue was going to get complicated.

"We need to find it before he does," she said. "Keeps our life simple."

Cole's stare raked over her for a silent moment. "There's something you're not telling me."

She tried not to flinch. She couldn't let him see her fear. "There are plenty of things I'm not telling you," she said, going on the offensive. "But I *am* doing everything in my power to find your brooch. I won't lie to you, if the brooch is already on the black market, Bradley's a threat."

"How big of a threat?"

"He's after it. But we've got Gwen. And Gwen is good."

Cole's expression turned speculative. "What about you, Sydney?"

"What about me?"

"Are you good?"

"At finding antiquities? I'm very good."

He nodded toward the antique store they'd just left. "So why does this feel like amateur hour?"

She struggled to keep from squirming under his gaze. "Because we haven't gotten started yet."

"Then let's get started."

Sydney nodded. "Right." She'd get the real search under way the very minute she ditched Cole.

He put the car into first gear and checked his side mirror. "Let's start with what Bradley is to you."

"A thorn in my ass."

Cole grinned, and another layer of tension dissipated.

"Ever slept with him?" asked Cole conversationally as he pulled into traffic.

"No!" She folded her arms across her chest. "And, by the way, that's none of your business."

"Sure it's my business."

"Why? Because we—" She stopped herself short.

"Because I want to know how deep this guy's vendetta goes."

Sydney puzzled over that one. "Would it be better if I'd slept with him, or worse?"

"A scorned lover makes a powerful enemy." He stopped at a red light.

She hesitated, then asked softly, "Are you my enemy, Cole?"

He turned his head. "Have I been scorned?"

She immediately realized her mistake. Reminding him of their lovemaking was a stupid idea. She cringed. "Sorry."

"For what?"

"Bringing it up."

The light changed and he pulled ahead. "What? You thought I'd forget?"

"This conversation is a bad idea."

He flipped on his signal and took a right turn. They accelerated past a sandy beach lined with palm trees and colorful umbrellas.

"Sydney," he said, keeping his attention fixed on the straight road. "Since you were there." He shifted to third. "And I was there." He pulled it into fourth. "And since we both have pretty damn good memories." He climbed on the brake pedal and swerved around a minivan exiting a parking stall. "I don't think it matters much whether we have this conversation or not."

She gripped the door handle. He made a good point. She remembered everything in vivid detail. Everything.

"We had sex," he said bluntly. "And that's that."

She pictured him mentally brushing his hands together. He was done with the subject and done with her.

Her stupid chest contracted. "Okay."

He was silent for a split second. "No hard feelings?"

"No hard feelings." None at all.

Chapter 8

It took Sydney the entire next morning to convince Cole they needed to split up. But she finally sent him to some antique dealers across town, freeing her up to walk to city hall.

Hunched over a microfiche reader in the bowels of the building's basement, she discovered Irene Cowan had paid taxes on a little house at Risotto Beach for ten years running. But Irene's trail disappeared in the early eighties. She could have started renting, or she might have moved away.

Sydney moved on to utility records. But she found nothing new. Then, two hours later, just when she was sure she'd hit a dead end, it occurred to her to check marriage licenses.

She moved to the State offices upstairs. There, finally, she had another lead. Irene Cowan had become Irene Robertson. She and her husband had paid taxes in Oceanside for a further fifteen years. Then they'd died in a car accident in the mid-nineties.

But they'd raised one son, Rupert Cowan. And according to the Oceanside *Gazette,* he'd graduated from Edison High School and won a small scholarship to Southwestern State Fashion Design College. The Southwestern State alumni newsletter revealed that he'd received his degree then taken a job in New York.

Then Google picked up a local fashion show from last year in Miami. Rupert Cowan's company, Zap, had been a contributing designer.

It was a break. A huge break.

Rupert could be in Miami.

Sydney needed to get there just as soon as possible. She began formulating a plan. She'd approach him the way she approached any other potential seller. Not on the phone, not with a letter, but in person. She needed to see his expression, gauge his mood, his interests, his weaknesses.

This was the most important antiquity purchase she'd ever make. She was doing it step by careful step.

Her heels clicked on the floor of the cavernous, marble foyer while she dialed Gwen's number.

"Hello?" Gwen answered.

"I need you to send us to Miami."

"Sydney?"

"Yeah. It's me."

"What's in Miami?"

"I can't explain, but you need to give us some kind of a lead for Miami."

"Whoa. A false lead?"

"Yes."

"What's going on?"

"You know I wouldn't ask if it wasn't important."

"You've got something. What've you got?"

"I've got a name," Sydney admitted.

"Who? Where? How?"

"I can't tell you that. It would give away a confidence."

"You have someone else working on this?"

"It's, ah, complicated."

"I'm reasonably intelligent."

"I know." But Sydney couldn't tell Gwen. She couldn't tell anybody Rupert's name. She'd given her word to Grandma.

"So, what exactly is it that I'm doing here?"

"You're sending us to Miami."

Gwen's tone hardened. "That's not what I meant."

Sydney sighed, not sure how to answer.

"So, what? I'm window decoration?"

"Right now. Yeah."

Gwen's voice rose, her exasperation coming through loud and clear. "You mean I can stop *calling in favors from Edinburgh to Rome?*"

"Yes."

"Sydney!"

"I didn't know until this very minute. I swear, I just found out—"

"Fine."

Sydney felt like crud. "I'm sorry."

Gwen's voice was flat. "Call me if you need help."

"I will. And, Gwen?"

"Yeah?"

"I'll tell you what I can later. But this is important."

"I hear you."

"I'll call you from Miami."

"I'll be asleep." Gwen disconnected.

Sydney ended the call and pushed open the glass door.

Out on the wide, concrete staircase, she swore under her breath. Gwen was a good friend, and a consummate professional. Maybe it would be safe to tell her…

Sydney trotted down the steps, rubbing her thumb over the keypad of her phone, trying to decide how much she could afford to tell Gwen. As she ran through the facts, Grandma's stricken expression flashed through her mind. Sydney heard her own heartfelt vow, and remembered her determination to do right by the woman.

Good friend or no good friend, she knew she'd take the secret to her grave.

"I gotta ask myself…" came a familiar, mocking voice.

Sydney blinked the world back into focus and stared directly into the face of Bradley Slander.

"…what does the Oceanside City Hall have to do with our little search?"

A cold wave of fear momentarily paralyzed her.

"This is the best one yet, Sydney." He chuckled. "Come on, tell ol' Bradley what you've got."

"Nothing." She gripped her phone, cursing herself as she increased her pace in an effort to get him away from the building.

She frantically cataloged her movements over the past few hours. Had she covered her tracks? Would the clerks remember her? Had she written anything down? Tossed evidence in the wastebasket?

How could she have been so careless as to let Bradley sneak up on her? He could have overheard her phone call to Gwen. He might already know about Miami.

"We can go fifty-fifty," he said, pacing along beside her.

"Get lost."

"Now, that's just rude."

Sydney stopped on the sidewalk and turned to stare at him, a horrible thought crossing her mind. What if he'd talked to Cole's grandmother? What if he'd gone to the ranch, lied about who he was and pumped the family for information.

"If you're so damn good, why do you need me anyway?" she asked, fishing to see how much he knew.

He moved in closer. "Because we're a *team,* Wainsbrook. It wouldn't be near as much fun without you."

"You mean, you don't want the entire profit?"

His beady eyes narrowed. "Yeah, right. You don't think for one minute I'm going to find it."

"Frankly," said Sydney, with what she hoped was an unconcerned toss of her hair, "I don't think either of us is going to find it."

"They why are you wasting your time?"

"It's my time to waste."

"What've you got?"

"I've got a missing brooch." She waited, hoping his ego would force him to give out his own information.

"We know the age of the fake," he said.

"Of course we do." She waited again.

"We know it's the Erickson family."

Sydney nodded, concentrating on keeping her expression neutral. Had he talked to Grandma? Had he been to Texas?

"You talked to them?" asked Bradley.

"I've got Cole Erickson with me now," she admitted. Maybe if she focused on Cole, Bradley wouldn't realize Grandma was of any significance.

If Bradley was surprised that she volunteered Cole's name, he didn't show it. He probably chalked it up to his superior interrogation techniques, thinking he had her right where he wanted her.

"He the guy on the phone?" Bradley asked.

"Yeah." Sydney gave a long sigh, trying to appear tired and vulnerable. "He hasn't given me anything. You want to give him a try?"

This time, Bradley did eye her with suspicion.

She hoped she hadn't overplayed her hand.

Then he grinned, reaching out to touch the bottom of her chin. "Not."

Relief shuddered through Sydney. By sheer force of will, she didn't brush his hand away. Instead she raised her eyebrows in a question.

"Don't want to make him nervous." Bradley chuckled. "I think he's got the hots for you. Not a good idea to bring him face-to-face with his competition."

She nearly choked on that one.

Bradley moved in closer, dropping his voice to an intimate level. "Why don't *you* talk to him? I can come up with a few questions for you, and you can tell me what he says, hmm?"

Sure didn't take much for the man to think they'd joined forces. "Okay." Sydney agreed with a nod. If Bradley focused on interrogation questions for Cole, he might just stay out of city hall wastepaper baskets.

Bradley snaked an arm around her waist and she forced herself to remain still.

"Don't be afraid to get persuasive," he whispered, his hot breath irritating her skin.

What? She was supposed to break Cole's legs?

"You know what I mean." Bradley rubbed his knuckles up and down her arm. "Flirt a little. Give a little."

Sydney tightened her jaw and swallowed hard against her scathing retort. "Right," she said instead.

"That's my girl." He gave her a kiss on the cheek.

Cole watched with disbelief as an overpolished, ridiculously urbane-looking man kissed Sydney right there on the sidewalk. He gripped the steering wheel and everything inside him clenched to stone. He reached for the door handle, intent on ripping the jerk's head off, but a horn sounded behind him.

He looked up to see the light had turned green. Then he glanced back at Sydney. She was smiling at the man, their posture intimate and telling. Cole's nostrils flared and he stuffed the transmission into First.

No wonder she'd been so anxious to get rid of him this morning. She had something going on the side, and he was in the way. Whether this guy was a lover or a secret contact, her interests obviously weren't those of the Erickson family.

Cole wasn't about to sit still for that. Miss New York's plotting days were over. He was taking over as of right now. He was calling up the best PI firm in the country and putting them on retainer until the job was complete. Sydney could get the hell out of his way.

He pulled into the hotel underground and parked the car. Then he grabbed an express elevator and stomped his way down the hallway. He'd call Kyle, see if his brother had come up with any leads from the neighbors. Then he'd call Joseph Neely and get some PI firm recommendations.

* * *

Kyle didn't have any new information, so Cole moved on to Neely. Five minutes later he was armed with a list of the top-ten firms.

"Cole?" Sydney's voice wafted through the connecting doorway.

He picked up the phone, planning to start with the L.A. firm.

Her footsteps sounded on the carpet behind him. "You find any… What are you doing?"

He turned to look at her lying, cheating, beautiful face. "Better question is, what are *you* doing?"

She glanced from him to the phone and back again. "I'm looking for the Thunderbolt."

"Find it?"

"Uh…no."

"Find anything new today?"

She shook her head.

"Nothing at all? Nothing interesting?"

"Cole?"

That was it. She'd blown her last chance.

"I'm calling P.I. firms," he said, punching in the last few numbers.

She took a step forward, but something in his expression made her hesitate. Smart woman.

"Why?" she asked.

"Amber and Associates," came the voice on the telephone.

"I'm interested in hiring a private investigator," said Cole. "I need to find some missing jewelry."

Sydney moved around the bed, stopping directly in front of him. "Don't."

He ignored her.

She shot a telltale glance at the disconnect button.

He covered the mouthpiece. "Don't even think about it."

"I'll put you through to Dean Skye," said the receptionist.

"Thank you," said Cole, warning Sydney with his eyes.

"Hang up," she insisted.

"No."

"Why are you doing this?"

"So I can find the Thunderbolt."

"We *are* finding the Thunderbolt."

Cole scoffed out a sound of disbelief.

"Cole!"

"Dean Skye speaking."

"Mr. Skye," said Cole, ignoring Sydney. "I have a situation involving—"

Sydney's hand shot out.

Cole grabbed her wrist. But he was too late. The line went dead.

He squeezed. "What the—"

She winced and he immediately let her go.

"What the hell do you *think you're doing?*" he bellowed, slamming down the receiver.

"You can't do this."

"Yes. As a matter of fact, I *can*. It's my brooch. It's my problem. You don't even need to be here."

"But—"

"You're dead weight, Sydney. Go home."

She blinked. "I don't understand. What happened?"

He'd seen her in the arms of another man. That's what happened.

And he knew in that instant that he couldn't trust her.

He also knew she was under his skin. He'd spent one single night in her arms, but there was no denying the acid spray of jealousy that burned through his body.

He was making decisions on emotion here. He had to send her away before he did something really stupid and compromised his family.

"Cole?"

"I know your little secret." He spat the words out.

All the color drained from her face. Her green eyes went wide, and her arms went slack by her side. "How…"

Well, if there was any doubt at all left over, *that* reaction sure confirmed that he'd seen what he'd thought he'd seen.

Cole sneered. "I saw you kissing him. Hugging him—"

"Who?"

"The guy on the sidewalk."

"Just now?"

What the hell kind of a question was that? "Yes, just now. How many guys did you kiss today?"

"You mean Bradley?"

"I don't know his name."

The color was coming back to her face. Now she looked more confused than scared. "You called in a P.I. firm because you saw Bradley Slander kiss me?"

"I called in a P.I. firm because you spent the afternoon with *Bradley* instead of doing your job."

"I was with him for two minutes."

Cole snorted. "That must have been disappointing. And, by the way, if that was Bradley Slander, he sure hasn't been scorned yet."

"You think I was having *sex with him?*" Her question ended in an incredulous shout. Then silence took over the room and she stared at him with impressive indignation.

Okay, if her reaction was anything to go by at this point…

"You kissed him goodbye," said Cole.

She paced across the room. "*He* kissed *me*. On the cheek. In public."

"You didn't exactly slap his face."

"I didn't exactly kiss him back, either. He's smart, and he's unpredictable. I just wanted him to go away."

"I saw what I saw," Cole insisted, but his voice was losing conviction.

"You saw him kiss me on the cheek, because that was all he did."

"You didn't have to smile."

"I was gritting my teeth."

Cole swallowed, allowing that he might not have connected the dots in precisely the right formation.

"Cole, I spent the afternoon researching the Thunderbolt. And I'd slit my wrists before I'd sleep with that man."

Something relaxed inside Cole. Bad sign, he knew. But there was nothing he could do about it.

Her eyes burned an emerald fire as she moved closer. "And I'm insulted that you jumped to that conclusion. Just because I slept with you—"

"I'm sorry."

"—doesn't make me—"

"I'm sorry."

She took a breath. "You're a cad, you know that?"

He nodded. "I'm a cad."

She poked him in the chest with her index finger. "You ought to be ashamed of yourself."

He nodded again. "I am."

She poked him, and this time he captured her hand.

She looked up into his eyes and her voice softened. "I'm a very reliable person. I could get references."

"I don't need references," he whispered.

She searched his expression. "Then what do you need?"

What did he need? He needed to be sure that emotion wasn't overriding reason when it came to her. He needed to know she was on his side. He needed to know she didn't have an ulterior motive.

She sighed into the silence. "Once, just *once,* do you think you could give me the benefit of the doubt?"

"Yeah," he answered. "I will."

"Good."

He inhaled the scent of her hair and something primal rose up inside him. She might not have been interested in Slander, but Slander was sure as hell interested in her. Cole felt an overpowering need to stamp out the other man's taint.

He needed to hold her, to kiss her, to remind himself that *he* was the one she'd made love with. It might be an overreaction, but the blood of pillaging Vikings pounded through his veins. Ericksons took what they wanted, and Cole wanted Sydney.

He wanted her bad.

He bent his head, bringing his lips down onto hers. He forced himself to keep his arms by his sides. She could step away if she wanted. He wasn't holding her, but he wasn't holding back, either. He was going to kiss her until she told him to stop.

But she didn't step away, and passion crested within him. His hands went to her hair. How he'd missed its satiny texture. He cradled her head, taking a small step forward, his body coming up against hers, her heat flaring against his skin.

"I missed you," he whispered, the words almost painful. "I missed you so much."

Had it only been a week since they'd made love? It seemed like an eternity.

"I missed you, too," she sighed, her soft body snuggling into the hollows of his own. "I know you're marrying someone else…"

"And I know this is just business for you…"

Their kiss deepened. He wished he could absorb her, keep her, bind her so tight she'd never touch another man. Never look at another man.

He plucked at the buttons of her blouse, needing to feel her satin skin once more.

Her blouse fell open and his fingertips skimmed their way over her stomach.

He covered one lacy cup, filling his hand with the weight of her breast. Her nipple poked into his palm and he wanted to rip off her clothes then and there. She wasn't going near another man. Ever. *Ever!*

He didn't care that it was only business. His hand convulsed around her breast, and the other went to her buttocks, dragging her tight against his body, leaving no question about the strength of his desire.

"Cole," she moaned, her body going lax.

He wrapped an arm around her waist, supporting her slight weight.

"What you do…" she groaned.

"What *you* do," he muttered back.

She wound her arms around his neck, holding him tight, her lips searing his skin.

"Cole, please," she gasped.

"Anything," he said. "Anything."

"We have to go."

"Huh?"

She stopped kissing, released him, her breath coming in short gasps. "We have to go to Miami."

Cole felt as though he'd been bucked off and hit the dirt sideways. "What?"

"I found out… Gwen called… We need to go to Miami."

He stared down at her open blouse, her lacy bra, the creamy breasts that mounded up like ambrosia. *"Now?"*

"Now. Bradley's here. We can't waste any time."

Cole pulled back, irrational anger bubbling up at the mere mention of Bradley's name. "Is that what you call this? A *waste of time?*"

She closed her eyes and let out an exasperated sigh. "Don't."

Fine. Forget it. They'd drop everything and fly across the country to play hurry up and wait. "Sure, we'll go to Miami."

"You think I *want* to stop?"

"Just say it—you're stopping, aren't you."

She tightened her jaw, bringing her hands up to her hips. "Cole Nathaniel—"

He froze at the intimate sound of his middle name.

"—I want you more than I've ever wanted any man in my life. And if I had my way—"

"You want me?"

"Yes."

"But we're leaving?"

"Yes! Bradley's going to stake out the hotel."

"But, you definitely want me." Suddenly life didn't

seem so bleak. Miami was only four hours away. They could be there before morning. Nothing to do before the antique stores opened up…

She shook her head. "Yes, I want you. Should I make up a sign or something?"

"And you'll still want me in Miami?" He'd take it in writing if she'd give it to him.

"Not if you don't shut up."

Cole grinned. "Shutting up now."

"Good. Grab your bag."

"Should I call a cab?"

"No. Let's duck out the back way and catch one a few blocks down."

He gave her a squeeze. "It's sexy when you go all secret agent on me."

She shot him a look of impatience. "Want meter is going down."

"Shutting up again."

"Good thinking."

Chapter 9

The minute the door swung shut on their Miami hotel suite, Cole pulled Sydney into his arms. Passion burst to life inside her, and she fumbled with the buttons at his collar, loosening his tie while he shucked his jacket.

She moaned her satisfaction, burrowing her face into his neck, inhaling deeply. She didn't know what it was about his scent, but if they could bottle it, they'd make a fortune. She flicked her tongue out to taste his skin, then she suckled a tender spot near his collarbone.

"You make me crazy," he rasped, running his hands through her hair.

She started on the buttons of his shirt. "You just make me want you."

"How is it I do that?"

"Breathing," she answered.

He returned her kisses, reaching for her blouse, popping the buttons and peeling it off her shoulders. He stood back and gazed once more at her lacy bra. "I like it when you breathe, too."

She unsnapped the hooks and dropped the wisp of fabric to the floor. His eyes darkened, and her body began to hum in earnest.

"Oh, man." He slowly pulled her in, pressing them skin to skin, holding her tight and setting off tiny explosions in her brain. His hands worked magic. His kisses grew harder, sweeter, ranging further and further.

She tangled her hands in his hair, loving the touch, loving the texture. "Stop time again," she begged.

He feathered his fingertips down her spine. "I'll do my best." He tasted her earlobe. He kissed her neck. He delved sweetly into her mouth, and she thought she never wanted him to stop.

How had she imagined she could live without this?

They'd wasted six whole days, avoiding each other when they could have been in paradise. It was almost criminal.

He peeled off the rest of their clothes, and his touch grew more intimate. A flush covered her body, and an overhead fan whirred a gentle breeze, cooling the heat, sensitizing her skin.

He scooped her into his arms once again and crossed through the French doors to the king-size bed.

"Tell me when to put you down," he said.

A shudder ran through her at his selfless memory. "Not yet."

She loved this. There was something about his strength, his caring, his bold masculinity that sent shivers to her core.

He smiled and kissed her lips. Then he kissed her

eyelids and the tip of her nose. "You really like this," he teased.

"I really like this," she agreed.

"Gotta figure out what fantasy it is."

She grinned. "Caveman?"

"Viking."

Her body convulsed. "That's it."

His eyes turned stormy. And he sobered, covering her lips in a long, deep kiss as he gently laid her back on the bed. He brushed her hair from her eyes. "You're beautiful."

She felt beautiful. She felt desirable and wonderful.

He kissed his way up her body beginning with her ankle, then the bend of her knee, gently flexing her leg until he had access to her inner thigh. His days' growth of beard gently abraded her tender skin, sending shivers of desire to her core. His lips nibbled and his tongue teased higher and higher while she gasped his name.

She tensed when he blew gently on her curls. But then she closed her eyes and bit down on her lip as sensation after sensation throbbed their way along her limbs.

This was Cole. She was safe. He wouldn't hurt her. He wouldn't hurt anyone.

Then his hand replaced his mouth, gently stretching and filling her as he moved on to kiss her stomach. Her hips came off the bed, and he murmured words of encouragement against her skin.

She grasped for his hair, her hands restless, needing something to do. He moved again and took one nipple into his mouth. She groaned, burying her fingers in his hair. Her entire body arched involuntarily, striving to get closer to the sensations that were driving her sweetly out of her mind.

She dug her fingernails into his shoulders, raking them down his back as he moved up to kiss her mouth.

She opened wide. Finally, finally. She wrapped her arms around his broad body, holding him tight against her breasts. She kissed his mouth, kissed his cheeks, kissed his eyelids, then buried her face in his neck and inhaled.

He kissed the top of her head, one hand stroking down her glistening body, coming to rest on her bottom. "Slow and you just don't go together, do they?" he gasped.

"Get over it, cowboy," she rumbled, reveling in the salty taste of his neck.

She felt his deep chuckle.

"I'll try," he promised, easing her thighs apart. "I'll try really, really hard."

He eased inside her inch by careful inch. She bit down hard on her bottom lip. Time was stopping again.

He did slow it down. Then he sped it up. Then slowed it down again, holding her shimmering until she was sure she'd cry out in desperation. He whispered her name over and over, until the city lights blurred and streamed together, melting into the hot, humid ground.

Hours later, the rising sun turned the edge of the ocean a pearly pink. The champagne bottle was three quarters empty. And the lazy ceiling fan pushed a breeze down on Cole's bare skin.

He dipped a fresh strawberry into the bowl of whipped cream on the bedside table and held it to Sydney's lips.

She bit down, smiling her appreciation of the delicacy.

He popped the other half into his own mouth, thinking he could happily stay here for the rest of his life.

"So," she continued around the berry. "Your great-great-granddaddy, the infamous and sexy Jarred Erickson—"

"I believe I take after him," said Cole, pushing himself into a sitting position, striking a pose among half a dozen plump, white pillows and a billowing comforter.

"The sexy part or the infamous part?" she asked, bending her knees to cross her ankles in the air and resting her chin on her interlaced fingers.

Cole took in her tousled hair and her bare buttocks. Yep. Definitely forever. "I'm thinking both," he said.

She grinned and reached for her champagne flute. "So you're telling me Jarred decreed that the ranch should stay as one parcel into perpetuity?"

Cole nodded. "My ancestors were big on decrees. Every few generations, somebody comes up with something that wreaks havoc for a couple hundred years."

He figured most of them were lunatics, particularly those who had taken to piracy.

She took a sip of the champagne, and he had to curb an urge to kiss the sweetness from her mouth.

"And your solution is to come up with some new decrees?" she asked.

"Damn straight. It's my turn. I complied with theirs—"

Sydney coughed out a laugh.

"What?"

"You complied with *what,* exactly?"

"Passing on the Thunderbolt."

"Ha. You had to be railroaded into marriage."

That was unfair. He frowned at her. "It's completely voluntary."

"As a last resort."

He reached for his own champagne, leaning back against the birch headboard. "Point is, it'll get the job done."

"You're also splitting the ranch in half, in defiance of Great-great-granddaddy Jarred."

"That's just common sense. Keeping it intact was a stupid idea."

"Are you always this determined that you're right and everyone else is wrong?"

"Of course."

"Of course," she mimicked.

"Hey, if a man doesn't trust his own judgment, what's left?"

She laughed again, nearly spilling her champagne. Then she twisted into a sitting position, rearranging the comforter over her lap. "You know, whoever came up with the wenches and ale rule, sure had you Erickson men pegged."

"Wenches and ale?"

"Yeah. You know. The wenches and ale."

"I have no idea what you're talking about."

"Didn't your grandma tell you?"

Cole shook his head.

Sydney leaned across him, snagging another strawberry and dipping it in the cream. "That's why the women get the brooch." She popped the berry into her mouth. "Somebody back in the fourteenth century decided you guys might sell it for wenches and ale. You know, the Erickson of the day would change the tradition. And, poof, there would go the Thunderbolt."

Cole couldn't help but grin.

"What?" she asked.

"Who needs wenches and ale?" He lifted his flute in a mock toast. "I've got champagne and—"

"Watch it, cowboy."

He leaned forward and kissed her strawberry lips, taking the safe route. "A princess."

She pulled back. "A *princess?*"

Okay, too sappy. "A hot babe?"

She raised her eyebrows.

He decided to go with the truth. "A beautiful, intelligent, funny, gracious lady?"

"That's not bad."

He took the champagne from her hand and set both glasses down on the bedside table. "Come here," he said, needing to feel her all over again. He gathered her into his arms and they stretched out on the comforter.

She sighed and rested her head on his shoulder.

He stroked her hair, releasing its scent. "Wenches and ale. How is it you know more about my family than I do?"

"I'm nosey. I ask lots of questions."

He settled his arm more comfortably around her. Traffic sounds came to life on the street below, and the rising sun flashed its orange rays through the balcony doors.

"Let me ask *you* a question," he said, twirling a lock of her hair around his index finger.

"Fire away."

"You said you had foster parents."

She nodded. "I lost my parents in a house fire when I was five."

Cole tightened his arm around her, and the ceiling fan whooshed into the silence.

"My foster parents were friends of the family. Nanny Emma and Papa Hal raised me. But they were older. And they've both since passed away."

Cole's heart went out to her. He didn't know what he'd do without his family. "You must miss them all."

"Nanny and Papa, yes. But I don't really remember my parents at all. I have these vague images of them in my mind."

"What about pictures?"

"Burned in the fire. A few of the neighbors had shots of my father from a distance, but they tell me my mother was always behind the camera, not in front of it."

Cole's chest tightened at the injustice. Never to know what your mother looked like? At twenty, he'd ached for his mother. Sydney had been five.

Protective instincts welled up inside him. "What about newspapers? Her high-school yearbook? Surely somebody—"

"It's okay." Sydney reached over and stroked her palm across his beard-stubbled cheek, comforting him, when he should have done it for her.

"What *do* you remember?" he asked, covering her small hand with his own.

"My mother's locket." Sydney relaxed against him again, smiling at what was obviously a touchstone memory. "It was silver, oval-shaped. It had a flower, I think it was a rose, etched into the front. I don't know whose picture was inside, but it would dangle down when she bent over to hug me. I distinctly remember reaching for it. Her hair was blond, and it sort of haloed around the locket."

"Where's the locket now?"

"Destroyed by the fire."

"Oh, Sydney."

"It's really okay."

He tucked her hair behind one ear and gently kissed the top of her head. "I guess that explains a lot."

She tipped her chin to look up at him, green eyes narrowing. "Explains what?"

"Your profession. Your burning desire to locate antiquities."

She pulled back. "I locate antiquities because I have a master's degree in art history."

"You have a master's degree because you've spent your life looking for the locket."

"That's silly. The locket was destroyed more than twenty years ago."

He touched her temple with his index finger. "Maybe in here." He placed his hand over her heart. "But not in here."

"Did you minor in psychology?"

"Computer science. With a major in agriscience."

"Then you're completely unqualified to analyze me."

"I supposed you're right," he said to appease her. But qualified or not, he knew hers was a personal search.

She stifled a yawn.

"We need to sleep," he said.

"It's morning already."

"Not quite."

He sidled down the bed, keeping her wrapped in his arms.

"We do need to sleep," she agreed. Then she smiled as she closed her eyes.

Cole sucked in a deep breath. Sleeping with Sydney

in his arms. He could get used to this. He shouldn't. She had her career and he had his family.

Still, he could get used to this.

Eyes closed, Sydney waited until Cole's breathing was deep and even. Then she blinked away her fatigue and watched his profile in the gathering light. His tanned skin was stark against the white pillowcase, and she gave into an urge to run her fingertip along his rough chin. She wished she could be honest with him, take him with her, listen to his advice.

For a moment she considered waking him up and swearing him to secrecy. Then she could tell him all about his grandmother's problem, and they could solve it together.

But she couldn't do that. She wasn't even sure Cole would want her to do that. She had a feeling he'd consider a promise to any member of his family to be a sacred trust.

When she was sure he was sound asleep, she carefully inched out of the cradle of his hug and slipped from beneath the covers.

It was 8:00 a.m. in Miami, five in California and seven in Texas. She could only hope that Cole's late night and all those time zone changes would keep him unconscious a few more hours.

She tiptoed into the living room, carefully clicked the French door shut behind her and turned on a small lamp on the desktop. Then she opened her purse and retrieved the number for the Miami fashion show. Hopefully, they'd have contact information for Rupert Cowan.

She dialed the number, spoke to a show coordinator who had Rupert Cowan's business phone number and address. She jotted it down on the hotel notepad, peeled off the sheet and tucked the slip of paper into her purse.

She had no way of knowing if he was the right Rupert Cowan. Heading down there might be a waste of time. But she couldn't for the life of her come up with a way to broach the subject with him on the phone.

She had no choice but to approach him in person and keep her fingers crossed.

She might have one heck of a lot of explaining to do once she got back. But it was time to pull out all the stops. If Rupert Cowan did have the brooch, and if she could get her hands on it, Cole would probably be grateful enough not to question the details.

She unzipped her garment bag, retrieved a blazer and skirt that were only slightly wrinkled, then dressed and headed for the lobby.

When Cole woke up, Sydney was nowhere to be found. She wasn't in the suite. She wasn't in the hotel restaurant. And she wasn't in the lobby.

He knew he had to stop being suspicious of her, but it was unnerving to have her just up and disappear. They were supposed to be working together. Even though he'd promised to give her the benefit of the doubt, he couldn't help but wonder if she was up to something.

Okay, so there was every chance that she was investigating antique dealers, or maybe she'd just gone around the corner. She could easily show up any minute with coffee and bagels.

Still, he glanced around the suite, taking inventory. Her suitcase was open on the sofa. Her toiletries were in the main bathroom. She'd opened a bottle of water at the bar.

What else?

He glanced around for clues.

A pen lay haphazardly across the oak desk next to a hotel note pad. Nothing to say the housekeeping staff hadn't set them out crooked, but nothing to say Sydney hadn't used them, either.

Cole held the notepad up to the light, staring across the fibrous surface. There were a few indentations in the paper, so he took a trick from a television crime drama and shaded across them with a pencil.

Rupert Cowan—2713 Harper View Road. Didn't sound like a deli or a coffee shop to Cole.

Didn't sound like anything, he told himself. She could have a perfectly legitimate reason for writing that down and leaving.

After last night, he was giving her the benefit of the doubt if it killed him.

He crumpled the shaded paper in his fist.

It might even be left over from the last guest.

They'd probably laugh about it later.

He tossed the note into the wastepaper basket and sat down on the couch, bracing his fists on his knees.

He couldn't *wait* to laugh about it later.

Chapter 10

Sydney stepped cautiously into 2713 Harper View Road. Unlike the other commercial businesses on the block, this one had a solid gray door that was tucked into an uninviting little alcove.

Inside, hanging fluorescent lights buzzed in the cavernous space. The shoes of unseen employees shuffled against the gritty concrete floor between rows of beige, Arborite countertops and fabric-filled shelving. A few voices sounded in the distance, and a lone man paged through sketch sheets a few counters back.

"Hello?" Sydney ventured.

The man glanced up, pushing his long, graying hair back from his forehead. "Hey there."

She took a couple steps toward him. "I'm looking for Rupert Cowan?"

The man straightened to about five feet seven. He wore black slacks and a black, ribbed-knit turtleneck. "You found him."

Butterflies pirouetted in Sydney's stomach. "Oh, good."

He braced his hands against the countertop. "Something I can help you with?"

She moved forward and stretched out her hand. "I'm Sydney Wainsbrook."

He shook. His hand was pale and his grip noncommittal. "Nice to meet you, Sydney."

"I was wondering—" she glanced around, swallowing against her dry throat "—is there somewhere we can talk?"

He laced his fingers in front of his chest. "About?"

"It's a personal matter." Her heart rate was going up, and her palms were getting sweaty.

Thank goodness they'd already shaken hands.

"You looking for a job?" he asked.

Sydney shook her head. "It's... I'd feel better if we could sit down somewhere."

Rupert glanced at his watch. "Well, I'm a little—"

"Please?"

He hesitated. "We could go next door for coffee."

She nodded eagerly. "Perfect."

"Patrice?" Rupert called over his shoulder.

"Yeah?" came a woman's gruff voice from the back of the shop.

"I'm out for a bit. If the agency calls, tell them we'll need all ten girls there by Sunday for rehearsal."

"Okay," came the voice.

Rupert gestured to the door with an open palm.

Sydney gave him a shaky smile, then led the way outside and around the corner, into a small, glass-fronted coffee bar.

"Frappachino? Mochachino?" asked Rupert.

"Let me," said Sydney, pulling out her wallet.

Rupert addressed the clerk. "Small half-caf, two sugars, extra foam."

"Just black for me," said Sydney as she pulled out a few bills.

They took a corner table with a checkered plastic tablecloth and a metal napkin dispenser. The whine of the coffee machine filled the silence.

"Are we through being mysterious?" asked Rupert.

Sydney took a bracing breath. Then, making a firm decision, she opened her purse and took out the picture of the fake Thunderbolt.

"Do you recognize this?" she asked Rupert.

Rupert took the picture between his fingers and sat back in his red leather seat. "You must be one of the Ericksons."

Sydney's stomach bounced clear to the floor.

He *knew* about the Ericksons?

"So, you recognize it?" she asked, struggling to re-craft her approach. She hadn't counted on him knowing the story. Did he know about Grandma? About his father? About his mother's extortion?

"It's the heirloom brooch," said Rupert, dropping it on the table top. "My mother warned me you'd come looking for it one day."

If he'd known about the Ericksons, why hadn't he come out of the woodwork before now?

"What, exactly, did she tell you?" asked Sydney.

He stroked his chin as if he'd once had a beard. "You know, you're not what I expected."

"What did you expect?"

The waitress set their coffee cups in front of them,

and Rupert shrugged. "Someone a little less classy, a little more West Texas."

"I'm not an Erickson," said Sydney.

"Ah-hh."

She resented his tone. Cole had looked damn classy in his suit yesterday.

"I'm a…friend of the family," she offered. She wouldn't mention the Laurent if she could get away with it. If he thought there was interest from a museum, his price would probably go up.

"And you want the brooch."

She nodded. "I'm prepared to pay."

He shook his head. "Not for sale."

Damn. He was sentimental.

She kept a poker face. "You don't know how much I'm offering."

He propped his elbows on the table and rested his chin on his laced knuckles. "It's pretty valuable to me at the moment."

"For sentimental reasons?"

He let out a cold laugh. "Sentimental? Me? About them?"

"Then, why…?"

He leaned forward. "Ever heard of Thunder Women's Wear?"

Sydney shook her head.

"Don't worry. You will. We caused quite a stir in Miami last season, and we're scheduled for Milan in ten days."

She paused. "I don't understand."

"That little brooch? That stupid little brooch that my mother practically worshiped, is the centerpiece of my new line—the bold, crisp colors, the angular lines, the drama and majesty of it. We reproduced the jewel using embroidery thread and my final model wears the brooch itself in every show."

"A fashion line?"

He nodded. "Years, I've been slaving away in this fashion backwater. Then, one night, I'm hunting through the drawer for a pair of cuff links and out drops the brooch…"

Looking for a pair of cuff links? The man kept the Thunderbolt in his *dresser drawer?*

Sydney was going to have a heart attack right here and now.

He picked some lint from his sleeve. "So, you see. It may not have sentimental value, but it has business value to me."

Sydney took a sip of her coffee, searching her brain for a new tactic. She could blurt out a lucrative price— Grandma had arranged a line of credit. But instinct told her it was too soon to talk numbers.

"Did your mother ever tell you how she got the brooch?"

He cracked a knowing smile. "A gift from dear, old Dad. I figured it was hush money."

"Is that why you never contacted the Ericksons?"

Rupert tipped back his head and laughed. "That would presuppose I gave a damn about his reputation. I just figured those cowpokes would have no more interest in me than I have in them."

Sydney nodded. That was good. If Rupert didn't want anything to do with the family, all the better.

She took another drink of her coffee, choosing her words carefully. "You've probably guessed it has sentimental value to them."

Rupert sipped his frothy brew. "That would be why they sent you."

She nodded, toying with the handle of her mug. "I'm prepared to offer you a hundred thousand dollars."

Rupert didn't react. Not even a flicker.

Sydney swore silently. Maybe he'd had it appraised.

Unexpectedly, the chair beside her squeaked against the floor and a shadow loomed large.

"Whatever she just offered you," said Bradley, plunking himself down and crossing one ankle over the opposite knee. "I'll double it."

Sydney felt like she'd been sucker punched. "How did you…"

He cocked his head. "*Please.* Double-o-seven, you're not."

Sydney could have decked him.

Bradley picked up Sydney's coffee cup and took a deliberate swig. "I assume we're getting down to brass tacks?"

"Who are you?" asked Rupert.

Bradley stuck out his hand. "Bradley Slander. I deal in antiques."

"And I've got a bidding war?" asked Rupert with an impressive air of unconcern.

"If she makes another offer, I'll top that, too." Bradley took another defiant swig of her coffee and slanted her a cold look.

It was official. The man had no soul.

Grandma's line of credit went as high as three hundred thousand. Bradley could easily match that. Even if Sydney added her own savings, there was no way she'd beat him.

"Exciting as this is—" said Rupert, pushing his chair

back from the table "—and much as I'd love to add six figures to my bank account today, the Thunderbolt is not for sale."

Sydney reached toward him. "But—"

He stared down his aquiline nose. "Sorry, Sydney."

"Four hundred thousand," said Bradley.

Rupert hesitated.

Sydney swallowed. Should she match it? It would take all of her savings…

"Sorry," said Rupert, taking another step.

Sydney jumped up, nearly knocking over the heavy chair.

She absolutely, positively could not let Rupert out the door without making a deal. Bradley wouldn't give up. He'd be on the phone to Oslo within the hour, upping the ante. He'd eventually win Rupert over, and Grandma would never see the brooch again.

"Really, Rupert—" Sydney began, trying not to gasp for air. "It's a family heirloom."

Rupert shook his head. "And I give a damn, because?"

Should she tell him the truth? That his mother was an extortionist? Put her cards on the table and betray Grandma?

Betraying Grandma would be better than losing the Thunderbolt forever. Wouldn't it?

Her heart was pounding and her palms were sweating. She needed time to think. Somewhere out of the heat, away from that infernal coffee grinder.

Rupert started for the door.

"Wait!" she called in a dry, hoarse voice.

He turned and gave her a salute. "I need it for Milan, Sydney. Milan and beyond."

The fake! The idea slammed into her brain with the force of an anvil.

"I can replace it," she blurted.

He paused with his hand on the knob.

She moved toward him. "I have a replica."

His brow furrowed.

"It's good," she assured him. "It's *very* good. Flawless diamonds, five-carat rubies. You could have the cash *and* the Thunderbolt."

"Half a million," drawled Bradley.

"I'd have to see it," Rupert said to Sydney.

"I'll have it here this afternoon."

Bradley stood up, clattering his chair against the floor. "For half a million you can make two fakes, and then some."

Rupert arched a brow. "Within the week?"

A muscle ticked in Bradley's jaw, and his eyes beaded down to brown dots.

Rupert shook a warning finger at Sydney. "I'll look at it, but it would have to be perfect."

"It's perfect," said Sydney, counting on the fact that the faceted diamonds were only a historical flaw.

He hesitated for a long minute. Then he nodded his head. "Here. Two o'clock. Right now, I have a conference call."

As soon as he disappeared, Sydney groped for her cell phone. Bradley pulled his out of his pocket and left the café. Calling Oslo no doubt. He'd be back with a higher offer this afternoon.

Never mind Norway, thought Sydney as she punched in Grandma's number.

* * *

By two o'clock, Cole was forced to face the fact that he'd been duped.

Sydney wasn't coming back. Whatever it was that had brought her flying to Miami must have been a damn good lead. She'd obviously decided she didn't need him anymore, and she'd had no compunction about ditching him.

Maybe she was going to sell the Thunderbolt on the black market. Maybe she'd decided that one big score was worth giving up her career. Maybe she'd never been from the Laurent Museum in the first place.

Lies upon lies upon lies.

Whatever it was she'd decided, it definitely included screwing him.

He stood up from the sofa and crossed the room to retrieve the address from the wastepaper basket. *Twenty-seven thirteen Harper View Road.* There wasn't an explanation in the world that would get her out of this one.

One of Joseph Neely's clerks personally delivered the fake Thunderbolt to the Miami airport. Sydney met him there and made it back to the café with less than five minutes to spare. Where, to her surprise, Rupert pulled out a jeweler's loupe and began inspecting the brooch.

Bradley sat next to her, drumming his fingers against the plastic tablecloth, all traces of his flirtatious persona gone.

"Five hundred and fifty thousand," he ventured, and she knew his profit margin was diminishing. He was going for pride now, pure and simple.

Sydney stared directly into Bradley's eyes. "Four hundred thousand, plus the replica."

Rupert paused, looking up from his inspection. "Will you two *stop*."

The muscle in Bradley's jaw began ticking again.

After an excruciating fifteen minutes, Rupert returned the loupe to his jacket pocket. He closed the case on the fake Thunderbolt, and Sydney held her breath.

Finally, he put his hand out to Sydney, palm up. "Four hundred thousand."

"A cashier's check?" she asked, her heart smacking against her rib cage.

Bradley swore, but Rupert silenced him with a glare.

"A cashier's check will be fine." He pulled a sheaf of papers from his breast pocket. "And you can sign here."

It was Sydney's turn to hold out her hand, palm up.

Rupert smiled his admiration, then he reached into the same pocket and pulled out a worn jewelry case.

She clicked it open, and her entire body shuddered in relief.

"May I?" she asked, pointing to the pocket that held the loupe.

He retrieved it. "Be my guest."

She checked the jewels, then she turned the brooch over to check the casting. A deep sense of satisfaction settled in the pit of her stomach. The Thunderbolt was going home.

She pulled out the envelope containing the two cashiers' checks—one from Grandma's line of credit, the other from Sydney's savings account.

Rupert handed her the pen.

Bradley smacked his fist down on the table.

The transaction was over with surprising speed, and all three of them stood.

"You need an escort to a taxi?" asked Rupert, slanting a glance at Bradley.

Sydney chuckled, enjoying the moment. Glad to have thwarted Bradley, excited about telling Cole, and absolutely thrilled for Grandma.

"I don't think he'll mug me," she answered.

"Man," muttered Bradley. "You're a freakin' lunatic," he said to Rupert.

"It was interesting to meet you, Sydney," said Rupert, ignoring Bradley's pithy comment and striding for the door.

Sydney zipped her purse securely shut and tucked it under her arm.

"Don't look so smug," said Bradley.

"I'm not smug," she returned as they paced for the exit. "I'm happy for the Erickson family."

"Don't you ever gag over all that syrupy sweetness you call a personality?"

Sydney opened the glass door and glanced back at him over her shoulder. "Been nice doing business with you, Bradley." Then she turned her head and took a step, walking straight into Cole's broad chest.

He grabbed her by the upper arms and put her away from him. "You lying, cheating, little—"

"Cole!"

He was dressed like Texas again. A denim shirt, his sleeves rolled up, with faded blue jeans riding low on his hips. His boots gave him an extra inch, and he looked truly dangerous.

He glared past her, eyes hardening on Bradley. "Looks like you changed your mind about slitting your wrists."

No. Oh, no.

Her stomach turned to a block of concrete. She had to explain. She had to make him understand. "It's not—"

Cole shut her up with a look of ice. "Don't even bother."

"But—"

"Do you actually think I'd listen to *anything* you have to say right now?"

Bradley made a move.

"Keep walking," Cole barked, squaring his shoulders and shifting himself between Sydney and Bradley.

Bradley hesitated for a split second. Then he held up his palms and took a step back. "Hey. Nothing to do with me. I've got bigger fish to fry." He turned to walk away.

"Hand it over," Cole demanded in a cold voice.

"You have to let me explain," she pleaded, searching her brain for something that would work as an explanation. She still couldn't give Grandma away.

"Explain?" He laughed coldly. "Explain why you ditched me in a hotel and bought the Thunderbolt for yourself."

"It's not for—"

"You've been stringing me along from the beginning."

"Will you *listen* to me?" What could she say? What would make sense? If only Bradley hadn't shown up. If only Cole had stayed back at the hotel.

He threw up his hands. "I can actually *see* you making up the lies."

"I'm not—" Okay, well, actually, she was.

He shook his head. Then he swiped his thumb across her bottom lip. "As far as I'm concerned, every word that comes out of your pretty little mouth is a lie."

"I never lied to you."

"Yeah? Then what the hell happened to 'Cole. I've got a lead on the brooch. I know who's got it. We can buy it back.' Did I miss that part? Was I not paying attention?"

"It's not that simple."

He folded his arms over his chest, gazing down at her with contempt. "It's *exactly* that simple. Now hand it over before I call the cops."

"You'd have me *arrested?*"

His blue eyes glittered like frozen sapphires. "Damn straight."

"What if—" What could she say? How could she explain it without betraying Grandma?

"You going to give me *another* logical story, Sydney? Been there. Done that." He held out his hand. "Give."

Sydney's shoulders drooped. It didn't matter what she said. It didn't matter what she did. "You've tried, convicted and executed me, haven't you?"

"I may be a little slow on the uptake, but I like to think I'm not a complete idiot."

Sydney yanked the purse from under her arm, fighting back a surge of stinging tears. At least Grandma would have the brooch, she told herself. And Cole would have his inheritance.

She dragged open the zipper. Maybe he would get married someday. Maybe some beautiful bride would give him beautiful children, and he'd pass all the traditions on to them.

She should be happy about that. But she just felt hollow and nauseous as she retrieved the jewel case.

"This the real one?" he asked with a derisive sneer.

She glared at him without speaking.

His voice dropped to a menacing growl as he clicked open the case. "If it's not, you know I'll come after you."

She wasn't about to dignify his accusation. "Tell Grandma…" She stuffed her purse back under her arm, squeezing it down tight. "Tell your grandmother I'm sorry."

His blue eyes hardened to stone in the bright sunshine, and he snapped the case shut. "I don't think so."

Sydney winced.

She'd lost the Thunderbolt. And she'd lost Cole.

Her body suddenly felt too heavy for her frame.

She searched his face, but there wasn't a crack of compassion, no sign of conciliation. Anything she said now would be a waste of breath.

She blinked once, then turned away. She took a couple of wooden steps toward the curb and put up her hand to hail a cab.

Cole didn't call her name, and she didn't look back.

Chapter 11

Cole wheeled his pickup into a wide spot in front of Grandma's house. The flowers were still blooming. The barns were still standing. And the horses still grazed in the fields.

He'd been to Heaven, then Hell, then home again, but the Texas landscape stuck to its own rhythm, not even missing his presence. He killed the engine, trying to shake the vacant feeling that had built up inside him, forcing himself to drum up some enthusiasm for the good news he was about to give his grandma.

He felt the breast pocket of his shirt for the hard, rectangular package, reassuring himself that the last four days hadn't been a dream—or a nightmare.

He kicked open the driver's door, snapping himself out of his mood. Nobody needed to know he'd been taken for a fool. They only needed to know the brooch was back. He'd gloss over Sydney's betrayal and gloss over his own gullibility.

He crossed the dirt driveway and took the front stairs two at a time.

"Grandma?" he called as he opened the door.

She appeared in the foyer, wiping her hands on a dish towel. "I heard your truck. Do you have news?"

He forced himself to smile as he slipped the case out of his shirt pocket. "I have great news. I found it."

She searched his face for a moment. "And everything's okay?"

That wasn't exactly the reaction he was expecting. He smiled wider. "Of course it's okay. We have the Thunderbolt." He held the case out to her.

Her pale blue eyes shimmered with tears and she reached for the case, opening it carefully to gaze at the brooch. "Where's Sydney?" she asked, glancing to the open doorway behind him.

Cole inhaled, turning to close the door. "She's in New York."

Grandma stilled. "Why? Why didn't she come home?"

"She had things to do."

"What things?"

"Grandma…"

"What things? Cole Nathaniel? This is her triumph—"

Cole winced and bit back a sharp denial.

"—her achievement—"

He clenched his jaw tight to keep himself silent.

"She needs to be here with us to celebrate."

"Grandma."

"Don't you 'Grandma' me." She snapped the case shut.

"She's gone."

"What did you do?"

"Sydney is not our friend," he said as gently as he could.

His grandmother glared up at him, waving the Thunderbolt case. "That's ridiculous. You're marrying her."

Cole ran a hand through his hair, gripping the base of his neck. He needed to get out of here. He needed some air. He needed *not* to be answering questions about Sydney right now. "No, I'm not marrying her."

"Oh, yes, you are." Grandma nodded. "I'm not letting you talk yourself out of this girl. It's time to grow up, Cole. It's time to take on your responsibilities."

"I'll marry someone else. I promise."

Grandma shook her head and clicked her cheeks.

Cole sucked in a breath, calming himself down. The sooner he got it over with, the better. "I didn't want to have to tell you this, Grandma."

"Tell me what? What did you do to that wonderful girl?"

That was it. Cole had had about enough. "That *wonderful girl* tried to *steal the Thunderbolt*."

"She did not."

Oh, great. Denial. That was helpful. "I watched her do it."

Grandma waved a dismissive hand. "Not possible."

"She's a stranger, Grandma. You can't have such blind faith in her." As Cole had done.

He'd been taken in by her sexy smile and her sultry voice. This was what happened when you started letting emotions mess around with your logic. Or maybe it was his libido that had messed around with his logic.

"She may be a stranger to you, Cole." Grandma

tapped the case against Cole's chest. "But I know that woman. She did *not* betray us."

Sydney was amazing, a con artist of incredible talent. She probably duped old people all the time. Her and that partner, Bradley Slander.

"You do *not* know her," said Cole.

"Go get her."

Cole sputtered for a moment. "I will not go get her. Grandma, she ditched me in a hotel room to go and make a deal."

"I'm sure she had a perfectly logical explanation."

"Yeah. It was logical, all right. She wanted to steal the Thunderbolt out from under us."

Grandma waved away his words.

"I waited five hours," he explained. "I took the address from the trash bin. I followed her, and caught her and her partner red-handed, bribing some black market criminal."

The color drained from Grandma's face.

Cole was sorry to disillusion Grandma, but Sydney had to be stopped. She wasn't a good person. She was a thief. "I saw them through the window. The three of them."

"Cole." Grandma's voice turned to a hoarse whisper.

"I'm sorry, Grandma." Nobody wished more than Cole that things had turned out differently. The fake Sydney was one of the most compelling women he'd ever met. Even now, even after everything she'd done to him, he still remembered her laughing voice, her gentle caresses and her emerald-dark eyes. His stomach contracted with regret.

Grandma blinked at him. She gripped the jewel case

against her chest. Then she squared her shoulders. "Sit down, Cole. There's something I have to tell you."

Perched on the couch, Cole listened with growing incredulity to his grandmother's confession.

His grandfather?

His *grandma?*

When she got to the part where she'd taken Sydney into her confidence, he jerked up and paced across the room.

With every word, with every passing second, his muscles tightened into harder balls of anger.

He didn't blame Grandma, and he didn't blame Sydney. He blamed his grandfather. And he blamed himself. It was their job to protect the family, to keep them safe.

"She bought it from your half-uncle," Grandma finished. "Then she didn't explain it to you, because I'd sworn her to secrecy. She kept my secret, Cole. She let you hate her, and she kept my secret."

Cole stopped in front of the fireplace mantel, fixing his furious gaze on the picture of his grandfather.

The man was grinning.

Grinning.

Before he was even aware of the impulse, Cole slammed his fist into the wood paneling next to the picture, cracking the veneer, putting four deep dents into the grain.

Strangely, he didn't feel the slightest pain.

"Did I miss something?" came Kyle's voice from the foyer.

A deafening silence swept the room.

"Cole and Sydney had an argument," said Grandma.

"You never punched a wall over Melanie," said Kyle.

As Cole stared at his grandfather, everything inside him turned to stone. Then his chest swelled with an ache, and his throat went raw.

He was just as bad as the old man.

He'd failed.

He wasn't there for Grandma, and he'd sent Sydney packing when he should have been down on his knees thanking her.

She'd done his job for him.

"Cole?" Kyle's voice seemed to come from a long way off. "Any news on the Thunderbolt?"

"It's here," said Grandma, holding out the case.

"Isn't that mission accomplished?" asked Kyle. "So what's wrong?"

What was wrong? Everything was wrong.

A family crisis had unfolded right under Cole's nose, and he hadn't even noticed. And he'd destroyed the woman of his dreams. She was back in New York right now, shutting down the Viking show and killing her career. She didn't deserve this. She'd stepped in to help, and what did she get in return?

He cringed remembering the insults he'd hurled at her on the sidewalk. He'd actually threatened to have her arrested.

And she hadn't said a thing. She'd kept his grandmother's confidence in spite of everything. Everything.

"Cole?" Kyle repeated, moving into the room, all humor gone from his tone.

Cole ignored his brother, slowly turning to meet Grandma's eyes.

When a man could no longer trust his own judgment, what was left? "I don't know what to do," he said.

Grandma took a step forward. "Give her the Thunderbolt."

He shook his head. It was too late. Sydney was canceling the show, and she'd never speak to him again.

"I thought you were marrying her," said Kyle, glancing from one to the other.

"They had a fight," said Grandma. "Get on the next plane, Cole. Go to New York and fix it."

"I can't fix it."

"Yes, you can."

Could he? Would an abject apology help at all? Would the Thunderbolt help, even now?

There was only one way to find out.

Cole straightened.

He filled his lungs.

"What the hell happened?" asked Kyle.

Cole turned on his heel and brushed past his brother. Grandma could tell Kyle, or not tell Kyle about the forgery. Cole would respect her decision. But right now, he had one thing to do, and one thing only.

He banged his way out the door and practically sprinted to the pickup truck.

In her cramped office on the mezzanine floor of the Laurent, Sydney hugged her arms around her chilled body.

"You fell for him, didn't you?" asked Gwen as she perched herself on the window ledge.

Sydney closed her eyes and nodded. At least there was one area where she could be honest with her friend. "I couldn't tell Cole what was really going on, either, and then Bradley showed up…."

"And Bradley's the reason Cole thinks you tried to steal his brooch?"

Sydney nodded again, struggling against the overwhelming weight of defeat. How had Cole found her? How in a city the size of Miami had he happened on that little coffee bar?

She'd thought she was home free. She would have come up with a story, any story. But when she placed the brooch in his hands, he would have known she was on his side.

Instead. Instead…

She groaned out loud. "I wish I could tell you more."

"Hey." Gwen gave a sad laugh. "It's really okay. I don't need to know. But what are you going to tell the boss? He's pretty upset, what with your promises and my promises…"

"That they wouldn't lend it to me, I guess." She shrugged. What did it matter? Her career was over. They were already scrambling to book another show for the front gallery.

Sydney had broken a cardinal rule. She'd made a promise she couldn't keep. She should have called her boss as soon as the brooch went missing. No. She should never have offered it in the first place.

She should never have offered up an item she didn't already have in her hand. But she'd trusted Cole. She knew that if he said he had the Thunderbolt, and he said he'd give her the Thunderbolt, it was as good as done.

Not quite, as it turned out. Not that it was Cole's fault. It was her fault. All her fault.

"Maybe we can replace the Thunderbolt," Gwen suggested. "Use one of the ruby necklaces."

"There's not enough public interest. It had to be a new piece. It had to be a fantastic piece."

"It's not fair that you should get hung out to dry."

Sydney gave a hollow laugh. "It's official. Life's not fair." She knew she should care a lot more about the demise of her career, but she couldn't seem to get past losing Cole.

Every time she closed her eyes, she saw him in the Miami hotel room—the sympathy in his blue eyes when she talked about Nanny and Papa, the twinkle when he fed her a strawberry, and the dark passion when he reached out to touch her hair and pull her in for a kiss.

Stop. She had to stop—

"For the record," came the voice that was haunting her brain, "I gave you the benefit of the doubt."

Gwen's eyes went wide. She quickly slipped down off the window ledge.

Sydney pivoted to see Cole, big as life, lounging against the jamb of her office door.

"I'll…uh…" Gwen quickly brushed past Cole to exit the room.

Sydney blinked, trying to adjust her focus to something that made sense.

"I waited five hours in that hotel room," he said. "It took me *five* hours to convince myself you actually had betrayed me."

"What are you doing here?" Her fingers curled convulsively into the palms of her hands. The Thunderbolt was genuine. He had no excuse to show up and torture her.

He took a couple of steps into the room, swinging the door shut behind him. "Grandma told me."

"Grandma told you what?"

"She told me the truth."

Sydney backed up, shaking her head. That couldn't be. They were home free. Grandma would never have given away her secret once she had the Thunderbolt back.

Sydney's butt came up against her small desk. "No," she whispered.

"Yes." Cole nodded. "Why didn't you tell me, Sydney?"

What kind of a question was that? "I gave her my word. My vow."

"I could have helped you."

"You were the one she was keeping it from."

"She's my responsibility," he snapped.

Sydney recoiled from the shout.

She wished she knew how to help him. This had to be hell on his pride. You took away what a man like Cole needed to protect, and he was lost.

He raked a hand through his hair. "I'm sorry."

"It's okay. I know you're upset."

He moved closer, shaking his head. "No. I'm not sorry I yelled. I mean, I *am* sorry I yelled." He stopped. "But I'm really sorry I mistrusted you. I'm sorry I treated you so badly. I'm sorry we…" His gaze drifted away from hers.

Some of the tension went out of Sydney. "Yeah? Well, I'm sorry about that part, too." They'd played with fire and they'd both been burned. She'd known all along that Cole was temporary, but she hadn't been able to resist him. And now any man she slept with from here on in was going to be held up to his standard.

Even now, his elusive scent teased her.

She shook herself. "Why are you here?"

He hesitated. "I'm here to give you the Thunderbolt."

Her throat went dry. "You can't do that."

"Oh, yes I can."

"But—"

He reached out and took both of her hands.

Her chest contracted with the touch.

"I'm proposing, Sydney."

Her heart skipped a beat. Proposing? For real?

"How do you mean?" she ventured, not daring to believe it could be true. She'd already had that dream crushed once.

"Just like we planned. You show the Thunderbolt. And then…" He shrugged his shoulders and glanced down at the floor.

The faint hope leeched out of her body. "A marriage of convenience, Cole?"

He nodded. "It is the only answer."

She'd once thought so, too. But she'd been wrong. Cole loving her was the only answer. Cole wanting to marry her and spend the rest of his life with her was the only answer she'd accept now.

He'd once asked her if she was ready to walk down the aisle in a white dress, promise to love him, then kiss him, throw a bouquet—and then go their separate ways.

She'd been prepared to do it then. She couldn't do it now.

"I don't think it's the answer anymore," she told him, her throat aching with disappointment.

"You've earned it," he said.

She raised her hand to her lips to stifle a bitter laugh. "By lying to you? By sleeping with you?"

"Don't."

She shook her head. "Thanks for the offer, Cole. But I think I'll pass."

She couldn't show the Thunderbolt under these circumstances. And she wasn't even sure she wanted to show it. The brooch was exactly where it was supposed to be, safe with Grandma, safe with Cole, someday safe with Cole's real bride.

"I'm not taking no for an answer," he insisted. "You're the reason we found it. You're the reason we even knew where to look. You were there for Grandma when she couldn't trust me—"

"Oh, Cole." Sydney's heart instantly ached for him. "It wasn't a matter of trust."

"No?"

"She was embarrassed beyond belief. I was a stranger. She didn't care about my opinion the way she cared about yours."

"That's not how I see it."

"You're not thinking clearly."

"I'm thinking perfectly clearly. I want you to marry me. I want you to reap the professional benefits of showing the Thunderbolt. It's all I can offer to make up for…"

Sydney fought the chill that moved over her soul. "I don't want it." Did he think they could just erase the past two weeks? He'd shown her the moon and the stars, then he'd yanked it all away. She'd watched the way he'd treated his family, felt the way he loved them, felt the way life might be if he might have loved her. But he didn't, and he never would, and there was nothing she could do about that.

"You're lying."

"The answer is no, Cole."

"You'll break Grandma's heart."

"Low blow," she retorted, a weak smile cresting his lips.

"You ain't seen nothing yet." He clamped his jaw. "Marry me, or I'll fight dirty."

She folded her arms across her chest, not about to give an inch. "Go ahead. Give it your best shot."

"I'll call Bradley."

Sydney pulled back in horror.

"I'm sure he'll have some ideas about showing the Thunderbolt."

She shook her head. "Cole. No. You don't know what he'll—"

"I'll do it. Either you marry me, or I make a deal with Bradley."

"You're bluffing."

"I don't bluff."

"That man's evil."

"Then marry me."

"No."

He threw up his hands. "I'm not asking you to walk the plank. You only have to put up with me for an hour or two. Give me one little kiss, pretend you like me at the reception, then we each go our own way. You'll find reasons to be in New York. I'll find reasons to be on the ranch. And, after a decent interval, we tell everyone it didn't work out."

"Could a proposal get any less romantic?" she asked.

He glared at her.

"I mean, really, Cole. Is there anything you could add that would make a girl feel less desirable?"

He stared hard into her eyes. "My desire for you was never in question."

Familiar stirrings rose up in Sydney's chest. For a

split second she considered saying yes and hauling him off on a real honeymoon. But she couldn't do that. It would only put off the heartbreak, maybe make the pain even worse.

"You're thinking about it," he said. "I can tell you're thinking about it."

She shook her head.

"Say yes, Sydney. You can do it."

Could she?

If she didn't get past her feelings for Cole, she'd go insane. She needed to focus on something else. And her career was the only reasonable distraction. And at least she'd have the satisfaction of thwarting Bradley.

She gazed into Cole's eyes, studied those flecks of storm-tossed gray for the last time.

"Fine," she said, suddenly tired of fighting, tired of feeling, tired of wishing for something he'd never be able to give her. "I'll marry you."

"Yeah?"

"Yeah." She tossed her hair behind her shoulders. "After all, it's the professional coup of a lifetime."

Chapter 12

Two weeks later Sydney was seriously rethinking her decision to marry Cole. But the Laurent was already poised for the Viking antique show, Grandma had already pinned the Thunderbolt to the bodice of Sydney's wedding gown and, most importantly, Sydney had already said "I do."

In the brand-new hay barn down the driveway from Cole's cabin, all eyes were on the bride and groom. The small band launched into the bridal waltz, and Cole pulled Sydney into his arms.

The floor was rough, and the walls were bare wood. But the acoustics were impressive, and they danced together like they made love together, every movement in sync, every breath in harmony. She could swear their heartbeats had synchronized.

"Relax," he whispered into her ear, gathering her close.

"I'm trying."

"Think about the Thunderbolt," he advised. "You're going to be a very famous woman."

"And so, I'm a success," she said on a forced laugh, fighting to keep it from turning into a tear.

His hand stroked up and down her back, just barely touching her exposed skin where the dress veed between her shoulder blades. Ironic that the very man who was tearing her heart out was also comforting her.

She subconsciously moved closer to the heat of his body, his scent taking her back days and weeks to the tiny bedroom on the shores of Blue Creek. She could almost hear the clock ticking as he messed with time.

He settled his arm more securely across the small of her back while the singer crooned his way through a wholly inappropriate country tune.

"Are you remembering?" Cole whispered.

"No," she lied.

He bent closer to her ear, his breath puffing in warm bursts. "I sure am."

"Don't." Memories could kill her. They were killing her.

"No matter what happened," he rasped, swaying to the strains of promises and love for the rest of their lives. "No matter what I said and did that can never be fixed. I want you to know that you rocked my world."

"Cole," she moaned.

"For as long as I live, I'll see you in that billowing bed with strawberry-stained lips and tousled hair, sharing my secrets, looking out for my family."

"Please stop."

"I'm so sorry, Sydney."

She shook her head. "It's not you."

He gathered her closer still. "Well, it's sure as hell not you."

"Maybe it's us."

"Maybe it was circumstances."

She dared to look up at him. "Does it really matter anymore?"

It was over between them. Not that they'd ever had a chance. He was her ticket to the Thunderbolt, nothing more. That he was the lover of a lifetime had messed things up, and that she had to lie to him had messed things up. But even without the lies, without the love-making, the best she could have hoped for is exactly where they were now—going into a sham marriage to circumvent a will.

He sighed against the top her head. "I hate leaving things unsettled between us."

"We're settled." She was getting better and better at lying.

"No, we're not."

The band moved into the third chorus, and the lyrics all but pierced Sydney's heart.

"What do you need to settle it, Cole? To know that I'm sorry I lied to you?"

"No." He pulled back, cupping her face in his palms. "That's not what I meant."

To her surprise, he captured her lips in a long, soulful kiss.

Ridiculous hope fluttered to life as the song built to a crescendo of everlasting love.

She pulled back, intent on saving her sanity. "There are two hundred people watching us."

"Lucky them."

"Cole."

"Just tell me you forgive me."

"For what?"

He chuckled softly as the band held the final note. "Right."

"Seriously, Cole. What?"

He stared into her eyes.

The note faded to silence and the audience burst into applause.

Kyle appeared next to Cole's shoulder. "I believe it's the best man's turn."

Cole plucked an ice-cold beer from the bar in the corner of his new barn.

Sydney needed to forgive him for insulting her. She needed to forgive him for threatening to have her arrested. And she also needed to forgive him for not recognizing she was the most wonderful woman on the planet.

He'd picked that sappy song himself, hoping by some miracle she'd know he meant it.

She hadn't.

He briefly acknowledged the congratulations from one of his neighbors, but he didn't engage Clyde in conversation. He wanted to fade into the shadows and watch Sydney sway in Kyle's arms, since tonight might be the last time he saw her.

The song ended and he checked the impulse to rush back to her side.

She glanced around, then glided across the floor, her dress flowing softly around her ankles. A few people stopped her to exchange words, Cole's neighbors, Sydney's co-workers. Then a man cut in front of her, and

Cole squinted. He didn't recognize the guest, but something prickled along his spine.

Her back was to him, but her shoulders tensed as the two began to speak. Cole ditched the beer bottle and headed across the floor.

Halfway there, he recognized Bradley Slander.

He swore under his breath and quickened his pace, shouldering his way between guests. He still couldn't see Sydney's expression, but Bradley was way too close.

When Cole got into range, he heard Bradley's tone dripping with malevolence. "—and so I'm wondering what it feels like to whore yourself for an antique."

Sydney recoiled, and something exploded inside Cole's brain. Instinct took over as he crossed the last few yards on a dead run. He grabbed Slander by the collar and slammed him up against the wood wall.

He held him there, nose to nose, forearm jammed against his sternum while Slander's face turned an interesting shade of maroon.

"I don't know how things work up in New York," stormed Cole. "But here in Texas, y'all 've got two choices. You can apologize to my wife and get the hell off my land. Or I can blow off your balls and feed them to the dogs."

Slander's mouth worked, but nothing came out except raspy squeaks.

"Cole?" came Kyle's warning voice.

Cole would have broken Slander's nose for good measure, but he'd already wasted too many minutes of his life on the man, and he needed to make sure Sydney was okay.

He jerked back and let Slander crumple to the floor. Then he turned to look for her.

She stood frozen, a few yards away, her eyes wide as a few people tried to engage her in conversation.

Cole marched to her side and wrapped an arm around her waist, pulling her away from the curious guests.

She was shaking.

Fortunately, the band hadn't seen the altercation, and they played on. He guided Sydney into the middle of the dance floor and gathered her into his arms.

Her glance went to the doorway where Kyle was escorting Slander outside.

Cole turned her so she wouldn't have to look.

Her voice quavered. "He—"

"He sends his apologies," said Cole.

She nodded against Cole's shoulder, her body stiff as a board.

"It's okay," he whispered, rubbing a hand up and down her back. "Relax. It's over. Just dance with me."

She shook her head against his chest. "He just said what they're all thinking."

"No, he didn't."

"That I married you for the brooch."

"They're all thinking you're a beautiful bride."

"They're wondering why you agreed to marry me. They're thinking I'm a mercenary."

"No, they're not."

"That's what Katie thought."

He tipped her chin up. "For a short time, maybe. But then she got to know you. She knows you're not a mercenary."

"But I am." There was a catch in her voice, and his heart ached.

"We both know the truth, and that's all that matters."

She shook her head once more.

He kissed the softness of her hair. "Stop. Just stop."

"But we don't, Cole."

"We don't what?"

She tilted her chin to look up, eyes glassy and tearful. "*You* don't know the truth."

He squinted at her. Oh, no.

"The truth is, I didn't marry you for the brooch."

A chill of fear iced Cole's spine. He couldn't take another one of her deceptions. Not here. Not now.

She bit her bottom lip, and her chest rose once, then fell. "I married you because I love you."

The fear in Cole's body plummeted through the floorboards. He gave his head a little shake. She couldn't have just said those words. It was his own wishful thinking.

"Say that again," he rasped, fighting the roaring in his ears.

"I love you, Cole," she repeated.

He squeezed her tight. "Oh, Sydney. I have loved you for…" He stroked his hand slowly over her fragrant hair, marveling that his dreams had actually come true. "Forever, I think."

Her voice lifted. "You do?"

He kissed her temple. "I do."

A soft sigh escaped from her, she seemed to melt against him.

"Oh, Cole.

"I know."

"We're married."

"I meant the song." He cradled her face in his hands. "For as long as I live. I meant every word."

"I meant my vows," she whispered.

"I will love you," he whispered back, "cherish you, honor and keep you."

"Till death do us part," she said, finding his hand with her own and twining their fingers together.

"Till death do us part," he repeated, pulling their joined hands between their bodies as the music swelled. The yellow lights shone through her hair and the scent of the wedding roses filled the new barn.

"I guess we'll be building that house now," said Cole, feathering light kisses down her cheek, heading for her soft lips.

"With the turret and the dormer windows." She sighed against him. "And a breakfast bar and some of those high stools with the curved backs."

He chuckled. "I guess if I'm going to be a patriarch, I'll need a big house."

"A patriarch?"

"Yeah."

"Oh, great. You're going to start issuing decrees now, aren't you?"

"You bet." He nodded. "Starting tonight, I'm whipping this family into shape."

"Kyle will never take the land."

"I know he won't." Cole smiled to himself. He'd been working on that one for a while.

"What?" Sydney prompted.

"I'm leaving it to his children."

"You're devious."

"That I am. But you love me, right?"

"I love you," she said.

"Say it again."

She pulled back and cupped his face between her soft hands. "I love you, Cole Erickson."

He sighed. He could listen to that all night long.

"Isn't there something you want to say to me?" she prompted.

He kissed her softly on the lips. "Hmm. Let me think."

She dug her elbow into his ribs.

"I love you Sydney…Erickson," he rumbled.

A funny expression flitted across her face.

"I guess we didn't talk about names, did we?" He wasn't going to insist. After all, traditions had to change sometime.

"Sydney Erickson." She rocked her head back and forth. "I think I like that." Her lips curved into a smile.

Cole grinned right back, smoothing her hair, kissing her again. They could have a real honeymoon now. He'd planned to hide out in Montana for a week, but he'd go wherever she wanted.

"Hey, Cole." Kyle danced up to them with Katie in his arms.

Cole nodded to his brother, hugging Sydney close.

"Who was that guy?" Katie asked Sydney.

"Antique vulture," Sydney answered, and Cole was proud of how quickly she'd recovered from the altercation.

"Won't *ever* be back to the Valley," said Kyle.

Cole nodded his thanks. He should've broken Slander's nose. But then the sheriff might have had to lock him up on his wedding night.

"Thought you two might like to know the wedding worked," said Katie with a wide smile.

"Sure did," said Cole, though he wasn't sure how Katie knew that already. He kissed Sydney's temple.

"Looks like along about April," said Katie.

Sydney let out a sudden squeal and pulled away from Cole's arms.

"What?" asked Cole as his wife embraced his sister-in-law.

"New little Erickson," said Kyle with wide, sappy grin.

Cole let out a whoop. He reached out and clapped Kyle on the shoulder. "That's fantastic! Congratulations, little brother."

"Thanks," said Kyle.

"Can we talk about splitting the land now?" asked Cole.

"No," said Kyle.

Cole smiled as he shook his head. "I'm going to win this one."

Someone tapped his shoulder and he turned.

"Hey, Grandma." He pulled Sydney back into his arms as Kyle danced off with Katie. "Don't you just love a good wedding?"

"You know I do," said Grandma. "And I have something for Sydney."

Sydney tipped her head questioningly. "For me?"

"This way," said Grandma with a mysterious wink. "Both of you."

They followed her through the crowd, past the band, toward the back of the barn where the light was dim and the air was a few degrees cooler.

Cole held Sydney's hand as they walked, unable to resist sending goofy smiles her way. He couldn't wait to get her alone.

Or maybe he could. It was fun to show her off. His wife. His *wife*. And tonight was the first of thousands together.

Yeah, he could wait.

He lifted her hand to his lips and kissed each of her knuckles. He was going to relish every single hour with this woman.

Grandma came to a stop at a back table, rattling something out of a paper bag.

She turned to face Sydney with a very serious expression on her face. "Sydney Erickson."

Cole squeezed Sydney's hand. He loved her new name.

"It is my honor," said Grandma, "to present you with the providence and chronicles of the Thunderbolt of the North." She handed Sydney a large, leather-bound book.

Sydney's forearms sagged with the weight of the dark, heavy volume. Cole started to take it from her, then checked the impulse. Her eyes were wide with wonder as she stared down.

Cole blinked in amazement as well. He hadn't even known such a thing existed.

"It was translated in the mid-1700s," said Grandma, patting her hand gently on the cover. "I've never been sure if it was taken from a written account, or if Sigrid wrote down the oral history. In any event, it's all here. The life and times of the Thunderbolt."

Sydney ran her fingers over the embossed cover. "This is absolutely amazing," she whispered, glancing up at Cole. "It's priceless."

Grandma smiled with obvious satisfaction. "And it's your turn to continue the saga."

Sydney's jaw dropped open.

"And I suggest you start with the Thunderbolt's latest adventure."

"Are you sure?" asked Sydney. "The *entire* adventure?"

Grandma patted the book again. "Yes. The whole adventure. The diary deserves no less than the truth."

Cole wrapped an arm around his grandmother's thin shoulders and gave her an affectionate squeeze. "Thank you, Grandma."

Her eyes shimmered bright as she smiled up at him.

"For everything," he said.

"I was right about Sydney, wasn't I?"

"You were absolutely right about Sydney."

"Good. Well, I'll leave you two alone now," she said with a quick smile.

"I can't believe it," said Sydney, her voice hoarse with awe.

"It couldn't be in better hands," said Cole, loving her more by the second.

She shook her head, and her eyes shimmered jewel-bright under the lights. Then she pressed the big book more tightly against her chest. "I never thought it could happen," she whispered. "But you did it, Cole."

"I did what?" He searched her eyes. "I fell in love with you?"

She shook her head. "That, too." Then she reached up and stroked her soft palm against his cheek. "What I meant was, you found my silver locket."

Ah. His gaze went to the brooch, nestled against the beaded fabric of her wedding dress. "The Thunderbolt."

She shook her head again. "No. It was never the jewelry." She smiled. "It was never the things."

"Then…"

"It was the heritage, the home. I finally realized."

She swayed toward him, and his arms automatically wrapped around her.

"I was searching for the family I never had. And you gave it to me."

His chest expanded almost painfully.

She was his. She was here forever.

"Welcome home, Sydney," he whispered against her hair. "We've been waiting for you all along."

* * * * *

#1 *New York Times* bestselling author

LINDA LAEL MILLER

returns to the Arizona frontier in a tale of passion, adventure and dangerous promises...

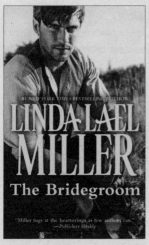

Undercover agent Gideon Yarbro is renowned for stopping outlaws almost before they commit a crime. But now he must stop a wedding— despite the bride's resistance. Lydia Fairmont will lose everything if she doesn't honor her betrothal to a heartless banker. Unless she marries someone else instead... whether it's a love match or not.

Determined to honor his own decade-old promise to help Lydia, Gideon carries her off to Stone Creek and makes her his reluctant wife. Forget a honeymoon for "show"—not with a vengeful ex-fiancé on their trail and a hired gun on the loose. But there just might be hope for the marriage... and two hearts meant for each other.

HARLEQUIN®

Desire

ALWAYS POWERFUL, PASSIONATE AND PROVOCATIVE.

THE LAST COWBOY STANDING
Colorado Cattle Barons
by Barbara Dunlop

After a disastrous first meeting, Colorado rancher Travis and city gal Danielle don't expect to cross paths again. But when they end up in a Vegas hotel suite together, there's no denying the depths of their desires. Could she finally manage to lasso the last cowboy standing?

Look for THE LAST COWBOY STANDING
in May 2014 from Harlequin Desire!
Wherever books and ebooks are sold.

Don't miss other exciting titles from the
Colorado Cattle Barons miniseries by Barbara Dunlop,
available now wherever ebooks are sold.

A COWBOY'S TEMPTATION

MILLIONAIRE IN A STETSON

AN INTIMATE BARGAIN

A COWBOY IN MANHATTAN
A COWBOY COMES HOME

Colorado Cattle Barons: From the mountains to the boardroom, these men have everything under control—except their hearts.